Sapphires in Snow

Sapphires in Snow

By Amy Schisler

ISBN-13: 979-8-9852232-7-9

Published by:
Chesapeake Sunrise Publishing
Amy Schisler
Bozman, MD
2022

Acknowledgements

A few years ago, I was toying with the idea of writing a book about former female Navy SEAL. I didn't know her name or her story, but bits and pieces were beginning to come to me. I couldn't find any direction and didn't feel like the character was talking to me as I sat at my desk in my office on the Eastern Shore of Maryland. I needed a break to clear my head. Some time away with a good friend was just what I was hoping for.

When I arrived in the Arkansas Ozarks, my dear friend, Tammi, assured me that I would one day write a series that takes place in one of the picturesque towns in the area. I was dead set against writing a series, but I went with an open mind. After several days of driving around and visiting many of the towns, I was even more convinced that I was not meant to write a series, and my character was still hiding in my brain, refusing to show herself. Then we drove through a town that broke my heart.

The sidewalks were cracked, most of the windows were boarded up, and the fountain in the center of town was dry and crumbling. Suddenly, I saw Andi, arriving home from the Navy, standing in the middle of town with a hole in her heart. She was dying inside, and the one place she thought could revive her was dying as well.

Here we are, three years later, and Andi is happily married and living in Buffalo Springs, the town she helped restore. Her sister, Helena, is engaged to the town doctor and piloting every organization in town. Their brother, Jackson, well… he's trying to find his way out of Buffalo Springs as fast as he can.

This is the second book I have written with the help, advice, and keen eye of editor, Cayley Ross. Thank you, Cayley, for coming on board. I am so pleased by and impressed with your knowledge and editing talents. I know we can do great things together in the future!

I have wonderful beta readers and proofreaders, my Aunt Debbie Nisson, Anne Novey, Jeanne Stockmeyer, and Olivia Deboeck. I could not put out a quality product without you all. Thank you for never saying no to my pleas for help and guidance.

Thank you again, Tammi. Without you, I would never have found Andi or the rest of her family. The same can be said of so many others who have supported my writing over the past fifteen years. First, my mom and dad have been encouraging me to follow my dreams for over fifty years. They proofread every manuscript, approve every cover, attend every event, and sell books out of their houses, out of their cars, in their club meetings, in grocery store aisles, and anywhere else they can get people to listen to them brag about their daughter. I would be lost without them.

My husband, Ken, and our daughters, Rebecca, Katie Ann, and Morgan have been my biggest supporters and cheering section. I have to say a special thank you to Katie Ann who is my website advisor, social media marketing guru, and entire technical support team.

Last, but never least, I have been blessed with the most wonderful and faithful readers. You all have a very special place in my heart. I wish I could meet every single one of you face-to-face to let you know how much your support means to me. I do this for you.

Thank you all. I love you. God bless you.

One

A cold wind—the precursor of a coming storm—shook the trees and rattled the shingles, but the flames flickered in the fireplace, and the house smelled of freshly baked bread and roasting, Thanksgiving turkey. Jackson slipped out the front door and leaned against one of the columns that framed the steps of the only place he'd ever called home. He took a sip from the bottle in his hand and heard the door open behind him.

"Cold night to be stargazing," Jackson's father said as he slowly moved to stand beside his son, using the furniture and porch railing to guide his steps. He hated using his walker.

"Cold but clear. The best kind of night to see the stars." He gestured at the sky with the bottle.

"I guess you don't see many stars in the city," his father said.

Jackson took another sip. "Not as many as here," he agreed. "But there are a lot of things the city has that Buffalo Springs doesn't."

"I suppose I probably thought that way when I was your age."

Jackson ignored the comment and leaned closer to the man whom he had always admired. He asked quietly, "How're you holding up, Daddy? Are you feeling okay?"

Joshua beamed up at his son. "Never better."

"I'm glad to hear that," Jackson said though he doubted there was much truth to his father's statement. "We just don't want you overdoing it."

"Nonsense," Joshua said, waving his hand in dismissal. "I'm as fit as a fiddle."

Jackson wished that was true, but one look told him otherwise. His father had aged at least ten years since his stroke back in June, and though Jackson had seen his progress from then through the month of August, he was shocked to see how fragile his father had become while Jackson was at school.

Joshua Nelson's blue eyes seemed dimmer, and he had lost more than seventy pounds. His arms were thin with none of the muscle he had built up after years of heavy lifting in the town's paper mill. When the mill shut down a few years back, Joshua had no problem getting a job lifting and carrying loads at the local hardware store. It was only after he was laid off, during the town's bad years, that Joshua's health had declined. Now, he stood stooped over, his face sagged with wrinkles and empty skin, and his legs didn't always work the way they should.

"Daddy, you must be freezing out here. Let's go back inside. I'm sure Mama could use some help, and your game shows will be on soon."

Jackson remained alert, his arms ready to give aid, as his father shuffled back toward the door. His heart broke to see his strong, capable father reduced to half his size and a quarter of his strength.

"Your mother's the one who always overdoes it," Joshua said. "I told her to wait to cook that bird in the morning when the girls are here, but she insisted that she always cooks it the night before. Says it's easier for me to carve it that way."

That was something Jackson hadn't thought of. Was his father capable of carving the turkey? Could he even hold the knife steady? Maybe Jackson should suggest that it was high time for him to learn to do the job. After all, he'd be a college graduate in less than a month. Time to start taking on some more responsibility around here, for what little time he'd be around here anyway.

After helping his father get settled in his armchair, Jackson's eyes fell on the carpet where the repair stood out, the threads bright and colorful. He recalled the day a fireball had been thrown through the window and onto the rug. He frowned, remembering the men who tried to burn down his parents' house and attack his sister, Andi, when she and Jackson devised a plan to save the town from the drug lords who were running it. It was during that time that Andi convinced Mayor Wade Montgomery to join their efforts, and Wade went from being a figurehead who bowed to the crooked town council to a legitimate mayor who fought for the best interests of Buffalo Springs. Both Andi and Wade came close to being killed by the men who thought they ran the town, and Jackson's already high admiration of his sister had grown even more.

"There you are." Grace's voice pulled Jackson back to the present. "I called from the kitchen, but y'all didn't answer."

"Sorry, Mama. We were on the porch. Do you need help with something?"

"Can you lift the bird from the oven for me? It gets heavier every year."

Jackson smiled. "Sure, Mama." He started toward the kitchen.

"Just put it on top of the stove for now," Grace called.

The aroma of spice-laden skin and toasted stuffing filled the air, and Jackson's stomach growled despite the hearty supper they'd eaten only an hour before.

He hefted the turkey onto the stove and turned off the oven. Before he returned to the living room, he gazed around the bright kitchen with its yellow walls and lacy curtains. Nothing about this room had changed in at least fifteen years, but instead of comforting Jackson, it made him uneasy. Not much in this town ever changed even with all the new businesses that his sister and her husband were bringing in. It was no place for a young man just starting out in life, and as much as he would hate to break the news to his family, Jackson knew that come New Year's, he would be long gone from here. He didn't plan on ever coming back.

***

Jackson was pleased with his carving efforts even if Andi teased him about his lack of butchering skills. He smiled to himself as he walked down the hall from the kitchen.

"You, uh, are only having one glass, right, Joshua?" Jackson looked over at Dr. Blake, Helena's fiancé. The doctor was looking at his patient and future father-in-law with concern.

Joshua held up the whiskey glass and nodded. "I'm following doctor's orders, son. No need to worry."

"Oh, Joe," Helena said, her blue eyes sparkling and dirty blonde curls bouncing. "You know Daddy is a model patient."

"Not according to the staff at the rehab center." Joshua's wife, Grace, reached for the glass in her husband's hand. "Dinner is ready, and I don't want you worn out before we cut into that pie Andi made for dessert. Let's all head into the dining room."

"Pumpkin pie, right?" Jackson asked his sister, Andi, as he walked with her toward the dining room. Andi was the owner of the local bakery, and pies were her specialty.

"Pumpkin with cinnamon custard."

Jackson's face broke into a wide grin. "My favorite."

Everyone took their seats at the table as Grace and Helena finished adding food to the wide assortment already on display. A tan tablecloth dotted with orange, yellow, and brown leaves lay beneath the bounty, and an arrangement of pinecones and gourds surrounded glowing candles.

"This is quite the feast, Mama." Jackson's eyes roved from the roasted turkey to the mashed potatoes then over the succotash, cornbread, and green bean salad. "I feel like it's already Christmas."

Joshua reached out to take Grace's hand on one side and Andi's on the other, and everyone took each other's hands as they bowed for the blessing. After a resounding *Amen*, the joyous noise of passing bowls and tinkling utensils filled the room.

"Wait until you see the menu Joe has started planning for Christmas," Helena said as she passed the cornbread. "Y'all are going to love it. I am so lucky to be engaged to a man who likes to cook." She looked over at Joe, and Jackson watched as their eyes locked. Sparks of love emanated between them. He swallowed hard, looking back and forth between both of his sisters and the men they loved.

He was getting ready to turn twenty-four and was almost two years behind most of his friends. They had graduated in May of the previous year and were now getting engaged and planning the next phase of their lives. Jackson didn't regret leaving school for a time. His father had been laid off, and his parents needed him. And if he hadn't been home when Andi returned from the Navy, he never would've given Andi the ideas and vision that prompted her and Wade to revive the town and turn it into the tourist destination it was quickly becoming. He loved his family, and he loved this town, but he knew that there was nothing here for him.

How would he ever become a successful investment banker living in a tiny town in the middle of the Ozarks? How would he make enough money to support a family? How would he find the woman with whom to create that family? The only answer was to leave Buffalo Springs.

He painted on a smile as he looked around the table. His heart ached as the biggest questions of all weighed on his mind and soul. How would he ever be able to leave his family behind, and how could he break the news to them?

***

Cindy wiped the tears from her eyes and tried to concentrate on the dark, winding road. She wasn't used to driving in the mountains. Cities she could handle, and freeways were a breeze, but she'd never been on a road like this, and the weather wasn't helping. A light drizzle fell, making it difficult to see through the already foggy windshield. The worn wipers screeched as they moved back and forth like a metronome, and Cindy reached to change the station on the radio without taking her eyes from the road. She was a Lady Gaga fan all the way, but she was in no mood to hear the song, *I'll Never Love Again,* from the hit movie, *A Star Is Born.* The only thing worse would have been to hear *Before You* by Fortunate Ones. That had been their song—hers and Evan's—and she couldn't bear to hear it even though it had been eighteen months since...

She swallowed and forced herself to bring to mind the happy memory of the night they'd met.

The small bar in her hometown of La Mesa, California, was dark and crowded. Since she rarely drank, she was the DD that night; and while her friends were tossing back the drinks, she was watching the men play pool across the room. They seemed to be military, and she assumed Marines, since Camp Pendleton was nearby, though she knew that sometimes Navy sailors wandered inland to get away from the expense and tourism of Coronado. Out of her league either way, she told herself. Still, the tall one with the great smile was cute, and she found herself glancing his way more often than she should.

She had just picked up another Sprite from the bar when she turned around and caught his eye. Her heart skipped a beat, and she realized that really was a thing. He gave her a shy smile before turning back to the game. Cindy took a quick sip of her soda and returned to her friends, feeling the heat rise in her cheeks. She tried to stop herself from looking toward the guys again, but she felt an irresistible pull that had her raising her eyes ever so slightly to the far corner of the room. Another shy smile greeted her when their eyes met, and she quickly turned away.

A slow song began playing on the old-fashioned juke box, one she'd never heard before, but it had a beautiful rhythm, and she found herself closing her eyes and swaying to the music. A light touch on her shoulder caused her to turn her head and look at the man standing behind her. Her face warmed as the table became silent. She felt the eyes of all her friends glued to her, but she only saw his eyes. Violet. They were violet. She'd heard of eyes that color but had never actually seen them.

"Would you like to dance?" he asked quietly in a Mid-Western accent.

Without answering, she slid her hand into the one on her shoulder and let him lead her to the dance floor. She ignored the drunken squeals from her friends and the whistling and catcalling from the pool table area. Blocking out everyone and everything else, she stared into those violet eyes and listened to the lyrics of the song that she now knew was "Before you."

I remember nights I'd lie awake
Fighting shadows of all my mistakes
In and out they come like tides
Upon some angry ocean blue
But I can't remember my life before you.

Maybe it was the song. Maybe it was his eyes. Maybe it was the thrill of being in the arms of a complete stranger, but suddenly, the lyrics rang true. Cindy remembered nothing before that moment, before he held her in his arms, before he became her everything.

A long, loud honk shook her from her memory, and Cindy squeezed the wheel, correcting her drift into the other lane. She let out a long breath and blinked, becoming aware that the tears were now flowing down her face like a tropical waterfall. She glanced at the older model phone attached to the mount on her dashboard. She had thirty more miles to go before she reached Buffalo Springs and the only person who could help her.

Cindy knew what the others thought of her, the girl who chased the *Officer and a Gentleman*. She was the ultimate Paula Pokrifki, the poor, uneducated blue-collar daughter of a single mother, who landed the dashing, darling Zach Mayo, officer and gentleman. She knew that the other wives saw her as a Tag Chaser and tried to warn Evan just as Zach had been warned about Paula. Ironically, she and Debra Winger's movie character were nothing alike. The dark-haired Paula had spunk and nerve. She drank and smoked and spent her days in a factory and her nights chasing sailors.

Cindy was quiet and shy with strawberry-blonde hair and little to no confidence. She was smart. Brains had never been her problem. She did well in school, read voraciously, and understood world affairs and politics. But she was poor, more than poor. As a teenager, she went to school and then to work and then back to school with little sleep in between. She supported herself and her mother from the time her father left them when she was only twelve, starting her first job at thirteen. And good riddance to the man.

The windshield wipers slapped back and forth, beating a rhythm that almost perfectly matched the more upbeat song now playing on the radio. Cindy peered through the foggy glass as she thought about all that her father's leaving had cost her. Her mother had never been a great role model, caring more about her next drink than about Cindy, and her father had been no better. Though she was old enough that she should have remembered more about him, she had only vague memories of the man. What she remembered most about her childhood was never feeling loved or wanted by either of her parents. One only loved the bottle, and the other only wanted to be rid of both mother and daughter.

All Cindy ever wanted when she was growing up was to go to college, find a job she enjoyed, and be content with life. She didn't even care if there was a man in the picture. After watching her parents for twelve years, she didn't believe in love. Not until she met Evan. That's when her desire to have a family really took hold.

Nobody else believed that Cindy and Evan were soulmates, destined to be together from the moment their eyes met. Not even her mother thought she was good enough for him. She couldn't compete with the Coronado girls, with their perfect blonde hair, expensive clothes, and good educations. And though none of the other SEAL wives were from California, they all came from solid homes, had college degrees, and gave off the air of being far more sophisticated than Cindy. Or maybe she just felt that way.

Only Andi, the sole female on the tight-knit SEAL Team, accepted Cindy unconditionally. Only Andi saw the hurt in her eyes and came to her defense, included her in conversation, and made sure she was invited to the picnics and christenings and parties even when Andi and the boys were away on assignment. She never went when Andi or Evan wasn't there, but she was invited just the same, and she knew it was Andi who insisted upon it. Andi had been her rock during that one, short, fraction of a year she and Evan had been together. But Andi had her own demons to deal with after the crash that took all the men from their lives.

Since then, Andi had rebuilt her life, opened a bakery, and found her true love. Cindy, on the other hand, was still alone and more of a mess than ever. Her mother had passed away shortly after she lost Evan— liver failure from years of alcohol abuse. Cindy had no friends, not the girls she knew from school who turned against her when she 'landed' Evan, and certainly not the SEAL wives. She needed to get away from California, to find herself, to figure out her life, and she thought Andi might be the only person who could help her find her way.

Cindy hoped that Andi would be okay with her showing up out of the blue. Because if Andi turned her away, there was no place else to go.

***

Jackson was beat, but his sisters were lingering, waiting out the pounding rain that fell between the warm house and their cold cars. The younger generation gathered back in front of the fire after telling Grace and Joshua goodnight. Stifling a yawn, Jackson saw Andi glance at her phone and frown. She excused herself and slipped out the front door onto the porch. He wondered if everything was okay.

Taking a blanket from the back of the couch, he went outside just as Andi said, "Cindy, of course it's okay. Whatever you need."

Jackson held out the blanket with a raised brow.

"Cindy, hold on a minute." She cupped her hand over the bottom of the phone. "I won't be long. A friend is in town and needs some help. Can you tell Wade we need to head home?"

Jackson started to ask if everything was all right, but figuring it wasn't any of his business, he simply nodded and went inside, blanket in hand.

"Andi says it's time to go," he told Wade. "Something about a friend being in town and needing help."

Wade's brow rose in the same manner Jackson's had, but he didn't ask questions. He told Jackson, Helena, and Joe he'd see them later and retrieved his and Andi's coats from the closet.

"How's the rain?" Helena asked.

"Pretty light at the moment," Jackson answered though, in truth, he hadn't really looked. He was just anxious to go to bed.

Joe stood and offered a hand to Helena. "Come on, Pix, Jackson looks ready to collapse." Jackson had never understood the nickname Joe used with Helena, something about Cornish Pixies, but he'd gotten used to it. And right now all he cared about was closing his eyes and welcoming a nice, long sleep.

After Andi stuck her head inside to say goodbye, the four of them hastened out the door. Jackson bolted the door with a smile. With peace in the town now restored, the house was never locked except when they slept at night. It was his mother's belief that the only time there was anything worth protecting inside the four walls was when her family was in their beds fast asleep. He switched off the lights and headed upstairs, not remembering a thing once his head sunk into his pillow.

***

Cindy curled up in the warm, comfortable bed and closed her eyes. She inhaled, relishing the soft scent of clean sheets and the cold mountain air that crept in from the slightly open window. She hadn't had time to explain her sudden presence or even ask Andi for her advice.

When she arrived at the mailbox on the main road, and drove down the long, pitch black lane, she was sure she was at the wrong place. It was a farm of some sort with fields flanking both sides and rows of young, bald trees standing along the drive like tall, thin soldiers standing guard in the dark night. As she neared the house, she gasped. It was enormous—a three story white house with a wrap-around porch and balconies gracing the second level. Multiple chimneys rose above the many gables that protruded from the roof. Soft light glowed behind some of the windows, and it looked like something out of an historical fiction novel—grand and opulent but at the same time warm and welcoming.

The moment Andi opened the front door, Cindy burst into tears.

"Oh, sweetie, it's okay." Andi wrapped her arms around Cindy, and for the first time since losing Evan, Cindy felt protected and accepted.

A nudge at her leg caused Cindy to jump, and Andi released her. "Boomer, down." Andi scolded the penitent-looking dog who looked up at Cindy with an apology in its eyes. Cindy reached down to pet the dog on the head.

"It's okay, Boomer. I like dogs."

"You must be Cindy," a voice said, and she looked up to see one of the most handsome men she'd ever laid eyes on. He had dark brown eyes and a warm smile, and he was even taller than Evan had been. She reached her hand toward him.

"Yes, Sir. I'm Cindy."

"It's Wade, just Wade." He looked her up and down, waving off her outstretched hand. "No formalities here. And you must be freezing. You're not in California anymore. Andi, get her into the house. It's cold here by the door."

Cindy looked down at the threadbare jeans and light sweater she wore under her jacket. She supposed it was cold outside, but the heater in her car barely worked, so she'd gotten used to the dropping temperatures after a while.

Wade gestured toward the small bag she had dropped at her feet. "Can I take that upstairs for you?"

"Oh! I, um, are you sure it's okay?"

"Cindy, of course it's okay. I told you on the phone that you're welcome to stay here. Now, come on in and get warmed up. Wade's right. It's cold here in the foyer."

She looked from Andi to Wade and back to Andi. "If you're sure. I mean, I know I just showed up out of the blue, and it's Thanksgiving. I hope I didn't interrupt your plans."

"We insist on it," Wade said. "Until we fill this house with kids, it's much too big for just the two of us."

"And we were leaving Mom and Dad's when you called," Andi said, one arm still looped across Cindy's shoulders. "Besides, I've always told you that you're welcome here."

"It's a beautiful house," Cindy said as they walked farther inside. Wade began toward the stairs, which were carpeted in a rich red hue and enclosed with an intricately carved bannister of dark, expensive-looking wood.

"It's been in Wade's family for generations," Andi said, taking her hand. "Feel free to wander around tomorrow. You must be exhausted after all that driving in the rain."

Cindy yawned and suddenly felt the weight of exhaustion bearing down on her. "I am," she said, the surprising realization evident in her voice.

Andi took her arm and led her up the stairs with Boomer close at their heels. As she talked, Cindy gazed at the family photos that lined the curved stairwell.

"Let's get you settled, and you and I can talk tomorrow. I have to be at the bakery early. I was just about cleaned out of everything yesterday, and we were closed today, so I've got a lot of baking to do. But you can sleep as long as you want and give me a call when you're up and about. Wade leaves for his office around eight, so the house will be nice and quiet. Take your time getting up."

They'd only been back in each other's company for a few minutes, and already Andi seemed to know just what Cindy needed. That's how it had been since the day they met. Though not more than ten or twelve years older than Cindy, Andi had quickly become the mother figure Cindy never had. It felt so good to be back with her. It felt safe and welcoming—the kind of feeling Cindy always imagined other people felt when at home with their families.

Once in bed, she let the cool air, the soft sheets, and the sound of the light rain lull her to sleep. She had no idea what she would do tomorrow, but for tonight, she would sleep like a baby.

Two

Jackson hefted the bag of seed from the pallet onto the bed of the customer's truck. Farming never stops, no matter what the calendar reads, and Jackson was kept busy by farmers stocking up on seed and fertilizer for the busy growing season. He wasn't expected to work since he was just home for the weekend, but he needed the money.

Despite the chill in the air, Jackson wiped sweat from his brow. He told the farmer to have a nice day, and watched the man pull his truck out of the lot. He closed the bay doors, grabbed his water bottle, and took a long drink. The warehouse was cold, and the cloudy sky didn't help. It was almost always cloudy in the late fall and winter in Buffalo Springs, but snowfall wasn't bad at all, especially considering they were in the mountains.

Jackson looked out through the windows of the bay doors. Though it was cloudy, he could make out the peaks of the nearby mountains and wondered what it was like to look out and see nothing but skyscrapers and smog. He'd heard that a lot of people were leaving the big cities and opting for small towns and telecommuting, but he knew a young, inexperienced guy could not make it as a real estate investor without a network, mentors, and colleagues to help him succeed. He wanted—no he needed—the big city, the bright lights, the late nights and busy weekends, and everything he could never find here in Northwest Arkansas.

He set the water bottle back down on the table and stood as a bell signaled another truck backing up to the bay. He tightened the gloves he was wearing and shook off the cold. The sooner he started applying to investment firms, the better. He had more in mind for his future than loading fifty-pound bags into pickup trucks all day.

***

Cindy explored the grand old house on her own with warm socks on her feet and cream-diluted, hot coffee in her hand. Boomer followed her wherever she went, and Cindy couldn't help wondering if he just wanted attention, or he had a sixth sense about how lost and lonely she felt. Cindy didn't mind either way. The house was huge and reminded her of the ones in the old classic horror movies she used to watch, though this one was considerably homier despite its size and grandeur.

The living room had her mesmerized with its rows and rows of books on shelves that went all the way to the ceiling. She felt like Belle exploring the castle and discovering the Beast's library. She fingered the spines, seeing everything from law school texts to romances to international cookbooks. The room's décor was rich and dark but not foreboding. On the contrary, the soft, plush furniture, the paneled walls, and the ornate fireplace came together in a way that made her want to curl up in a corner of the sofa and stay there forever. The vast windows brought sunlight into the room brightening the dark décor, despite the clouds that hung over the mountains. Heavy draperies hung around the windows, and she resisted the urge to close them to protect the books and the rich colors in the furniture.

She wandered down the hall to what she would call the sunroom but probably had some fancier name like the conservatory. She felt like she'd fallen asleep and woken up as a game piece in Clue. There was a music room, a study—nobody would refer to that simply as an office—a magnificent dining room, a large and sprawling kitchen, and even a billiards room containing a pool table, poker table, and a dart board. The room looked as though it had been decorated by a teenager, with its framed sports car posters and beer can collection, and she wondered if this was Wade's high school hangout.

Upstairs, Cindy found an enormous master bedroom, which she imagined must contain his and hers dressing rooms and a luxurious bathroom with a jacuzzi, but she didn't dare enter. She did have boundaries after all. Besides, she still wasn't sure if Boomer was sizing her up, not that he could tell anyone where she went or what she did. She looked down at her companion and smiled.

"Don't worry, boy. I won't go where I don't belong."

He tilted his head and lifted an ear, either in understanding or total bewilderment.

In addition to the room where she had slept, there were three other bedrooms on that floor. Two had their own small bathrooms, and two shared a Jack and Jill bathroom that reminded her of that old sitcom, *The Brady Bunch*. Was that the show? Or was it *The Partridge Family*? She'd seen both on TV Land but hadn't ever really gotten into either one. She never believed that families like that existed in the real world. When a parent died or went away and left the other parent and kid or kids behind, everything didn't fall magically into place. New parents didn't walk into their lives bringing with them sound advice and camping trips and hit records. Only with Evan, and only for a brief moment in time, did she think that maybe, just maybe, those families could exist; but that dream was shattered like all her others.

She continued to explore, following another set of stairs. The third floor was essentially just an attic, but it was spacious and well-lit, and Cindy was impressed by the well-thought-out organization of the room and its contents. She wandered through the shelves and boxes, reading the carefully hand-printed labels: **Wade's baby clothes, Christmas decorations - 1 of 10**—ten whole boxes of Christmas decorations?—and **Jolene's baby clothes**. Jolene? Who was she?

Cindy went to the neatly arranged shelves lined with dozens of old family photo albums and metal boxes organized by date. Curiosity got the better of her, and she gently lifted the lid off one of the boxes. Inside were old movie reels. Family movies, perhaps? She took one out and squinted to examine the small print. *Casablanca.*

Cindy blinked. No. That's not what it said. Surely, she misread it. She looked again. What was this? A family vacation? She reached for another. *The Pride of the Yankees. Yankee Doodle Dandy. Lassie.*

Cindy quickly closed the lid and stood back. She looked down at Boomer. "Do Wade and Andi know these are up here?" He tilted his head again and narrowed his eyes. "They must be worth a fortune. What do you think, Boomer?" He blinked, then yawned, clearly unimpressed with her find.

Cindy felt guilty even knowing about the film reels and began to feel bad for taking such liberties in the house. Andi had invited her to wander around. She hadn't said she could become Nancy Drew and dig into every closet and corner.

She turned to head back downstairs, but the glow of morning sunlight at the other end of the attic caught her attention, and she found herself walking toward it. She leaned toward the oval window and gazed out onto the fields. She could see the rows of trees along the driveway more clearly now and wondered why some seemed hundreds of years old while others were mere saplings.

The fields were expansive and bare. What did they hold during the summer? She had no idea what kind of crops grew in the Ozarks or anywhere else in Arkansas for that matter. She knew nothing about Arkansas, nothing about farming, nothing really about any way of life or any places outside of Southern California. At twenty-one, she crossed the border into Mexico for the first time for a quick weekend getaway with Evan in Baja. So far, Buffalo Springs, Arkansas, was the only other place she'd ever been.

Sighing, Cindy turned from the window and retreated down the stairs. Andi had left her a note with the address of the bakery though Cindy doubted it would be difficult to find. From the little she'd seen the night before, Buffalo Springs could fit onto one side street of La Mesa.

She stopped in the bathroom adjacent to the room where she'd slept and brushed her teeth and hair. She'd showered and dressed before she went in search of food and coffee, so she was ready to head out. In the kitchen, she rinsed her mug and dropped it into the dishwasher with the plate she'd used for her bagel and fruit.

When she was ready to go, she bid Boomer goodbye and pulled on her jacket. The big dog, obviously accustomed to being left alone, sighed and loped off to his pillow in front of the floor-to-ceiling window. She took a deep breath herself before opening the door and stepping onto the front porch. From now on, she would look back on this day as being the start of a new chapter. She just had no idea what the rest of her story was going to look like.

***

The bakery smelled like a little corner of Heaven on Earth. Cindy inhaled the scents of pumpkin pies, apple turnovers, something chocolate, and fresh baked bagels.

"The bagel I had for breakfast…did you make it?"

"I did. I usually bring home the ones that don't sell within a day or two." Andi pulled a tray of chocolate cookies from the oven.

"Those smell amazing."

"They've always been my favorites—double chocolate chunk cookies. You've never had them before?"

Cindy shook her head. "Not yours. Only your pies."

"I guess that makes sense. Most of the wives requested pie whenever we got together."

Cindy frowned.

"What? Are they still being mean to you?"

She shook her head. "No. They're all gone now. Janet was the last to leave, and she's been gone about six months."

"I guess I hadn't realized that." Andi carefully moved the cookies to a cooling rack and blew from her forehead a lock of hair that had escaped from her hairnet. "Makes sense though. I mean, they were only there because of…" She glanced at Cindy. "And you? Did you move back home?"

"Yeah. No place else to go really. And Mom needed me."

Andi set aside the small metal spatula and laid her hand over Cindy's. "I'm so sorry about your mama. I wish I had been there."

"It's okay. I didn't tell anybody about it until after the funeral. I knew nobody would come anyway."

Andi squeezed Cindy's hand. "That's not true. I would've come."

Cindy managed a small smile. "You would have," she agreed. "But it was better this way. Mama didn't have any friends, and by then, neither did I. A small, simple burial was all we needed."

"Cindy, you must have friends. You lived in the same town your whole life until you met Evan. Surely, there's somebody there you can count on."

She bit back the tears. "Not anymore. When I met Evan, everything changed. My friends were so happy for me at first, but then…I don't know. Once they realized we were serious and Evan was the one, they started distancing themselves. It was like I got what they all wanted, and I hadn't even been trying. I didn't want to meet a man, any man, not to mention a sailor. A SEAL no less! I never even wanted to get married. Then suddenly, there he was, and he was all I ever wanted without even knowing it."

Andi smiled. "I understand. I never fit in around here. All I wanted was to be in the Navy, to serve our country, to travel, to have adventures. The other girls around here didn't get it. Well, Helena did, but she's my sister, and my Daddy always encouraged us to think outside the box. Anyway, contrary to popular belief, I did not enter the Navy to meet a man. When Jeremy and I—" Andi stopped abruptly, and Cindy saw something she'd never seen or picked up on before.

"You and Jeremy? What? When? How?" Cindy was at a loss. Andi was involved with the leader of the team? Andi, who traveled as part the team, who gave the intelligence to the men, who heard the last radio transmission… "Oh my gosh, I'm so sorry. I had no idea."

Andi waved her off. "Nobody did. I mean, nothing ever happened. The night before the crash…" Andi looked away and blinked. She went back to her work, transferring the cookies from the cooling rack to a tray for the display case. "The night before, he kissed me. That was it." She looked at Cindy and smiled. "That's as far as it ever got."

"But you're happy now right?" Cindy desperately needed to know that happiness could be found. Somehow, it had to be possible.

Andi broke into a radiant smile. "I'm happier than I've ever been. Ever. Wade and Jeremy are polar opposites, but I've never loved anyone more."

Her words struck Cindy and pushed a lump into her throat. She couldn't imagine ever loving anyone more than she loved Evan. It wasn't possible. Just a little bit of happiness in her life would be more than she could ask for, and she was going to find it somehow. Though she longed for a family, for a real connection to people who loved her, she was resigned to the fact that it just wasn't meant to be, and that was okay. Cindy was a survivor, albeit a lone one.

***

"Do I have to?" Jackson groaned into the phone as he put the truck into gear. He tapped the speaker button and tossed the phone onto the seat beside him.

"Yes, you have to. Please, Jackson? For me?"

"Why can't you do it?"

"Because I've got orders on top of orders, *and* I'm baking the desserts for the hospice Christmas tree lighting on Sunday. Come on, Jackson, it's just one night. All I'm asking is that you keep her company. Wade's meeting up with a friend who's in town for the holiday, and Mama has Daddy to keep an eye on, and—"

"I just don't get why you can't ask Amanda or Melanie or one of the other women in town to give up an evening to entertain a total stranger."

"Amanda's in Nashville with her family. Melanie has a date, and Allie and Paige are taking a trip to Nashville themselves to see the Opryland Christmas display. They want to bring back some new ideas for the town's decorations."

"Isn't that what that Pinterest thing is for? Can't they just find decorating ideas there?"

"Jacksuuuun," she said, drawing out the second syllable of his name.

He turned onto the street where he'd grown up and technically still lived when not at school. Where he wished he was now so that he could avoid moments like this.

"Okay, fine. I'll do it. But you owe me big time."

"For what? Can you tell me you had a better offer?"

He wished he could. He wished he had plans to do anything that evening other than eat dinner with his parents and then watch *Wheel of Fortune* and *Jeopardy* and some lame chick flick on TV with his mother. Tanner was working late at the hardware store, swapping out Black Friday signs for Small Business Saturday signs, and there wasn't anybody else Jackson would've had plans with. He sighed.

"No, I can't."

"Jackson, it won't be so bad. Cindy's a lovely girl."

"A 'lovely girl'? What's that supposed to mean?" He sat in the driveway with the truck running and the heat cranked on high.

"Exactly what I said. She's really a wonderful girl, and she's had a hard life, Jackson. Her father left when she was twelve, her mother was an alcoholic, her fiancé was killed in a helicopter crash leaving her practically widowed at the age of twenty-one, and then her mother died shortly after that. Please, be nice to her. Even if it's just for this one evening."

"She was only twenty-one?" he asked quietly, "when she lost her fiancé and then her mom?"

"Yes. She and Evan were supposed to get married right after her birthday, but he got called away, and they had to postpone. He used to tease her that she had to be legal to partake of their toast. He was a good guy."

Jackson could tell by her voice that she was thinking about all the guys his sister had lost in the crash. They had meant everything to her.

"Where is she now?"

"I'm not sure. She hung out with me for a while, and then said she was going to wander around town. I can't thank you enough, little brother. I'm going to text you her number. Just tell her that I asked you to take her out since I'll be working late."

"Wait. She doesn't even know about this?"

"I didn't realize how much more work I have to do until a little while ago. I thought maybe she'd come back when she was done walking around town, but I haven't seen her."

"And you didn't want her to tell you no." He cut the engine. "What if she tells me no?"

"Then talk her into it."

"How?" He picked up the phone and opened the door.

"I don't know. Use your charm."

Jackson rolled his eyes. "This is going to be a disaster." He slammed the truck door and walked up the porch steps. "Just send the number. But if she says no,

I'm not begging." He disconnected the call and went inside.

The smell of hot soup and baked bread hit him like the hot breeze of a roaring fire, warming his insides without even touching his lips. His phone buzzed, and he lifted it to look at the number Andi had sent. A smile crept onto his face as an idea struck him. He hit the screen and pressed the button to make a call.

"Hello?" A tentative voice answered.

"Is this Cindy?"

"Yes?" He assumed the questioning tone was meant to ask who he was and not to question her own identity.

"Hey, this is Jackson, Andi's brother. My mama asked me to call you. Andi has to work late, and Mama made a big pot of soup and homemade bread, and she wants you to come for dinner. We eat at 6:30. Can I tell Mama you said yes? She'd be awfully disappointed if you didn't come."

In the void between them, he thought he could hear her slow intake of breath and possibly even the sticky sound of her licking her lips. "Um, okay. If you're sure."

"I'm absolutely sure. Mama is looking forward to meeting you. I'll text you the address."

She answered with a quiet, "Okay" before thanking him and saying goodbye.

"I sure am looking forward to it," said the voice from behind.

Jackson turned to face his mother who stood in the room holding a blanket-in-progress and a crochet hook with a dangling thread. He felt his face growing hot. "Mama, I didn't know you were standing there."

"And I didn't know I'd invited someone to dinner. Care to let me know who I'm sharing our meal with?"

"Her name is Cindy. She's a friend of Andi's. She called after you went to bed last night and apparently showed up at the house sometime after that. Andi has to work late at the bakery, and Wade has plans, and it looks like I'm the only person in the whole town not doing anything this evening."

As he said the words, he realized how it made him feel. He missed out on so much of his college life, bouncing back and forth between school and home, between work and class, and then doing an entire semester after all his friends had moved on, even the ones beneath him in school. His friends from home had moved away, gone to graduate school, or were getting married. The more he thought about it, the more he knew he had to move on, too.

Grace looked at Jackson in that way that only mothers can—sympathetically and lovingly but without a dose of pity. She knew he'd lost a lot, but she had confidence things would get better. She always had the faith that things would get better no matter what. She trusted in God completely. When Andi was in the Middle East, Mama trusted that God would keep her safe. When Daddy was laid off, Mama trusted that God would find him work. When it looked like Helena would never find the right man, Mama trusted that God would bring her a soulmate. When Daddy had his stroke, Mama trusted that God would heal him. Jackson wished he had her unshakable faith.

"Well, I guess I need to set another place at the table. This will be good for you. You need to have more contact with people outside this house once you move back home."

Jackson wanted to argue with her, to tell her that most people he knew wouldn't be caught dead in this town, to tell her that he planned to move out; but he loved his mama, and the look of love and concern in her eyes kept him from answering with an angry retort she didn't deserve.

"I need a shower. Mind if I do that before dinner?"

"I'd prefer it," she said with a smile and a sniff. "You smell like fertilizer."

As he dressed, clean and smelling like Irish Spring—the only soap he ever remembered his mama buying—he heard the doorbell ring. It was an odd sound to his ears. Nobody used doorbells around here. Not even the postman who had delivered their mail and packages since Jackson was five. At the Nelson home, the door was always open, and people tended to just wander in, sometimes hollering out a greeting, and sometimes just showing up in the kitchen where Grace spent the majority of her time when not tending her gardens.

He pulled on a long-sleeved shirt that read, University of Arkansas, and his nicest pair of blue jeans. He wore socks but no shoes. He wasn't trying to impress anyone after all. Still, he found himself slapping on just a bit of aftershave. His parents drilled into the three of them that they should always strive to make a good impression no matter whom they were meeting. He just hoped that this *meeting* would go by quickly. He had no desire to spend the evening entertaining some friend of Andi's even if she did have a heartbreaking past.

***

Cindy looked around the cozy room. It was so different from the living room she had known most of her life, littered with cigarette butts and empty bottles. This room had warm, fuzzy blankets thrown across the furniture, photographs on every surface, and a popping, sizzling fire in the fireplace.

She removed her jacket and handed it to Andi's mother then took the seat that was offered on the couch and smiled at the older gentleman in the recliner.

"It's nice to meet you, Mr. Nelson. Thank you for having me."

"No need to thank us. Any friend of Andi's is always welcome here. Besides, I think Grace makes enough food to feed an army in the hopes that someone will drop by in time for dinner. Feeding people makes her feel good."

"Here you go," Mrs. Nelson said, handing Cindy a glass of water. "Our well water is real good. It comes straight from the mountains."

"Thank you," Cindy said, accepting the glass. She'd been offered wine or a cocktail, but she declined.

"Where are you from, Cindy?" Mrs. Nelson took a seat in the other recliner, a cocktail of some sort in her hand, and a basket of yarn at her feet.

"I'm from California, a suburb called La Mesa. It's about a half hour from Coronado."

"How did you and Andi meet?"

"Mama, don't give the poor girl the third degree."

Cindy looked toward the steps where a pair of legs appeared, presumably attached to the voice that had just spoken. She watched as the jean-clad legs gave way to a college t-shirt and then to a face that looked remarkably like Andi's, only with no trace of girlishness. He had dark, close cropped hair, but it appeared to have a touch of curl to it. Andi's dark hair was as straight as a stick. He didn't have her blue eyes either. His were dark, but he had the same contours around his eyes, and he shared Andi's smile. She felt her mouth go dry when his eyes met hers. She tried to swallow but couldn't. She took a sip of water and returned his smile.

"You must be Jackson," she forced herself to say. It wasn't easy for her to talk to strangers, especially to be the first one to speak, but that familiar smile urged her on. "Thank you for calling me. I, uh, wasn't sure what my dinner plans were going to be."

He stood at the bottom of the steps for a moment as if unsure what to do or say next, but that Nelson confidence she'd seen so many times in his sister must have kicked in because he strode into the room and took a seat next to her.

"Would you like a drink, Jackson?" his mother asked.

"I'll have a beer with dinner if that's okay."

Did he just ask his mother permission to drink? Was that polite or weird?

"That's fine, dear. Are you hungry?"

"Starving." He turned toward Cindy. "You?"

Her stomach growled at that very moment, and she felt her lightly freckled cheeks turn pink. "I guess so."

Jackson laughed, and she felt a familiar tug that both thrilled and alarmed her. Evan had been gone less than two years, and it still felt like it was yesterday. Plus, this was Andi's baby brother. What was wrong with her?

"Mama, can I help with anything in the kitchen?"

Is he for real? What guy asks that?

"It's all done, Jackson, but thank you."

There was no surprise in his mother's voice, no blinking of the eye. His offer was genuine; he was a man who helped his mother in the kitchen.

"Come on, then. Let's go eat." Mrs. Nelson and Jackson both stood and went in unison to Mr. Nelson's chair. "Are you ready, Joshua?"

"I'm ready. Let me do it."

Cindy watched as Andi and Jackson's father placed both hands on the arms of the chair and pushed with all his might. His face turned red and his knuckles turned white, and Cindy stood, trying to figure out what she could do to help. It was painful to watch, but after some intense effort, the man stood and smiled at his wife and then his son.

"It's getting easier," he told them, and Cindy wondered what hard looked like.

Jackson reached behind the chair for a walker, opened it, and placed it in front of his father.

"After you," Mr. Nelson gestured toward Cindy.

"Go ahead, ladies," Jackson said. "I'll follow Daddy down the hall."

Daddy. It was strange to hear a grown man call his father 'Daddy' and his mother 'Mama,' and Cindy tried to remember calling her mother anything other than Gloria. Gloria was not the motherly type.

Cindy looked at the family photos in the hall, reminding her of the ones that hung along the stairwell at Andi and Wade's house. Did her family ever take any pictures? She doubted it. She'd never seen any, not even a baby picture of herself.

The kitchen was as cozy as the living room. It looked neat and well organized—organization was something Cindy always noticed for some reason, perhaps because her life had never been neat and organized—and had a long table big enough to fit at least ten people. It reminded her of the one in that old show about the family in the mountains. What was it called? It was another totally unrealistic show about a family who weathered the Great Depression, and all came out better for it. She'd turned that one off, too, once she'd seen enough episodes to know that it was too fake to waste her time on. But looking around, she was beginning to wonder… Was it just in the mountains that families were like this? Was it even real? Maybe it was all an act.

But as she gazed between Jackson and his parents, she began to realize that all the things Evan told her might actually be true. Maybe there were some families who didn't drink too much, didn't yell and scream, didn't hit, and didn't constantly disappoint each other. She'd seen glimpses of that at the homes of friends when she was growing up, but it never lasted. There was always divorce, infidelity, secrets, and lies.

Here, though, all she saw was love. All she felt was warmth and gratitude and respect. And when they bowed their heads to pray before their meal, she felt peace.

***

Cindy was quiet during dinner. She spoke when spoken to and obliged them when they asked questions, but she offered no more than minimal answers. Jackson didn't know if she was shy or just secretive. While they ate, she answered his father's question about how she and Andi met and became friends. It was painful to hear her tell how she met and was engaged to one of Andi's SEAL Team members only to lose him just a few weeks after their postponed wedding date. She blinked her green eyes a few times but never shed tears, and he wondered if she was putting up a brave front or if she was stronger than she looked.

Because she didn't look strong at all. She looked so fragile, he thought she would shatter into thousands of tiny pieces if he made even the slightest touch on her arm. Her light reddish hair and pale skin made it seem as though he could look right through her, especially in the worn jeans and too-light-for-December top she was wearing. Long wisps of hair that trailed into slight curls gave the impression that she was much younger than twenty-one or twenty-two. He noticed her fingernails, neat and trimmed but almost translucent without any polish or even natural color or shine. Her hands had a slight tremble when she lifted her knife and fork or took a sip of her water, and her smile didn't reach her cheeks.

"Jackson?" His mother broke into his thoughts.

"I'm sorry? What did you say?"

"I asked you what your plans are for this evening. Are you going out?"

He eyed his mother for a moment. When was the last time he'd gone out? He thought it was Wade's bachelor party back in September. His monthly night with the guys consisted of online game playing where he, Tanner, and their friend, Austin, battled monsters, giants, and raptors.

"Um, no. I didn't have any specific plans."

"Then why don't we clean up and have some dessert in front of the fire. I made a bourbon sweet potato pie earlier. I must have had a notion we'd have company tonight." His mother smiled at Cindy, and Jackson felt both love and pride for his mother. She embodied what she had always preached to them, *Do unto others as you would have them do unto you.*

Jackson laughed. "Mama, when are you not making some kind of pie or fancy dessert?"

"You must be the one who taught Andi to bake pies. I've never had any that are better than hers."

"Mama and Andi sure do have a gift when it comes to baking pies." He watched the blush rise in his mama's cheeks and knew she appreciated the compliment. Grace Nelson, like her daughter, loved to please people with her baking.

"Are you sure I'm not imposing?"

His parents answered in unison. "Of course not!"

Cindy turned to Jackson. "I'd hate to think I'm keeping you from anything."

He searched her face for clues as to what she was feeling. Was she looking for an excuse to leave? Was she tired, bored, in want of an escape? All he saw was uncertainty, and it made him feel guilty for giving Andi a hard time. This poor girl looked like a lost puppy in need of love and attention, and she'd come to the right place. There was nobody better at that than Grace and Joshua Nelson. And young Jackson always had a reputation for bringing home one lost puppy after another despite his father's severe asthma and allergies.

Jackson gave Cindy a warm smile. "I really don't have any plans, and I could never say no to one of Mama's pies."

He saw a flicker of relief pass over her features. No wonder Andi hadn't hesitated when Cindy called out of the blue. There was something about her that made a person want to wrap his arms around her and protect her from the many sufferings in her past.

A piece of pie in front of the fire turned into a heated competition when Grace turned on *Jeopardy*. Jackson was pleasantly surprised by how quickly and easily Cindy answered the questions, beating him and his parents to the response nearly every time once she figured out that there were no rules to their family style of play—as soon as you know the answer, shout it out.

By the end of the episode, Cindy was grinning ear to ear, and Jackson saw her laugh more than once. He noticed how pretty she was when she smiled, how different she looked when she felt at ease and confident.

"Well, Cindy, you sure kicked our butts!" He saw her blush and liked how she looked with the bright color in her pale cheeks. As if a light had been switched off, though, she retreated back into the same, insecure person she had been when she first arrived.

"I don't have much education, but I like to read. I try to learn as much as I can."

"You need to meet our Helena," Grace said. "She runs the town library. I'll let her know that you'll be coming round tomorrow to see her."

Cindy's face went from pink to red. "Oh, that's awfully kind, but I don't know what I'll be doing tomorrow. I mean, I'm not sure how long I'll be in town."

"Where are you going?" Jackson asked before he even realized he was wondering it.

"I…" She looked from one face to another as if searching for the answer in their expressions. "I don't have any idea."

***

For just a short time, Cindy was able to forget that she was motherless, childless, friendless—completely alone. She felt at home and could easily see how Andi had turned out to be the person she was. Grace and Joshua, as they insisted on being called, were all that she'd imagined parents could and should be. Jackson was sweet—attentive but not patronizing. They welcomed her and made her feel like she belonged, and she so desperately wanted to belong. Sometimes she was surprised at how much she wanted to belong.

"I mean, I don't really have anywhere to go. When I got engaged to Evan, I moved into his house with him, but when he died in the crash, I moved back in with Gloria. She was sick by then. Anyway, I had to sell the house after she passed, and I can't afford a place on my own. I had a small savings to get me through the past year or so, but now…" She sighed and gave a small shrug.

"What about your family?" Grace asked, her eyes conveying sympathy.

"I don't have any. Like I said, my mother died not long after Evan did, in July of last year, and my father left when I was twelve. I haven't seen or heard from him since. They weren't…" She met Grace's eyes with a degree of defiance and strength. She would not be embarrassed or judged by her parents' faults. "My parents weren't very nurturing. Gloria was an alcoholic."

Grace frowned. "Gloria?"

"My mother. She didn't like being called mom. She said it would make people think she was old. She wasn't." Cindy said without shame. "She was seventeen when she had me."

She met Grace's eyes again, and again, all she saw was acceptance. She went on. "My father was just one of many though he did stick around for longer than she thought he would. One day, I just woke up, and he was gone. To be honest, I couldn't say for sure that he was my father though Gloria always maintained that he was, and he was the only man I remember from my childhood. But after he disappeared, I realized my mother had many men who came and left."

Tamping down any animosity or shame she might have felt, Cindy continued to watch Grace. She'd spent twenty-two years telling herself that she wasn't her parents and wouldn't make the same mistakes they made, and she hadn't. She wasn't going to shoulder the blame for what they did, and she fought hard against the sting of knowing what others thought of her.

Rather than recoil, Grace offered a kind smile. "Well, nobody leaves this house without having a place to go. If for some reason Andi can't put you up in that giant house of hers, you're always welcome here."

Cindy was mortified. "Oh, Mrs. Nelson. I mean, Grace. I would never impose on any of you like that. I didn't mean for it to sound like I was—"

"Oh, hush now. I know you're not anglin' for a place to stay. Don't you think that for a minute. We've been blessed, and we all have the extra room. It would be a sin not to offer you a place to stay until you get on your feet. Whatsoever you do for the least of my brother, you know."

Cindy didn't know what to say. "You don't even know me. What if I was—"

"Bless your heart, child. What if you were what? A serial killer? I don't think we have anything to worry about. I bet you don't weigh a hundred pounds soaking wet. And you don't seem like the thieving type to me. You just take some time to figure out what you're going to do next and make yourself a plan. Things always go more smoothly when you've got a plan. Once you've got that figured out, I reckon we'll go from there."

Cindy looked from Grace to Jackson. He raised his hands and shoulders in a pronounced shrug. "Don't try arguing with Mama. She's always right."

"I'm always right because I've got God in my corner. He tells me which way to go." Grace looked at Cindy. "You remember that, no matter what your past looks like, no matter how alone you feel, God is there, and he'll make sure you're okay. Just follow him, and you will find your way."

Cindy blinked. She was at a loss as to what to say. Nobody had ever talked to her about God. Nobody had ever told her that her past didn't matter. Nobody ever told her that she wasn't alone. At a loss as to how to accept this unaccustomed kindness, she did the only thing she could.

"Thank you, Grace. I appreciate the kind words and the dinner invitation. It was wonderful. Jackson?" She looked over at Andi's brother. "Thank you for calling me. I've had a great time, but I'm awfully tired. Maybe I'll see you around."

She stood and looked for her jacket.

Jackson got up and went to the small closet just inside the front door and took out her jacket.

"Be careful driving back to Andi's. The streets can be awfully slick at night once the temperature drops."

She took the jacket he offered. "Thank you." She looked into his eyes, hoping he could see how much the evening meant to her. "Thank you for everything."

At her car, she felt his eyes on her as she fumbled with her keys, but she managed to get the door unlocked. She backed out of the driveway and found her way back to Andi's house. As she sat in the car and stared up at the big house, she thought about Grace's advice to come up with a plan. How could she devise a plan that would lead her to this? To a house, a family, a life like the one Andi and Jackson and their parents had, a life she had barely had time to imagine having with Evan. How could she plan for the future when even the present was so unknown?

Three

"Thank you, and have a nice day." Andi turned to Jackson after her customers left the bakery. "Shouldn't you be at work?"

"I'm working this afternoon. Besides, I'm technically on vacation this weekend." He lifted the glass dome from the platter of doughnuts and chose a shiny, golden one with chocolate glaze, no sprinkles.

"Hey, are you paying for that?"

"I did you a favor last night, remember?"

Andi frowned and crossed her arms across her chest. "And Mama said y'all had a real nice time. So, what's up?"

Jackson chewed the pastry, enjoying the still warm sensation and sweet taste. "What's her story?"

"Why?" She eyed him with suspicion.

He popped the rest of the doughnut into his mouth and licked his fingers. "She seems kind of lost. I feel sorry for her."

Andi stared at her brother for a moment. "She's not a stray dog, Jackson. You can't just feed her, take her on a walk, and make her life better."

He winced. "Ouch. I never compared her to a dog."

"You've never been able to resist helping a dog or a cat or even a person who was in need. You're just like Mama through and through."

"Look who's talking, Miss I'm Going to Save the World."

She rolled her eyes. "Okay, so maybe we all three got a bit of that from Mama, but Helena and I didn't spend our entire childhood wandering the neighborhood looking for lost animals."

"I only did that because Daddy never let me have a pet."

"He's allergic to cats, Jackson."

"I know that, Andi, but we could've had a dog at least." He sighed. He was getting off subject. "Besides, I'm not talking about a cat or a dog. I know she lost her mother to alcoholism, her father was apparently a loser, and her fiancé died. But none of that tells me anything about her as a person. You're always the first one to point out that our pasts should not define us, but I'd like to know more about hers."

"You spent the evening with her. You tell me." She walked into the back where Naomi, her employee, was boxing up pies.

"Hey, Jackson."

"Hey, Naomi." He gave her a quick nod. "Hospice orders?"

"Yeah. Your sister must have been up half the night baking these."

"Jackson and I are going to be in the office for a bit. Can you listen out for the bell?"

"Sure thing, Andi."

Jackson followed his sister to the closet she called an office. Andi sat in the chair behind the little desk where she did her bookkeeping and took online orders. Jackson leaned against the closed door. There was no room for another chair.

"Look, Cindy doesn't talk a whole lot about her personal life. The fact that you know about her father surprises me. What did she say?"

"That he may or may not have been her real father and that he left them when she was twelve. She said her mother had her when she was just seventeen. She had to sell the house she and her mom lived in, and she doesn't have anywhere to go."

"Hmm…She told y'all as much in one night as she told me in a whole year. Cindy's had it rough, but she's a fighter." She leaned her elbows on the desk and looked at him. "When she and Evan got together, she had plans and dreams that he encouraged. He was going to use his GI Bill to let her go to college. She's really smart"

Jackson thought about Cindy's competitiveness and abilities during *Jeopardy* the previous evening.

"Yeah, I picked up on that."

Andi nodded. "She's a hard worker and has a lot of spunk and determination when she's not letting others get her down. The other wives, they weren't kind to her. I don't think she fit their definition of 'military wife'."

"What do you think she'll do now?"

"I heard her just beginning to stir when I left the house. I haven't asked her how long she's staying, but based on what you just said, it doesn't sound like she's going to be in a hurry to move on."

"Is that a problem for you? Or for Wade?"

Andi frowned. "I don't think so. I always liked Cindy, and Boomer adores her, but she can't stay forever. That won't help her get on her feet. I wonder what her plans are."

"Now you sound like Mama. She told Cindy that the first thing she needs to do is come up with a plan for her future."

Andi smiled. "Sounds like Mama. She always has a plan of some sort even if it's just her daily to-do list."

"Mama and Helena, two peas in a pod." He smiled. "Speaking of whom, Cindy said she loves to read and learn. Mama suggested she go by the library today to meet Helena. They'll hit it off like a pig and a mud bath."

Andi made a noise of amusement. "They will. In fact, Cindy always kind of reminded me of Helena with her pale skin and hair, her love of books, and her willingness to jump in and try new things despite her insecurities."

"Yeah, I can see that." Their sister came across as a highly intelligent, upbeat, sometimes annoyingly perky person; but Jackson knew that underneath, she saw herself as inadequate, overweight, and under experienced in the ways of the world. "But I can't see Cindy suddenly announcing that she's going to Europe alone for the summer. She doesn't seem to know what to do next."

Andi took a deep breath and slowly let it out. "That trip made a world of difference for Helena. It was just the confidence booster she needed." She squinted her eyes and stared at the door behind Jackson, a look of deep concentration furrowing her brow.

"What are you thinking?"

"That Cindy needs a trip to Europe, so to speak."

"Meaning what?"

"Something to boost her spirits and her confidence. What can she do that would make her feel better about herself and her situation?"

"Hmm… Who's searching for stray dogs now?" Jackson asked.

Andi gave him a look that he'd seen many times when she was annoyed with him.

"Let's think, Jackson. There must be something she can do."

"I'm going to go out on a limb here and guess that she never made it to college, since Evan died, and doesn't have much work experience."

"I honestly don't know about college, but she has plenty of work experience. She's been supporting herself and her mother since her father left them. She's worked as a waitress, a cashier, and a housekeeper at a hotel."

"With all the new businesses coming to town, she shouldn't have a problem getting a job. Maybe the

Russos could use another waitress at Al Forna. Hey! I saw a sign in the window at the Shop-a-Lot the other day. They're looking for help."

Andi shook her head. "No, it's not just a job that she needs. She needs a calling."

"Andi, I hate to break it to you, but you can't find someone's calling for them. They have to discover it for themselves."

She waved him away with a flick of her hand. "I know, but we can steer her in the right direction."

"You're wrong, Andi. Cindy needs to figure this one out on her own. Even I can see that."

"Then why did you come by?" she asked, her voice conveying annoyance.

"Because I was curious, and sure, I thought maybe I could help her, but I'm not sure Buffalo Springs is going to have what she needs."

"What she needs, Little Brother, is a family, a group of people she can rely on, a community she feels a part of. Those are the things she's never had that everyone needs."

"Okay, I agree with that. The question is, how can she find that? And where?"

"I don't know, but I bet if we all put our heads together, we can figure it out. Christmas is less than a month away. I'll convince her that we want her to stay here through the holidays. I know she'll like that. Lots of places will need extra help. We can feel her out, see what she'd like to do with her life, and determine how we can help. Maybe we can pull off a Christmas miracle of some sort."

Jackson left without quite knowing how he felt about his sister's plan. There wasn't anything wrong with it on the surface, but he felt like they were playing God, and he didn't like that. Then again, he'd been brought up to believe that all humans were put on the earth to do God's work. Maybe he and Andi were being called into action. Again.

***

"Are you Helena?"

The woman behind the counter looked up in surprise. "Me? No, I'm Sarah. Helena's in the office. Would you like me to get her for you?"

"Um, no, that's okay. I, uh, I'm a friend of her sister, and their mom suggested I come here."

"Oh, okay. Hold on." Sarah turned and hurried toward the back of the library before Cindy could stop her.

Cindy turned and looked around. It was a magnificent building—an old converted house with a spiral staircase and wide windows.

"Can I help you?"

Cindy spun around, her heart in her throat.

"I'm sorry. I didn't mean to startle you." There was absolutely no resemblance whatsoever between this blonde-haired beauty and her dark-haired siblings.

Though she and Andi both had blue eyes, and Jackson had brown, Andi and Jackson looked much more alike.

"Are you Helena?"

The woman beamed. "I am. And you must be Cindy."

"How…?"

"Mama called. It's so nice to meet you. You're staying with Andi and Wade, right?"

"Well, I stayed last night and the night before. But staying, as in the future tense? Well, I'm not sure. I mean, I'm not sure for how long."

"I'm sure Andi is thrilled to have you here." Helena's smile was so genuine and welcoming, Cindy felt right at ease, like she'd known her for ages.

"Thank you. I really appreciate her letting me stay. I'm trying, I mean, I'm hoping… Well, I'm just trying to figure out where to go from here. And your mom said I should come by because I told her I love to read."

"Then we have that in common," Helena said. "What do you like to read?"

Now this was a subject Cindy had no problem expanding upon. "Anything and everything. On the ride here, I listened to the latest Kristin Hannah book, but I'm currently reading a book I picked up at a yard sale. It's an old Anne Perry mystery."

"Oh, those are so much fun. We have a great mystery section. Sarah and I both just adore a good mystery. Let me show you."

Cindy followed Helena to the mystery section of the library where, indeed, she was treated to quite the collection of old and new. They chatted about the titles, their favorite mystery writers, and what they liked best in a good whodunit. They expanded their talk to their favorite movies once they discovered they both loved movies as much as they loved books. Books and movies had been Cindy's only escapes from the life she lived before Evan.

Before they knew it, Helena was looking at her watch and declaring that she was way overdue to cover the desk so Sarah could eat lunch.

"Feel free to hang out and pick out a title or two."

"But I don't have a card."

"It only takes a few minutes to fix that," Helena assured her. "Just come see me when you're ready. If you're not busy, you can join me for lunch when Sarah gets back."

Away she went like a magician disappearing in a cloud of smoke. Cindy shook her head. Helena and Andi were nothing alike, but she liked them both. Helena was obviously the dreamer, a girl given to fancy and romance, while Andi and Jackson both seemed so serious and practical. What fun it must have been to grow up with siblings. Cindy hoped to have a whole house full of kids some—

She stopped and straightened, her hand grazing a book on a plastic display stand and knocking it to the floor. She shook her head as she picked it up and replaced the book and stand on the shelf.

Children. Siblings. Family. Things that Cindy knew nothing about and probably never would. She'd had her chance at true love, and it was taken from her just like everything else she'd ever had—a mother, a father, a home, a life. If there was one thing Cindy had learned in her short time on earth, it was that she wasn't meant to have anything permanent in her life. She was destined to be alone, and she had no choice but to accept that and move on. She wouldn't allow herself to think otherwise.

***

Jackson put his car into park and sat in the back of the lot, looking at the Tractor Supply. He'd been working there every summer and school break since he was fifteen, and he was more than ready to move on. He hadn't planned on working all weekend, but the warehouse manager, Pete, had texted him last week that they'd be shorthanded because of the holiday and asked if he wanted to pick up a few hours. Knowing he needed the money, Jackson agreed.

All afternoon, his thoughts drifted to Andi's friend. He'd never thought about how lucky he was that his mama and daddy were good people, that they had a good marriage, that he had sisters he actually loved *and liked* and enjoyed being with. He took for granted the way he was raised, the lessons his father taught him, and even the education he'd worked so hard to pay for. Sure, he'd done it himself, but at least he had the opportunity to do it. Not everyone got to go to college or learn a trade or know, beyond a doubt, what they were going to do with their life.

In two weeks, Jackson would be a college graduate. Finally. He could go anywhere he wanted, do anything he wanted. He'd have a degree, a good education, the support of his parents, and even a little money in the bank. Not enough to move right away, but once he had a job secured, he'd be able to go.

What would Cindy do? Where would she go? How could she make plans without money or a degree or a support system?

Though Jackson told himself that it was none of his business and that once he left to go back to school the next day, he'd never see her again, he couldn't stop thinking about Cindy and how lost and alone she looked when she rushed out the night before.

****

Cindy couldn't remember the last time she laughed so hard. Helena had a wicked sense of humor that perfectly matched Cindy's wit. She took a long, slow drink of her hot chocolate as Helena continued her story about growing up with Jackson and Andi.

"Do you want the rest of my fries? I'm trying to cut back." Helena pushed what was left toward Cindy.

"Are you sure?"

"Absolutely. I'm engaged to a fabulous cook, and between his cooking and Andi's pies, I'll never be able to find a wedding dress that fits come spring."

"You look fine to me," Cindy told her. "I'm sorry I missed Andi's wedding. The pictures were beautiful."

"She made a beautiful bride. She and Wade are so good together."

Cindy thought of Jeremy. She had no idea until a few days ago that there had been anything between him and Andi. She didn't know him well. He was quiet, introspective, always thinking about their next assignment. It was hard to picture them together. But in just the few minutes she'd spent with Wade, she could see how perfectly suited he and Andi were for each other.

"Wade seems really nice. I'm glad he and Andi found each other."

"Me, too, but it wasn't love at first sight. Believe me. They had a long road ahead of them when they first met. Andi didn't trust Wade, and he didn't care for Andi at all."

Cindy was surprised. "Really? Why? Everyone likes Andi."

"Andi didn't tell you about what was going on when she first got home? With the town, I mean?"

Cindy shook her head. "No. But I was dealing with my own stuff back then, losing Evan. And then I had Gloria's illness and death to deal with."

"I'm sorry about that. All of it. It must have been really hard on you."

Cindy smiled. "It was, but I'm trying to move past it."

Helena looked at her watch. "I need to get back. This was so much fun. I'd love to get together again."

"That would be nice, but I'm not sure how long I'll be around."

"Where are you heading?"

She shrugged. "I don't know, but I can't live in Andi's spare bedroom forever."

Helena's eyes lit up. "Then move in with me. I have an extra room, and I really miss having a roommate. I didn't know how much I missed having someone around until Andi moved in, and now that she's married, I'm alone again. You don't have any plans, and Christmas is coming. You might as well stay here for a little while."

"But I'm just about broke, and I don't have a job, and you barely know me."

"And look how well we've hit it off already. Come on, Cindy. This town is going to be booming come springtime. There will be lots of opportunities here. Why not stick around for a while and see how it goes?"

Cindy bit her lip. "Well, maybe I could move in just through the holidays and then see what happens. I really need to get a job."

"Then start looking! Come back to the library with me, and I'll point you toward the want ads. There's got to be something that'll interest you. Everyone needs help at Christmas time."

Helena's excitement was contagious, and Cindy found herself being pulled across the deli.

"I guess I could at least take a look at the job listings."

"Of course, you can. You said yourself, you've got no place to go."

"Are you always this spontaneous and enthusiastic?"

"I try to be," Helena said with a laugh. "I like to keep Joe on his toes."

Cindy followed Helena back to the library. Why not? She could at least stay through the holidays. Maybe she'd find a job, maybe not. She'd be no worse off than she already was, and she'd finally have a real family to be with for Christmas.

***

"You're not upset, are you?"

"Upset?" Andi asked. "I'm thrilled! I knew you and Helena would hit it off, but Boomer sure will miss you." Cindy helped Andi pull off the sheets from the guest bed back at the house.

"I'll miss him, too." Cindy let out a sigh of relief. "I didn't know if this would cause some sort of sibling rivalry. I'm not sure how that stuff works." She made a face of exaggerated confusion, and Andi laughed.

"There's nothing like that with us. Helena and I are four years apart, but we share a number of friends. In fact, she should introduce you to our other friends. Well, they're mostly her friends, but we all hang out. We have kind of a… club? I guess you'd call it that."

"What kind of club?"

"Mostly a love and support club, I guess," Andi said with a laugh. Cindy followed her to the laundry room on the first floor where they loaded Cindy's towels and sheets into the washer. "We get together once every two weeks, usually at Rick's, talk about whatever is going on in our lives—vent about men or jobs or whatever is bugging us mostly—and we drink. Nothing over the top, just a few social drinks. Helena, Allie, and Paige—Helena's two best friends—started this years ago. They call themselves, and the rest of us now, I guess, the Comfort and Aid Society."

Cindy raised her brow. "The Comfort and Aid Society?"

"Yeah, because when they were teens sneaking around, they drank Southern Comfort in lemonade. They still do on hot summer days, but their tastes have matured. Some." Andi grinned.

Cindy wondered what it would be like to have a group of women to count on like that. She'd had friends in high school, but she always felt the need to be guarded around them. Her home was not the kind you invited other kids into. When she met Evan, she thought she'd finally found a group of women with whom she had things in common, but they refused to accept her. She was always the outsider. She tried not to let that bother her, but other women could be so cruel.

Cindy watched Andi add soap and press the digital buttons on the washing machine. "These friends of yours…what do they do?"

"Allie recently helped Paige open a souvenir shop in town, but Allie works for an abuse shelter, and Paige is a freelance graphic designer. Paige's brother runs the store, and Paige designs the souvenirs. Sarah, well you met her, she's kind of new to the group and doesn't really come that often now that she's met other gals her age." Andi stopped and narrowed her eyes. "Actually, Sarah's about your age, so I'll text her and make sure she comes and see if she wants to bring the other gals. Amanda is new, too. She's the other doctor at the clinic with Joe."

"That's Helena's fiancé, right?"

"Right. He's Jeremy's brother. Did you know that?" Andi leaned back against the washer as the sound of water rushed into the tub.

Cindy's eyes widened. "Jeremy's brother?"

"Twin brother."

"Oh my gosh," Cindy breathed. "Twin?"

"Yeah." Andi nodded. "It kind of freaked me out when he first showed up in town, but it didn't take long for us all to become friends. Well, more than friends in their case."

"How did he and Helena get together?"

"That's a story I'm sure she would love to tell you." Andi pushed away from the washer and headed back upstairs. Cindy followed. Andi pulled an extra set of sheets from the closet, and she and Cindy went back to the guest room.

"Your family has been awfully nice to me, Andi. I really appreciate it."

Andi stopped, and the sheet in her hands fluttered onto the bed. "Cindy, we're happy to have you. Don't start thinking for a minute that we aren't."

Cindy's heart stirred a bit. She was falling in love with every member of Andi's family. She just hoped she didn't wear out her welcome before she figured out where on earth she could go next.

***

"Busy day?" Mama asked after they'd helped put Daddy to bed. Jackson was on his way to his room when her voice stopped him.

"Not really." Jackson ate a late supper in the living room, watching television with his parents, but had been preoccupied throughout the evening.

"Something bothering you?"

He took a long, deep breath, held it for a moment, then let it out in a slow stream. "I'm not sure right now is a good time to talk about it."

His mother's brow creased in concern. "What is it, Jackson?"

"Maybe we should sit down." He opened the door to his room and let his mother pass by. He closed the door and sat on his bed, gesturing toward his desk chair. His mama took a seat in the chair.

"You're worrying me, Jackson."

"I don't mean to, Mama." He rubbed his hand across his forehead, then looked up at his mother. "Mama, you know I love you and Daddy."

"Of course, I know that. What a silly thing to say."

"You know I'd love to stay right here, in Buffalo Springs, forever."

She smiled. "Well, I wouldn't go that far. I reckon most young men have a desire to leave their hometown and explore the world, find new horizons, all that stuff."

"Yeah, but you know what I mean. I was never one to complain about life in a small town or wish I could grow up and get out of here."

"But now…"

He sighed. "But now." He should be excited about venturing out, starting a new life, seeking his path, but he wasn't. "I can't do what I want to do here. I need to be somewhere I can find bigger and better opportunities. I need to do what Wade did and go to New York. I want to join an investment firm."

His mother nodded, her expression giving nothing away.

"It's not that I want to go, but I have to. I—"

"Jackson, don't you think we know that, your father and me? This town is finally starting to become something, to hold opportunities it never held before, but not for you. We know that your career path dictates that you leave Arkansas. You don't have to feel bad or feel that you need to break it to us. We've known that for a while now."

"Really?" He felt relieved while at the same time, a little sad. He wanted their blessing, but he also wanted to stay near them. Maybe it was because he was the youngest. Maybe it was because he'd always been a mama's boy, holding onto the hem of her skirt, crying when she first took him to school, always seeking her approval. Maybe he just liked it that his sisters were both home, and their family was in a really good place for the first time in a long time.

"Sugar, don't you think we want what's best for you and what's going to make you happy? We support you, no matter where the road takes you. We know you'll always have a connection to home."

Jackson was nearly twenty-four years old, yet he fought the urge to cry like a baby. He hid his face in his hands, massaging his temple. He felt the bed give and his mother's arms circle around him.

"I know it's hard to leave. It will be hard to let you go. But look at your sister. I cried all the way back from Annapolis, and she cried through her first year at the academy, but she loved what she did. And when it was time to leave, she came home, and she's never been happier. Going out into the world is a good thing. It's what everyone needs to do at some point in their lives whether it's for twelve years like Andi or four weeks like Helena. This is your chance to find out who you are, what you can accomplish, and where you're heading in life." Reaching out, she smoothed back his hair like she'd done when he was a little boy, and suddenly, he felt like that five-year-old first-day-of-schooler, standing in the doorway, tears streaming down his face, watching his mother walk away.

"I know, Mama. I guess I just needed to hear you say it."

"This is what you've waited for your whole life. There's no need to be sad. Daddy and I will be fine, and this here bed will be waiting for you whenever you want to come home for a spell."

"Thanks, Mama. You always know just what to say, you know that?"

His mother pointed above. "Not me, Jackson. Every morning, I pray to the Holy Spirit to give me the right words I'll need for the day. He hasn't failed me yet."

They hugged and said good night, and it suddenly felt bittersweet. This was the last night Jackson would spend in his bed before he became a college graduate. But that was okay. He was ready, and so were his parents.

As Jackson drifted off to sleep in his childhood room with one of his mother's handmade afghans draped over him, he felt the weight of the world slide away, washed away like the chalk drawings he and Helena used to cover the sidewalks with. He felt ready to go wherever the Spirit led him.

Four

The following week, Andi stood on the sidewalk, gazing at the candy store with her mouth hanging open. Cindy held her breath, waiting for a reaction. Finally, Andi let out a long lungful of air and shook her head.

"It's like…it's like a Hallmark movie."

"Really?" Cindy asked, still not sure. "Not too over the top?"

"Not at all," Andi reassured her, her eyes still roaming over every inch of the window display and the decorations along the roof and front porch. "I absolutely love it."

"I wasn't sure what to do when Mrs. Franklin asked if I would be willing to do it, but I figured, if she was going to pay me, I'd make it worth her while. Helena suggested I talk to her and said she'd vouch for me, which was really nice of her considering I didn't have time to put together any references, and she hardly knows me even though I am living with her." She forced herself to stop babbling and took a deep breath. She was a bundle of nerves, and Andi's opinion meant the world to her.

"Well, you won't need references after this. I can't believe what a spectacular job you did in just a couple days. It looks like something out of a Dickens novel."

Cindy joined Andi on the sidewalk and looked through the windows at the display. After seeing the ad at the library for someone to help with Christmas decorations, Cindy went by the store to talk to the owner, Mrs. Franklin. The woman's husband passed away that year, and she wasn't in the state of mind to decorate. She wanted to pay someone to do it for her. Cindy felt a kinship with the woman, under the circumstance, and agreed to do the short-term assignment. When she brought up the job to Andi and her friends the night they went out, they all encouraged her to give it a try. Their support, without even knowing her, was both surprising and uplifting.

After getting permission from Mrs. Franklin to use anything she found in the back of the store, Cindy repurposed an old, antique scale. She took it apart and hung the scales from the top of the window display area then filled them with old-fashioned candies. She took garlands that she found in a beat-up cardboard box and lined the window all the way around, tucking in shiny, red Christmas balls that looked like giant jawbreakers. Soft white lights twinkled in the greenery. Faux gingerbread Santas stood at attention on the left side of the display, and a basket overflowing with candy canes in various sizes filled the right side. In between, bow-wrapped boxes of vintage candies were stacked in towers and drew the eyes to the assortment of confections.

Above the window, the gutter was lined with more lighted garland that trailed down each side of the door and along the step railings. The door boasted a giant evergreen wreath with all sorts of candies tucked into its fronds. A generous plaid bow glistened from the bottom right side of the wreath.

"You've created something magical," Andi said with amazement.

Cindy was delighted with her friend's assessment. She wanted so badly to please Andi and everyone else. She needed to make money, but more importantly, she needed to feel accepted. Why this sudden need after all these years, she didn't know, but she wanted it badly.

"You'd better watch out. Everyone else in town is going to be after you to set up their displays."

Cindy felt her insides grow warm with happiness. "You think so?"

"I do, but I have a problem with that."

Disappointment flooded her. Why would Andi not want Cindy to make money? "You do?" she asked with annoyance.

Andi laughed. "I sure do! I get you first! For my bakery and my house. You should see the number of boxes of Christmas stuff Wade's got in the attic. I didn't even try to decorate last year. It was too overwhelming."

Cindy's smile was so wide, it almost hurt. She didn't mention that she'd already seen the boxes in the attic, but the thought of digging into them made her giddy with excitement.

"When do you want me to start?"

***

Jackson stared at the photo on his phone for the tenth time that afternoon. He was supposed to be studying for finals, but his mind was back in Buffalo Springs. Andi had sent a photo in the family group chat of a display in the candy store window, saying what an amazing job Cindy had done. The rest of the family responded with praise for the decorations, and he longed to be home where he could see it in person. The question was, why?

The first year Jackson was away at school was a struggle. He put on a brave face, but he missed his mama. He knew that made him a complete wimp, but he couldn't help it. He'd never been away from her before. Add to that the facts that Andi was always away on some secret military mission with the Navy SEALS, and his father had lost his job at the factory. Jackson found it hard to enjoy college life.

By his second semester, though, he'd come to like having a life away from the small town where there were no secrets. He liked that he could date someone without a thousand questions from his mother and Helena. He liked that if he had a little too much to drink, which he was not proud to admit had happened more than once, he didn't have to answer to his daddy. He liked that he had his own life and made his own decisions. Once he came to that conclusion, his eyes were opened to another revelation. There was a whole world out there much bigger, brighter, and busier than Buffalo Springs.

When Joshua lost his job at the hardware store—a job with low pay and few benefits that he'd been forced to take after the factory closed—Jackson reluctantly took off a couple semesters and went home to help with the family finances. It was then that he realized he could never go home again, not permanently. Sure, the town was growing as fast as grass in early June, but he didn't see how there could be any real possibilities for him there. So, why was he feeling homesick now with only one more week of classes and a few days of finals? He was graduating in a little more than a week and was making plans to head to New York. Why was he suddenly longing for home?

New York. That must be it, he told himself. He knew that after the first of the year, he would be leaving, probably for good. He was going to have to say goodbye to everyone he loved and start over again just like he did when he went away to school. Only this time, Andi was out of the military and back home, happily married to the mayor, his father was improving—slowly, but improving—and Helena would soon be married to the town doctor. His family was safe, the town was booming, and his life was just getting ready to begin.

Satisfied that his impending move was all that was bothering him but knowing that it was what he'd worked so hard for, Jackson put his phone on do not disturb and turned back to his studying. An image of the store window flickered in his mind followed by the memory of Cindy's shy smile, and Jackson thought, perhaps he should make a trip home that weekend. To take home some of his clothes and things, of course.

***

"You look amazing," Helena told Cindy.

The red dress she'd borrowed from Sarah fit perfectly, and Cindy felt like a different person as she spun around in front of the mirror.

"This is so much fun. I've never dressed up and gone to the theater before."

Helena laughed. "Well, don't get too excited. This is Buffalo Springs, not Broadway. How do I look?" She turned around to show off the sparkly green dress she'd ordered online. "Is it too much?"

"Not at all! It looks like it was made for you."

"I hope we're not overdoing it. This is the first production since the old movie theater was renovated into a stage theater, so I know they're going all out to make it a grand and festive affair, but like I said, it's not Broadway."

"Who cares?" Cindy said. "Just because we're not in a big, fancy city doesn't mean we can't get dressed up and go out and enjoy the arts."

"Pix, I'm here! Are you ladies decent?"

"We're almost ready, Joe," Helena called. She frowned and looked around the room. "Have you seen my silver shoes?" She lifted the trailing cover of the unmade bed and looked underneath.

"I don't know how you find anything in here," Cindy said then gasped at her own words. "I'm so sorry! I shouldn't have said that."

Helena threw her hand up in triumph, a silver pump dangling from her finger. She hauled herself up from the floor. "Don't worry. It's nothing Andi hasn't said to me a million times." She frowned. "I guess I'll have to work on that before Joe and I get married."

"Is he very neat?"

Helena rolled her eyes. "As neat and clean as a surgical unit."

Cindy looked around the bedroom. Not a surface could be seen anywhere. Dirty clothes were scattered on the floor, and clean ones were piled in a chair. The closet doors were open, revealing clothes, shoes, purses, and scarves haphazardly stashed throughout. The rest of the rancher was spotless and meticulously organized, but the bedroom looked like a tornado had gone through it.

"It's a good thing you've got until June to mend your ways. You know, I could help you. I'm really good at cleaning, and I like to organize. I always feel this need to make things neat and tidy." Cindy was sure a therapist would have a field day with that revelation.

"If you're half as good at cleaning and organizing as you are at decorating for Christmas, I may take you up on it. You did an amazing job on the display at the candy store, and Andi and Wade's house looks like something from a movie set."

Cindy blushed. "It was fun, and I really do love planning, organizing, and decorating. I'm sorry if I offended you. I was trying to help."

Helena laughed. "One thing you should know about me, I don't offend easily. And though I'm a master planner, list-maker, and event organizer, I could use some help cleaning and organizing in my personal life, but not tonight. As far as this stuff goes, for tonight, and I'm borrowing a phrase from a new friend here..." Helena looped her arm through Cindy's. "Who cares? Let's go enjoy our night at the theater. I hear the Christmas decorations are amazing."

Cindy's smile widened. She didn't know what was more exciting—a night at the theater or having everyone in town see the lobby she had worked so hard on for the past two days.

***

The Nelson family, minus Joshua, met them on the sidewalk outside the theater. Jackson did a double take when Joe walked up with Helena on one arm and Cindy on the other. She looked stunning, and he was momentarily at a loss for words. Luckily, he'd always been one to recover quickly in awkward or shocking situations.

"Well, aren't you the lucky one. Not just one beautiful woman, but two." He spoke to Joe, but his eyes never left Cindy's. He saw the heat rise in her face and he smiled, hoping to put her at ease.

"Jackson, you are nothing but a flirt," Helena teased her brother before reaching for a hug.

"Cindy, you look beautiful," his mother said. "I'm tickled pink you agreed to join us."

"Oh, I'm so excited to be here. I've never been to a real live play before."

"You grew up in California but never saw a stage show?" Wade asked, and Jackson saw Andi elbow him in the ribs.

"Well, my high school put on shows, and I saw a couple of those, but I never had the occasion to go to a real theater."

Jackson saw the humiliation in her eyes and felt a pang of regret.

"Don't feel bad, Cindy." He slid her arm out from Joe's hold and looped it through his own. "I've never seen a show in a theater either. It will be a first for both of us."

Jackson saw Andi arch her brow, and he shot her a look. His family never missed a new show at the Sight and Sound Theater in Branson, but Cindy didn't know that. He'd recognized right away, the night they had dinner, that she was self-conscious about her upbringing, and he didn't want her insecurities to ruin her evening.

"Where's your father this evening?" Cindy asked as Jackson led her inside.

"He's not up to big outings like this. It wears him out. He's content to sit home and watch the History Channel. It worked out perfectly though since nobody knew I was coming home for the weekend. Daddy was happy to give me his ticket."

They waited in line to enter the theater behind Helena and Joe. When Joe casually slipped his arm around Helena's shoulder, his mangled hand was in full view, and Jackson heard Cindy gasp. He leaned down and whispered to her.

"It's a long, gruesome story. He's had several surgeries, and he's able to do almost everything he could before, even minor surgeries, but it will never be one hundred percent again."

"What happened?" Cindy asked.

Before Jackson could answer, it was their turn to present their tickets, and the conversation was forgotten. Jackson handed their tickets to the usher and was surprised when the young man beamed at Cindy and said, "Nice job in there, Cindy." Jackson noticed the red in the man's cheeks and felt a stir in his gut but didn't have time to think about it.

He watched Cindy as they entered the renovated movie house. Her eyes were wide with excitement when they walked on the red carpet toward the pair of double doors leading into the theater.

As he entered the lobby, Helena grabbed Cindy's arm and began gushing about the tree in the center of the high-ceilinged room.

"Cindy, it's spectacular. I'm at a loss for words."

That's a first, Jackson thought as his gaze focused on the tree. And what a tree it was!

The magnificent fir tree stood at least twenty feet tall, the top nearly brushing the mural on the theater ceiling. It glistened with thousands of white lights and sparkling glass Christmas balls as large as duckpin bowling balls. The tree was wrapped with red ribbons and bows as well as old celluloid movie reels. Round, metal reel casings were strategically placed around the tree along with glass drama masks in gold and silver.

Jackson's eyes roamed to the balcony behind the tree. Garlands of greenery, Christmas balls, and white lights ran along the railing while white lights covered the balusters. An enormous wreath hung in the center, adorned with a giant red bow. Along the stairs leading up to the balcony were giant poinsettias. Bow- and ball-ladened arrangements sat on top of the posts at the foot of the stairs.

It took Jackson several minutes to pick up on the conversation around him. Everyone in the lobby, not just his family, lauded Cindy with praise and commented on what a marvelous job she had done. Jackson looked at her with his mouth agape. Their eyes locked, and Jackson saw her swallow. He noticed how her neck was smooth and pale, as elegant as a swan's.

Wade appeared at Cindy's side and pointed up to the cascading lights above them. "The tree and all the lights and glittering decorations draw the eyes right to the ceiling lights." Wade said to her. "They don't just fade into the background. How did you manage that? My mama would be so pleased. Those lights were hung in 1937, just in time for the premier of *Gone With the Wind*."

Cindy turned toward him, fascination showing on her face. "That's amazing. Nobody told me that. I just thought they were so beautiful, I didn't want the decorations to overshadow them. I choose the location of the tree for just that reason." She followed his gaze and looked at the lights for a moment before turning back to Wade. "I know this theater meant a lot to your family."

"It did. My family opened this place back in the early 1930s. My mama—she passed away last month—was the last owner and operator of the movie house. We sold it to the Prestons last year. They've worked around the clock to convert it from a movie house into a performing arts theater. It's what Mama would have wanted—for the theater to still be used as a theater in some way. She and Daddy loved this place, and I remember bringing my little sister here to see Disney movies before we lost her…" His voice trailed off as he looked back at the tree. "The film reels look great, by the way."

Jackson understood his need to change the subject and wondered if Cindy knew that Wade's sister had been hit by a car and killed when she was not yet thirteen.

Cindy's eyes softened in understanding as she looked at Wade and then shifted her attention toward the tree. "Thanks. You know, when I was decorating your house, I came across some reels of famous classic movies—*Casablanca*, *Yankee Doodle Dandy*, and some others. Did you know you had those?"

"Yeah. Unfortunately, they were never stored properly, and they're pretty worthless, but they were Mama's favorites, so I haven't had the heart to get rid of them."

"I'm so sorry. About your mother, I mean."

Jackson wondered if she thought of her own mother and pondered, not for the first time, how she had managed to be so sweet and kind after what sounded to him like a terrible childhood.

"Thank you, but she's in a better place now. Though I have a feeling she's here with us in spirit tonight."

"I'm sure you're right."

Wade smiled. "I can't think of a better way to celebrate the opening than with a family Christmas play. Mama loved movies, and she loved books. I remember watching the movie, *The Best Christmas Pageant Ever*, right here when I was a little boy."

The lights dimmed. "We'd better take our seats," Wade advised.

Cindy began to walk toward the main entrance to the theater, but Jackson tugged on her arm and gestured toward Wade and Andi who were walking through a door on the far side of the lobby.

They entered a small hallway and took a narrow flight of stairs to a box in the center of the hall.

"Where are we?" Cindy whispered.

"Wade has box seats. The Prestons wanted to gift them to him in appreciation for the nearly one-hundred years his family owned the theater, but he refused. He purchased the box and told them he insisted on buying any and all tickets for the box as well."

"Wade's, um…"

"Loaded? Yeah. His family is one of the few in town that always had money, and then he made a lot of money as an attorney in New York. Apparently, he even lived in a penthouse. He put all that on hold to move back here to take care of his mama, and then he met Andi, and well, he decided to stay." There were few people in the world Jackson truly admired, and Wade was one of them, but the life he gave up was just the life Jackson wanted.

Cindy gazed at Wade admiringly, and they all took their seats just as the theater went dark.

"I remember reading this book when I was little," Cindy whispered, leaning into Jackson as she spoke. He detected the scent of strawberries—a shampoo just right for her strawberry blonde hair—and it made him feel slightly heady. He nodded, unable to find his words.

Much of the show was lost on Jackson. He couldn't take his eyes off Cindy. She laughed, she cried, she clapped and cheered. When intermission came, she reached over and squeezed Jackson's hand.

"This is just wonderful. I can't believe I'm here."

Jackson could only smile. It was like watching a little kid on Christmas morning. Her enthusiasm and excitement radiated from her beaming face, and Jackson wondered what else they could do to keep her feeling and looking this way.

He watched as she eagerly bounded from her seat and went to talk to Helena and his mother.

"It's fun to watch someone come alive, isn't it?" Joe asked.

Jackson nodded and turned to Wade. "Thank you. I think this is just what we all needed."

"It's just what Mama would have wanted," Wade said. "Everyone in Buffalo Springs is here. The theater is full and bright and looking brand new. It's times like this that make me glad I came back to town." Wade looked over at Andi and his eyes lit up as his smile widened. "Well, I guess there are several reasons I'm glad I came back to town."

Jackson felt a tug in his gut as he observed the adoring way Wade looked at Andi. He hoped he'd someday find what his sister and Wade had. He glanced at Cindy just as a voice in his head reminded him: someday, but not today.

Jackson had too many other dreams to make a reality before he would be ready for that.

***

"And unto you a child is born!" The child actor belted out the play's most robust line with all the enthusiasm he could muster.

It was all Cindy could do not to jump to her feet and applaud. She laughed and clapped along with the rest of the audience. When the play was over, she went with the Nelson family to the town drug store that boasted an old-fashioned ice cream parlor and soda fountain in the back of the store. The proprietor had kept the doors open late to welcome the theatergoers.

"What would you like?" Jackson asked as Cindy eyed the many choices written on the blackboard.

"There are too many to choose just one."

Jackson laughed. "Andi is partial to anything with peanut butter, and Helena always goes for something super sweet and fruity like cherry or raspberry. Mama likes plain old chocolate."

She looked at Jackson. "And what do you like, Jackson?"

She saw his expression falter for just a moment, and a curtain of pink danced across his features, reminiscent of the curtains that closed at the end of the show. He blinked and just as quickly as the odd look appeared, it disappeared, and he broke into a wide grin.

"I always go for a good, old-fashioned root beer float with vanilla ice cream."

"Would you believe, I've never had a root beer float?"

The look he gave her was one of exaggerated shock. "What? That might be the most un-American thing I've ever heard." He clutched at his chest. "A shot to the heart."

Cindy laughed, and Andi inserted herself between them to grab some extra napkins from the top of the ice cream display case.

"Is this guy bothering you?" she asked with a mock scowl.

Cindy shook her head. "Not at all. This has been one of the best nights of my life, and I'm going to top it off with my very first root beer float."

Andi smiled. "I think that's a great idea."

On their turn, Jackson ordered for them both then reached for his wallet to pay, but Cindy put her hand on his arm.

"Jackson, no, I can't let you do that."

"Why not?"

"Because I can pay for my own ice cream. You all have been so generous already."

"Sorry, Cindy, but my daddy would skin me alive if he heard that I allowed a female to pay for her own ice cream."

She frowned and said in a firm voice, "Jackson, this isn't a date. I can pay for my own ice cream."

Again, she saw his face redden. "I never said it was a date, and you should accept an act of kindness when presented with one."

The cashier cleared her throat, and Cindy realized they were holding up the line. Embarrassed for drawing attention, she said, "You're right. Go ahead and pay, but I owe you."

"That's fair. On the next family outing, you can buy me ice cream."

Cindy accepted her root beer float from the young girl behind the counter and took a sip. She didn't know how to respond to Jackson. She wasn't part of the 'family' and didn't know if she'd be there for the next outing. Rather than agree, she concentrated on her float and sat quietly while listening to the rest of them banter about Christmas and New Year's and the June wedding. She couldn't help but wonder what she would be doing by then and where she would be.

As she ate, Cindy felt a peculiar tingling on the back of her neck. She looked around, peering up and down the streets. Other families hovered nearby, eating ice cream, and several couples walked along the sidewalk. It looked like everyone in town had come out to see the play. None of the other theater goers paid any attention to Cindy or the Nelsons, and Cindy had no reason to be paranoid, but she could not shake the eerie feeling that she was being watched.

Five

Jackson sat at the kitchen table, his elbows planted, and his chin resting on his clasped hands. His cereal was long past mush.

Grace sat down across from him, "Everything okay, Sugar?"

"Yeah. Everything is fine."

"Studying going all right?"

"Yep. I'm ready for finals." He looked up at his mother. "We're really blessed, Mama, you know that?"

His mother smiled. "I do know that, Jackson. The Lord has been very good to us over the years. Now, what makes you so introspective and grateful this morning?"

"I was just thinking. Wade lost his sister at a young age, then he lost his father, a fiancée, and finally his mother. Joe lost his twin brother. It doesn't sound like Cindy ever really had anybody, but still, to lose her mother and her fiancé so close together..." He lifted his eyes to hers. "How did we get so lucky? Or, is everything going to come crashing down around us without any warning?"

"Oh, Jackson, such heavy thoughts on this beautiful Sunday morning."

"I know, and I'm sorry. I just can't stop thinking about last night. I've never seen anyone so excited about a play. And when she said she'd never even had a root beer float, I mean, what has she been doing all her life? Has her whole life just been a means of survival without any pleasure or happiness?"

"Sugar, I don't know what kind of life Cindy had, but I'll admit, it doesn't sound like a happy one. We may never know all the trials she's had to endure, but what we do know is that God put her here right now. Her coming here is part of her journey. Maybe we're just signposts along the road that she will pass and look back on with good thoughts someday. Maybe we're a rest stop for her to take her eyes and mind off the road for a spell. Maybe we're just a pit stop for her to find the gas to keep going. Or maybe we're the place where she will put the car into park and stick around for a while. Only the good Lord knows. But while she's here, we can show her love and respect and what it means to be a family, and I bet we can learn as much from her as she can from us."

"Do you think that's what she's searching for? A family?"

"I think that's one thing. Just like all those stray dogs and cats you used to bring home and hide in the tornado cellar. You always did try to give every one of God's creatures a home, but you can't do that for everyone, Jackson."

"You sound like Andi."

"Maybe so, but I know my baby boy. Just keep this in mind, Jackson. Not everyone is meant to stay in your life. Some people are meant to just pass through, and it's not always the passersby that are in need. Always keep an open mind. Sometimes, those people passing through bring us what we need when we need it."

"How so?" He pushed aside his soggy cereal and looked at his mother with interest.

"Let me give you an example. Every one of us carries crosses in life. Sometimes the cross is so small, we hardly notice we're carrying it. Sometimes, it's so large, we can't handle it by ourselves. Just when Jesus was at his lowest, after he'd been beaten and scourged and had fallen on the road more than once, Simon the Cyrenian was passing by and was told to help carry the cross. It doesn't appear that Simon knew Jesus or had ever met him before. We know that Jesus died, so they never met again, not on this earth anyway. Simon was just there for those precious moments when Jesus needed him the most. We all have a Simon or two who show up in our lives when we need them. They help us in some way or teach us something we need to know, and then they're gone."

"And you think Cindy is a Simon to one or all of us? That at some point, she'll just go away?"

"Now that, Sugar, is not for me to say. What I am saying is that we all need to play a part in helping others carry their crosses. We may never know what comes of it, but both you and the cross-bearer will come out better for it. Whether she stays around or not. Now, finish eating. We need to leave for church soon."

Jackson watched his mother as she stood and walked toward the hallway. Before she left the room, she turned back to him. "Jackson, you have a good heart. You brought home so many animals, I lost count of them, but you can't save everyone. Sometimes, helping to bear their burden for a little while is the best you can do."

He nodded, and she left for the living room where his father was deeply entrenched in a documentary about the Christmas truce of 1914. He heard her give a warning, "Ten minutes, Joshua, then we're all heading to church."

Jackson understood where his mother was coming from. He had plans to leave town and make his mark in the big city. Cindy was on a quest to find herself, and that could take years. If she was still around when he got back home, he would do his part to make sure she had the best Christmas of her life, but after the first of the year, he would move on, and she'd have to find a way to carry her cross on her own.

***

"You really need to get out more." Sarah took a seat at the library table next to Cindy. "You're here all the time."

"I don't have anywhere to go. I finished all the jobs I was hired to do." She placed a bookmark between the pages and closed the book. "It's too cold to explore the outdoors, and I need to save the little bit of money I've made."

There was little left in her bank account after paying for her mother's burial, and even less from the sale of the few meager items she'd managed to sell after the funeral. Most of the things in the house went to Goodwill. Her mother's electronics and few pieces of jewelry had been pawned, and Gloria's car had been sold, but the car money and the money from the sale of the house had gone to pay the outstanding bills. Cindy was packing away all the money she made decorating. She had no idea when everything would come tumbling down around her, so she needed to save every penny for when it did. She'd been working since she was twelve, but there was never any money when she needed it. Life was expensive, Gloria had no life insurance, and Cindy had no more savings and no backup plan.

"It's hard, I know. When I first moved here, the town was just beginning to attract new businesses and a handful of tourists, but with winter now setting in, it's practically a ghost town."

"What do you do for fun?" Cindy asked the question though she had all but forgotten what fun really was. The play was the first night she'd gone out and enjoyed herself in ages.

Sarah shrugged. "I've managed to make a few friends. I get together with Andi and Helena's group at

Rick's sometimes, but mostly, I hang out with Mel and Trudy and watch movies and drink wine. You should join us next time."

Cindy hesitated. She didn't want to show up somewhere and find that she wasn't welcomed by everyone else. She'd been there and done that. Then again, Andi and Helena's friends had been quite welcoming. Should she take a chance with Sarah's friends as well?

"Come on, we won't bite. Seriously, Mel and Trudy are awesome. And while Helena is great, she's a little older."

Cindy frowned. "She's not that much older."

"She's twenty-nine. I'm twenty-four. It's not much, but it's enough, plus she's engaged, so that adds a whole other layer to the age difference. Tru and Mel are single. Mel's my age while Tru's a year older than you. You should give us a chance."

"I'll think about it."

"Tell you what. Helena will be going to the holiday dance this weekend at the firehouse with Joe, but Mel, Trudy, and I are going as a group. Meet me at my place, and we'll go to Trudy's and all get ready together. You can be part of our stag group." She made a face. "Do you still call it stag if you're all female?"

A chuckle broke through Cindy's reservedness. "What's the female equivalent of stag? I don't think it's a doe."

"As long as it's not a cow." Sarah rolled her eyes and stood. "Anyway, I mean it. Come to my apartment. It's above the deli. We can ride over to Trudy's together. You'll love the other gals. I promise."

"Can I ask you a question?" Cindy asked.

"Sure." Sarah put her hand on a chair and waited.

"Helena's fiancé, Joe. What happened to his hand? When we were at the theater the other night, I noticed it and wondered…"

"Oh, that. It's a long story, but his crazy ex-fiancée came to town and started stalking him and Helena. She was a total psycho. She tried to cripple his hand to ruin his career. It didn't work though. Helena and Dale—do you know Dale? The sheriff?—anyway, they figured out where she'd taken him and got him to the hospital in time to save him and his hand."

"Wow," Cindy breathed. "That's like something out of a horror movie."

"Yeah, it was, but she died during the rescue, and Joe and Helena are happy." She shrugged. "So, I guess, all's well that ends well."

Sarah began to walk away, and Cindy thought over her offer. She really wanted to go to the dance, but she didn't want to go alone, nor did she want to be a third wheel with Helena and Joe. Maybe she should go with the other girls. It would be better than being at the house by herself.

"Sarah," Cindy whispered loudly and waited for Sarah to turn around. "What do people wear to the dance? I really don't have anything fancy with me." Nor had she ever owned anything she'd consider nice.

"It's the first one, so I imagine there will be a mix. Come a little early, and you can look through my clothes. I was in a sorority in college, so I have plenty of options."

"What time?"

Sarah smiled widely as she told Cindy what time to be at her house. The dance was only three days away, and Cindy had never met Mel or Trudy, but she was already looking forward to a night out with the girls.

***

The bubbling champagne sent a warmth through Jackson as everyone toasted him on his big night.

"To the newest college graduate," Andi said, raising her own glass in yet another toast to her brother. "May he prove to be the wisest of us all by actually making money instead of spending it."

"Cheers!" and "Hear, hear!" rippled around the restaurant along with the clinking of glasses.

"Who wants more?" Joshua asked, raising another bottle as far as his weak arm would allow him. "I'm finally through paying college tuitions!"

Jackson took the bottle and watched his father sink back into the chair, still smiling but showing signs of becoming tired.

"Since when did you pay my tuition?" Helena asked. "I paid for both my undergrad and my master's in library science."

"Well, we all paid for Andi's," Joshua said, pointing to the oldest of his three children.

"Our taxpayer dollars at work," Jackson agreed, winking at Andi, a Naval Academy graduate. "But I'm with Helena, Daddy. I'm pretty sure I paid for my degree which is why it took so long!" His words were true, but his smile showed no anger or regret, and the slap on his father's back was done with great love and admiration for the man they almost lost six months earlier.

"Well, I paid for your clothes, your food, your car insurance…"

"Fair enough," Jackson said, eyeing his father. He took another sip before turning to Helena. "So, what's Cindy doing tonight?"

"She's home. She didn't want to intrude on the family celebration."

"Nonsense," Grace said. "Since when have we ever turned anyone away?"

Helena shrugged. "You know, Mama, her upbringing was pretty different from ours. I don't think she's used to all the family togetherness and being welcome to join in, family or not."

Jackson thought about Cindy sitting home alone in Helena's house. This time of year, nobody should be alone. Maybe he'd ask her to the dance.

As if reading his thoughts, Helena said, "She's made plans to go to the holiday dance with Melanie, Trudy, and Sarah. I think that will be good for her. She needs to meet people."

"Are you thinking of kicking her out?" Jackson asked in surprise. He couldn't imagine his sister doing that, but she was gearing up to put the house on the market in a few months.

"No, of course not. I just think she needs to enlarge her circle. Hey…" She turned to him. "You're about the same age, you could introduce her to some of your friends."

Andi laughed. "Helena, do you remember what pests Jackson and his friends were when we were little? Do you really want any of them putting the moves on Cindy?"

"Hey, there's nothing wrong with my friends," Jackson said, more testily than he meant. There wasn't anything wrong with his friends, but the thought of any of them dating Cindy made his gut clench.

"I've got a nice, big T-bone steak here for the graduate," their waitress, Alice, said. "Cooked just the way you like it," she added with a smile.

"I think she's hitting on you, little brother," Andi said with a nudge of her elbow.

"You know it," Alice said, beaming at Jackson. "I always did like them young and good looking."

Alice fluffed her grey hair and bent down to give Jackson a kiss on the cheek. "That's my congratulations to you, Honeypie."

Jackson put his hand to his cheek and closed his eyes with an exaggerated sigh. "That's the best gift I've ever received."

They all laughed while Alice passed out the rest of the plates. "Y'all enjoy your dinner. I'll be back to check on you in a bit."

Jackson savored his steak, cooked to perfection, and looked around the table. He'd never felt so blessed.

The thought of Cindy at home alone drifted through his mind, but he shook it off. In a few weeks, he'd be gone. Helena was right that she needed to meet more people. Maybe Jackson would introduce her to some of the other people his age. Everyone should feel like they belonged somewhere.

***

Cindy stared at the page, not sure she had read any of the words. It was a Christmas romance that Helena read and said was cute, but Cindy wasn't in the mood for romance. She was lonely, kind of regretting that she didn't take up the offer to attend Jackson's graduation dinner, and wished she had a friend, a real friend, something she hadn't had in a very long time—not since she had become Evan's girl and an outsider to everyone else.

She put the book down on the couch, leaned back, closed her eyes, and breathed deeply. She tried to recall the one and only Christmas she'd spent with Evan, but her memories of him were beginning to become muddled, and the guilt she felt about that was as bad as the heartache over losing him.

They hadn't been together for very long, but she loved him with all her heart. So why was her mind betraying her? Why was the image of him in her head, once so vivid and full of life, beginning to fade? Why were their conversations and the little moments they shared starting to crumble like a sandcastle drying in the sun?

Did this happen to couples who had been together for years? Did everyone lose their images and memories of important people in their lives?

She thought of her father. She could vaguely recall what he looked like, but she hadn't seen him in ten years. Would he look the same if she saw him tomorrow?

She sometimes wondered about his life. Had he remarried? Did she have siblings she didn't know about? Maybe he was dead, killed in an accident or crumpled in some ditch after another binge. He'd never tried to contact her or her mother, as far as she knew, after the day he disappeared. If his life had turned out anything like her mother's, he probably was dead, or dying at least.

Cindy sighed and stood, padding across the thick, warm rug to the window, a fire crackling in the fireplace. It was cold out, colder than anything she had ever experienced. She thought of the California sun and the people who would be having bonfires on the beach even at this time of year. She couldn't help but wonder if she'd made a mistake coming here.

At the thought, she felt that tingling on the back of her neck again, like somebody breathing on her. She shivered and reached up to close the blinds. A sudden chill raced through her, despite the fire, as though someone had walked across her grave.

***

"Jackson, this is—"

"Mac." The bearded man in a lambskin-lined denim coat reached for Jackson's hand and shook it hard. His grip was firm, almost painful. He was twice Jackson's size, hefty with the kind of bulk you don't get from eating moon pies. This man worked out. A lot. "Everyone just calls me Mac."

"Nice to meet you, Mac. You're working out here with me?"

"He is," Pete, the warehouse manager, confirmed. "Figured you could show him the ropes."

"No problem," Jackson said. The man's size and obvious strength would be a help. He turned to Mac. "First thing, you're going to want a good pair of gloves. They have to be durable enough for lots of lifting and hauling and thick enough to keep your hands warm. If you don't have any, I'd go back inside and buy a pair."

The man nodded. "Okay. Anything else I should get while I'm inside?"

"A good water bottle. It's cold out here, but we work up a sweat. Good to stay hydrated. Is your coat warm?"

"Warm enough." The man looked hard at Jackson, sizing him up, and making him feel uncomfortable. "You been working here long?"

"Off and on since I was fifteen. Just graduated from college a couple days ago. Not sure what's up next. How about you? Where'd you come from?"

The man took his time answering. He reached up and scratched his head, and Jackson caught a glimpse of a rather large tattoo peeking out from under the man's sleeve. "Here and there. I guess I'm what you'd call a drifter. I don't like staying in one place for too long. I'm just trying to enjoy my freedom."

Jackson wasn't sure what that meant, but he didn't care. He was just biding his time, working through the holidays, and moving on. Most likely this guy, Mac, was doing the same.

"I guess I'll go inside and get those gloves and a water bottle."

Jackson watched him go with an uneasy feeling stirring in his gut. As soon as the holidays were over, and people were back at work, Jackson hoped to get some calls from New York. He wasn't keen on working with this Mac fella for any longer than necessary, and he was more than ready to give up his rawhide gloves for a suit and tie.

***

"I love your necklace," Mel said, eying the heart pendant.

Cindy lifted the pendant and looked down at it. "Thanks. My fiancé gave it to me."

"You're engaged?" Mel exclaimed.

"No," Cindy said quietly, letting the pendant drop onto her sweater. "He was killed in an accident. Military." She held out her hands and shrugged, trying to be casual, noticing that the tears didn't come so easily anymore when she mentioned Evan's death.

Cindy sat at a high-top table across from Melanie. Trudy sat to her left, and Sarah to her right. Country music played in the background, competing with the sounds of clinking pool balls and surrounding chatter. When Sarah called that morning to ask if she wanted to join them for dinner and drinks, Cindy didn't hesitate at the chance for a night out with people her age. She had come to the realization that she truly missed this.

"I'm sorry," Mel hastened to say, and the table grew quiet for several seconds.

"It's okay. It's been a while now." She fingered the pendant. "I just haven't been able to stop wearing this yet."

"Of course, you haven't," Trudy said before hastily changing the subject. "Sarah tells us you're going to go to the dance with us Friday night. I hope you're up for a night of shaking your groove thing."

"Trudy," Melanie said with a laugh. "Seriously, you sound like you were raised in the last century."

Ignoring her friend, Trudy reached over and picked up one of Cindy's strawberry-colored tresses. "You should let me fix your hair for the dance. I love fixing hair, just not enough to do it for a living."

"What do you do?" Cindy asked, settling back into the bar-height chair.

"I'm Wade's assistant in the mayor's office."

"Really? I didn't know you knew Wade."

Trudy let out a loud, melodious laugh. "Know him? He's my first cousin. But I had that job before he was mayor. I've worked in the office since I was sixteen."

"Wow. That's impressive. When I was sixteen, I was asking, 'Do you want fries with that?'"

Cindy had learned that Melanie was a nurse at Joe's clinic. With the news that Trudy worked for Wade, she wondered how many other people had connections with Andi's family. Talk about a small town!

"No chance of that here. I'd kill to have a McDonald's less than an hour away," Trudy said.

"Consider yourself lucky. I always smelled like fries no matter how many showers I took. I'd have loved to work for the town mayor, even if he was my cousin."

"He wasn't mayor when I started there. I was just a file clerk, but I moved up to assistant after I graduated and the previous one retired. Wade kept me on. I love my job, but lately, he's been getting on me to get more organized. I don't know why. My system works for me, but he says it's just organized chaos."

"I've always had the opposite problem," Cindy said. "I'm organized to a fault."

"No such thing," Sarah said.

"Coming from a librarian," Trudy said. Mel laughed, and the two clinked their glasses over the table.

"Anyway, how 'bout you stop by the office tomorrow morning and take a look? If your help gets

Wade off my back, I'd be happier than a pig in the sunshine."

"Is that good?" Cindy asked with a laugh.

Trudy leaned close and looked at Cindy across the table. "Sugar, it don't get any better than that."

"Then, I guess I'll be there," Cindy said, taking a large gulp of wine. "After I stop at the clinic. Joe wants me to look at something for him."

"Thank Heaven," Mel said. "I can't find a thing I need. Dotty is the best receptionist ever, but her organization needs some help."

Cindy smiled. She seemed to be getting one job after another, which was a very good thing.

As the evening went on, she relaxed more and more. She really liked these girls and started looking forward to the dance. Some time with other women her age was exactly what she needed, and she was going to enjoy these moments for as long as she stayed in town.

***

"Isn't that wonderful news?" Grace handed Jackson a bowl of mashed potatoes. "Helena says everyone in town is just buzzing to hire her. I'm glad she found a career she enjoys."

"I don't know that I'd go as far as saying it's a career, Mama. Helena said Melanie wants her to help reorganize the medical supply closet at the clinic, not hire her to build a new wing."

"Jackson, this is a really big business now. Have you seen that Marie woman on Netflix? She's become a national celebrity because of her organization efforts."

Jackson chewed politely before speaking. "Can't say that I have, but do you really think it's something sustainable around here? As a career?"

"Lots of new businesses are starting, and people are moving into town," Joshua offered. "Cindy did a bang-up job of decorating those windows in the shops, so she's got some talent in making things look nice and orderly. Everybody could use a little help getting their lives in order and being more efficient." He smiled at Grace. "Except your mother, of course. She's the most organized person I know."

"Oh, I don't know about that, but I have been doing some cleaning in the attic, and I've got several boxes that need to go to the Salvation Army. Jackson, are you going to Harrison any time soon?"

"Not that I know of, but I can make a trip up there for you. Just label which ones you want taken."

"Thank you. Oh! And I have a box for Helena. Can you take it to her? I'd rather not lift and haul boxes. My back isn't what it used to be."

"Sure, Mama. I'll take it tonight and drop it off as soon as I get a chance. I'm working from open to close the next few days, trying to make some extra money and help with the Christmas rush."

"Saving for a New York apartment, I suppose," Joshua said, wiping his mouth with a napkin.

Jackson looked at his mother in surprise.

"Now, Jackson, you know your daddy and I don't keep secrets from each other."

"Besides," Joshua interjected. "What's the big deal? Nobody expected you to stay here forever once you got that degree."

"I'm just not ready to tell everyone."

"Not ready to tell or not ready to accept?" Grace asked with a knowing look.

"Both, I reckon."

"You know what I always recommend when someone is faced with a major decision—pray about it. You'll get the answer you're looking for, though keep in mind, it's not always the answer you want."

"I'll try that, Mama. Thanks."

"Oh, Jackson, if Cindy is at Helena's when you go over there, could you let her know that we expect her for Christmas Eve and Christmas Day?"

Jackson felt a slight stir in his stomach. "Sure, I can tell her. That's awfully nice of you."

"Well, what did you expect? That girl doesn't have anyone but us. It's hard being all alone."

All alone. The words hit Jackson harder than he would have expected. Was he feeling bad for Cindy or thinking about what it was going to be like for him once he's away from home?

Six

It was early when Cindy finished at the clinic and headed to the mayor's office. She knocked on the door and stuck her head inside, putting on the face she wore so well, the one that hid her anxiety.

"Hi!" Trudy said enthusiastically. "Come on in." She stood and hurried to give Cindy a hug, a move that almost brought tears to Cindy's eyes. Other than Andi, she couldn't remember the last time she'd been greeted with such kinship and familiarity. Her anxiety quickly disappeared.

"I'm here to take a look at your organized chaos." As she spoke, Cindy looked at the desk. There were four separate piles of papers on the desk, a couple framed photos, a mug with what appeared to be heavily creamed coffee, a tape dispenser, a stapler, several pens and pencils in various colors, a scented candle, and peeking out from the middle of the mess, a computer and two monitors. The keyboard was barely visible under the papers, and to finish it off, a large flowering plant towered over the workspace. A small stand sat next to the desk with a printer on top and various types of copy paper on a shelf underneath,

Cindy stood with her mouth agape.

"Is it that bad?" Trudy asked with a frown.

"Not bad, necessarily. I'm just amazed you can fit everything onto one desk. Where do you work?"

"I'm mostly on the computer. Well…" She knitted her brow and tightened her lips as she, too, looked at the desk. "Kind of. I have a lot of paperwork, too."

"And where do you work on that?"

Trudy shrugged. "Well, I kind of move this and that until I find a clear surface.

"I see," Cindy said. She walked to the other side of the desk where Trudy's chair sat. "You know, this would all be so easy to organize." She looked up at Trudy. "Really organize. We'd need a few supplies and a longer table to form an L-shape. That will greatly expand your workspace. We just need to make sure you have all the proper components so that it doesn't became a collection spot." She reached for the center drawer. "Do you mind?"

"Go ahead," Trudy encouraged.

Cindy tried to open the drawer, but it was jammed. She gave it several tugs until it burst open, the contents bouncing into the air an inch or two and then settling back into the drawer. She widened her eyes at what she saw inside. Pens and pencils were strewn everywhere along with plastic food containers holding paper clips, staples, and other small, assorted things—a medal or pendant of some sort, a key, a few nails, a picture hanging nail and holder, a few USB devices, and some spare change. Bookmarks, staple removers, a hole punch, highlighters, glue sticks, nail files, and a couple matchbooks swam around in the shallow drawer as well.

Trudy stood beside her, looking at the mess. "I know. I keep saying I'm gonna clean it out."

"That won't help, I'm afraid."

"You mean, it's hopeless?" Trudy's shoulders sagged.

"No," Cindy laughed, her confidence at an all-time high. "I mean, cleaning it out won't keep it from getting like this again. You need a system both on the desk and inside of it."

"Okay, I'm ready. What do you suggest?"

"What are you doing after work?"

"Whatever you tell me I'm doing."

"Good. We're heading to the closest Walmart. This is Arkansas. I know you must have one nearby."

Trudy grinned. "One town over, they have three."

"Good. The first thing we need to do is take some measurements. Then we're going to make a list of what we need." Cindy stood, walked to the closet, and opened the door. It had regular closet-length shelves from floor to ceiling, and all the office supplies were stacked on the shelves. Some paper stacks were toppling over, and others blended into each other. Cardboard boxes held extra rolls of tape and other supplies.

"Do you know a good carpenter?"

"I do. Why?"

"We could try to organize this with a few containers, but a custom build-in would work so much better. Then you could use magazine files to organize things like these folders, stackable file holders for the paper, and baskets for the loose supplies. These shelves could work, but you don't have the ability to make them different sizes or heights. Plus, you want some floor space, about three or four feet high, beneath a set of shelves, for things like those rolls of contact paper that don't sit on the shelves easily, as well as space for those." She pointed to the large Post-It boards standing in the corner of the room.

When Cindy turned back to Trudy, she was met with wide eyes and an open mouth.

"What?"

"I should be paying you for this."

"Come on. We're friends. Besides, I'm not a professional decorator or anything."

"Yet you've been getting paid to decorate. Your work is the talk of the town, and I bet decorating isn't even your specialty. You're a born organizer. You should be doing this for every business in town. And I'm going to pay you to organize my house. If Wade says we don't have the budget to pay you for this, then we'll take pictures and put together a portfolio for you so that you get something out of it. We should have Paige come in and take the pictures and design a website. Do you have Instagram? You need to upload before and after photos of every job—"

"Trudy, slow down. I don't have any jobs." Her mind was reeling. What was Trudy thinking? She had no education, no real experience, and no training. When her mother was on a bender, which was pretty often, Cindy locked herself in her room and rearranged and reorganized. She supposed a therapist would say that she needed to find order in her life. When her mother got sick, Cindy spent those few months taking apart and reorganizing every room of the house; and when she passed away, Cindy threw herself into staging the house for sale just like on HGTV. Those instances were far from being a job, but… Cindy knew what she was doing.

"Cindy, I mean it." Trudy took hold of her shoulders to emphasize her seriousness. "You could make a living doing this. A real living. Here or anywhere. You have real talent and gut instinct. Don't throw that away."

Cindy blinked several times as reality began to take hold. Trudy might be right. "Do you really think so?"

Trudy nodded slowly. "I know so." She let go and took a step back. "Now, wait right here. I'm going to talk to Wade."

Cindy looked around the office and smiled at what Trudy said. She knew Trudy was right. She could do this. She'd worked at a department store for a while before Gloria got sick, and she watched the professional decorators set up displays. She often thought they lacked imagination and originality. Organizing was a step beyond that, but Cindy knew she was good at it. She'd seen shows on TV about organizing spaces. She thought some of the suggestions were good. Others, she knew would never work in the real world. You couldn't organize just by looking for joy in your possessions. You had to think things through, analyze, plot and plan, and determine the best use for a space. You had to customize the space according to the needs of the user. What worked for Dick would not work for Jane. She'd seen this over and over when she'd worked in busy restaurants with poorly planned kitchens and storerooms. She'd witnessed managers fumble around their desks for simple things like pencils and paperclips, take the time to tidy up, and then have the same problem the following week. It was almost never the person or their habits that were the problem. The issue was always how they organized the space they had to work with. And the organization couldn't be done for them. It had to be done with them. One person could never successfully organize another person's space without careful planning and a meeting of the minds.

The more she thought about it, the more she knew Trudy and Mel were on to something. She felt it when she was at the clinic, and she felt it now as she surmised the mayor's office. Cindy had already established a reputation as someone who was good at decorating and creating displays. So, did she have the confidence, the tools, and the money to take on organizing and decorating as a career? She was going to try and find out.

***

"You have plans for Christmas?" Jackson asked Mac on Friday morning while they waited for a truck to drive around from the front of the store to pick up a purchase.

"Not really. A frozen dinner in front of the TV most likely."

Jackson wasn't sure how to respond to that. "I guess it's hard to celebrate the holidays without any family around."

Mac gave him a hard look. "You got family here?"

"My whole family. Well, my mother's sister lives near Little Rock, and her family is all there or beyond, but my parents and sisters are here. We'll all be together on Christmas Eve and Christmas Day."

"Just your family? No girlfriend for you?"

Jackson pictured Cindy and quickly pushed the image from his mind. Why would he think of her? Having a girlfriend in Buffalo Springs, Cindy or anyone, was not what he needed or wanted right now.

"Nope. Not really a good time for me. I've got some interviews pending now that I have my degree. Not planning on staying here much longer." He looked up at the customer and smiled. "Mornin' Cooper. How are things going?"

Cooper, a friend of Andi's, stepped away from the driver's side of the truck. He wore the standard lime green shirt of the Arkansas Search and Rescue Association. He took off his matching lime green cap, wiped his brow, and replaced the cap.

"Going well. I need to replace some chain."

"Why wouldn't you just get chain inside?" Mac asked.

"He needs heavy duty chain, too big and heavy to have inside." Jackson went right to the supply. "How much?" He looked at Cooper for an answer.

Once the men had the heavy chain loaded into the back of the truck, barely a chore for Mac, Jackson said, "I heard about the little girl who got separated from her family on their hike. Must have been scary."

"Her parents were frantic, but we found her pretty quickly, all things considered. Would have been worse if the weather hadn't cooperated. Good thing it's not that cold yet."

"You're right about that. You coming to the dance tonight?"

"For sure. Unless there's an SAR emergency, I'll be there. Have to make an appearance at least since we'll receive part of the funds."

"Yeah, I figured. Hopefully there's a good turnout. Take care, Coop."

"See you around Jackson. Tell Andi I said hi."

"Will do."

Cooper drove away, and the men busied themselves with unpacking products while waiting for the bell to signal the arrival of another customer.

"Friend of yours, I take it. The guy with the chain."

Jackson shrugged. "I guess. More like a friend of my sister. They graduated from high school together. His brother is Dale, the chief of police."

"I guess everyone knows everyone around here."

"Pretty much. New people are starting to become interested in relocating here, but it's mostly the same folks who've lived here forever."

"New people? Anyone interesting."

"Well, you, for one. What's your story? Where did you come from? Other than 'here and there'."

Mac was silent for a moment before answering. "Last place I lived was Arizona, in a little place just south of Phoenix."

"Never been there. Is it nice?"

"Not the parts I saw."

"What did you do there? For work, I mean."

Mac seemed to give this question some thought. "I worked in sanitation."

Jackson pictured Mac on the back of a garbage truck. "Not much need for that around here. Most people outside of town burn their trash, and in town, we have receptacles that get picked up by the county."

"Yeah, well, I was looking for a change."

Jackson nodded. Mac was a man of few words who didn't seem to like talking about himself, so Jackson let the conversation go while they saw to the inventory. To his surprise, Mac spoke up after a few minutes of silence.

"What do newcomers do around here?"

"For fun?"

"Or work. Whatever."

"Well, there are several new businesses opening, so I guess the newcomers are either opening the businesses or getting jobs at one of them. Lots of potential in Buffalo Springs these days."

"Where do most people live? The ones who are just arriving."

"Depends, I guess. There are some houses for sale. A lot of single people rent apartments above the shops or rent houses together. Most of the buildings are old houses that have been converted into businesses. They have living spaces on the upper floors. You lookin' for something?"

"Nah. I've got a little camper out at the campground off the highway. Suits me just fine. I just noticed there aren't any apartment buildings here. For a town that's having an influx of people, seems like they'd need a place to stay."

This was the most Jackson had heard Mac speak in the past three days. "I guess so. Like I said, there are some houses for sale. Some developer recently bought a large parcel outside the city limits. I suppose there'll be a neighborhood there before long."

"Apartments over the shops, you say?" Mac's thoughts seemed to drift as he looked toward town.

"I can hook you up with somebody if you'd like to see one, maybe move out of the campground."

Mac shook his head. "Thanks but no thanks. I'm happy living away from town. Not used to being around civilization a whole lot."

"A country man at heart, huh? I hear ya. I'm going to miss the country when I move to New York."

"You mentioned that. Moving to the Big Apple, huh?"

"That's the plan." He stopped working and took a long drink from his water bottle. "Applying for some finance jobs up there. We'll see."

Mac nodded, and the conversation ended when another truck backed up to the doors. They didn't talk much for the rest of the day, and Jackson felt like he didn't know the man any better than he had on day one; and though Jackson wasn't planning on sticking around much longer, something about the man's evasiveness bothered him.

*****

The house was dark that night when Cindy pulled up in front after being at the library all afternoon. She spent the morning surfing the web, marking things on Pinterest, and signing up for a few free webinars on organization techniques. She'd even watched an episode of *Hot Mess* on HGTV. She went to the library after assessing the supply closet at the clinic.

Helena had plans with Joe that night, so Cindy picked up a carry-out meal from the Smoke Pit. She balanced the takeout container in one hand and her large, metal water bottle in the other. A bag of supplies—she could hardly believe she had her own bag of supplies for a legitimate business—hung heavily on her shoulder. With the key held precariously in her fingers beneath the takeout container, she tried to unlock the door, but it gently opened on its own as she was inserting the key.

"That's odd," she said out loud. "Helena never leaves the door unlocked." Helena had told Cindy that it was a strict rule she had abided by ever since she moved out of the family home. She promised her father that she would never leave her house unlocked, especially after Joe's crazy ex-girlfriend had broken in the previous summer. Coming from urban California, unlocked doors weren't something Cindy had ever considered.

"Hello," she called, pushing open the door. "Helena?"

There was no answer.

Cindy went inside, every nerve in her body on edge. Something didn't feel right, though she couldn't have said what it was. Then she smelled it—the acrid smell of a man who hadn't showered or had been working hard and sweating profusely. Her heart began to race. Was someone in the dark house waiting for her or Helena to come home?

She started to back toward the door. She could barely hear a sound over the beating of her heart as she took a step backwards into the open doorway and bumped into a tall, hard body. She screamed and dropped her water bottle and dinner. On instinct, she turned, kneed the man hard where it hurt and, when he doubled over, knocked him upside his head with her heavy bag of notebooks, tape measures, pencil case of pencils, pens, and markers, and the books she'd checked out from the library. The man gasped, and she ran for the kitchen, fumbling in the dark for a knife from the wooden block on the counter.

"Cindy," the man wheezed. "It's me."

The familiar voice stopped her.

"Jackson?" She lowered the knife and took a tentative step toward him.

"What is wrong with you?" He took several deep breaths but stayed bent over, reaching for the nearby table to steady himself. A small lamp rocked back and forth as he gripped the table.

"I'm so sorry. The door was unlocked, and I smelled…" She felt ridiculous now. The only thing she smelled was her own fear and the aroma of the dinner that was now spewed across the entryway. The plastic container of barbecue sauce had opened when it hit the hardwood, splashing red on the floor and wall in a pattern that reminded her of blood splatter in a horror movie.

"You smelled something, so you decided to take away my manhood?"

Her face turned red. "I smelled a man. His sweat, I mean. And the door was unlocked."

The words finally got his attention. Holding onto the table, he straightened some and looked at her. In the pale moonlight leaking through the windows, she watched the lamp wobble again as he pressed his weight onto the table.

"The door was unlocked?"

She reached for the nearby light switch and turned on the overhead light. "Yes, and, I know this sounds crazy, but I could have sworn I smelled sweat. Like from someone who badly needed a shower."

"Should I check the place out?"

Suddenly reminded that someone could still be in the house, Cindy's heart returned to its accelerated beat. She looked around.

"Can you? I mean, are you okay?"

He took a long swallow and nodded. "I'll live." He looked around before pointing to the back door. That was when Cindy saw that it was ajar. "Go back outside and call Dale," he whispered, handing her his phone after glancing at the screen to unlock it. "The intruder is probably gone, but…"

She wanted to protest. She couldn't just leave him, but she found herself taking the phone and walking onto the front porch. She found his contacts and searched for Dale's number, trying not to be nosy and to concentrate on the task at hand.

Jackson appeared in the doorway just as she disconnected the call.

"Dale's on the way. He's gone?"

"Looks like it." His jaw tensed as he stared at her.

"What?"

"You're pretty organized, right? Keep a clean room and make your bed and all?"

That was an odd question. "Yes," she answered slowly.

"I thought as much."

"Jackson, what's—" She was cut off by the sound of the car pulling behind Jackson's truck at the curb.

"That was fast," Jackson said when Dale exited the car.

"I was at home. Jamie and Suzy are doing homework. I figured they could be alone for a few minutes. I called Eric to come take over. I'll leave when he arrives. Cindy said someone broke into the house." He looked from Jackson to Cindy.

"Well, I don't know if he broke in. The door was unlocked." She proceeded to tell Dale what she found when she arrived at the house. They walked through the house to the back door which Dale inspected.

"No sign of forced entry at either door. But the locks aren't the highest quality. Anybody in the world can watch YouTube videos these days on how to jimmy open a door."

The thought sent a chill down her spine.

"Helena can check her security footage," Jackson offered. He looked at Cindy. "You know she has cameras, right? Joe installed them last year after…"

Cindy nodded. "Yeah," she said, wondering just how many crazy people lived in this small town.

"There's something you should see," Jackson said to Dale, and Cindy felt a twinge in her gut as he led them to her bedroom.

At the sight of the room, Cindy sucked in her breath and clutched her chest.

The bedding and pillows were tossed aside haphazardly, the comforter thrown up to reveal the empty space under the bed. The few clothes she owned hung from the open drawers, and what hair and makeup accessories weren't on the floor were strewn across the top of the dresser. The closet doors were open, her meager wardrobe exposed.

"I take it, this isn't how you left it."

Cindy couldn't find the words to answer. She shook her head.

"Dale?" A voice called from the other part of the house.

"Back here, Eric," Dale called. When the other officer stood next to them, Dale said, "I need photos of this room as well as the front and back door. Check outside for shoe prints or any signs of trespassing. Get the security footage from Helena." He looked at Jackson. "Any other rooms touched?"

"Not that I can tell. Helena's pretty much always looks like that." He looked away sheepishly, and Cindy knew he wished he could save his sister some embarrassment.

"Eric, can you take a look upstairs?"

"Yes, Sir," he responded and took the attic stairs two by two.

"Where's Helena?" Dale asked.

Jackson shrugged and shook his head, then looked at Cindy.

"With Joe. His house, maybe? They were having dinner. That's all I know. Hey, Sarah told me Joe's ex is dead. Is that right? I mean, she couldn't have…"

"Not unless she's a ghost," Dale said. "I can guarantee you, she's deader than a doornail."

"Attic looks good. She uses it for storage?" Eric asked Jackson and Cindy.

"Yes. I've only been up there once, to put my suitcase away. It was pretty straight."

"Still is. Doesn't look like anything has been moved."

"Look, I've got to get back to the kids. I'll call Helena and ask her to come home. She can tell us if her room was hit, too, and get the recordings. Eric, you good?"

Cindy missed the rest of the exchange. Her mind went to the attic and her supposedly empty suitcase. Should she ask if he'd seen it? Should she go up and see if it was still there? She decided against it. Even if the suitcase was gone, there was nothing valuable inside of it. Not of monetary value anyway.

***

Following orders, Jackson led Cindy out to the living room and sat next to her on the couch after they answered a series of Eric's questions. Cindy was adamant that nothing was missing, insisting that she didn't have anything of value to begin with. Her eyes were filled with fear, and she held her arms tightly around her body as though she was trying to ward off an Arctic blast.

"You okay?"

She swallowed and nodded.

"I'm assuming that food that's now all over the floor was your dinner. Are you hungry?"

She shook her head.

She looked lost, lonely, and afraid. She was so thin and pale, she looked like a little child huddling on the couch like that, and he had the strongest impulse to wrap her in his arms and tell her it would be okay, but would it? Was someone after her? Who? Someone from her past or someone she came across since coming to town? Did she have any idea who it could be?

"Jackson! Cindy! What happened?"

He looked up and saw Helena sidestep the spilled food as she walked swiftly toward them. Joe was just a step behind her.

"We're not sure," Jackson answered. "Looks like someone got in. We don't know how. Cindy's room is trashed. We weren't sure about yours…" He looked away while she interpreted his words.

"Helena." They turned toward Eric. "Can you, um, come tell me if this is the way you left your room this morning?"

After a few minutes, Helena returned, looking embarrassed. "Eric says we can't stay here tonight." She looked at Joe. "Boy, if this doesn't bring back bad memories."

"Let's not think about that. Why don't you both come to my house?" Joe offered. "I have plenty of room."

"I don't want to intrude," Cindy began before Jackson broke in.

"I'll take Cindy to Mama's. She hasn't eaten, and we know Mama will have plenty of food."

"Jackson, I—"

"It's settled," he said, expecting the same protest he would have gotten from Andi or Helena. Instead, she simply nodded and looked back down at her lap.

"Do you need to get anything before we go?" Joe asked.

"Let me see if we can take some things with us." Helena went to see Eric, and an uncomfortable silence filled the room.

When she returned, she had a small bag of things. "Cindy, Eric's waiting. You can get a few things to get you through the next twenty-four hours. He thinks we can come back after that."

Cindy mumbled what sounded like, "thank you" and went to her room.

Helena turned to Jackson and said quietly, "I checked my app, and it showed someone breaking in the front door and then leaving by the back door when Cindy got home, but he did a good job of hiding his face. Nothing about him was familiar or distinguishable. She's lucky he left when she got home. What is going on?" Jackson couldn't tell if her tone was concerned or accusatory, but the hair on the back of his neck stood when he thought of Cindy being so close to a burglar.

"Why didn't your alarm go off?"

Helena's face reddened. "I haven't used the alarm in months. I didn't think I needed to." She shook her head. "Does Cindy have any clue who did this?"

"I don't think so. She hasn't said much. Just that she came home, and the door was unlocked. She seemed genuinely shocked by the condition of her room."

Cindy returned quickly, and they hurried out into the cold, evening air. Cindy grabbed the same bag she had hit Jackson with and didn't protest when Jackson took it from her. He knew how heavy it was.

"Oh, Helena. I've got a box in the backseat of my truck for you. Mama's cleaning out the attic. I was going to drop it off, but when I saw the house was all dark, and the door was open, I just went inside."

"Thanks, Jackson. I'll get it tomorrow."

They said goodbye, and Jackson led Cindy to his truck. Before he could open the door, she stopped him.

"I need my car."

"I can bring you back on my way to work in the morning."

"Thank you, but I would feel better having it with me."

Jackson frowned but decided not to argue. "If you're sure you're up to driving. You've had quite the shock."

It was her turn to frown. "It's only around the block."

Which is precisely why he didn't understand her insistence, but why belabor things?

He waited for her to get into the car and start the engine, then he followed her to his house, all the while wondering if she had any inkling as to the who's and what's of the evening.

Seven

Cindy looked at herself in the mirror. She wore a lightweight, green sweater that looked nice with her hair and her green eyes. The other girls chose tight jeans for her to pair with the sweater. She completed the outfit with black cowboy boots she'd bought at the church thrift shop. She frowned as she eyed her outfit.

"I don't know. Are you sure this is okay for a Christmas dance?"

"Around here? It's perfect," Sarah assured her. "Look how good your curves look, and the sweater is the perfect style for you. It says, 'I'm cute and single but not showy."

Cindy thought of the bikinis, cropped tops, and short shorts she and her high school friends wore back in Southern California. Until Evan, she'd never considered whether she was giving off a showy or not showy signal. What did that even mean?

"Time for me to fix your hair," Trudy offered. "Take a seat."

Cindy sat in the chair Trudy had dragged in from the kitchen. She watched in the mirror as Trudy tried out several styles before she got to work. Cindy let her eyes roam around the reflection of the room in the mirror.

Trudy's dresser and desk were cluttered with makeup, hair accessories, and framed photos. Her dresser drawers were closed, but earlier, Cindy had spied an odd combination of clothing all stuffed into the same drawer. Her closet was neat but could be much better. It was nothing like Helena's room, but it needed some attention.

"Can I be honest?" Cindy began tentatively.

"You hate it already?" Trudy asked, holding a handful of Cindy's hair in one hand and a curling iron in the other.

Cindy laughed. "No, so far, so good." She paused, and Trudy continued creating long spirals of hair. Cindy gestured toward the dressing table. "You know everything I explained to you the other day about your office?" Cindy gestured toward the dressing table with one hand. "The same goes for here. All this stuff could be grouped in a more manageable and attractive way. It would give you some space on the table and let you see exactly what you've got." She held her breath as all three of the other women stared at the dressing table. She hoped she hadn't overstepped.

"She's right, Tru," Mel said. "Your organized chaos is what the rest of the world calls clutter."

"Honestly, I'm not sure what needs organizing more, your office or your bedroom." Cindy said and then immediately regretted saying anything.

"It's a toss-up," Trudy said without resentment.

Cindy took that as agreement and smiled as Trudy added layers of curls to her hair.

"Cindy, what's the latest on the break-in?" Sarah asked, coming in from the bathroom wearing a pair of red jeans with a gold top and red cowboy boots. "Helena says nothing was taken and that you were able to go back in."

Cindy gave a small shiver as Trudy let a curl drop onto the back of her neck. Trudy pulled some of her hair back and laced tiny white flowers into the strands that were gathered at the back of her head.

"Nothing at all," Cindy answered Sarah. "It was so strange. Dale thinks it might have been someone looking for prescription meds." Though that didn't explain why it was her bedroom that was hit so hard.

"Wouldn't be the first time around here," Trudy said. "Now, what do you think?"

Cindy eyed Trudy's handiwork in the mirror. She'd never seen it with so much body. Most of the time, she wore it pulled back or just let it hang loose without thinking much about it. She turned her head this way and that, looking in the mirror. "I love it! Trudy, you're amazing."

"Cindy, you look amazing," Sarah said. "We're gonna have to put a fence around you to keep all the guys away, or you'll never have a moment's peace all night."

"She's right," Mel agreed. "You look stunning."

"Ladies, I think our job is done here. Let's grab something to eat and head to the dance." Trudy herded them from her room and down to the kitchen.

As they walked through the house, Cindy looked around at the tasteful wooden furniture and pretty area rugs. The living area was large enough for a chair, couch, and converted hutch that held a modest sized television. The space was fairly open with a kitchen table and chairs at the other end in an area that led into the kitchen. A beautiful red brick wall separated the kitchen and living room. Despite the shoes, jackets and sweaters, and paperwork strewn everywhere, the house was lovely.

"Trudy, your house is so nice. I can't believe you live here all by yourself. However did you come to own it?"

"It was my grandmother's on my father's side. When she decided to move to Florida, I asked her if I could buy it." Trudy's eyes twinkled. "She did one better and gave it to me."

"Wade and Trudy's families established the town. Their money is what we Southerners call, *old money*," Mel said.

"Wade's side of the family has a heckuva lot more money than mine does." Trudy opened the oven, and the scintillating aroma of barbecue wafted through the room. "I've had the pork on warm. Mel, can you get the slaw from the fridge?" She pulled the covered dish from the oven and set it on top of the stove. "We're going light y'all—just pulled pork and slaw—so that we can dance the night away and not feel full. But make sure you grab a biscuit or two. I don't want to carry anybody home at the end of the night."

Cindy obeyed and ate enough to satisfy her without making her feel too full. She was looking forward to dancing the night away.

***

"I can't believe I let you drag me to this," Austin complained as Jackson followed him and Tanner through the door of the fire station.

"Come on, Austin, how often do you come home to visit?"

"Too often," Austin muttered loudly enough for Jackson to hear him.

Jackson laughed and clapped Austin on the back. "What's your problem? It's a good cause."

"I guess, but I can think of a lot of other things I'd rather be doing than attending a dance."

"Like what?" Jackson faced his oldest friend. "We're in Buffalo Springs. The most we ever did on weekends was drink and shoot at targets and try to stay out of trouble."

"We were actually pretty good at staying out of trouble despite a little drinking now and then."

"You were the one who drank," Tanner said. "Jackson and I were too scared of our daddies to take the chance."

Jackson had to agree. The three of them were pretty good kids. They had big plans and bright futures, so they did their best to toe the line, and Tanner and Jackson were always worried about getting caught. Austin was a bit more rebellious—not unlike Helena—but he was still a decent guy.

Austin came up short and held his arm out to stop Jackson. "Who's that?" he asked, his eyes wide.

Jackson followed his gaze and sucked in a sharp breath. Actually, it was more like she took his breath away. Her full strawberry blonde hair stood out in large curls that were dotted with little white flowers. The strawberry blonde tresses were accentuated by the green sweater, and her long legs stretched up forever from a pair of black cowboy boots. She was with Trudy, Sarah, and Melanie, and she was clearly having a good time. The ladies laughed and clinked their glasses together. As she took a sip, her eyes caught his. She smiled, and his heart skipped a beat.

"Hey, man, she's smiling at me."

Jackson turned to look at Austin.

"At *you*?"

"Yeah. Do you know who she is?"

"She's the girl who went to the play with your family, isn't she?" Tanner asked. "Cindy?"

"Um, yeah, she's a friend of Andi's. She's actually staying with Helena right now. I'm not sure how long she's in town." He felt a protective urge though he didn't know why. Austin was a good guy. Kind of. Good, but on the wild side when it came to women and booze.

"Can you introduce us?"

"I'm not sure she's your type, Austin. She's kind of—"

"Oh, she's my type all right. Come on."

Austin grabbed Jackson's arm and pulled him through the crowd of people. Tanner followed.

"Hi, Jackson," Cindy said with a wide grin. "I didn't know you were coming."

"Of course, I came. I'm all for supporting the fire station and other emergency services." Austin elbowed Jackson in the ribs. "Cindy, these are my best friends, Tanner and Austin. Austin lives in Nashville. He's just here for the weekend."

Austin gave Jackson a look that said, 'too much information' before smiling broadly at Cindy. As if they were starring in one of those stupid chick flicks Helena always watched, a slow song began to play.

"Would you care to dance?"

Cindy looked at Jackson and then back at Austin.

"Say yes," Sarah whispered and nudged her.

"I'd love to," Cindy said, taking the hand he held out to her.

"That Austin Porter," Trudy said, fanning herself. "He always was one tall glass of iced tea."

"He's not all that," Jackson said before turning on his heel and heading toward the bar, leaving Tanner behind.

As he sipped his beer, he turned so that Cindy and Austin were just inside his peripheral vision. They were dancing close, looking into each other's eyes and talking. Cindy laughed, and Austin pulled her a little closer.

"Jackson!"

Jackson jumped, and a small splash of beer rose from the bottle, running down his fingers and onto his hand.

"Dang, Helena. What'd you do that for?" He shook his hand and reached for a napkin.

"I said your name three times. You were in another world." She followed where his gaze had been. "Is that Austin? My, he sure did turn out fine, didn't he?"

"Why does everyone keep saying that?" He took a long drink while Helena looked at him, back to Austin and Cindy, and then back at him.

"What?"

"Well, I'll be. Little brother, are you jealous?"

"Jealous? Of what?" He finished the beer and set it down a little too loudly on the bar.

Helena tsked her tongue and shook her head. "Not a good idea, Jackson. Not a good idea."

"What's not?" She had his full attention now.

"She's got a lot of baggage. Don't get me wrong. I like her. She's as sweet as one of Andi's fruit pies, but she still has a lot of baggage. And I doubt she'll stay around for long."

"You think she's leaving soon?" He didn't know why that bothered him. After all, his mama had said as much, and he was leaving himself as soon as he got a job.

"I don't see any reason why she'd stay, especially after what happened at the house."

"Yeah, well, Austin's the heartbreaker in the room. Maybe he's the one you should be talking to. I'm not the one who asked her to dance."

"Uh-huh." Helena rolled her eyes and headed back toward the table.

The slow song ended, but the couple stayed on the dance floor when the rhythm of the music sped up. Cindy danced while Austin stood with his hands on her waist, his body swaying out of beat with the music. Jackson watched as Cindy and Austin stopped dancing and made their way back over to Tanner and the other girls. Austin kept his hand on the small of her back, and Jackson ordered another beer before heading in their direction.

***

Cindy could not remember the last time she had just relaxed and had fun. She and the other girls were true to their word and spent most of the night on the dance floor. Each time a slow song played, Austin was there by her side, leading her to the middle of the floor, and it made her feel good. She noticed that Tanner asked Trudy and Melanie to dance a few times. They'd all been friends back in high school, according to Mel. Cindy saw Jackson dance with Mel and then with Sarah, but despite the great band, the flowing drinks, and the festive mood, he hadn't looked happy all night.

"What's with Jackson?" she asked Austin, her arms around his neck.

"Huh?"

"He seems upset about something. Did something happen?"

Austin looked up and moved his eyes around the room until they settled on Jackson and Melanie. They seemed to be making small talk, swaying with the music. "Jackson's a bit of an introvert. We tended to stay away from most social functions when we were growing up. Though he and Melanie went to our junior prom together, and we used to go line dancing now and then. He was actually pretty good at that."

Cindy looked again at the two people dancing and felt a pang of something in her gut she couldn't quite name. "Really? Melanie never mentioned that."

"Well, why would she? I mean, I wouldn't expect Jackson Nelson to come up in normal conversation. Oh wait." He nodded in realization. "You're living with his sister, right?"

"Temporarily. I'm not sure how long I'll be in town."

"Oh? Are you heading home soon?"

"Home?" She scoffed. "Hardly."

"Why? What's wrong with home?"

She felt his arms grip her waist a little tighter, pulling her closer. He'd been doing that all evening, and while it felt nice, she'd found subtle ways to loosen his grip each time. He was fun to dance with, and she felt pretty when he looked at her the way he was looking at her now, but she didn't want to lead him on. She just wasn't attracted to him.

"Nothing if you live here. Or if you have family. Or friends." She shook her head. "Never mind all that. I'm a free spirit, just trying to figure out where to go next." *And how to pay for it.*

"You should come to Nashville. There's so much going on there. What do you do for a living?"

Cindy told Austin about the jobs she'd been doing around town, but as she talked, she spied Jackson with his friend, Tanner, at the bar. Whatever Austin was saying faded out as she gazed at Andi and Helena's brother.

***

"What's wrong with you?" Tanner asked Jackson as they stood by the bar.

"What are you talking about?"

Tanner gestured toward the straw in Jackson's hand. It was bent a dozen ways, and the paper wrapper was shredded on the bar. "You're destroying that straw. You only fiddle with things like that when you're upset."

Jackson tossed the straw onto the bar. "You're imagining things."

"Am I?" He gestured toward Cindy. "Come on. Just admit you like her."

"I told you, it's not like that." He picked the straw up again and twisted it between his fingers.

"Then what is it like, Jackson, because I've known you since the first day of kindergarten, and you've never been this weird about a girl before."

"Weird? How so?"

"You hate seeing her with Austin. It's written all over your face. You talk about her all the time, and you've been acting strange ever since she came to town."

Jackson glanced toward Cindy.

Tanner followed his gaze. "Man, you've got it worse than I thought. Look, if you're that into her, then why are you still standing here beside me? Go say hi and get her out on the dance floor."

As if on cue, the band announced that the line dancing portion of the night was about to begin.

***

Cindy couldn't ever remember having this much fun in a place involving country music. Sweat ran down her back, and her feet were killing her, but she stomped, heel-toed, and grapevined, keeping up with the crowd and laughing the whole time. Mel was right. Jackson was really good at line dancing. When the song ended, he leaned over and asked if she wanted a drink.

"I'm so out of breath," she said as they waited in line at the bar. "I must be out of shape."

She saw Jackson give her a once over, and she felt heat rise into her cheeks.

"What do you wanna drink. And I'm paying, so don't bother arguing."

She rolled her eyes but didn't argue. She'd learned that it was no use arguing with Jackson over who was paying. "I'll just have a water."

"Are you saying that because it's free?"

"No. I'm actually dying of thirst. I've had enough to drink already."

Jackson squinted at her for a moment before giving her a smirk, and his scrutiny, along with the crack of a smile made her stomach do flips.

"Okay, water it is."

Once she had her water and he had his beer, they made their way over to the area their large group had commandeered all night. Just as they made it to the others, everyone hollered and ran onto the floor. Cindy turned to watch them for a moment before tugging on Jackson's sleeve.

"Jackson, this one looks like fun. Do you know it? Can you teach me?"

He glanced at the dance floor where Austin was the center of attention and nodded. "Sure can." He put his bottle down on the table and took her hand, leading her back to the dance floor.

She tried to keep up with Jackson and the others, but it was difficult. The dance was much more complicated than she bargained for. After several heel and toe tappings, they swayed their hips back and forth and then circled them before doing some kind of little walk forward, then back a couple times, all at a frenzied pace. Next, they turned and did the little walks facing the other way and somehow ended up facing backwards. Her head was spinning as she tried to keep up. On top of that, something was going on between Jackson and Austin. They seemed to be trying to outdo each other, both adding in extra turns and looking determined to take the dance to a higher level.

When it was clear she wasn't getting the hang of it, Jackson took it down a notch while Austin kept going. Jackson beckoned to Cindy. She moved closer to him, and he wrapped his arm around her, telling her the moves as they went along. By the time the song ended, she'd done a few rounds and was laughing hard. Jackson grabbed her hand, spun her around, and tilted her back. Their fellow dancers laughed and clapped, except for Austin, who was glaring at his friend. When Jackson pulled Cindy back to standing, their eyes locked, and she felt a jolt to her entire body.

"What was that?" she asked breathlessly.

Jackson gave her an odd look before smiling. "You mean the dance? It's the tush push."

"The what?" she asked with a laugh. He led her from the dance floor back toward their corner.

"The tush push. You'll need to learn it. It's probably the most popular line dance in America."

"I've never heard of it before."

"It's probably not on the regular dance circuit where you come from."

Whistles and hollers greeted them as they joined the rest of their friends. Austin smiled at Jackson and nodded. Whatever was going on between them, Austin seemed ready for a truce. She glanced at Jackson who just grinned.

"You two looked good out there," said Trudy, who had pretty much danced to every dance, including the tush push, like an expert.

"Thanks." Cindy looked around and leaned toward Trudy. "Where's that guy you like?"

"Coop?" Trudy said quietly. "He and Amanda went to get drinks. He's never even looked my way. Oh well." She shrugged. "But you and Jackson? Something going on there?"

Cindy looked over at Jackson who smiled broadly at her, and her stomach flipped again. She couldn't stop herself from breaking into a wide grin.

"Never mind," Trudy said with a knowing look. "I can figure that out for myself."

Cindy felt a sharp pang in her chest. "No, Trudy, it's not—"

"Uh-huh. Whatever you say, sugar." And Trudy headed back to the dance floor, leaving Cindy wondering if coming to the dance at all had been a good idea.

***

When the tapping of drums and singing of fiddles came to an end, the band lapsed into a rendition of a very old song Jackson recognized as a favorite of his father's. He thought the singer was named Keith something.

Jackson looked up, and his vision telescoped in on Cindy so that he saw nothing but her, swaying to the music as she listened to something Trudy said. Cindy looked up and smiled, but something seemed wrong. Jackson tipped his head toward the dance floor, and after a brief hesitation, she moved toward him like a fish on a line. Without a word, he took her hand, led her to the dance floor, and wrapped his arms around her.

"You know, I was told that you weren't much of a dancer."

"And I was told you didn't like country music."

"Maybe it's growing on me," Cindy said with a tentative smile.

Jackson pulled her close and listened to the words of the song.

Don't close your eyes, let it be me
Don't pretend it's him, in some fantasy
Darling just once, let yesterday go
And you'll find more love than you'll ever know
Just hold me tight, when you love me tonight
And don't close your eyes.

He wondered if Cindy still thought about her deceased fiancé. Was she ready to move on? Was she ready to love again? The thought made him tense. What was he thinking? What happened to moving to New York?

Before he could dwell on any of the questions swirling in his mind, Cindy stepped back and looked at him, her face stricken with emotion.

"I'm sorry, Jackson. I have to go." With that, she ran to the table, grabbed her coat, and dashed out the door.

Maybe he had his answer after all.

Jackson reached for his own coat and followed her. He called her name when he spotted her walking toward the road, and she hesitated for a long moment before she turned around.

"Please tell everyone I had a great time." She suddenly looked like she was going to cry. Was it something he did or said?

"Where are you going?"

"Back to the house. It's late, and I'm feeling pretty tired."

"Let me drive you. It's not safe to be out this late alone. Besides, maybe you shouldn't go into the house alone." He knew that wasn't fair. Why scare her when she'd been having such a fun night?

But it worked. Rather than protest, she nodded and began walking to the parking lot. He hurried to keep up with her.

Jackson couldn't get over the change in the December air. Only a week before, they had walked casually to the play. Tonight, it was bitter, and a wind howled as they hastened through the lot. It appeared that there was more than one change in the air.

"You have fun?"

"I did. It's been a long time since I hung out with friends and just let myself enjoy it. I really enjoyed the line dancing, too."

He went to the passenger door and held it open for her. She climbed inside the truck and thanked him with a smile.

Jackson got in the driver's seat, started the engine, and backed out of the spot. Once on the road, he spoke. "When you left, I was afraid something was wrong. You didn't even tell anyone goodbye."

She was quiet for a moment before replying. "I think it's time for me to move on. Please, tell Austin I said thanks for being so nice, and thank you for teaching me all the line dances."

Jackson felt his heart stop. "Move on? You're not happy here?"

"Oh, I'm very happy here. Everyone has been really nice to me. I've loved getting to know your family. I just need to figure out what I'm supposed to do next."

Jackson nodded in understanding. His mother had been right. Cindy wasn't meant to be a part of their lives forever. Besides, he knew where she was coming from.

"I get it."

"You do?" she asked in surprise.

"Yeah. I haven't told anyone but Mama, but I'm leaving, too."

He thought he heard a quiet, "oh" escape from her lips as he eased to a stop in front of his sister's house.

"I'm applying for jobs in New York. It's always been my dream. As soon as I can find something, I'll be on my way."

"New York. Wow. That's a big change from Buffalo Springs."

He frowned. "Yeah, I know." He looked down at his hands, calloused from working at the Tractor Supply all these years. No more, though. Soon, he'd be sitting behind a desk.

"Will you miss it? Home, I mean?"

He looked up and met her green eyes, and in that moment, the world fell away.

"I'll miss everything about it," he said quietly.

He leaned closer, his eyes still locked on hers. She didn't blink, didn't move. He could feel the warmth of her body as he drew closer, could smell the strawberries in her shampoo, could see something unreadable in her eyes… and he stopped.

Kissing her on the cheek, he whispered, "Good luck, Cindy. I hope you find everything you're searching for."

Her top teeth tugged at her bottom lip, and she nodded. She reached up as if she was going to touch his face, but she pulled her hand back and smiled.

"Thank you, Jackson. I hope the same for you."

Without a goodbye, she opened the door and ran up the steps to the house.

Jackson waited for her to get safely inside, meaning what he said about her not going in alone but wanting to give her space, then he put the car in reverse and checked behind him.

As he was pulling out, his phone vibrated. For a split second, he thought maybe it was her, but when he stopped and looked at his screen, it was Austin.

Jackson hit the button to silence the phone and headed home. Tomorrow, he'd text Austin and ask his friend if he wanted to get together when he came back.

For tonight, Jackson was going to go to sleep while the feel of Cindy's skin still lingered on his lips.

****

"Good morning, is this Ms. Cynthia Kline?"

The man's voice was unfamiliar, old and gravelly, but not unfriendly, with a thick Latino accent.

"Yes," she said warily, staring down into her bowl of cereal.

"This is Sheriff Jose Ramírez with the San Diego County Sheriff's Department. I try to make it my business to alert people when a family member has been released from a federal penitentiary."

"I'm sorry. I don't think you have the right person. I don't have any family." She was about to hang up when…

"Is your father Reginald—"

"Reginald?" Cindy interrupted. That was a name she hadn't heard in a long time. Nobody ever called her father that from what she could remember. A memory floated to the surface. She was about seven and was the one to answer the door when a local police officer brought her father home, drunk as a skunk. He called him, 'Reginald,' which sounded foreign to Cindy.

The sheriff continued, giving her father's entire name, and she knew he had the right person.

"Did you say, 'released from a federal penitentiary'?"

"Yes, ma'am. Several weeks ago. You're not an easy person to track down. Different last name and leaving the area and all."

"Yes, I use my mother's maiden name. She changed our names after…" She didn't say, *after my dad left us.* "My father was in prison? What did he do?"

"Armed robbery with a deadly weapon. He was suspected of being involved in other robberies, too."

She pushed away the bowl of soggy flakes.

"And he was released?" She wasn't sure what was more shocking—the fact that her father had been in prison, was involved in an armed robbery, or was being released.

"He served his time, or most of it. He got time off for good behavior. Claims he found God."

"Where is he now?"

"I don't have that information, ma'am. Just thought you'd like to know. I take it you haven't heard from him."

"I haven't. Should I let you know if I do?"

"That's not necessary. As long as he checks in with the parole board, he's a free man."

"Okay. And you're just calling to let me know?'

"Yes, ma'am. Felt it was my duty to do so. You, uh, sure you haven't heard from him?"

"I haven't."

"Okay, then. You have a nice day."

Cindy wished him the same, thanked him, and said goodbye. She disconnected the call with an uneasy feeling in her gut. So, that's why her father had abandoned them. What other secrets had her mother been hiding?

Maybe I have the answers right here and didn't know it.

She glanced at the clock. No time to look now. She had a few things she wanted to do before she left town. Besides, she wasn't quite ready to open that can of worms.

As she left the house, she couldn't help but wonder. Could her father's release and the break-in be related?

***

"Hey, Austin was pretty ticked last night," Tanner told Jackson over burgers at Rick's.

"What for? He looked like he was having the time of his life."

"Until you and Cindy disappeared together at the end of the night after you stole her right out from under him with your line dancing moves. What happened?"

Jackson took a sip of beer. "She was tired and wanted to go home. I had to work today, and I didn't want her going into the house by herself, so I gave her a ride. It was no big deal."

Tanner eyed his friend. "Jackson, I've known you since we were skimming the pond for tadpoles no bigger than my little toe. Most of the night, you acted like someone licked the red off your candy. What was your problem?"

"Nothing. I just wasn't in the mood to be out. I shoulda stayed home." He took a bite of his burger and avoided making eye contact with Tanner.

"Look, man, if you like her, then do something about it."

"Like who?" he asked with a mouthful of food.

"You know who. Cindy. If you like her, then ask her out yourself. Otherwise, you can't be mad if someone else does it first."

"You don't get it. She's a friend of Helena's."

"And from what I recall, Joe was a friend of Andi's. Who cares? We're adults, not middle schoolers."

Jackson turned toward Tanner. "You really think I should ask her out?"

"I think you're a fool if you don't."

Eight

Cindy should have slept like a baby. Her body should've been physically spent. She should've had the best sleep of her life. Instead, she had tossed and turned throughout the night. She hadn't been sleeping well before the dance either, so it had nothing to do with the way Jackson had looked at her before she jumped from the car.

She kept thinking about the break-in and wondering if it had anything to do with the phone call from the sheriff. She'd never had any dealings with criminals or anyone who broke into houses and robbed people. At least, she thought that was the case before that call. Knowing who and what her father was changed everything and had her looking at the break-in in a whole new light.

Around three in the morning, she tiptoed down the stairs and out the front door. Stopping at the back of her car, she looked around before quietly opening the trunk. She moved the blanket and pulled open the carboard that covered the spare tire. Lifting the tire, she reached her hand underneath and breathed a sigh of relief when she felt the small, flat bag she'd hidden there when she left California. The key was still in it. Could this be what they wanted? Could this mean something to her father?

With another glance around, she re-covered the tire and, as silently as possible, closed the trunk.

Later that morning, after a very large mug of coffee, she was hunched over Helena's kitchen table making sketches and diagrams for Trudy's office and laying out some ideas for a website. She logged into her Instagram account for the first time in months and started a Pinterest board for organizing tips.

At eleven o'clock, she opened the door to Paige's design studio. "Are you ready?"

"Cindy! Come on in." Paige waved her inside. "You've got perfect timing."

Cindy looked around the converted pole building. It was neat and tidy, extremely well organized, and smelled like cinnamon and vanilla. She spotted a diffuser on a small table with a stream of vapor emanating from the hole in the top. A college diploma hung on the wall amid nature photos.

"I'm so sorry to make you work on a Saturday."

Paige laughed. "When you own two businesses, you work every day."

Cindy gestured toward one of the framed prints. "I love this. It's beautiful. Did you take these?"

"I did. Just a little hobby of mine. We use my photos of local spots on all the shirts and souvenirs at the shop. Saves us a lot of copyright costs."

Cindy stepped closer to look at a photograph of a river disappearing into the side of a mountain. Leaves of red, orange, yellow, and green filled the photo with splashes of color. The water sparkled with glistening sunlight.

"This is magnificent. Where is it?"

"The state park down the road. That's the Buffalo River. You'll have to go there when the weather is nicer. We all love having it so close."

Posters advertising an upcoming play at the theater and a Valentine's dance at the high school stood on one wall, and stacks of menus were in a box on a table. Cindy spotted a narrow staircase in the corner.

"Do you have more studio space up there?"

"No, that's home sweet home. Daddy and I worked together to turn the second floor into an apartment. I wanted to move back here after college, but there just wasn't anywhere to live, and I wasn't sure I'd stick around. I just needed to figure out a way to put aside some cash and apply for jobs. With the town now bouncing back, I've gotten more jobs than I ever dreamed would be possible here, plus there's the shop, so it looks like I'm staying."

"I'm sure Helena is happy to have you around."

"And I'm happy to be here. What about you? Are you going to stick around?"

"I guess what you and I come up with today will help decide that."

"Then let's get working. We've got a website to set up."

Cindy still wasn't sure she was doing the right thing, but everyone was so willing to help her make it work, she felt like she had no choice but to give it a try.

***

Jackson spent Monday researching job openings. After getting lost in cyberspace for more time than he wanted to admit, he decided to take a walk downtown. It was cold, but the air felt good on his face. He did a little Christmas shopping—a scarf for Helena, a pair of gloves for Andi, and a bottle of Scotch for Wade. He was stumped when it came to Joe. They were just getting to know each other since Jackson had been at school for the fall. He also needed to come up with something for his parents. There were only so many places to shop in Buffalo Springs.

The town needs more shops, he thought, and a gym. He wondered if there was a good space for one. He looked at the empty buildings as he went by. There weren't many left, and the few he saw weren't conducive to the needs of a gym.

His mind wandered as he thought about the other needs of the growing town. Helena was complaining over Thanksgiving dinner that there was no local florist. She had to drive an hour to the closest one. There wasn't a bridal shop either, but he didn't know if Buffalo Springs could sustain one of those yet. An automotive garage would be a good thing for any town, and another nice restaurant would be perfect. They had the café, Rick's Saloon, and The Smoke Pit, but La Forna was the only nice restaurant.

Lost in thought, Jackson almost missed his brother-in-law heading to the mayor's office, but he caught sight of Wade just ahead.

"Wade, hey!"

Wade turned and smiled. "Hey, Jackson. How's it going?" Jackson fell into step with Wade, and they continued down the sidewalk.

"Okay, I guess."

Wade looked sidelong at Jackson. "What's up?"

Jackson thought about it for just a split second before telling Wade what was on his mind. "Andi doesn't know this. Only Mama does, and she wouldn't say anything before I did." He took a deep breath. "I'm applying for jobs. In New York. I'm planning on leaving town as soon as the first of the year if something comes up."

They stopped outside the town hall. "Really? Well, good for you."

"I hope so." Jackson sighed.

Jackson felt the weight of Wade's hand lay on his shoulder. "Jackson, what's going on?"

He gave his shoulders a slight lift and let them fall. "I don't know. I know I have to go. I can't be involved in real estate investing here. I've got to go where the action is, I reckon, but it's hard. I mean, you know, you did it. Was it hard leaving Buffalo Springs, your friends, your Mama?"

Wade inhaled and let it out slowly. "It was, and it wasn't. I had a hard couple years after Jolene's death."

Jackson thought about what it might be like to lose Andi or Helena. Jolene, Wade's only sibling, had been hit by a truck and killed while walking home in the dark when she was just twelve. "I can only imagine."

"Daddy was still alive, so Mama was taken care of, and she wasn't sick yet. Still, it wasn't easy to go to Notre Dame and then head straight to New York. Life in the city is much different from here. There's no fresh air, or stars at night, or sunshine unblocked by tall buildings, and there's so much smog. But there are a lot of good things about it, too. I could order take-out any time, day or night. I could see a show." He grinned at Jackson. "Date night was never hard to plan. There were endless possibilities. And I learned a lot about my job from my colleagues and supervisors."

"So, it was worth it?"

"It was. Until it wasn't."

Jackson waited.

"I got pretty involved in work, to say the least. I stopped coming home for holidays, slept only a few hours at my apartment before grabbing a fast shower and heading back to the office, and made some business decisions I'm not proud of. I was gone so long, I forgot who I was. And it didn't get any better when I moved home after Daddy died. I convinced myself I was doing the right thing by becoming mayor and looking the other way when Ted Mitchem and his minions tried to shut down the town. I had blinders on to what I'd been missing and didn't think I deserved what I have now. If it hadn't been for your sister, I could've caused a lot of people a lot of pain, and I could've ended up in jail."

"But none of that really had anything to do with your going to New York or with the job you had."

"Didn't it?" Wade asked. "Look, I'm not trying to talk you out of going. The experience I got, and the people I met, they were all worth it, one hundred percent. And I loved the work so much that I'm… well, never mind about that. Just don't lose yourself, Jackson. Don't let the suits make you forget who you are and where you come from. Go to church, pray, keep being a good person. Don't let greed take you down the wrong road. It's a long, bumpy ride back."

Jackson nodded while many thoughts clouded his mind. "Thanks, Wade. I appreciate the advice."

"You're welcome. Now, I've got to get back to the office before Trudy and Cindy bankrupt the town."

"Cindy?"

"Trudy had me hire her to reorganize the office. So far, the expense has been minimal, but they've got Stan up there right now measuring things and making plans to start constructing some kind of table and a custom closet as soon as he can fit it in. I had to get out for a few minutes. I was way out of my element." Wade leaned close to Jackson and held up a small shopping bag from the little boutique on the other side of the street. "I did some Christmas shopping." He smiled conspiratorially. "But I'd better get back upstairs. See ya later, Jackson."

Jackson bid Wade goodbye and stared up at the second-floor windows where the mayor's office was. Trudy had Wade hire Cindy to organize? How did that come about? Maybe his mama was right after all about this decorating and organizing thing she was doing actually being a career. Well, good for her. Now, he just needed to secure a career of his own.

***

The moon was full outside Cindy's window. All the lights in the house were off except her bedroom lamp. Helena was with Joe, as usual, and Cindy was alone. She sat on the floor of the bedroom staring at the beat up, leather-worn Louis Vuitton luggage. The rancher had a small loft with a wide, dormer window that Helena used as an attic and where Cindy had stored her suitcase. She'd told herself she was just getting it out of the way. Now, after the break-in, she wondered if there had been some part of her subconscious that had warned her to hide it.

She carefully opened the vintage luggage, which she remembered giving to her mother for Mother's Day when she was fifteen. She'd been so excited to have found it in a thrift shop and was sure her mother would like it. Instead, her mother laughed at her and asked,

"When do you think I'll ever be able to use this? Not until you get yourself married at least." Cindy had slunk to her room, hiding her tears. But Gloria had held onto the suitcase, and when Cindy was getting rid of the house and everything in it, she'd come across it in her mother's closet.

Sitting on the floor, in the pale light, she ran her hand across the yellow sweater her mother wore nearly every day. It was frayed and stained and held no good memories for Cindy other than Gloria had loved it. It was the only piece of Gloria's clothing Cindy had kept after washing it twice and hanging it in the sun to get rid of the smell of cigarette smoke. Removing the sweater, she carefully unwrapped the tissue paper around the champagne glasses her mother and father had used to toast their marriage. It was the same set she and Evan planned to use at their wedding—the only gift her mother had ever lovingly given her even though she originally accused Cindy of having been pregnant, which she was not.

She took out an old CD, kept in its hand-labeled case, with love songs her parents had liked. It still amazed Cindy that her father had made this for her mother and that Gloria had kept it all these years. Knowing what she did now, she wondered if her father had continued loving her mother for the past twenty years. Had her mother loved him? She never spoke about him, never told stories or said she missed him. She just told Cindy, at the age of twelve, that he'd left and was never coming back. He was never spoken of in the house again. She assumed Gloria knew that he was in prison, and most likely why. Had she been trying to protect Cindy—an instinct that Gloria had never seemed to possess—or was she simply angry that he'd gotten caught and sentenced for so long?

Cindy put the CD back and picked up the framed photograph of her parents from their wedding day. She had found it in the bottom of a drawer in Gloria's bedroom. She sat back against the bed and stared at the picture.

Her mother was absolutely beautiful with big green eyes and a warm smile. Cindy wasn't sure she'd ever seen that smile in real life. Her father was taller than her mother, but not much over six feet. He was lean, almost scrawny, and had a thin mustache. His eyes were hazel, like hers, and looked like the eyes of a man who had everything he'd ever wanted. What had happened to them? To him? Had they already been drinking and using drugs when they married? Did they ever wish for more for themselves and for her? Was she wanted at all? And what had driven her father to armed robbery and her mother to obliterating him so completely from their lives?

She sighed and put the photo back into the suitcase. She rifled through odds and ends—a few old school pictures she'd found when packing things up, a small, ceramic dog with a broken ear that had been a gift from her grandmother before she passed away, the stuffed rabbit she slept with every night until she was twenty, and the three books she'd saved from her childhood—

the first and last books in the *Series of Unfortunate Events* saga, her favorite *Princess Diaries* book, and S. E. Hinton's, *The Outsiders*.

Finally, she pulled out the wooden box with the fancy scrolled pattern carved into the top. Cindy rubbed her finger along the grooves in the wood and wondered, once again, if Gloria had intended for her to find the box tucked away among the dust bunnies and cobwebs under the far corner of Gloria's bed, or if she had wanted it to stay hidden forever.

Taking a deep breath, Cindy lifted the lid and peered at the contents. She hadn't been able to go through them until now. It was too painful when she first came across the box. She couldn't figure out why her mother kept them from her. She was angry at them both, angry at her mother for concealing the photos of her and her father from birth to age twelve, and angry with her father for leaving them. Though the letters may have told a different story, she now realized. They may have given her a clue, let her know he didn't leave on purpose, told her he loved her after all. But she couldn't read them, couldn't look at their smiling faces in the pictures and reconcile them with what she knew—that her father had turned his back on them, on her. Now, though, she wondered…

She set the letters aside and reached into her pocket for the little bag that, until that evening, was hidden in the trunk of her car. She opened the envelope she mysteriously received on her twenty-first birthday and took out the key and the note. She read the note for the hundredth time.

Cindy, this is yours. It's all I have to give. I love you.

She held the note up to one of the envelopes and compared her name. The writing was the same. This mysterious note and key were from her father. She uttered a small cry—whether of frustration, sadness, or contempt, she didn't know.

For over a year, she had wondered what the note meant and what the key opened, and these letters may have had the answer all along. Maybe it was time to see what other secrets they contained.

"Cindy! I'm home!"

Cindy quickly shoved everything back into the suitcase and pushed it under her bed. Reading the letters would have to wait.

***

"Yes, this is Jackson Nelson." He held the phone to his ear and stepped outside of the warehouse. The sky was coyote grey, and he could smell the snow in the low-hanging clouds. At any moment, the flakes would descend upon the town.

"Mr. Jackson, this is Denise Stewart, personal assistant to Mr. Kramer of North American Bank in New York. Mr. Kramer would like to bring you in for an interview. Are you able to travel to New York next week? I realize that's only a few days before Christmas, and it's a busy time for most, but Mr. Kramer has some space in his schedule then."

"Yes, Ma'am. I can be in New York next week."

They agreed upon a day and time, and Jackson thanked her for the call. He returned to checking in inventory with a smile on his face.

"Good news?" Mac asked.

"I hope so." He relayed the information, becoming more comfortable with Mac and his reserved ways.

"Ever been to New York?"

"Nope. Been to Baltimore, St. Louis, and Little Rock. And to Nashville once to visit a friend. Those are the only big cities my boots have walked in. You?"

"Nah. I lived in a city for the first thirty-some years of my life. Not for me."

"Phoenix, right?"

"Huh?"

"You said you were from somewhere near Phoenix."

Mac's features became pensive for a moment. "No, Phoenix was nearby, but I never lived there."

Jackson waited, but Mac didn't offer any other details about his life.

"Ever been married?"

Mac looked at Jackson with suspicion. "You writing a book?"

"Just curious. You know more about me than I do about you."

"I find that most folks share too much information. What with that face thing people are always on and that snap photo thing. Too much info."

"So, you don't like to share, don't have a family, from what I've gathered, and don't live in one place for too long. Don't you get lonely?"

Mac seemed to think about that for a long time. He gazed out the wide-open bay doors, his denim coat ruffling in the breeze, and something in his expression gave Jackson a sense of deja vu. He watched as Mac took a long drink from his water bottle and tightened his gloves before turning back to Jackson.

"I've got the Lord," he said, surprising Jackson. He hadn't pegged Mac for a religious man. "All I need, I suppose."

"I didn't know you were religious."

"I wasn't for the better part of my life. Found God later than most, I suppose. He helped me become a better man. But I've still got a lot to make up for in my life."

"I reckon we all do."

Mac eyed Jackson warily. "I doubt you've got much to make up for, son. You're still young enough to get it right. The wife and kid thing, the good job, the smart decisions. Don't screw up like I did."

"Care to enlighten me?"

"Nope. Just make sure you let the good Lord lead you through life. That's the best any of us can do."

Mac stood and stretched his back as a light snow began falling outside the doors, and Mac walked slowly to look out. Jackson knew that the conversation was over. He chastised himself for judging Mac too harshly. Maybe the man wasn't so bad after all.

***

"I must say, I had my doubts, but everything looks great," Wade said with a look of genuine surprise.

It had taken Stan a couple days to find the time, but once he gathered the supplies and got to work, it was an easy job. Cindy was very pleased with the results. Without so much as a brush of paint on the walls, the office looked like an entirely new space.

"Good morning, Mr. Mayor, Trudy." An older woman, quite short with a grey bob haircut and an air of superiority glanced from one to the other before holding her gaze on Cindy. She wore a long grey coat over dark pants and a bulky sweater, but her clothes didn't tell the whole story, nor did her height reveal her stature. She was a formidable woman just by her countenance and her stare. "You must be Ms. Kline."

Cindy swallowed and nodded. "It's just Cindy, Ma'am."

"Cindy," Wade said. "This is Madam Mayor, Imogene Baker."

"Mayor? But I thought—"

"Former mayor," the woman supplied in her authoritative voice. "I heard you were making some changes to the office and thought I'd see what's going on." She stepped into the room and walked to the closet.

Cindy held her breath while the woman inspected the neatly organized build-in, the plastic baskets and magazine files, and the space for the presentation boards.

"I like it," she said after a few minutes. "It's a good use of the space, not too fancy, and not too expensive from the looks of it. Stan always does fine work, no matter how large or small the project."

"Stan made this table, too," Trudy said, gesturing to the table next to her desk.

Mrs. Baker walked to the desk and surveyed the setup. "Very nice. An L-shaped work area is almost always the most ideal way to go." She looked at Trudy. "And I can actually see the top of the desk. Haven't been able to do that since I promoted you from file girl to my assistant."

Trudy looked quite pleased, and Cindy was amazed by how this woman, who couldn't be a day less than eighty, had walked in like she still ran the place and made her opinions known. More amazing was the fact that Wade and Trudy seemed to hang on her every word. If Buffalo Springs was a realm of Middle-earth, Mrs. Baker was no doubt the Galadriel of the realm. Cindy had to hide her smile as she realized she had mentally compared the very short woman to Tolkien's elf queen. Before she could erase the thought from her mind, the woman turned toward Cindy.

"You do good work. I was impressed with the window displays, and I'm just as impressed with this. When are you available for your next job?"

"Oh, this was just—"

"She's available now," Trudy said. "What do you need her to organize?"

"I have a hobby room that is completely out of control. I need you to tame it for me."

Cindy saw the look of astonishment on the faces of both Wade and Trudy and wondered if they were surprised that Mrs. Baker hired her, that the woman could ever let anything be out of her control, or that she had hobbies to begin with. Cindy looked at Trudy, her heart in her throat. What should she do?

"Well? Are you available or not?" Mrs. Baker asked impatiently.

Trudy nodded vigorously at Cindy, and Cindy found herself nodding back. "It appears that I am."

"Good. I'd like you to be at my house by 8AM sharp. I will have a cup of coffee ready for you, but eat before you come. And be prepared to leave your shoes at the door. I don't allow them inside the house." And with that, Imogene Baker, former mayor of Buffalo Springs, turned and walked out the door.

The room seemed to suddenly deflate. "What was that?" Cindy asked in amazement.

"That, Cindy, was the former mayor of Buffalo Springs and your new client," Trudy said.

"She's scary," Cindy said in a low voice.

"You haven't seen scary. Believe, me. I've been on the receiving end of her scary," Wade told her.

Cindy stared at the doorway, contemplating the tornado that was Imogene Baker. Tomorrow was going to be interesting. Cindy just hoped she could live up to the mayor's expectations.

***

Jackson followed Andi into the kitchen, a much more subdued room than most of the others in the grand house. The old wooden table, antique butcher block island, and cheery yellow walls always made Jackson feel as though this room was in a different house entirely.

"Wade's on his way. Sit down." She gestured to the chairs around the table. "Can I get you something? A Coke? A snack? I'm not sure what I'm making for dinner yet." She opened the freezer and stuck her head inside, shifting and moving items around. Jackson reached down and gave Boomer a hard knuckle rub on the top of his head, and the dog's tail thumped the hardwood floor in appreciation.

"I'm fine, thanks. Actually, on second thought, a Coke would be great."

Andi closed the freezer, opened the fridge, and poured her brother a Coke with ice. She made herself an ice water and sat across from him at the table, shifting so she could prop her feet on another chair.

"So, what's going on, little brother? Why do you need to talk to Wade?"

"It's about work."

She made a face. "What does Wade know about working at the Tractor Supply?"

"Andi, do you think I plan on working there forever?"

She frowned. "Did he talk to you about—"

Before she could finish, Wade walked into the kitchen, took hold of her shoulders, and leaned down to give her a kiss on the cheek. "Hey, Jackson," he said, looking up.

He went to the fridge and took out a beer. "Want one?"

"No, thanks." He held up his Coke. "I'm good."

Wade sat down at the head of the table between Jackson and Andi. "So, what's up?"

Jackson briefly looked at his sister and then back at Wade. "I've got a job interview the Monday before Christmas. With North American Bank. In New York."

"Well, I'll be!' Wade exclaimed, clapping him on the back. "Good for you."

"New York?" Andi asked.

Jackson nodded. "I've applied to several banks that do real estate investing, but this one sounds the most interesting to me. It's a good, entry-level position. I'd be doing financial modeling, deal screening, providing support for meetings, preparing LIOs and RFPs, structuring RBC transactions, writing investment summaries, that kind of stuff. Of course, I have to actually get the job first."

Andi looked at Wade. "Do you understand what he just said?"

Wade smiled. "Oh, to be young and writing summaries and preparing LOIs again."

"Forget all that," Andi said. She turned to her brother. "Are you excited?"

"I am. At least I think so. It's a big change."

Wade laughed heartily. "That's an understatement."

"Yeah, that's kind of why I'm here. I have no idea what the best way to get there is. Flying, I reckon. Or where to stay or how to dress or if I should take anything with me. I spent the last five years of my life preparing for this, and I feel like I know nothing."

"No problem, Jackson. I've got you covered. Andi, why don't we order a pizza? Jackson and I have a lot to discuss."

***

Mrs. Baker lived in a stately log house just inside the town limits on a large tract of wooded land that sat high on a ledge overlooking a valley. Cindy arrived at the house at 7:59. Imogene took only a few seconds to answer the door. When she answered, she was wearing what looked to be the same dark blue pants as before, but she had on an off-white V-neck sweater with a striped, button-down shirt underneath. With her round glasses, she reminded Cindy of the older woman who used to be Red's murder scene cleaner on the television show, *Blacklist*. Only Mrs. Baker actually smiled when she opened the door, and the woman on the show only scowled.

"Good morning," Cindy greeted her, trying to hide the nervousness in her voice.

"Well, don't just stand there. Come in. We've got lots of work to do, and there's snow on the way."

Several hours later, they had emptied the contents of the hobby room, as Mrs. Baker called it, into the open floor space of the downstairs. The log house was two-stories, though the second story consisted of just an L-shaped balcony with rooms lining it and an opening in the middle that looked down into the large living area. A modern re-creation of a pot-bellied stove gave off enough heat to reach into the surrounding rooms. Skylights were framed overhead, and Cindy could see the clouds as they moved across the grey sky.

The open plan provided a roomy kitchen with a long wooden table and living room. A master bedroom was placed behind the kitchen, and an office—now the hobby room—was off the living room. A beautiful back deck boasted a breath-taking view of the Ozark Mountains. The heads of deer, elk, and even a buffalo hung on the walls. When Mrs. Baker noticed the startled look on Cindy's face at the sight of them, she said, "My husband was a hunter. I haven't the heart to take them down."

The hobby room wasn't as disorganized as it was cluttered. Mrs. Baker explained, "I've spent fifteen lonely years trying to find something that holds my attention. The only one that really satisfied me was being mayor."

"Why did you quit?"

"Who says I quit?" she asked sharply. "Maybe I was defeated in a bid for re-election."

Cindy laughed. "I doubt that. Who would be brave enough to run against you?"

Mrs. Baker eyed her for a moment before a laugh burst forth from her belly. "I knew I liked you from the moment I saw you. And you're right. I want you to know that I am not a quitter, but my doctor told me it was time to retire, take it easy, find a hobby." She looked around. "Look where that got me."

They worked in companionable silence, concentrating on their task, unless Cindy had a question. Taking a cue from one of the shows she remembered seeing on television as a child, Cindy had Mrs. Baker sort everything into three piles—keep, toss, or give away. Once they had everything sorted, they broke for lunch.

Over grilled cheese and tomato soup, they talked as they watched the snow fall on the deck, creating a curtain of flakes that hung between them and the next mountain over. Cindy found Mrs. Baker very easy to talk to and surprised herself by sharing some of the painful details of her own life.

"Well, you're certainly doing the right thing by coming here and starting this business of yours."

"You think so?" Cindy asked, sipping the hot tea Mrs. Baker insisted she try. Hot tea was not a popular drink in Southern California, but Cindy liked the flavor she was offered—spicy with a hint of orange.

"Of course. It sounds as though you had nothing to lose by setting out on a new track, and it's always good to make a fresh start. Now, the question is, do you plan to stick around or continue on your journey?"

Cindy thought for a moment. "Well, I guess it depends upon how many jobs I have here."

Mrs. Baker nodded. "I think it depends upon a great deal more than that. You've got to think about more than a job when you look at the future. What kind of life do you want to live? What kind of man do you want to marry?" She stopped and looked appraisingly at Cindy. "I assume it would be a man."

Cindy smiled. "Yes, Ma'am. It would be a man."

"Very well. What kind of man? Will he be content with living out here? Will you be? This is a much slower life than what you're used to in California."

"I'm okay with slower. In fact, I think I prefer it."

"What about kids? What do you want for them? This town had a terrible drug problem for a long time. Took many of our youth. If not for Andi and Wade's slow, eventual growth of intelligence and balls, if you'll pardon my French, we'd still be burying one young person after another. Things are better now, but there's not much for them to do. What would you propose to keep our kids safe and healthy and away from that…stuff."

Cindy got the impression that Mrs. Baker didn't censor her words often.

"I'll be honest. These aren't things I've ever thought of."

"They'll have to be if you're going to be a fruitful contributor to society and raise a good family."

"I'm not sure I'm even close to being able to do either." Why this line of questioning didn't bother her, Cindy couldn't say. She felt like she was sitting with the

Dali Lama, being given the secret of the meaning of life. "I've already been engaged, and it didn't work out. Maybe I'm not meant to find that kind of happiness."

"That wasn't your fault, and you were young and probably not together long enough to get a feel for it. Your business is a good way to make a new start. I'll be letting others know that your services are worth spending money on. They'll listen to me."

Cindy had no doubt.

"Speaking of which, we have a lot to do. Break's over."

Cindy resisted the urge to salute and doubted that Evan had encountered personalities as commanding in his entire tenure in the service.

By the time they were done for the day, measurements were taken, plans for new furniture and organizers were made, and a shopping trip was planned. Mrs. Baker was prepared to spare no expense and even told Cindy that her quote was much too low and not to underestimate herself or her talent. Cindy was looking forward to a nice, fat paycheck just in time for Christmas.

Nine

"Good morning, Mrs. Baker," Jackson said cheerfully. "Need more pellets today?"

"I do, Jackson. That snow the other day nearly wiped me out. Though I must say, that Cindy has me working up a sweat."

Jackson laughed. "Wade told me you hired her. How's the organizing coming?"

"It's coming. She's quite impressive, that girl. She knows what she's doing. I plan on recommending her to everyone in town."

Jackson looked at her receipt and went to fetch the correct brand and size of the wood fuel pellets she had purchased.

"And who are you?" she looked at Mac, obviously taking in his beard, tattoos, and worn denim coat, and asked pointedly.

"The name's Mac." He stood and reached out his hand which she eyed suspiciously but then accepted and shook vigorously.

"Mac, huh? New around here?"

"Yes, Ma'am. Arrived just after Thanksgiving."

"You look familiar…" She arched her brow as she looked him over, scrutinizing him from head to toe. "Did I see you in the back of the Church on Sunday?"

"You might have," he said noncommittally.

Jackson returned with the pellets and hefted the bag into the back of the truck that once belonged to Mr. Baker and closed the tailgate. "I'll come by after work and take this inside for you. Don't you try to take it in yourself."

"Jackson, my boy, you know I have a cart that does all the hard work for me. All I have to do is roll the bag across the bed of the truck and let it fall into the cart."

"And climb into the back, and bend over, and push the bag, and haul the cart around the house. Yes, I know what needs to be done, and I'll be there before eight tonight to do it. You need to watch that bad back of yours."

She gave him a look of exasperation. "Are you trying to tell me I'm incapable of doing this myself?"

"I would never dream of it. I know quite well how capable you are. That doesn't mean you should be doing it."

"Well, seeing as how I have other things to do today, I'll let you come by and take care of this for me."

It was a song and dance they'd played for years, and Jackson enjoyed it each time. He also enjoyed the twenty-dollar bill she always shoved into his hand before he left, which he'd stopped trying to refuse a long time ago. Mrs. Baker had money, and lots of it. If it made her feel good to spread it around, then he should let her, or so his mama told him.

"She's a trouper, that Cindy. She's had a hard life, but she's managed to overcome every obstacle that's been put in her way. Except for college. Not being able to go is her one regret. Not counting losing her fiancé, but there wasn't much she could've done about that. Anyway, there's something really special about that gal."

"I'm glad you two are getting along so well," Jackson said, and Mrs. Baker gave him a hard stare.

"Sometimes, Jackson, we need to appreciate the gifts God has given us, especially the ones we least expect."

She waved goodbye to both men and climbed into the truck.

"I never can figure out what that woman is trying to tell me," Jackson said.

"Who is she?"

"Former mayor of Buffalo Springs and still the most formidable woman in town. If she likes you, you've got it made. If not, she'll have you run out on a rail. She and Wade got off to a rough start, but he straightened up, and she came around to liking him."

"Wade?"

"My brother-in-law."

"And who's this Cindy person she talked about? She sure had a lot to say about her."

"Friend of my sister's. Well, a friend of the whole family now, I reckon."

"Sounds like she's had it rough."

"Yeah, she had a tough childhood—father abandoned them; mother was an alcoholic. Cindy was engaged to a guy in my sister's SEAL unit, but he was killed in a helicopter crash. A few weeks ago, she showed up in town alone and not really knowing where to go or what to do."

Mac eyed Jackson for a long minute. "You like her?"

"Who? Cindy? Sure, what's not to like? She's pretty and nice and smart. Everyone likes her."

"I mean, do you *like* her."

Jackson felt an uneasy stir in his gut. It was the very question he had avoided asking himself ever since Tanner brought it up after the dance. With her being so lost and unsure of her future, and him heading to the Big Apple, what good did it do to start looking for feelings where it was best there should be none? Ever since the break-in, he'd been thinking about her a lot. Seeing her so scared and vulnerable really got to him. Then, after almost kissing her the night of the dance, his feelings had kicked up like leaves in a windstorm, swirling around him all day and all night.

Rather than answering, Jackson looked away and pointed toward the incoming clouds. "Might have more snow tonight."

"I'm going to take that as a yes."

Jackson turned back to Mac and clenched his jaw. He inhaled and shook his head. "I don't have time for that stuff, Mac. Mama says Cindy is just passing by, like Simon. He was just passing by, helped carry the cross, and kept going."

"Or did he?"

Jackson raised one brow questioningly. "Excuse me?"

"Did he keep going? From what I've read, there's mention of Simon's son in Acts, one of the new followers. Could be that Simon stayed around, made a home, found a new way of life."

"And? What's your point?"

Mac took a long, deep breath, turned to look at the clouds, and let out a stream of air that turned white and curled in front of them. "Sometimes, we can't see the life we're meant to lead even if it's planted right in front of us. We spend so much time looking for a sure thing, our big break, the road to riches, when all we really needed was right there all along just waiting for us to stop being stupid and start living like the men we were meant to be."

"It sounds like you're speaking from experience."

"Maybe I am, son."

"Yeah, well, I wouldn't know about any of that. I'm just starting to figure out what my life is going to be like. Besides, as far as Cindy goes, I think Mama's right. I don't think she'll stick around after what happened."

"Something happened?"

"Helena's house was broken into last week, and Cindy's room was trashed. Looked like they were trying to find something specific. Cindy was scared to death."

"Does she know what they wanted?"

"I have no clue. If she does, she's not saying."

Mac was silent then. He stood staring into the distance, a pensive look on his face. The bell rang, and another truck backed in, prompting them to return to work. Neither man had much to say for the rest of the day. Each seemed lost in his own thoughts.

***

"This is it, then? You've made a decision?"

Cindy stood next to Mrs. Baker as she surveyed the pile of paintbrushes, canvases, oil paints, and easels lumped together with dozens of boxes of puzzles. The larger pile behind them was a mingling of dozens of skeins of yarn, embroidery thread in every color under the sun, stacks of paper, rolls and sheets of stickers, fancy scissors, punches, and slicers, as well as crochet hooks, knitting needles, sewing hoops, and a smattering of craft odds and ends.

"Yes," Imogene said firmly. "I'm too old to scrapbook, my eyes can't see those little sewing patterns and needle eyes, and I can't get the hang of knitting or crocheting. I like to paint. It's fun. And if I mess up, I can just paint over it. No fuss or waste." She gestured to the puzzles. "And I like doing puzzles. Keeps my mind sharp, and I can do it while I watch TV. Helps pass the time in the winter."

"Okay, then. I think we need to organize your supplies in the closet, grouping items by the type of paint and type of supplies. You'll need a small cabinet of some sort to keep at hand the supplies you're using at that moment. We'll keep that table you have in there, but you're going to need a better chair. You need to protect your back."

Mrs. Baker looked at her, one eye widening. "You been talking to Jackson?"

"Excuse me?"

The older woman shook her head. "Never mind. What else?"

"Lighting. You've got plenty of natural lighting during the day for your painting, but you're going to need some hanging lights over the puzzle table and some lights over the painting area for days and times when the natural lighting isn't enough."

"You know a lot about what a painter needs."

"My grandmother was an artist. I didn't inherit any of her talent, and she died when I was very young, but she liked to talk while she painted. She tried to impart her knowledge on me just in case that gene suddenly appeared." She returned to the subject of the room. "You're also going to need a shelving unit for the puzzles. Will you break them up when you're finished or glue and display them?"

"I'll break them up and put them away for another time. Hey, I should start a trade group. I know several other ladies who like to do puzzles."

"I like that idea. Like a lending library but for puzzles."

"So, what do we do now?"

"I think it's time for that shopping trip we talked about making."

"I'll grab my purse."

Cindy smiled as she watched Mrs. Baker hurry to get her things. She felt good about herself and the impact she was making on people's lives. Once she was finished here, she had three more jobs lined up, and she wanted to surprise Helena by organizing her kitchen.

"Ready?" Mrs. Baker asked.

"I am," Cindy said with more confidence than she ever felt in her life. However, when she put on her coat, the key in her pocket felt like a weight pulling her down. Tonight, she would look at the letters. She'd put it off long enough.

***

Cindy was exhausted. She'd spent the afternoon shopping with Mrs. Baker, and that woman had energy to burn. They'd gone into every home store and discount store in Harrison and two different Walmarts. Her feet ached, her head pounded, and all she wanted to do was take a long bath and go to bed. That, and take a look at those letters.

What did they say? Would she finally find out who her father really was? Did she want to know?

She blew her bangs from her face and went to her room to retrieve a ponytail holder. She pulled her hair back as she walked to the kitchen where she shoveled in a bowl of cereal. She flipped the stations on the television while she ate, but she felt restless and turned it off, welcoming the silence.

She put the bowl in the dishwasher, wiped down the counter, and went to her room. Hunched on the floor, she reached under the bed and dragged out the suitcase. She had just pulled out the box when she thought she heard a knock on the front door. She listened but didn't hear anything else, so she sat on the bed and opened the box.

Before she had a chance to open the first envelope, she heard louder knocking. She jumped from the bed, stashed the box back into the suitcase, and shoved the suitcase under her bed. She hurried to the door and flung it open.

***

Jackson knocked on the door and waited for Cindy to answer. Her car was in the driveway as was Helena's, but he'd passed Joe and Helena in Joe's car, presumably on their way to dinner somewhere.

After a moment or two passed, Jackson knocked again. Helena really needed to fix her doorbell. Maybe, with the break-in, she should invest in one of those systems that sends a message and picture to her phone, showing her who was at the door.

He was about to give up when the door swung open, and an out-of-breath Cindy appeared.

"I'm sorry. Were you busy?"

She shook her head, a ponytail swaying behind her. "No, just tidying up."

Jackson laughed. "You live with Helena. Tidying up is an understatement, I'm sure."

Cindy frowned. "She's not that bad. Honestly, you and Andi give her such a hard time, but she's really quite neat everywhere but in her bedroom. And she has a right to have at least one space where she doesn't have to worry about being judged all the time."

Wow. He sure had struck a chord. "I'm really sorry. I didn't mean to come down on her like that. And I didn't mean to bother you. I have another box from Mama, but I can come back another time."

Cindy shook her head dismissively. "No, no, it's fine. You can bring it in. I'm sorry. I'm just in a bit of a mood tonight."

"Spending all day with Mrs. Baker can do that to a person."

Her forehead crinkled, and her eyes narrowed. "Mrs. Baker is a wonderful person who cares about people and only wants what's best for them and for this town."

He put his hand out defensively. "Hey, I'm not trying to get into an argument with you about Helena or Mrs. Baker or anything else. I just came to bring Helena this stuff. If it's a bad time—"

"I'm sorry," she said hastily. "I really do have a lot on my mind. Please don't take it personally."

"If you say so," Jackson mumbled. "How about I just bring in this box and then be on my way?"

She nodded, and he went to his truck to retrieve the box full of unknown contents from his sister's childhood. He was irritated, but he also felt bad. Cindy had been through a lot, and she had the right to be in a funk once in a while. From what he'd seen, she put a lot of effort into being cheery and nice and accommodating all the time. That had to wear on a person after a while.

Cindy held the door open, and Jackson deposited the box on the floor next to the big armchair. He turned toward Cindy who still stood next to the front door.

"Have you eaten? Food always makes me feel better."

She bit her lips together and inhaled through her nose. "I had a bowl of cereal."

"That's not dinner," Jackson said, shaking his head. "Helena is really rubbing off on you. Cereal is her go-to meal when she doesn't feel like cooking. I'm asking if you want to have a real dinner."

"I don't know…"

"You don't know if you want to eat dinner, or you don't know if you want to eat with me? I don't bite, you know." He smiled as a flood of uncertainty washed across her face. Was that about him or about whatever had her in a bad mood?

"I suppose I could eat something."

"Great. Order in or go out?"

"What were your plans?"

"Well, I didn't really have any. It's leftover night at home, and I'd rather have something else." He pulled his phone from his pocket. "Let me just tell Mama that I won't be home for dinner." He texted his mother, smiling at her rapid response. She was getting better at texting, and it pleased him to no end. He knew it was going to be hard on both of them when he left town.

As if reading his mind, Cindy said, "You seem to be awfully close to your mother." Her voice was more curious than accusatory.

"I guess I am. Mama and I seem to have a connection that's different from my sisters. Actually, Mama has a connection with all of us, but I think being the only boy makes me more protective of her, especially after Daddy's stroke. We were all just as worried about Mama as we were about Daddy."

"What's it like? Having parents who love you and stick around?" From the sudden change in her expression, she was just as surprised with her question as he was.

"Well…" How was he supposed to answer that? "I mean, I reckon I don't really know what to compare it to. I've never thought about it before."

Her voice was wistful when she sighed and said, "That must be really nice."

"Hey, let's get out of here. The Russos have quite the menu and an atmosphere to match. It's like stepping off the sidewalk in Buffalo Springs and stepping into a restaurant in Italy, not that I've ever been to Italy, but I imagine their place is pretty close to what it's like. Have you been there?"

She shook her head.

"Then, what are we waiting for?"

***

He'd given her time to change clothes and comb her hair, but she still felt disheveled. Jackson didn't seem to notice. A true gentleman, he led her to the passenger side of his truck and opened and closed the door for her. They chatted lightly on the short drive to La Forna on Main Street.

"What does it mean?" Cindy asked, pointing to the sign.

"I have no idea," Jackson said. "We'll have to ask."

He was around the truck in a flash and offered his hand to her as she climbed down from the passenger seat. She hesitated for a moment but took it and felt his touch all the way to her toes. She looked up and saw him staring at her. Their eyes locked, and a butterfly took flight in her stomach. A swarm of butterflies. For a second, she couldn't breathe, but then Jackson blinked and cleared his throat, letting go of her hand and ending the brief moment.

Jackson gestured for her to go first, and Cindy felt the light touch of his hand on her lower back as they walked up the steps to the restaurant. As soon as they entered the lobby, Cindy saw what Jackson meant.

The inside of the restaurant looked nothing like the outside. White brick covered the walls, and columns that stretched up into arches made it feel as though they'd stepped back in time. Ornate carvings adorned the columns, and Cindy imagined that this was what the Pantheon looked like on the inside. Or was it the Parthenon? In her mind, she heard the words of her ninth-grade history teacher, *Think of pan as in pizza.* Ah, yes, the Pantheon was in Italy.

The lighting was dim, but large rings of round bulbs hung in a long line down the center of the restaurant, and small lamps sat on the tables which were covered with white cloths and set for an elegant meal. Soft Italian music danced in the air and mingled with the aroma of garlic, olive oil, and marinara sauce, creating a lovely, intoxicating ambiance.

"Jackson, dear, buona serata," said a woman with a thick Italian accent. She greeted Jackson with an air kiss to each cheek.

"Good evening, Senora Russo. This is my friend, Cindy. We'd like your best table."

Cindy looked around. There weren't many others there, no surprise for a weeknight, and she wondered what table would be considered 'the best.'

"Ciao, Cindy," Mrs. Russo said, leaning in and pecking the air by both of Cindy's cheeks. Cindy blushed and smiled at Jackson, familiar with the custom but never having experienced it. "Follow me."

They were led to a table at the back of the restaurant in a cozy corner. There was no one else nearby. Mrs.

Russo handed them their menus. "I will send my daughter, Gabriella, over. She will see that you are well taken care of."

Cindy waited for her to be out of earshot before leaning toward Jackson. "I could listen to her talk all night. Her accent is so beautiful."

Jackson laughed. "It does sound nice, doesn't it?"

"How on earth did she end up here?" Cindy gasped at the sound of her own words. "I'm so sorry! I didn't mean—"

Jackson laughed. "It's okay. I know what you mean. She and her husband, Leonardo, immigrated to New York when they were around our age. They worked their way up through the restaurant business, and he went to the culinary school up there for a while where, I imagine, he taught them a thing or two! They decided they didn't like New York and started searching for a small town where they could open a restaurant. They thought this would be a great place to live and work. Their adult children even came with them."

"How'd you learn all that?"

"Buona serata, Jackson!"

Cindy blinked as she looked up at the stunning young woman. Her accent was slightly more New York than Italy, but it still had the same beautiful lilt. She could have been a model, with her perfect bone structure, olive skin tone, and big brown eyes.

"Hey, Gabriella. How are you?" Jackson stood and hugged her, and Cindy felt a twinge of jealousy. "Cindy, meet Gabriella. She and her family go to our church."

Cindy smiled and reached out her hand. "It's nice to meet you." She felt self-conscious with her reddish hair and pale skin next to this raven-haired beauty.

"It's my pleasure," Gabriella said with a genuine smile. "I've seen you with Sarah. You were at the holiday dance, right?"

"I was," Cindy answered.

"I thought so. You're new in town, too. Do you plan to stay long?"

Jackson looked at her with the same curious expression.

"I'm not sure. I mean, I'm doing some work around town right now, so I guess I'm here for as long as that takes."

"What kind of work?"

"I'm…" She had never said the words out loud and wasn't sure how true they would sound.

As though recognizing her uncertainty, Jackson spoke up. "Cindy's a professional organizer. She's helping people clean out, rearrange, organize, that kind of stuff. She's a decorator, too. You've probably seen her work in some of the store windows."

"Oh, that's you? Your displays are beautiful! And you organize, too? You and my mother would get along famously. Unlike most Italians, she is the most organized and most punctual woman I know."

"Probably why she and Mama hit it off so well," Jackson said.

Jackson sat back down, and Gabriella told them the specials. He ordered a bottle of red wine and an antipasti of caprese tomatoes with mozzarella and olive pesto. Cindy was impressed by his knowledge of what to order.

"Do you come here often?"

"Not really. There was a great Italian restaurant near campus that I frequented a lot. I took a class on restaurant economics, and I got to know the owner pretty well while I was doing research for an assignment."

"I didn't know there was such a class."

Jackson shrugged. "I didn't either. I thought it would be different and fun, and it was. It made me think about all small businesses in a different and more concrete way."

She took a sip of her water. "You're an interesting person, Jackson Nelson."

He smiled broadly. "Now that's really saying something. I doubt I'm all that interesting next to the surfer dudes you used to know back in California."

"I didn't hang out with many surfer dudes." She took great care in laying her napkin in her lap. She did know lots of kids who surfed, and that was a big part of her life growing up, but that all seemed so distant now. She hadn't really thought about those people since dating Evan.

"So, what did you do in California?" Jackson leaned across the table, his hands folded on top of the white charger plate in front of him.

Cindy shrugged. "I mean, I did surf. We all did. It just wasn't a big part of my social scene. To be honest..." She looked up at him. "I didn't have the money for a nice board or the right wetsuits or the wax and other necessary equipment. When I did surf, it was usually with a borrowed board and borrowed clothes. Things were tight for us."

"I'm sorry," he said quietly. "I don't mean to pry or make you uncomfortable. To tell the truth. Things have always been tight for us, too. I had to drop out of school for a while when my father got laid off, and Helena and I both had to pay for college, and she paid for grad school. I think it's one of the reasons Andi wanted to go to the Naval Academy so badly."

"Thanks, Jackson. I appreciate your honesty."

"Well, about that. I have a confession."

She looked at him and waited.

"I lied to you the night of the play. I have been to plays before."

Cindy laughed. "If that's all you have to confess, then I think we're okay. And I have a confession, too."

He raised his brow.

"I knew that already. There was no way you understood so much about the theater without having gone to see a show or two."

Gabriella brought their wine, and Jackson raised his glass in a toast. "To your new job and new future."

Cindy clinked his glass. "Thanks. I hope it's as successful as Trudy says it's going to be. Then I can stay in town."

"Is that what you want?"

Cindy nodded. "I do, I really do."

"So, you like it here? I mean, you feel comfortable? At home?"

"As at home as I can be living in a borrowed room in someone else's house. Don't get me wrong, Helena's awesome, but…"

"But you'd rather have something that's yours."

She thought about those words. She'd never had something that was completely hers. She guessed she could count her car, but it barely got her from one place to another. It was a miracle that it made it all the way to Arkansas and was still running. Even the house she and Evan had lived in hadn't belonged to them. They rented it, and she gave up the lease when Gloria got sick.

"I guess it sounds selfish." She ran her finger around the rim of her wine glass.

"I think it sounds normal," he said quietly. When she raised her eyes to meet his, there was an intensity there that caused a burning in her gut. She swallowed, unable to look away.

"Here's your antipasti," Gabriella said as she placed the plate between them, breaking off their gaze. "Are you ready to order?"

"I haven't even looked," Cindy suddenly realized.

"I know what I want," Jackson said. "Do you want some more time to look?"

"What do you recommend?" she asked him and then turned her gaze to Gabriella.

"Do you like steak?"

"I love it, but—"

"She'll have the Tuscan rib-eye and vegetables," Jackson said, handing his menu to Gabriella. "And I'll have the chicken parmigiana with capellini and tomatoes."

"Excellent choices. How would you like your steak cooked?" she asked, and Cindy told her medium. Gabriella nodded. "Let me know if you need anything."

"Jackson!" Cindy scolded as soon as Gabriella was gone. "Did you see the price on the rib-eye? I can't order that. I'll be completely broke."

"Cindy, what did I tell you the night of the play? My Mama would kill me if I let you pay."

"Jackson, I can't let you do that."

"Why not? You protested that night that it wasn't a date. Look around, Cindy. What does this look like to you?"

For the first time, she thought about their evening. He had asked her to go to dinner. He had driven them to a very nice restaurant. He ordered a bottle of wine. They were having an intimate conversation in which she divulged things she had never admitted to anyone other than Evan.

"I… I guess I…"

"What would you call this?" His smirk should have been annoying, but instead, it was endearing.

"Well, I guess if I'm honest, I'd have to call it a date."

"Exactly," he said triumphantly, raising his glass again. "To our first date."

She hesitantly raised her glass and gently tapped it against his. Their first date. That implied that there would be more. Was she ready for that?

She sipped her wine and let herself admit the truth—yes, yes she was ready for that.

Ten

Jackson's alarm went off the next morning, and he rolled over to face the window. It was still dark outside, but there was a faint glow that signaled that dawn was not far off. He stared at the ceiling and thought about the previous night.

He'd learned that Cindy knew how to surf but couldn't afford to make the sport a regular part of her life. She was estranged from her high school friends for reasons that sounded petty and childish on their part but, he could tell, were painful for Cindy. She'd been together with Evan for less than a year, but happily together was a stretch with all the outside pressures they had on them. His parents were nice to her but leery. They were guarded in their few conversations, and Cindy seemed to understand their reluctance in accepting the woman their son met and was engaged to just weeks later. She longed to go to college but assumed it wasn't in the cards. Organizing was something she loved to do, though, and she was thrilled that she could use her skill to help others and make money at the same time.

For someone whose father abandoned her at a young age, who was raised by an uncaring, alcoholic mother, rejected by friends and peers, and had no place to truly call home, Cindy seemed remarkably resilient. Or maybe that was because of and not in spite of the life she'd lived.

As the room began to illuminate with the orange glow of the sunrise, Jackson rose from bed. He showered and dressed, all the while thinking about the enigma that was Cindy Kline. They had spent the better part of the evening together, and he now knew slightly more about her past, but he knew almost nothing about her as a person.

She liked movies, all genres and all eras. She loved little more than cozying up with a good book. She loved steak and preferred lemon in her water, no ice. But what kept her awake at night? Did she like dogs or cats? Cake or pie? Mountains or beaches? What was her favorite song? Color? Did she want kids? How many?

Those last questions caused the hand holding the razor to stop, the blade just below his chin.

What did it matter? He would soon be gone, and she was making a home for herself here. And he believed she would make a good home for herself here. She seemed happy. She was making friends. She was showing some real promise with her unexpected business enterprise. They would barely have time to get to know each other.

Still… He was curious and a little more than entranced by her. He once heard Joe say that Helena seemed to cast a spell over him that he couldn't explain and couldn't shake. Jackson thought he was being patronizing, but… There was something to be said for the growing feelings Jackson had when he was around Cindy.

He finished shaving and headed downstairs for breakfast.

"You were out late last night," his mother said as she leaned up and gave him a kiss on the cheek.

"Keeping tabs on me, Mama?"

"Of course not." She placed two pieces of bacon, a spoonful of scrambled eggs, and a pile of grits on a plate while Jackson poured himself a large mug of black coffee.

"Are you ready for your interview?"

"I think so. Wade's helping me prepare. I just wish I'd heard from more than one place. I hate going all the way up there for just one interview."

"One is all it takes," she told him.

Jackson smiled. "I guess you're right." He snapped one of the slices of bacon in half and nibbled at it. "I ate at La Forna last night."

"Oh? I assume you didn't go there alone." She made a plate for Joshua who made his way to the table.

"I took Cindy. She hadn't eaten when I took that box to Helena, and I thought she could use a night out."

"So, you did that as a favor, like a good Samaritan?" She placed Joshua's plate on the table and began making one for herself.

"Well, I don't know if I'd put it that way."

"She seems to be getting on real well, from what I hear," Joshua said.

"She is. Her business is really taking off." He swallowed a mouthful of coffee and dug into his grits. "I wouldn't be surprised if she ended up sticking around town."

"Well, it would be nice for her to have a place to put down roots. Darn shame it's happening just when you're getting ready to flap your wings."

Jackson stopped chewing and looked at his mother. "What's that supposed to mean? I thought you said she was just passing through my life."

"Seems like you spend a lot of time thinking and talking about someone who's just passing through," Joshua said before spooning a large helping of grits into his mouth.

"I said, we didn't know if this was a short stop on her journey or a permanent one. From what I hear around town, she's making friends, making a name for herself in business, and starting to feel at home. Mrs. Baker sure has taken a shine to her. She's bragging about her to everyone from Sue down at the Shop-A-Lot to Father Michael. You'd think the girl was her long-lost daughter."

"Cindy thinks a lot of Mrs. Baker, too. What's that got to do with anything?"

"Just how many folk do you think Mrs. Baker takes under her wing? How many does she invite into her home to tell *her* how to live and what to do with her stuff? Does that sound like Imogene Baker to you?"

Jackson smiled. "No, I guess not. But what does that have to do with me?"

Grace looked at her son for a long time, and he began to feel hot under her gaze.

"Nothing, I reckon. I just thought maybe I was seeing something. Might could be wrong about that."

Jackson finished eating and hurried from the table. He understood full well what his mother was getting at, but it was no use. Jackson was heading to the city, and the last thing he would ever do was pull Cindy away from what could be the first real home she'd ever had.

***

Cindy was due at Paige's to work on the website at eleven, so she had the morning to do some research and outline some ideas. She had work to do, and she didn't want to put it off, but she had something else on her mind.

As soon as Helena left for the library, Cindy slipped into her room and slid the suitcase out from under her bed. She didn't really have time to read a letter and ponder it, so she took the key from her pocket. She held it up. What could it belong to? There was nothing in the suitcase that had a lock on it besides the box of letters, and it didn't go to that. Had she thrown out something important?

She thought back to the time she spent cleaning out her mother's house. No, there was nothing else. She was sure of it. So, if the key didn't fit the box, what did it go to? What was her father trying to give her? She closed her eyes and thought back all those years, but there was nothing she could remember him ever telling her about a key. She was just a child when he left, and he was almost never home before that. Her memories of him were fleeting.

She turned her attention to the box. The brown, wooden box with the beautifully carved scrolling design on the front. She'd been avoiding reading the letters she'd found inside, but maybe it was time. The answer to the key must be in those letters. She glanced at her phone and noted the time. Maybe just one…

With trembling hands, she held the stack of envelopes, tied loosely together with a piece of twine. She undid the twine and lifted the first letter from the top of the pile. She opened it and saw the date at the top. It was about a month after her father disappeared.

My dearest, Cindy,

I know I haven't been the best father I couldve been, and I'm real sorry bout that. Your mother and I never gave you the time and attention you deserved. We were young and stupid when you came along. Just kids ourselves. we didn't know how to be parents. Now I'll probably never have the chance to be a father to you. I hope you forgive me someday. For what its worth, I love you.

Love,

Dad

A teardrop fell on the letter, the word *Dad* becoming a mere blot as the water spread. While there was remorse, there was no excuse. Maybe he didn't have one or didn't feel he owed her one.

With a heavy sigh, she reached for the next letter. It was then that she noticed the return address, some place called FCI. She'd never seen or heard of anything with that name. She reached into her sweater pocket for her phone and looked it up. Just as the sheriff had said, the address was that of a maximum-security United States penitentiary. According to Wikipedia, the prison held an Al-Queda operative, Hamid Hayat, and several former rock band members who were imprisoned for assault.

She looked up her father online as well. According to the posts, her father was charged with robbing three small, locally owned banks in California and Arizona. He was suspected of robbing more, but prosecutors were unable to successfully tie him to the others. In the final robbery, a six-year-old boy had been shot in the crossfire but thankfully survived the shooting and subsequent surgery.

Cindy put down her phone. She thought she was going to be sick. Her father played a part in shooting a little boy. Had he pulled the trigger? Was he capable of shooting someone? The testimonies were unclear as to whom actually shot the child. In one account, he was the shooter, but in another, he was the one taking the money while someone else fired. The men wore masks and gloves and all looked the same in the grainy pictures provided.

The suspects constantly changed their stories, even on the stand. Only her father stuck to his story and maintained his innocence in the shooting. In the end, the jury found each one of the men guilty of robbery with a deadly weapon and intent to kill. There wasn't conclusive evidence to convict any one of the men for attempted murder though clearly one of them had shot an innocent child. There had to be more information. Someone knew the truth. She started to look at the next link but stopped. Did she really want to know? Did she really want to find out that her father had shot a little boy?

There was a reason she'd never looked up her father online before. Once he left, she didn't care what he was doing, and she'd never really been sure he was her father. There were so many men… She always figured that was why he was able to just walk away. Heck, her mother even changed their last name shortly after he disappeared, a sign Cindy took as proof that she hadn't been his.

She looked down at the stack of letters. Whether he was her biological father or not, he loved her, or said he did anyway. Maybe she'd been wrong to completely erase him from her life.

Surprised to find her cheeks wet, she wiped her eyes with the back of her hand and reached for the next letter. She held it out and thought long and hard before gently unsealing the envelope.

Dear Cindy,

Today is your 13th birthday. My little girl is a teenager. I'm sorry I won't be there to see you grow up, drive a car, go to the prom, or get married. I expect I'll be in here until the day I die. I wish things could be different. I really do. I told Gloria to divorce me, find someone new, someone who will love you like his own and be there for you the way I never could.

I look back now and wonder what I was thinking. It all sounded so glamorous, so easy. Make a few hits, stash some dough, then go back to living a normal life with a whole lot of money under the mattress. To tell the truth, though, it was never really about the money. Not once I did it anyway. But the thrill of the heist? The thrill of getting away from the police? Those were the things that got me. Hooked me right in.

I don't know why I found that so appealing at the time. Maybe I was tired of living a boring life with a wife and a kid. Maybe I was tired of being married to a ~~dru~~. Never mind. I never did much like those people who said bad things about their husbands and wives.

I don't know why I robbed that bank or why I kept doing it. But I do know one thing. I never thought about what it would do to you. You are the best thing I ever did and I let you down.

I hope you have a good birthday. Know that daddy loves you. Always.

Cindy tried to take a deep breath, but her inhale was blocked by her choking sobs. The man in the letters, he sounded so normal, so much like any father who loves his daughter. Except this father wrote about robbing banks and living for the thrill of it. He didn't mention the little boy who…

She gasped several times, trying to catch her breath and slow her cries. When her phone buzzed, she nearly jumped through the roof. It was a text from Jackson telling her he had a good time at dinner and asking if she'd like to go to Harrison to see a movie when they were finished work later that day.

It was then that she saw the time on her phone. She quickly grabbed the letters, shoved them back in the box, and stashed everything back into the suitcase. Once the suitcase was back under the bed, she hurried from the room. She grabbed her things and rushed onto the porch, making sure she locked the new deadbolt that Joe had installed.

Dale was no closer to figuring out who broke into the house, but Cindy couldn't help but wonder. Was it a coincidence that her bedroom had been ransacked around the same time her father had been released from prison? And if it was him, what was he hoping to find?

***

Jackson checked his phone several times, but there was no answer. Cindy didn't use the *read* feature, so he had no way of knowing if she'd gotten his text. Maybe she had, and she just didn't want to go. Maybe that was for the best. After all, he'd already decided not to start anything other than a nice, casual friendship.

"You expecting a call?" Mac asked.

"No, not really. Just checking on something."

"Must be something important. You haven't stopped checking every minute for the past ten minutes."

"It's nothing. Just waiting to hear from a friend about going to see a movie tonight."

"A friend? Or a *friend?*"

The more they worked together, the more Jackson liked Mac. They got along well. They were good at reading each other's moods and knowing when the other didn't want to talk. They chit chatted about this and that, but it was rarely serious. It was light and fun, and it made the long, cold days go by faster. Jackson often wondered why his boss hired Mac. They didn't need another person in the warehouse, especially this time of year. Still, Jackson was glad for the company.

"Just a friend. Remember, I told you I'm leaving town soon. I don't have time to make any *friends*, as you put it."

They re-stacked bags of feed and seed, looking for anything to do to stay busy and warm.

"Whatever happened to that girl you were friends with whose house was broken into? They find the guy?"

Jackson shook his head. "Not yet. No leads or clues at all. The guy knew what he was doing. He avoided the security camera and left no fingerprints."

"And she still doesn't know why he broke in or what he wanted?"

"Not that I know of. I haven't asked to tell the truth. I reckon she'd tell me if she wanted to."

Mac stopped and looked at Jackson. "Is somebody looking out for her? Making sure she's safe?"

"Well, I mean, Joe changed the locks on the house, and Helena said she'd spend more time at home so that Cindy isn't there alone." Though that wasn't happening as evidenced by his drop-in the night before.

"What's that look for?"

"Nothing. It's just… my sister said she'd be around more, but…"

"She's not."

"She's in love, and planning a wedding, and, well, I suppose she isn't really thinking about it. I mean, Cindy is an adult, and she's not the kind to want people looking out for her."

"Independent?"

"Yeah, you could say that. She's been on her own for a while, and I think she's pretty used to that."

"Anybody ever target this girl before?"

Jackson stopped and stood up straight. "I don't know. I don't think so. I mean, she was pretty shaken up. It didn't seem like she'd experienced anything like this before."

"When was the last time you saw her?"

"Last night. We went out to dinner."

Mac gave Jackson a long, hard look that made him uncomfortable. "You still gonna try to tell me that's not who you're waiting to hear from?"

"What difference does it make to you? You don't know me. You don't know her. Why do you care?" Jackson knew he was being unkind. Mac was just trying to be a friend, but the line of questioning and worry about Cindy were getting the best of him.

An unreadable expression crossed Mac's face before he shook his head and reached for another sack of feed. "You're right. It's nothing to me. Forget it."

Jackson tried to forget it, but Mac's words kept replaying in his head. Was Cindy in danger? Should he be checking on her more? Was Dale on top of the case? Was Helena leaving Cindy alone more than she should? Was somebody watching her?

The more he thought about it, the more worried he became. Maybe he wasn't planning on having a relationship with Cindy, but that didn't mean he wanted something to happen to her. He was itching for quitting time, but time moved like the hands on a broken clock.

When he finally felt his phone buzz, just before five, he couldn't get it out of his pocket quickly enough. He breathed a sigh of relief when he read the one-word answer.

"Sure."

Thank Heaven. If nothing else, at least she was okay, and he'd be able to see that she stayed that way for a few hours that evening.

***

"That was the funniest movie I've seen in a long time," Cindy said as she stood in the lobby and slid her arm into the sleeve of her coat. Gentleman that he was, Jackson took hold of the back of the coat and held it as she eased her other arm in. She liked that about him.

"Thanks," she said with a smile.

"You're welcome. Up for something to eat? I'm hungry."

"Jackson," she said with a laugh and a shake of her head. "We ate an entire large pizza, then we had a huge tub of popcorn, and you had a big box of candy with the popcorn." She stood back and gave him a once-over. "Where are you putting it all?"

"I'm a growing boy." He pulled on his jacket and started toward the door, but he stopped suddenly and looked around. Watching him, the hairs on the back of Cindy's neck stood, and she wondered if it was a reaction to his expression or to something else.

"What's wrong?"

There was a play of emotions on his face before he shook his head and smiled at her. "Nothing. Just a weird feeling I had for a moment."

A shiver made its way down her spine. "Like a somebody's-watching-you kind of feeling?"

He looked at her intently. "Yeah. That kind of feeling."

"I just had the same feeling."

They both stood and ran their gazes around the lobby.

"I don't see anyone," she said tentatively, but her heart was quickening.

"I don't either." He took her hand and began walking toward the door. "Let's get out of here. How about a McDonald's sundae?"

"Jackson, you're going to make me fat." She laughed, but it sounded forced even to her.

As they exited the theater, she looked back once more. Across the room stood a man with a dark, short, clean beard and a heavy denim coat. Their eyes met, and he held her gaze for a moment before turning away. She'd seen him before, but she didn't know where or when. She hurried to keep up with Jackson as he pulled her through the glass door. She told herself that it was her imagination and that the familiar-looking man hadn't been watching them leave.

***

"So, your interview is Monday, right? Are you ready?" Cindy stole another French fry while Jackson chewed his Big Mac.

He nodded and swallowed, then took a swig of his Coke before answering. "Yep. I fly out Sunday at noon. Wade hooked me up with a hotel room. It's some kind of business hotel, so he said it's going to be small and sparse, but it was cheap. Well, he said it was cheap. I'd hate to see expensive."

"It's New York."

"I guess so. Anyway, he used his membership to get me the room. I didn't know that was a thing— membership at a hotel."

"Me neither." She took another fry, and he smiled.

"I thought you weren't hungry.

"I thought we were just getting ice cream."

As she ate the French fry, he caught himself staring at her lips. He blinked and looked away, feeling color rise to his cheeks. If she noticed, she kept quiet about it.

"You'll be back by Christmas?" It was a question rather than a statement, and he wondered if it mattered to her whether he was there.

"I will. And you're coming over for Christmas Eve and Christmas Day?"

"Yep. I'm looking forward to it."

"Hey, have you heard from Dale about the break-in?"

She nodded. "He says there's nothing to go on. He thinks it was someone looking for prescription drugs. He thinks the guy probably hit Helena's room, too, but we couldn't tell because it was such a mess." She looked momentarily embarrassed, but then she smiled. "I guess that's not surprising to you. She is your sister."

"She is at that. And she's always been like that. Andi, on the other hand, was always as neat as a pin. I bet you could eat off her bathroom floor."

Cindy wrinkled her nose. "Uh, no thanks. I don't care how clean she is."

"That's the sixth fry you've stolen from me."

"I didn't know you were counting." She held her chin up and reached for one more, but Jackson grabbed her hand.

He leaned close to her face. "And just how many do you think I'm going to let you have?"

She leaned even closer. "As many as I want," she said with a twinkle in her eye and a smile on her lips.

"Oh yeah?" He inched closer.

"Yeah," she said, her voice low and husky.

Jackson leaned closer, so close he could hear her light intake of breath and feel the slow release of air from her soft, pink... He sat back abruptly as though a snake had bitten him.

"You can have them." He pushed the rest of the fries toward her and stood. "I'll be right back."

He hurried to the men's room, used the urinal, and washed his hands.

"Stupid. Stupid, stupid, stupid," he said aloud in the empty room. He looked at himself in the mirror. "What the heck are you thinking? She's off limits. You're leaving. She's just getting her life in order. She's friends with your sisters. Get a grip."

He took several calming breaths before returning to their booth.

"Sorry. I had to use the bathroom."

She looked as lost and sad as a homeless kitten in a dark alley. It made his heart ache, and he wanted to reach out and pull her to him, stroke her hair, smell her strawberry shampoo, breathe in the very essence of her, and then claim her mouth with his own.

He forced himself to look away and noticed she had cleaned up the table.

"Ready to go?" He asked.

"Sure," was all she said.

He wanted to take her hand like he'd done when they left the theater. Instead, he walked her to the passenger side of the car and saw her in. Before closing the door, he said, "I had fun tonight, Cindy. Thanks for coming with me."

Cindy's smile didn't reach her cheeks when she softly said, "Thanks. Me, too."

****

"Come on, Cindy. It could be fun. I'm so tired of living in that tiny apartment," Sarah begged.

Sarah and Cindy sat on Melanie's bed and faced Melanie who sat cross-legged on the floor.

"I don't know. I mean, I just moved in with Helena. How fair would it be for me to tell her I'm moving out?"

"She won't care," Melanie said. "We can't move into the house on Sycamore until the first of May, and she and Joe are getting married in June. She's going to be moving in with him. This house isn't going to be available for long, and it's perfect with three bedrooms. Someone else is going to move in and snatch it right up now that the owners have let it be known they're moving out in April. We have to make a decision this weekend, and we can't do it without you. Besides, we really like you and want you to stay in town."

Cindy's heart flipped at the statement, mostly because she knew Melanie meant it. She had really hit it off with them and with Trudy, and they all were spending a ridiculous amount of time texting during the day and hanging out at night.

"Unless you have somewhere better to live," Sarah said. "You did ditch us last night, and I've got it by good authority that you ditched us for Jackson Nelson."

"Oh, come on. I didn't ditch you."

"Did we agree on a girls night in?" Mel asked.

"Kind of." Cindy dragged out the words.

"There was no kind of," Sarah told her. "But we'll forgive you if you say yes to moving in with us. And Jackson can come over anytime."

"Sarah, shouldn't you be at work?"

She gave Cindy a look of mock annoyance. "I'm going, I'm going." She grabbed her coat and purse. "But this isn't over. Mel, work on her."

Melanie promised to keep at it, and she continued to bring up the subject the entire time they cleaned out her closet.

Around noon, Mel's mother stuck her head through the doorway. "This place looks worse than it did when you started."

"Don't worry," Cindy told her. "The results will be fabulous."

"Would you girls like some lunch?"

"Sounds good, Mama. Thanks. We'll be down in a minute." Melanie turned to Cindy. "See? She drives me crazy. I have to get out of this house. All my friends are on their own, but I'm still living at home. I'll finish college in May, Dr. Joe is going to hire me full-time, and I'll have enough money to pay my third of the rent. Sarah makes enough money for her third. We just need one more third." She widened her eyes and raised her eyebrows several times like Groucho Marx.

Cindy laughed. "I'll think about it, okay? No promises."

"But we need to know that we can afford it. We can't do it with just the two of us."

"Look, Mel, here's the deal. Right now, this little business thing of mine looks pretty good. I've got a few jobs, and I'm making a little money. But what happens when I've done all I can do here? I can't just keep redoing the same places over and over."

"That's why Paige is working on that website, remember? You're going to have jobs from here to the Missouri line."

"I'd love to believe that, but I can't go making any big financial decisions until I know for sure."

She promised herself that she would never do the four things her mother had done to her:

One – make promises she couldn't, or wouldn't, keep.

Two – get herself so deep in debt, she could never get out of it.

Three – Be a burden to other people.

Four – Let substances become more important than people.

"Will you keep thinking about it?" Mel asked.

"I'll think about it, but look, I left behind a bad situation. My mother was so far in debt, I had to sell everything she owned and give up our house just to pay off what I could. I used my entire savings, what little it was, to pay the rest. I will never let that happen to me. I've got to be in a better place before I sign a lease. Helena is letting me stay there for the cost of housekeeping, and believe me, she keeps me busy."

"I can imagine. Dr. Joe is so neat and tidy and incredibly organized. I hope they both know what they're in for."

"Helena's trying really hard to form new habits. She's getting there. He might just need to be patient with her at times. And I need you to do the same with me."

"Okay. I understand. I'll back off, and I'll tell Sarah the same. If the house is still available once you know where you stand, then we can talk about it. In the meantime, let's go get lunch before my mother starts hollerin' for us. And then you can tell me all about your *two* dates with Jackson."

***

It was dark by the time they finished the closet and Cindy said her goodbyes. She hummed a tune as she walked to her car, which was parked around the side of Melanie's family home where the driveway was. A few feet from the car, she stopped. Even though it was dark, she could make out the outline of the open trunk.

As she drew nearer, she saw the blankets piled onto the street. Papers blew by her, fluttering in the cold, night wind. Her heart lurched, and she thought she might be sick.

This was not the work of someone looking for prescription drugs, and it was not a random break-in. Someone was searching for something. Something they thought she had.

She ran to the car and looked inside. Sure enough, the tire had been lifted from its hold. Instinctively, she ran her hand on the outside of her jeans and felt the key in her front pocket. She quickly took her hand away in case she was being watched. She looked around, peering into the darkness.

Had she been watched that night? Had someone seen her checking the trunk and removing the key from beneath the tire? If so, they saw her put it back but didn't see her remove it again a few days later. Who was watching her?

She tried to hold her hands steady as she began dialing 911. Just before she hit the call button, she stopped, quickly backspaced to delete the numbers, and looked around. What were the police going to do? What could they do? And when would Helena decide that having Cindy around was too dangerous?

Quickly, she replaced the tire and threw the blankets and what few papers hadn't blown away back into the trunk. She slammed the lid shut and again looked around. The street was deserted, and the smell of burning wood emanating from the chimneys hung heavy in the air. Inside the houses, she could see dim lights, dancing fireplace flames, and flickering televisions, but she didn't see anybody looking out their windows or opening their doors. Nobody was walking a dog or taking a run, things that would have been normal back in California even at this time of night. Of course, it would have been warm there.

As if the thought reminded her that she was *not* in warm, sunny California, a violent shudder raced down her back, and her hands suddenly felt like ice. For the first time since coming outside, she noticed the patterns of her breath floating in front of her face. She breathed hot air into her cupped hands before hurrying to the driver's side of the car. She unlocked the door and got inside as quickly as possible, slamming the door shut with such intensity, she again looked at the nearby houses to be sure she hadn't disturbed anyone.

She locked the doors and started the car. She drove slowly back to Helena's, keenly aware of every turn, every light, and the black cat that raced across the road in front of her.

Why are they always black cats?

Cindy locked the car once she got out in front of the house and walked at a brisk pace to the front door. Helena's car was in the driveway, but the door was locked. Her hand shook as she turned the key and pushed open the door.

"Hey, there!" Helena said from the couch. "Long time, no see."

Cindy forced a laugh. "Yeah, I guess we've both been running in different directions. She recognized the Heath Ledger movie that was playing in the fire-lit room and wondered if watching a movie with Helena would help clear thoughts of break-ins and stalkers from her head.

"Sarah said you were at Melanie's."

Drawn from her thoughts, Cindy blinked and looked from the TV to Helena. "I was. We were cleaning out her closet." *Did Sarah tell Helena they want me to move in with them?*

"How were things at the library?" she asked casually, taking off her coat and hanging it on the coat rack in the space between the door and the living room.

"Busy. Lots of school assignments being handed out now that break has begun, and winter is a busy reading season."

Helena was sitting on one end of the couch, so Cindy took a seat on the opposite side, curling her legs under her. "Where's Joe?"

"He's home. He had some things he wanted to take care of, and I needed a night to myself."

"Oh! I'm sorry." Cindy began to stand.

"No, no, not like that. You're fine. I'm just tired of talking about wedding stuff and moving plans and all that. I love Joe to pieces, and I can't wait to marry him and move into his place, but I'm really going to miss this old house. I worked really hard to make it my own."

Cindy looked around. The little, two-bedroom house was nicely decorated with framed artwork of famous places—Rome, Athens, Paris. Helena had visited several European cities the previous summer. The furniture was nice but not expensive, comfortable and tasteful in solid colors with pretty, flowered pillows and soft blankets thrown around in a disorganized yet organized fashion. The gas fireplace gave off little heat but made the room feel cozy. The old, scratched table in the kitchen and farm style chairs added a layer of familiarity to the house, as if many generations had sat down in the room, talking and playing games and sharing meals. It was a life Cindy had only read about or seen on TV or in movies. "You did a really nice job. It's inviting and comfortable and shows your personality."

Helena smiled at Cindy. "Coming from you, that's high praise."

"Oh, no, not at all. I can organize, but I'm just learning about decorating."

"I don't know about that. From what I've seen, you're great at organizing but also have a really good eye for detail and design and aesthetics."

"Really?" Cindy was surprised Helena felt that way. She didn't feel like she'd done much with her few little jobs around town.

"Really. Everyone is still raving about the window displays, and they've been up for weeks. You know the theater was amazing, and Sarah showed me your website. It's very nice."

"Oh, that wasn't me. Paige did all of it. She's the one who's really good at design. And hey, I want to start paying rent. I can—"

"Don't be silly. I'm hardly here. It's more your house than mine these days."

"Precisely why I should be paying you something."

"Okay, but not a set amount. You can do what you can when you can, but seriously, you ought to look into taking some classes on interior design. The organizing stuff is a great little side job, but I'm not sure how many jobs you could realistically get, probably not enough to keep you fed with a roof over your head. Decorating, though, there's real money in that, and Northwest Arkansas is becoming more popular. You could do well."

Cindy thought about that. She didn't have the money to take classes, and she had no idea where she was going to live, but it was certainly something to think about. And she'd much rather think about that than about someone trying to find whatever they thought she had, especially since she had absolutely no idea what that something could be.

Eleven

There was a soft, white blanket of snow on the
ground and a chill in the air as Jackson walked across the
church parking lot on Sunday morning. He blessed
himself with holy water upon entering the church, made
his way up the aisle, and entered the pew to sit beside his
parents. Before kneeling to pray, he leaned forward to
give a small wave and smile to Andi and Wade who sat
on the other side of Grace and Joshua. When he'd said
to God all he could think of, he sat back in time to see
Joe entering the pew behind them. Just before Mass
began, Helena and, to his surprise, Cindy hurried into
the pew with Joe.

It took everything in him not to turn around, not to
move from his seat and sit beside her. No matter what
he did, the more he tried not to think about her, the
more she crept into his mind. His phone held a boarding
pass for a plane to New York, but his heart held her

smile, her laugh, and the memory of her hand in his when they walked from the movie theater to his truck. Unfortunately, he also remembered the look on her face when he abruptly left the table and returned to tell her it was time to leave.

Was it his imagination that each time they stood and then sat back down, he could smell that sweet, strawberry shampoo she used? It was wreaking havoc on his brain and causing him to lose focus.

God forgive me, I'm trying to hear your word!

He feared that the entire homily would be lost to thoughts of the woman sitting behind him, but when Father Michael began speaking, Jackson found himself hanging on every word.

"Today is the last Sunday of Advent," Father Michael began. "In the Gospel, we heard the account of Joseph taking Mary into his home. Joseph was, we believe, older, perhaps a widower, a man of the world, so to speak. Mary, on the other hand, was a young girl, just a teenager, with little to no knowledge of the world. Imagine, if you will, being in her shoes, your worry, your fears, your uncertainty. Yet Mary put her complete trust in the Lord. She knew he would provide for her.

"Nowhere in Matthew's Gospel does it tell us that Mary was worried that Joseph would abandon her. It never says that she begged him not to divorce her. We only read that Joseph, 'a righteous man,' unwilling to expose her to shame, was going to quietly divorce her. Does this mean that Mary had more faith in God than

Joseph did?" Father Michael paused and looked around the church before shaking his head.

"On the contrary, Joseph was a righteous man. He was only trying to do what was right by the law. Once the angel assured him that this was part of God's plan, Joseph took Mary into his home. He understood that he had a part to play in God's plan.

"My brothers and sisters, we all have a part to play in God's plan. We all have something we are meant to do in our lives to help others, to protect them from shame and uphold their dignity, or to provide shelter, a home, to those in need. We all have angels visit us with messages, telling us what God wants us to do with our lives. Who is your messenger? Are you listening to the message? Are you ready to be like Joseph, to awake and do as the angel of the Lord commands?"

Like so many times in his life, Jackson felt as if the priest was speaking directly to him. The problem was, who was Jackson's messenger, and exactly what was the message he was supposed to be hearing? Would he even know it when he heard it?

***

Cindy stood politely to the side while everyone told Jackson goodbye, a small knot in her stomach growing larger by the minute. As she watched the hugs and kisses shared by the family, she thought about what the priest had said.

This was only the second time in her life she had been to church. She'd attended a wedding inside a church once, but the ceremony had taken only twenty minutes, and there had been nothing like the prayers and songs and rituals she'd heard and seen today. This was a strange world to her—Arkansas, the South, the church, the Mass, especially the community and family aspects of it all.

She thought about Joseph being a righteous man. What did that even mean? It certainly didn't refer to men who robbed banks or left their families or went to jail.

She looked at Jackson and thought, *now, there is a righteous man.* She wasn't sure where the thought came from or how she could be so certain, but she knew it to the core of her being. Jackson was someone who cared for others, who tried to protect them, who took them into his home. Wasn't all of that what he had shown her, what he had done, the night of the break-in?

With those thoughts in mind, Cindy realized that this might be one of the last times she would ever see Jackson. Though he only planned to be gone for a couple days, and they would be together at Christmas, the next few days in New York could change his life forever. What if they offered him the job on the spot? Would he accept it and come home just long enough to celebrate Christmas and get his things? Would he forget that they ever met? They'd had such a brief amount of time to get to know each other, yet she felt as though she had known him forever, that he might be one of the few righteous men she'd ever known.

A movement from the other side of the churchyard caught her attention, and she turned just as a man slipped away behind the crowd of churchgoers. There was something about him… She craned her neck, but she could only see the back of his head as he hurried down the road and around the corner. What was it about him that seemed so familiar? Could he be the same man from the theater?

"Cindy?" Startled, she sucked in a quick breath and turned to see Jackson smiling at her. The rest of the family was already gone. "I told Helena I'd make sure you got home. I hope that's okay."

She smiled at Jackson, pushing thoughts of the man as far from her mind as possible. "That's more than okay."

Jackson took her gloved hand, and even through the thick cotton, she could feel his warmth melting away any uncertainty.

"I don't have long, but I wanted to say goodbye without my whole family standing there." Color appeared in his cheeks, and he bashfully looked away. He led her to his truck, and she stayed silent, not trusting herself to speak. She couldn't beg him to stay. That wasn't fair. And it wasn't like she wouldn't see him in a few days.

Jackson opened the door to the truck and chivalrously helped her inside as he had each time he'd driven her somewhere. She watched him run around to the other door and hop in behind the wheel. She shifted her eyes to his hand as he turned the key then reached over to turn up the heat. A hard, cold blast of air shot out at her and she jumped.

"It won't take long to heat up," he assured her, and she smiled. "I thought we could take a short drive." He glanced at her but looked away quickly, and she realized he was nervous. Well, that made two of them.

"You won't be late, will you? I don't want you to miss your flight." She suddenly realized that was a lie and kept her gaze locked on the windshield. If he missed his flight, would that change everything? She felt a stab of guilt at the thought. She would never wish for something that could jeopardize his future.

"We'll make sure it's a short drive." He put the car into gear, and she finally felt warm air on her face and on her legs through her tights. She'd worn a dress to church, one she'd found on one of her trips to Walmart. It wasn't fancy, but she thought the hunter green color looked nice on her, and it made her feel good to buy it with the money she'd made with her own business.

They drove only a few miles before Jackson turned off the road. He went a little further down the country lane until it ended in a clearing. Ahead, Cindy saw a frozen body of water and the outline of a mountain. It was covered in white as were all the trees that were scattered around the water, reflecting hundreds of colored beams of light from the icicles that clung to their branches. Cindy gasped.

"It's beautiful," she whispered.

"Very beautiful," Jackson whispered back, and when she turned toward him, his eyes were on her, not the wintery masterpiece outside the truck.

"Jackson…"

"Cindy…"

Their words bumped together in the air between them, and they both gave a small laugh.

"You go," Jackson said, inclining his head toward her with a brief nod.

"No, no. You go." She wasn't really sure what had been on the tip of her tongue.

He reached for her hand and rubbed the back of it lightly with his thumbs, staring intently at the black cotton. When he raised his eyes to hers, they held a question, but she couldn't tell what it was. There was a small tug at her stomach.

"I'll only be gone a few days."

She nodded, and he looked back down at her hands.

"Cindy, I'd like to see you again when I get back." He looked up at her through his long lashes without raising his head, and the look reminded her of a small puppy begging for attention. "Aside from Christmas, I mean. If you're planning on still being here after that." He looked back down as though he didn't want to know the answer.

"I'm not going anywhere, Jackson. Not anytime soon."

When he looked back up, there was no mistaking the joy on his face. "Really? You're going to stay?"

She thought about the person who had broken into the house and then her car. Was she making the wrong decision? Should she run, try to get away from whomever it was? Probably. She'd never forgive herself if her presence was putting Helena or anybody else in danger. But...

"I like it here. I'm happy here. I think I could get used to living in a small town and having my own little business. I'm not making much, but Helena thinks I should take some classes and expand my repertoire of skills. I'm thinking about it. I have friends, and your family has been so kind and welcoming, and, well...for the first time, I feel like I'm home."

If he hadn't been looking at her with such joy and anticipation, she would have missed it, the flash of disappointment, but she saw it even if only for a moment. What did that mean? She thought he'd be happy that she was staying, that she felt good here, at home. He recovered in an instant and smiled, though the smile wasn't as genuine as it had been before.

"Good. I'm glad. I want you to be happy and feel at home. You deserve that."

Why does that sound so empty? Like he's talking to a colleague or someone he just encountered on the street?

Jackson let go of her hand and looked back toward the windshield. "The snow doesn't stick around very long here, but it's pretty while it lasts. We might get more later today, so it should look nice for a few days." He looked at the clock on the dashboard. "I reckon I need to head to the airport." He put the truck in reverse and began backing out.

Cindy turned toward the window, fighting back the threatening tears. She was so confused. She didn't know what to think about what just happened.

They rode in silence back to Helena's house. When he pulled up, he put the truck into park and turned toward her, a friendly smile on his face, but not the smile he'd worn earlier.

"Well, I'll see you in a few days."

"Sure," she said. "Good luck with your interview. I hope you get everything you ever dreamed of."

She saw his smile falter before she turned and reached for the handle. She jumped out and turned back. "Have a safe trip, Jackson. Be careful up there." She closed the door and ran to the house, making it inside just as the tears began to fall.

***

The five-and-a-half-hour flight had been awful. Jackson was sandwiched between a snoring man on his right and a talkative, elderly woman on his left. At one point, he pulled out his phone and attempted to put his earbuds in his ears, but the woman extracted her phone from her pocket and began telling him all about her granddaughter's recent wedding. He hoped the girl hadn't paid thousands of dollars for a photographer, because her grandmother had managed to capture every possible shot, and though he hated to give the woman the credit, her iPhone pictures were actually pretty good.

Jackson heard all the stories about the rehearsal dinner, the groomsman who got so drunk he fell into the swimming pool at the fancy hotel they were staying at, and the missing earring that almost sent her granddaughter into hysterics just hours before the wedding. They were halfway through the reception pictures when the plane began its descent.

From the moment Jackson's feet hit the ground at LaGuardia, he felt unbalanced. He went with the flow of traffic through the airport to baggage claim though he only had a carry-on bag and his laptop case. He followed the signs to the taxi stand and gave the attendant the address of his hotel.

Once settled into the taxi, Jackson looked out his window. He watched as they passed gas stations and brick supermarkets and parks, and he wondered why everything looked so much different than he expected. This didn't look like the big city. It wasn't all that different from Harrison or Fayetteville.

After a while, the area took on a more distinct urban appearance with rows and rows of businesses in brick buildings, telephone and electric wires crisscrossing from every building and street corner, and cars—lots and lots of cars. It was well past dark, but lights were everywhere, and it felt surreal to not be able to see the sky, not to mention any mountains or wide-mouthed rivers.

They crossed a bridge and drove by nicer, newer buildings surrounded by quite a lot of green space. The next bridge they crossed, by way of an underpass with roads in every direction, took them onto a freeway of sorts, lined on one side by a body of water—a sign identified it as the Harlem River—and on the other by buildings that grew taller with every block. They continued the drive along the river, going in and out of tunnels and over and under other stretches of road. Looming ahead were the skyscrapers he had expected, lit up like giant Christmas trees reaching into the sky.

There were a lot more trees and more grass than Jackson thought there would be, but the cars, trucks, busses, and even bicycles—despite the dark and the frigid temperature he could read on the dashboard—far outnumbered the plants and trees. When they exited into the downtown, Jackson pressed his face against the glass, bending his neck to look up at the buildings that extended into the clouds. He lifted his hand and pointed to an extremely tall skyscraper with a tower on the top.

"Is that…?"

"The Freedom Tower," the driver replied in a heavy Middle Eastern accent. "One World Trade Center. Have you been?"

"No. First time in New York actually."

The man nodded. "You should go. To the top of the tower and to the museum. You can walk there from your hotel."

Jackson just nodded. He was overwhelmed by the thought of visiting either one. Though the attacks on the twin towers took place long before Andi went to the academy, long before he was even old enough to know about and understand them, he was part of the 9/11 generation, one of many children raised under the cloud of clearing smoke, the pile of metal debris, and the sound of Taps being played every September 11th on the courthouse steps.

"Here we are." The man came to a stop in front of the unassuming hotel. "Cash or charge?"

"Charge?"

"Yes, card or phone."

Jackson had no idea he could charge a New York taxi ride, but he had cash. "How much?"

"$37.50."

Jackson shook his head to clear his ears. "How much?"

The man repeated the amount, and Jackson decided to use his credit card. Then he remembered what Wade had told him about being very careful when using his card in the city.

"Um, I'll use Apple Pay."

The man handed Jackson a card reader and he paid the bill, rounding up for a tip. He thanked the driver and stepped out onto the street. It was his first night in the Big Apple, and he was tempted to walk around, but honestly, being in the city alone scared him, even at his age. He'd been to Little Rock plenty of times as well as St. Louis several times, but this was nothing like either of those. He felt completely out of his element, and he hadn't even been outside the cab for two full minutes.

He walked into the hotel and checked in. It was smooth and easy, and he soon found himself in his hotel room. The room was sparse, containing only a full-sized bed, a cushioned chair, small desk, and bathroom. It had a tiny alcove with a rod and hangers and two wall sconces above the bed with lights for reading. Wade warned him that it would not be fancy and that the hotel catered to no-nonsense business travelers. Jackson didn't mind. All he needed was a place to lay his head for a couple nights.

He pulled open the curtain and gasped. From the twenty-ninth floor, he could clearly see what he assumed was the New York Harbor. Three tall buildings, sparkling from top to bottom with yellow lights, loomed in front of him, with the harbor on the other side. Lights from across the harbor—*would that be New Jersey?*—cast a glow on the water.

As he looked out the window, he felt as well as heard the rumbling in his stomach. He let go of the curtain, grabbed his wallet and key card, and went in search of the rooftop restaurant the front desk attendant had mentioned. He was given a seat by the window and turned to look out after ordering a beer. If he thought the view from his room was something, he was amazed by the view from the restaurant. Below him, he caught a glimpse of one of the unmistakable large, square fountains that was in the place of, and now memorialized, one of the fallen towers. He'd seen the photos, and now he was looking down at the ground where one of the towers once stood. Several people walked along the gleaming gold sides of the fountains, and the area was well lit yet still aesthetic and soothing.

Jackson leaned back in his chair and looked down at his arms. Though he wore long sleeves, he could feel the gooseflesh rising along his skin. No matter how it turned out, his trip was going to be an unforgettable experience.

***

"Do you think it's too blue?" Trudy asked, holding a paint brush in her hand. A streak of blue ran down the white wall on the right side of her spare bedroom, and Cindy smelled the overwhelming scent of paint even though the sample jar was quite small.

Cindy, sitting on the floor cross-legged with a Coke in one hand and a decorating magazine in the other, scrunched her nose. "Well, it's blue, but what do you mean by too blue? What effect are you trying to achieve?"

Trudy tilted her head and stared at the wall. "Effect? I didn't know I was trying to achieve any kind of effect. I just want it to look pretty." The word pretty came out as 'purty' in Trudy's thick accent.

"Do you want it to be calm and soothing like a gently rocking wave or sobering like a dark night sky or eye-opening like the neon sign over the bar at Rick's?"

"Huh. I guess I never thought of it that way." She turned to face Cindy. "I guess different shades would give off different vibes."

"And they affect emotions and cause psychological effects and can even determine if one feels tired or anxious or hungry."

"Girl, I am always hungry!" Trudy said with a grin. "But seriously, what do you think? I don't want my guests sad or anxious. What does this blue say to you?"

"I would say it's a cobalt blue, which is really pretty, but it's going to make the room really bright, in a color-popping, eye-grabbing kind of way, which is fine if that's what you want."

Trudy stood back and looked at the wall, arms crossed, paint dripping onto the drop cloth she'd laid out. "I reckon I didn't think about that. If every wall is this color, that'll be awfully bright." She pursed her lips. "I just really like this color."

"If you really like it, what about using it as an accent color?"

"Like how?"

Cindy put down the magazine and stood. She set her Coke on the nearby dresser and took the paintbrush from Trudy. She laid the brush on a piece of newspaper next to the sample jar of paint.

"If you really want it to be a wall color, you could paint it on one wall, or even just part of a wall." She traced a space with her hands. "And put the bed there. It would act as a headboard of sorts. Or you could paint that white dresser and the base of the bed this color and buy sheets that have a pattern that will match it."

Trudy looked back and forth from the wall to the dresser. "If I decide I want a wall painted with this, what color do I do the other walls?"

"I'd do a matte white but use this blue and maybe other shades of blue or green in your accessories. You could even get a pretty rug to go by the bed with that color in it. Think pillows, bedspread, maybe a big comfy chair with a patterned slipcover. Another thing I've seen done is to paint half the wall blue." She went to the wall and placed her hand about a third of the way up. "Maybe up to here, and then paint the rest of the wall white. But I'd go with fewer patterned accessories because you don't want the room to be overwhelming."

"Wow. You are good. I mean, I knew you were, but, just, wow."

Cindy laughed. "I've been watching a lot of HGTV and buying too many magazines." Her phone buzzed, and she took it from the back pocket of her jeans and tapped on the screen. "Talk about wow."

Trudy leaned over. "Is that New York?"

"It is. Jackson says it's the Freedom Tower." Another text arrived. "Oh my gosh. Here's one of the 9/11 memorial fountains."

"Wow," Trudy gushed in a long, soft whisper. "Ask him how cold it is."

Cindy tapped on the keyboard, and Jackson quickly replied. "He says it's twenty-seven degrees."

"That's about what it is here."

"He says he's taking a walk along the memorials. It's right next to his hotel."

"That's kind of…scary. Don't you think?"

Cindy hadn't really thought about it, but now that Trudy had mentioned it, she felt a slight shiver. "I'm sure it's fine." She put her phone away and looked back at Trudy's wall. "So, what do you think about the paint?"

"I think you're changing the subject."

"I thought the paint was the subject."

"It was, but now the subject is Jackson."

"Nope. Off limits." Cindy picked up the paint sample and screwed the lid back on. "Do you want to get a can of this color, or what?"

"Don't you dare. I've asked twice about Jackson, and you've managed to avoid answering both times."

"Then that should tell you something." She crossed her arms and looked defiantly at Trudy.

"Come on. You know you want to talk about him."

The truth was, she did. She wanted to tell Trudy what happened and get her take on it, but she was afraid to. The last time she talked to friends about the man in her life, they ended up turning their backs on her. Besides, Jackson wasn't the 'man in her life.' He was just a friend. He'd made that perfectly clear.

"Cindy, you can't hold out forever. Why won't you tell me what's going on? I know he wasn't mean to you. I've known Jackson my whole life, and there's not a mean bone in his body."

"You're right," Cindy said with a sigh. "He's a really nice guy. Too nice for me, I think."

"What's that supposed to mean?"

Cindy shrugged. "I don't know. I think he's just being nice to make me feel welcome."

"Cindy, like I said, I've known Jackson since we were smaller than bullfrogs, and he's never looked at anyone the way he looks at you. I don't think he even had a serious girlfriend in college. I never saw him bring anyone 'round here."

Cindy sucked in a long breath, exhaled, and gave in, telling Trudy about their conversation in the truck that morning.

"Oh, sugar, I'm so sorry. I can't imagine what came over him. Did you ask him what was bothering him?"

"Of course not. I couldn't do that. If there was something he wanted to talk about or tell me, he could've done that."

"I think something's going on there, Cindy. I mean it. I know Jackson likes you just as sure as a possum likes sweet potatoes."

Cindy smirked. "And just how do you know that possums like sweet potatoes?"

"Why, sugar, everyone knows that."

Cindy shook her head and lifted the paint jar. "Let's get on with this. I'm getting hungry."

"Honey, forget about this for now. I'm so hungry, my belly thinks my throat's been cut."

Cindy didn't even try to keep a straight face. "Do you try to come up with these sayings just for my benefit?"

"Cindy, my dear, I'm fixin' to make a southern gal out of you yet. You just wait."

***

"Thank you, Sir. I appreciate your time." Jackson shook the man's hand and said goodbye before collecting his things and leaving the office. The interview went well, very well. The man was attentive, inquisitive, and approving. Jackson knew there were other candidates, but he felt good. As soon as he stepped off the elevator into the lobby of the building, he called Wade and relayed the details of the interview.

"Jackson, that's great. It sounds like you made a really good impression."

"I hope so," Jackson said, all the while wondering if he meant it. As good as it felt to know that he aced the interview, there was a nagging feeling in his gut he just couldn't shake. "I'm going to head out and take in some sights. Thanks for all your help."

"You're welcome. Stay warm."

"You, too."

Jackson hung up and walked outside into the bright day. The reflection of the sunlight combined with the steam coming from the buildings and the grates in the sidewalks, making the air seem warmer than it was. Rather than taking a taxi, Jackson walked away from Wall Street toward the harbor. He stopped after a few steps and flattened himself against a wall to plug in an address on his phone. A pungently sweet aroma wafted through the air, and Jackson recognized it from his college days. Though he'd never tried the stuff himself, he was well acquainted with the smell of burning marijuana. He hurried ahead and crossed the street amid a throng of people.

The navigation directions on his phone had him turning a corner, and he was hit with the stench of rotting garbage. He assumed it was trash pickup day because the sidewalk was crowded with piles of overflowing black bags. Trying to avoid one such pile, he bumped into a woman wearing a worn scarf with her hand out. He hesitated but reached into his pocket and handed her what little change he had.

He stopped to look at one of the store window displays and frowned. A giant LED screen filled the window, displaying an ad for clothing. Jackson looked up and down the street at the other windows. Most of them had similar screens with still or moving images. He recalled some of the movies he'd seen that took place in New York at Christmas and remembered how fancy the window displays were. He'd heard his grandmother talk about her one trip to New York and how even the windows were works of art. Visions of other store windows came into his mind—displays of gingerbread Santas and bow-wrapped boxes of vintage candies, the bakery window with pies, cakes, and cookies inside giant snow globes with snowflakes in all sizes hanging around them, and the library window with green and red houses constructed from books. Cindy's flare for decorating would be unappreciated in modern-day New York.

Jackson sighed and moved on. A gathering of pigeons hurried out of his way as he made his way through a tree-dotted park and followed the walkway to the water. The air was crisp, but the sun continued to warm him as he walked to the dock next to the ferry. He held his hand up to his forehead and chastised himself for not remembering his sunglasses as the bright sun reflected off the smooth, glassy water.

In the middle of the harbor stood the woman he'd known about since he was a toddler but had only seen in pictures. She towered above the little island and the many boats docked on the shore ferrying passengers from the mainland to the famed island that had once welcomed thousands of newcomers to the land of the free. She stood tall and proud, her tablet in one hand bearing the inscription, July IV MDCCLXXVI, and her torch raised high in the other hand. Jackson had already looked into going out to the island, but he had other things he wanted to do and see and decided that the view from Battery Park was as close as he would get on this trip. He marveled at the statue for a little longer, took a few pictures with his phone, and then headed back in the direction of his hotel.

The symbol of freedom, the woman beckoning to those who had nowhere else to go and were searching for a new home, a new life, and new start, prompted his thoughts to return to another woman who deserved a new home, a new life, and a new start. She was poor, yearning to be free, practically homeless, and in need of a guiding light. She was the kind of person his parents and his church taught him to never turn his back on, and he hadn't. So why did it feel like he had?

That nagging feeling in his gut returned. He had made the decision to let her go, to let her find her place and make her mark in the town that made him the man he was, while he was setting out to make his own mark in the city that never sleeps. He was at peace with his decision to say goodbye and go their separate ways. Wasn't he?

As Jackson turned at the same corner he had begun his day on, he came within sight of the Freedom Tower. He took a deep breath and followed the signs to the memorial museum on the other side of the tower. All thoughts of home, the interview, and even Cindy fled his mind as he handed the greeter his ticket and entered the building.

***

The house was quiet, and the cold outside outcompeted the gas fireplace inside, demanding that Cindy pull a sweatshirt over her long-sleeved shirt. She slept until nine that morning and had the house to herself. She was due at Mrs. Baker's at noon, so she finally had time to go through the letters that were constantly on her mind.

After spreading cream cheese on a blueberry bagel, Cindy took a seat at the kitchen table and wrapped her hands around a steaming mug of hot chocolate. On the table next to her was the box, already open, and several letters were scattered across the dark wood. She picked up the next one in the order she had arranged them based on the US Postal Service date stamps on the outside of the envelopes.

Dear Cindy,

I hope you and your mom are having a good life. Life inside these walls is terrible, but I guess I deserve it. I know you probably don't want to hear from me anymore, and I understand. I wouldn't want to know me either if I was you. But Cindy, you got to know that I'm not all that bad. Sure, I did some bad things, and I was a bad father, and I didn't take care of your mom like I should have, but I'm not a bad guy. You got to believe that. I thought that money would be good for us. It was supposed to make things better. I didn't know I'd feel the way I did about robbing and getting away with it, and we did get away with it for a while. Not that I'm bragging. Its just that it gave me a feeling like I've never had before, like I was good at something and was finally doing what I was meant to be doing. I know that don't sound good. I know I should be saying it was all bad, but it wasn't. I'm trying to figure out how I can find those same feelings for something good, but there aint no good in my life anymore.

Maybe I shouldn't be saying this to a kid, but I aint got anybody else. Your mom doesn't want me writing to her. She doesn't want me writing to you either, but I told her thats your call. So, if you want me to stop, then tell me. I'll keep writing for a while and hope that I hear from you.

Love,

Dad

Cindy didn't know what to think of the letter. Obviously, she'd never written him back. She didn't even know he was alive until a couple weeks ago. Would it have made a difference? Would she have written, begged her mother to let her see him, tried to have a relationship with him? She didn't think so. What teenaged girl wants to visit her father in prison or tell her friends that her father might have killed someone? As much as she wanted to be angry with her mother for hiding these, she understood. Wouldn't Cindy have done the same had she been in Gloria's shoes? It was better to grow up believing he wasn't her father, that she had no father at all.

She slid the letter back into the envelope, and question after question ran through her mind. Where was he now? What was he doing now that he was out of jail? Was it true that he'd found God, as the sheriff had put it? His letters made it sound like he wished he was a better father. Was that true? Was he looking for her? Did he want to make amends?

The biggest question of all was, did she even care?

***

Jackson had never been one of those people who thought that real men didn't cry, but he'd never been one to get all wishy washy with his emotions either. He usually kept his feelings inside, turning them over, weighing them, analyzing them, and deciding on his own what he should do or feel or say or how he should act or react. Jackson was usually pretty good at keeping his emotions in check.

That was not the case now.

Along with dozens of men and women, he quietly walked through the museum. Around him were people from all walks of life—some sporting tattoos, many with Veterans hats and jackets, some in wheelchairs or leaning on canes, some under the age of ten and others over the age of sixty. They were white, black, Latino, and Asian. Stopping in a darkened room, Jackson let the tears fall from his eyes as he listened to the recordings of phone calls from passengers on Flight 93 before it plummeted toward the ground in Shanksville, Pennsylvania.

After a full three hours spent wandering in and out of exhibits, reading plaques, listening to recordings and watching videos, and looking at the pieces of rubble, broken stairwells, and many tributes in art, sculpture, and writing, Jackson felt drained. He exited the building and headed straight into the subway inside an adjacent shopping mall called the Oculus. The strange design of the building made him feel like Jonah in the belly of the whale, its stark white flukes flapping out of the ground on the outside and its rib bones encasing the stores on the inside. After studying the map, he bought a ticket and boarded a train going uptown.

When the doors opened, he followed the crowd up and out into the flashing lights of Times Square. He stood for a moment, blinking and feeling dizzy amidst the neon lights, giant screens, honking horns, and throngs of tourists. Though it was in the middle of the week, in the middle of the winter, it was easy to see why the square was the pumping, throbbing, beating heart of Manhattan. Jackson saw stores, theaters, superheroes in costume, Minnie and Mickey, yellow cabs, emergency vehicles, and people—many, many people. His focus on the surroundings turned inward when he felt his stomach rumbling, reminding him that he hadn't eaten since breakfast at the hotel. He fished in his pocket for a few dollars and bought a hot dog from a street vendor.

He still smelled garbage and the occasional joint, but here, those scents were mingled with exhaust, hot dogs and gyros, cigarette smoke, and an unrecognizable aroma that he was beginning to think of as the city itself. He looked up at the skyscrapers and down to the dirty sidewalk. His gaze wandered along the streets where all he saw was metal, cement, asphalt, and glass as far as his eyes could take him. Overwhelmed, he closed his eyes and inhaled deeply, coughing on the exhaust of a passing car. Was this what he really wanted? To live the rest of his life closed in by glass walls on every side, staring out at concrete and steel, counting the days until someone or something took him from this earth?

He walked briskly away from the giant flashing ads, away from the mostly naked man holding a guitar, away from the blaring horns and the marquee signs and the people talking out loud into unseen microphones with white Air Pods dangling from their ears. When he was away from the chaos, he remembered a piece of advice Wade gave him and slid into a doorway to bring up the GPS on his phone. He got the desired directions, pocketed the phone, and zippered his coat pocket, feeling uneasy and exposed in this strange place. He headed west, stopping to check his phone's navigation every few minutes, trying to avoid bumping into other people or being pushed into the busy streets. His feet were just beginning to hurt when he looked up and found himself in front of Rockefeller Center. He walked around the famed office building, stopping just long enough to take in the gigantic Christmas tree, and continued to 5th Avenue where he turned toward the spires, hurrying to reach his destination.

He bolted up the steps as he prayed, literally, that the building would be unlocked and breathed a sigh of relief when he was able to push open the large wooden door. Despite the enormity of Saint Patrick's sanctuary, the towering beams and exalted arches, the height of the ceiling and depth of the aisle leading to the altar, Jackson felt at ease, and for the first time since leaving Buffalo Springs, at home. He no longer heard the sound of traffic. He smelled candles and incense and old wood. All was silent, and he felt the reverence settle upon him.

A Christmas tree stood just inside the cathedral, wreaths hung from every column, and poinsettias surrounded him, bunched together in front of each side altar and the main altar. A nearly life-sized manger scene filled the space to the left of the main altar.

Jackson slid into a pew and pulled out a kneeler. Closing his eyes, he bent his head and prayed.

Dear Lord, help me. Guide me. Show me the path I'm meant to take. Show me what you have in store for me. Is this where I belong? Is this where I can do your work and mine? Please, help me find my way.

He said the same words over and over until his breathing calmed and his heart stopped racing. He looked up, but he could barely see. For the second time that day, tears filled his eyes and streamed down his face.

On his way out, he spotted a full-sized replica of Michelangelo's Pieta, the statue of Mary holding the crucified Jesus in her arms. His thoughts went straight to his own mother, his beacon of light and wisdom, and he longed for home.

Twelve

"I love it, and don't think I say that very often, because I don't," the older woman said in her matter-of-fact voice.

Cindy stood next to Mrs. Baker in the former mayor's new hobby room. Just as Cindy had envisioned and described it, the room was awash with natural lighting, and recessed lights provided bright illumination over the puzzle table. Paints and supplies were set up and ready to be used, and a blank canvas sat on the easel. A new puzzle was open and laid out on the table, and the closet was perfectly organized to suit Mrs. Baker's needs.

"I'm so glad," Cindy told her. "It really did turn out nice. The guy Stan recommended did a fabulous job with the lighting, and the rug we ordered is my favorite part. The colors are just perfect in here."

"You have a good eye, Ms. Kline."

"You're not the first person to tell me that lately."

"And I won't be the last." Mrs. Baker turned to her. "I hope a check is all right. I don't believe in paying for business transactions in cash, and I don't know how to use all those fancy phone payment things."

"I expected no less, about paying by check, I mean. I just finished setting up my new account at the town bank. My old bank doesn't have a branch nearby."

Mrs. Baker used the table to fill out the check she had pulled from her pocket, and Cindy took it, putting it in her pocket without looking at it.

"You aren't going to check it?" Mrs. Baker asked in a disapproving voice with one eyebrow raised.

Cindy blushed. "I didn't want to be rude."

"Cindy, the first thing you need to learn about running your own business is, trust nobody. Always make sure you are being paid the right amount and that the check is properly filled out and legitimate."

"You're right. I'm sorry." She removed the check and looked at the amount. She felt her eyes bulging as she looked up at the older woman. "Th— this isn't right. It's way more than I quoted you."

"Yes, I've included a small amount as a retainer. The next time I need something done, I expect you to make time for me in your schedule."

"But, it's still too much, and I don't need you to pay me a retainer. I'm always happy to—"

"Cindy, rule number two: the customer is always right and should not be argued with."

Cindy's jaw hung open. "I don't know what to say. You gave me a chance. You fed me. You gave me advice. I should be paying you."

"And that's no way to do business. Now, the proper thing to say is, thank you."

Cindy closed her mouth and swallowed. "Yes, thank you. Thank you so much."

"You're welcome. Now, go deposit that this instant. Never leave checks lying around. Put them in the bank as soon as you receive them."

"I will, Mrs. Baker. Thank you." Cindy hesitated for just a moment before throwing her arms around Imogene. "Thank you so very much."

Mrs. Baker patted her back, and in the kindest voice Cindy had ever heard her use said, "You are very welcome, my dear. Please, come back and see me soon. We can work on a puzzle together."

"I'd like that very much." Cindy blinked back tears as she said goodbye and hurried outside.

She did just what she'd been told and deposited her check as soon as she left the house. She didn't use the newly installed app on her phone or the drive-up window. She parked her car and marched right into the bank feeling like J.D. Rockefeller with her check in hand.

It was when she was leaving the bank that she had the oddest sensation. A shiver ran down her back, and she pulled her coat on tighter to ward off the chill. But the shiver wasn't caused by the nip in the air.

Cindy looked this way and that, up and down Main Street, before she hurried to her car. Once again, she had that uncanny feeling that she was being watched.

***

It was early afternoon when Jackson's plane touched down at the Northwest Arkansas Airport in Fayetteville. He hadn't slept well the night before and rubbed his eyes as he made his way through the small terminal. He shivered when he walked outside. It was cloudy and colder than it had been in New York, but he was happy to be home.

He turned on the radio as he made the almost two-hour trip back to Buffalo Springs, a route he was familiar with after five years of college in Fayetteville. The country western melodies filled the truck, but Jackson couldn't have named which songs played. His mind was as tangled as the briar patches that grew around the blackberry bushes off the old county road.

As he pulled into town, Jackson found himself unsure of where to go. He was hungry but not ready to sit down with his parents and tell them about his interview or his trip to New York. He turned into a parking spot in front of the Country Café and went inside, taking a seat at a corner table.

"Jackson!"

He inwardly groaned as he turned to see his sister, Helena, picking up an order from the counter. She quickly made her way over and took a seat opposite him at the table.

"You're back. How was New York?"

He shrugged. "It was fine. Picking up lunch?"

"Yeah. I didn't feel like eating anything I've got at home, and Sarah didn't have time to pack this morning, so we're splitting the soup and sandwich special."

He looked around her to the white board that hung by the door. "Split pea soup and turkey club?"

"Yep. So? How'd the interview go?"

"It was fine, Helena. Everything was fine, okay?" He saw the hurt in her eyes and sighed. "Look, I'm sorry. I've just got a lot on my mind."

"Anything I can help with?" she asked kindly.

"Not really. I guess I'm just soul searching. So, how are things around here?"

"Good. Cold, but I'm sure it was cold up there, too."

"It was. I went to the 9/11 Memorial."

She nodded. "The pictures were amazing. I'd love to go there someday. What was it like?"

Good question. What was it like? He wasn't sure how to answer that. "Sobering. Sad. Unthinkable."

"I'm sure. Is that what has you thinking?"

"Not really. It was the whole thing, to be honest. The whole experience. I always thought I wanted that—the big city, the lights, the noise, the fast-paced life, the thrill of Wall Street."

"And now?"

"I hated it. The lights, the noise, the fast-paced life. The interview was great, and I left there feeling prouder than a peacock, but then… I don't know. I started walking around and taking it all in, smelling the reek of the city and the trash and the pot."

"The pot?"

"Yeah. Lots of it. Everywhere. Anyway…" He felt funny telling her, but this was Helena, his life-long confidant. "Without even thinking about it, I practically ran to St. Patrick's. You know, the cathedral."

She nodded.

"I just needed… well, I needed peace and quiet and some time to think things over."

"Did it help?"

"You know what? It did. But it left me even more confused. I mean, if I went to the city, that church would be there. God would be there. I know that. I wouldn't be leaving that behind. But everything else? You and Andi. Mama and Daddy. This Podunk little town." He shook his head, and in his mind's eye, he saw Cindy. "Everything."

Helena placed her hand on Jackson's. "You know, it's okay to not go, but it's also okay to give it a try. You need to decide what you'd regret more, what would ultimately make you happiest."

"I know. And the truth is, they might not even offer me the job. I might be getting all worked up over nothing."

"Then why worry about it now? Wait and see what happens. Maybe God will make the decision for you."

Jackson nodded. He liked that idea. "You're right. I can leave it in God's hands. See where the Spirit leads me, as they say."

"There you go." Helena glanced at her watch. "I've got to get back. I'm glad you're home safe and sound."

"Me, too, Sis. Me, too."

***

"Ms. Kline? This is Sheriff Ramírez. I called you a couple weeks back."

"Yes. I remember." How could she forget? His call had stirred up confusion, anger, and a whole host of other emotions that were only intensified by the discovery of her father's letters. She put her brand-new laptop aside on the couch and sat up.

"I'm just wondering if you've heard from your father."

"I thought you said there was nothing to worry about."

"Well, there's not, as far as I know."

"Then why are you calling and asking if I've heard from him?"

"I've learned that your father is living near Harrison, Arkansas. Ever heard of it?"

Cindy's heart thumped against the wall of her chest. Her eyes went immediately to the window as if she would see her father standing there, watching her. "He's here? In Arkansas?"

"So, you are there, huh? I suspected as much."

"Yes, not too far from Harrison. Do you think? I mean…"

"He hasn't tried to contact you?"

She shook her head and continued staring out the window.

"Ms. Kline, are you there?"

"I'm sorry. Yes, I'm here. No, he hasn't tried to contact me. Not since I was about fifteen. That's when the letters stopped."

"Letters?"

"Yes. He wrote to me from prison. I didn't know about them. My mother passed a year ago, but I only recently discovered the letters from my father."

"And what was in the letters?"

"Nothing really. Regrets. Apologies for not being a better father. That kind of stuff."

"Mmm. That's it?"

She stood and walked over to the fireplace, feeling a sudden chill. "Sheriff Ramírez, what aren't you telling me?"

"Well, there is one other thing you should know."

The sound of his voice made her clutch the phone tighter. "Yes?"

"Some of the money they stole, a lot of it actually, was never found. Now, your father claims he has no idea where it was hidden, but now that he's out…"

"Now that he's out, you want to know if he was lying and if he's got the money. Is that right? Is that why he was released early? So you could follow him to the money?"

"I wouldn't go that far. He did earn his parole, but… Well, there's an awful lot of people who'd like to know where it is. If he has it, he hasn't used it. Those serial numbers have been in the system for a long time, and there's been no trace of them, but with today's technology and global banking, well, we can't be sure that somebody hasn't found a way to use that cash."

Cindy shook her head. "Look, Sheriff, I'm sorry I can't help you, but I have no idea where my father is. I haven't seen him since I was twelve years old, and I haven't heard from him, other than those letters, since the day he left. I don't know anything about the money or about my father." And that was the truth. The more she read the letters and read about him online, the more of a stranger he was to her.

"I understand. I'm sorry to bother you."

"If I do hear from him, is there someone I should call?"

"No, he's in the system and checking in like he should. We know where he is. We just wish we knew what he was up to."

"Maybe, Sheriff, he's trying to lead a normal life, be a better person, make a new start."

There was silence on the line, and Cindy was sure that he was trying to read between the lines. Why she was defending her father, she didn't know, but it bothered her that this stranger thought that she knew something about her recently released father, his life of crime, or the money he stole. Then something occurred to her…

"Sheriff Ramírez, should I be concerned. I mean, is my father dangerous?"

There was a long pause before he answered. "Ms. Kline, your father was released on the belief that he has been rehabilitated. In my experience…" Again, he paused before letting out a long breath. "In my experience, when it's someone with your father's background, that rarely happens. Just do me and yourself a favor, and keep your eyes open, okay?"

Cindy swallowed the lump in her throat. "Okay. Thank you."

"Thank you for your time," Sheriff Ramírez said. "You have a nice day, and uh, be careful." He disconnected the call, and Cindy held out her phone, staring at it as if it somehow held all the answers.

She returned to the couch and picked up the computer she bought with the 'retainer' from Mrs. Baker. She tried to go back to reading the course offerings on the college website, but her mind was elsewhere.

Sighing, she closed the laptop and laid it on the coffee table. She went to her bedroom and opened the top dresser drawer. Pushing aside the bras and underwear, she lifted out the box. She sat on her bed and slowly unfolded the next letter.

Dear Cindy,

Did I ever tell you how proud I am of you? Your mother and me may not have been the best parents, but that didn't stop you. I saw you with those books and how much time and effort you put into your schoolwork. I know that your going to make a better life for yourself than your mother and me did.

When we first met, all we wanted was to get married, have a baby, and live in a little house where we could be part of the American dream. I'm sorry to say, things didn't go as we planned, and it was our own fault. You came along before the wedding did, a fact I'm sure you know. I thought I was doing the right thing by you and your mom, but I guess she didn't see it that way. We began to fight, and things got pretty ugly at times. I never wanted that to happen. I never wanted you to hear us shouting and cussing and saying the things we did. I feel real bad about that now.

I also feel bad that I let your mother find peace in a bottle instead of in me. I wasn't a good father or a good husband, and I let you both down. I'm sorry I didn't do better, and I'm sorry I went along with those men and did the things I did. You're going to hear a lot of bad things about me. You probably already have. But I want you to know that I didn't do everything they said I did. I didn't think about people maybe dying. I didn't know things would get so out of control. I thought

I could go with them one time and have enough money to take care of you and get your mom some help, but once I did it, I couldn't stop. ~~When I saw that little boy.~~ Well, anyway, I never thought things would go that far.

I guess now all I can do is say I'm sorry. I said it to the families. I said it to God. Now I'm saying it to you. I hope that someday you can find it in your heart to forgive me. I'm trying my hardest to be a better man. I'm reading the Good Book and talking to a priest, they call him a chaplain, and I'm doing all I can to serve my time and be a good person. I hope someday you will believe that.

I love you,

Dad

Cindy refolded the letter and wiped away her tears. She put it back, closed the box, and hid it in the bottom of the drawer. Feeling lost and alone, she went back to the living room and slumped down on the couch. She grabbed a throw pillow and hugged it tightly, thinking about her father's proximity to her. That was an awfully big coincidence. What did it mean? Was he the one she felt following her, the one who broke into the house and her car? What did he want, and why did he think she had whatever it was? Anybody could see that she had no money, and she certainly didn't know where he would have put it.

Besides, his letters made him sound like a different person, somebody who wouldn't care about the money anymore. He wrote that he was talking to a priest and reading the Bible. The Bible! She couldn't imagine the man she remembered ever doing that. Maybe he had found God, but why was he following her? Why break into the house and her car? Why not just reach out to her if he wanted something?

She looked down at the key that dangled from the chain she'd taken to wearing around her neck. She held the chain out and flicked the key with her finger, watching it twist and turn in the fading, late afternoon light. She pinched it between her fingers and brought it close to her face, squinting as she looked for any marks or clues as to what the key would open. Giving up, she tucked the key inside her sweater.

Wearing the key on her body was the only way she could think of to keep it safe in case someone broke in again. It was the only thing she had brought with her that could possibly be what the person was looking for. She still had no idea what it went to, but she was determined to hold onto it until she figured it out. Her father had made the key, or whatever it unlocked, sound important. Besides that, it was the only connection to him that she had other than the letters.

And why does it matter?

She asked herself that over and over again. Did she care where he was or if he was looking for her? She didn't owe him anything, and as far as she was concerned, he didn't owe her anything either. He hadn't shown his face, and he could keep it that way.

Despite the warm fire and the afternoon sun shining through the window, the room felt as cold as the sea caves along the beaches she and her friends used to explore when she was younger. And just like back then, Cindy saw nothing but darkness ahead.

***

"So, you're back from your interview, I see."

Jackson nodded at Mac and went right to work helping him pile wood stove pellets into the back of a customer's truck. When they were finished, Jackson took a long drink of the hot coffee with which his mother filled his tall thermos. He wiped his mouth and replaced the cap.

"Yep. Not sure when I'll hear from them, but I think it went well."

Mac surveyed Jackson for a moment before frowning. "You don't look too happy or relieved. Didn't you say it went well?"

"Yeah, actually, I think it went really well." Jackson fiddled with his glove as though it weren't tight enough.

"Then what's the issue?"

Jackson made a frustrated noise and shook his head. "I don't know. This is what I've always wanted, or so I thought, but once I was there, it wasn't as great as I thought it would be."

"You haven't even gotten the job yet. What's not so great at this point?"

Jackson propped himself against a tall stack of baled hay. "New York, the city, the smell, the high rises. It just wasn't…"

"Wasn't home."

Jackson looked at Mac and nodded. "Yeah. It wasn't home. And it didn't feel like home. Not at all."

"Don't you think that's normal, son? I mean, you don't know anyone up there, you've never been to a city that big, and you don't even have the job. I'd be surprised if it did feel like home."

"I know, but it was more than that. I keep wondering if maybe I'm not cut out for all that." He paused and looked down at his gloved hands. "Andi's husband, Wade, he left here and moved to New York. He was there about ten years or so. When he came back, he was a different man. He's the first to admit it. He was arrogant and self-absorbed and only cared about making money. I don't want to be like that."

"Son, I'll be honest with you. I don't think you could ever be like that."

"You'd say the same thing about Wade if you knew him. Something about that world changed him. It took him a long time to find himself again, and he says it took Andi to make it happen."

"Well, what about that gal you took out a few times. Couldn't she keep you grounded?"

Jackson smiled. "You see, that's part of the problem. Cindy likes it here. More than likes it. She wants to put down roots here, run her business, get to know her friends better, all that stuff. She says it's the first place that has ever felt like home to her. I can't ask her to leave to go to New York with me."

"First place that's ever felt like home, huh?" Mac looked wistful as he stared out at the mountain peaks.

"Yeah. And it's not like we're actually dating."

Mac looked back at Jackson. "But you like her, right?"

Before Jackson could answer, another truck began backing in. When they finished with their load, Mac took a long drink of water and turned to face Jackson.

"I'm not a good one to talk about how to treat a woman. I've done my share of wrong, and I mean wrong. But here's what I've learned. If you find a good woman, don't screw it up. Treat her right. Tell her how you feel. Do what you can to be a good, honest, hard-working person, no shortcuts or fast tracks to being rich. Just do the right thing and pray that the good Lord lets you have a long life together. A wife, a daughter, whatever, never let her down. It'd be the biggest regret of your life."

Jackson studied Mac for a long time. The man had a sadness about him that Jackson had never noticed before. He'd always thought the man was a loner, a drifter, not somebody's husband or father. There was something so familiar about that look… Jackson felt the need to try to fix things for Mac, like he always felt when someone was lost or alone.

"You screwed up, didn't you?"

"More than I can ever make up for."

"What'd you do?"

Mac took a deep breath; that far off look he so often got in his eyes returned. "I didn't think about how my actions would affect my family. I put myself and my own wants and needs first."

"Heck, lots of people do that."

Mac's hazel eyes met Jackson's and held them, boring into them like a drill. "Not the way I did, son. Not the way I did."

Jackson's phone interrupted their conversation.

"Mr. Nelson?"

"Yes, this is Jackson Nelson." He held the phone to his ear and walked to the other side of the warehouse.

"This is Elaine at North American Bank. I'm pleased to tell you that you've been short-listed. We'd like to set up another interview. This one will be conducted online with our Vice President of Banking Analysis. Are you able to set up an interview for one day next week? Maybe the 28th or 29th?"

Jackson held his breath for a moment. Was he? He still had no idea what he wanted, but he didn't want to look a gift horse in the mouth.

"Yes ma'am. I'd like to set that up now."

"Very well," she answered and then proceeded to list the times that the vice president was available for the interview. Jackson set up the interview for the following Thursday and prayed he was doing the right thing.

***

The sound of the front door closing caused Cindy to jump. With her hand to her heart, she puffed out a breath of air.

"Hey, Cindy? You home?"

She stood from the bed, went to the bedroom door, and opened it to Helena.

"I'm here. What's up?"

"Do you wanna have dinner together? Joe had an emergency, so I'm on my own. Unless you have plans…"

"No plans here. What are you in the mood for?" She followed Helena into the kitchen.

"Anything. What do we have?" Helena opened the refrigerator and looked inside, shuffling around items to see what she could find. She closed the door and opened the freezer.

"Anything good?" Cindy stood with her back against the counter, arms folded across her chest.

"Not much. How about a pizza?"

"Sure."

They popped a frozen pizza into the oven, opened a bottle of wine, then went into the living room to sit in front of the fire. They kept the lights off, letting the flickering flames and twinkling tree lights illuminate the room with a soft, warm glow.

"Jackson's home. Have you talked to him?"

Cindy took a sip of wine. "Nope. Did he tell you how things went?" She studied the inside of her glass.

"He said it went well. He wasn't crazy about New York though."

Cindy looked up at Helena in surprise. "I thought everyone loved New York."

"Apparently, not Jackson. He said something about not liking the smell." Helena rolled her eyes. "I don't know. Jackson's such a mama's boy. I can't really see him living that far from home."

"A mama's boy? How so?" Cindy curled her legs under her.

"He's always been Mama's favorite. It's fine." She waved her hand in the air. "Andi and I don't care. We know Mama loves us. They're just super close. Jackson has always had this need to protect Mama, and I think it goes both ways. Don't worry though, he can stand up to her if he needs to. He has the backbone. I think he just worries about her."

"From what I can tell, your mother doesn't need worrying over. She seems very strong and solid to me. Like she knows who she is and where she comes from."

Helena looked at Cindy and smiled. "You're right. My mama is the best." Helena made a face. "Do you miss your mama?"

Cindy swirled the wine around and watched it settle back into the glass. She took a deep breath. "Yes and no. I don't miss the drinking, the cleaning up after her, the adulting I had to do long before I should have, or the embarrassment I suffered from never wanting my friends to see her or come to the house. That kind of stuff. But Gloria wasn't all bad. When she was sober, she was kinda funny and a good listener. Those moments were few and far between, but that's what I miss."

"I'm sorry, Cindy, sorry that you didn't have a normal childhood."

"What's normal?" Cindy asked with a shrug. "It's all I ever knew. Would I do things the same? Heck no. If I had kids, I'd treat them like they were special, read to them, go on vacations, volunteer at school, punish them when they're bad but love them to pieces when they're good. I'd want them to have a good, kind, loving father who they could be proud of. I guess that's the hard part." She gave Helena a half-smile.

"Why is that hard?"

"In case you hadn't noticed, I didn't do too well in that regard."

"Cindy, you're young. You have lots of time to find the right guy."

"Maybe. Maybe it's just not meant to be for me." Sadness washed over her like a bucket of Gatorade.

"Oh, Cindy, I don't believe that. Not for one minute." Helena snapped her finger. "And we can't have anyone feeling sorry for herself this close to Christmas."

"About that." Cindy squirmed. "I'm not so sure I should attend your family's holiday get-together."

"What? Why not?"

"It's a family thing." Cindy hadn't seen Jackson since that awkward drive the day he left for New York. She didn't really want to spend Christmas with him after the way he got all weird with her.

Helena moved closer to her on the couch. "Come on! You're practically family. It'll be fun. I promise. Besides, what else are you going to do? You don't have any family nearby to spend the weekend with."

Cindy thought about her father. Did she have family nearby? The thought made her nervous and reluctant to be alone. "Okay, okay, I'll go."

Helena smiled. "Yay! You're going to have such a nice time. You'll see."

The oven timer rang, and Helena went to take out the pizza. Cindy took another drink of wine and hoped that this Christmas would turn out better than the last one when she sat by Gloria's side and waited for the inevitable to happen.

Thirteen

The early dusk of December was setting in as Cindy tilted her head and scrutinized the sale display. She'd been hired to put together a last-minute window display at the toy store to entice the harried parents who had waited until Christmas Eve to do their shopping.

"It looks good," a familiar voice said from behind her.

She turned and smiled, unable to help herself. "Hi, Jackson. I heard you were back."

He nodded. "Yeah."

She waited, but he didn't say more. "How was it?" she prodded.

Jackson shrugged. "The interview went well. Not sure I liked the big city though."

"Cindy," Dale's voice interrupted from behind, and his urgent tone put Cindy on alert. "I just got a call.

There's been another break-in at Helena's. I need you to come with me now."

Cindy felt the blood drain from her face. She blinked twice before looking at Jackson.

"I'm so sorry. This is all my fault." She turned and ran to Dale's car, leaving Jackson standing on the sidewalk outside the toy store.

***

Flashing red and blue lights bounced off the houses, and police cars lined the street in front of Helena's rancher. The house was lit up like there was a party going on inside. Cindy's breathing was shallow, and her heart raced as she listened to the men speak.

"A neighbor reported the sound of breaking glass," the officer told Dale. He was the same officer who had taken photos and asked them questions the last time— Eric, maybe? "She was out walking her dog and didn't think too much of it at the time, but when she returned and passed by the house again, it occurred to her that nobody was home and that maybe she should call it in."

"Are you sure someone broke in?" Helena asked.

He nodded. "It wasn't just the one room this time."

Cindy felt sick, and she could tell by Helena's gasp and look of horror that she felt the same.

"How much damage?" Dale asked.

"A fair amount." He looked at Helena. "I'm sorry, Helena. I know how hard you worked on the house.

"Thanks, Eric." Helena blinked, and Cindy saw the moisture in her eyes reflecting the flashing lights. "Can we go in?" she asked Dale who looked at Eric.

"It's secure, and photos have been taken. Your call," Eric said.

Dale scratched his head. "Do me a favor," Dale asked his brother, Cooper, who had appeared out of nowhere.

"Call Mama?"

"Yeah. Ask her if she can stay the night with the kids."

"Sure." Cooper disappeared into the shadows as quickly as he had appeared.

As Cindy watched Cooper walk away, she noticed Jackson leaning against a tree. It was dark under the tree except for the occasional flash of red or blue as the strobe lights continued to circle the air. She didn't know if he came for her or for Helena, but she was glad to know he was there.

"Let's go inside," Dale said to them. "But just as far as the entrance. You can see enough from there to get an idea as to how bad it is. I'm going to double check the scene, but I don't want either of you to go all the way inside. Understood?"

Helena and Cindy both nodded and followed Dale to the house. As they made their way up the walkway, Helena reached over and grabbed Cindy's hand and squeezed it.

"It's gonna be okay," Helena said quietly.

Cindy wanted to cry. How did Helena not hate her for the trouble she'd introduced into their lives? How was it that Helena was the one reassuring Cindy and not the other way around?

They stopped just inside the front door, and Helena gasped. She squeezed Cindy's hand tighter, and Cindy heard her sniffle. She felt like her heart was being ripped in two.

They could see into a small part of the kitchen where cabinets were open and dishes, pots, pans, and food items were strewn on the floor. In the living room, pillows and cushions littered the floor amidst stuffing and fabric. Everything had been slashed open. The Christmas tree had been toppled, and broken ornaments littered the floor. Gift boxes had been slashed open, their pretty paper and ribbons in tatters.

"Is the rest of the house this bad?" Helena asked in a broken voice. Cindy knew how much her ornaments meant to her. She'd been gathering them her entire life.

"Afraid so," Eric answered. "The mattresses were cut open, drawers emptied, closets gone through. We'll need an accounting of all your jewelry."

Helena nodded. Cindy couldn't move. She had been keeping the box of letters in the top drawer of her dresser.

"Did he… did he go through all the jewelry boxes?"

"Looks like it. Some were completely emptied. Others were just open."

"I need to check mine. It's important."

"Your what?" Eric asked, his eyes narrowing.

"My jewelry box. It was in the top drawer of my dresser."

"What did it look like?"

Cindy described the box, its light brown wood, the intricate scroll design, and the little lock.

"I'll double check."

She waited, wringing her hands, for Eric to return, but when he came into view, he shook his head.

"I'm sorry, Cindy. There wasn't a box like that anywhere in your room."

She sucked in air and almost choked. "What? It's…it's gone? What about the letters?"

Eric shook his head again. "I can look again, but I didn't see any letters anywhere."

"No, no, no, no," she repeated over and over, feeling the heaves in her chest and the moisture on her cheeks before she even realized she was crying. Not only were the letters gone, so was any doubt that her own presence had brought this on, and that her father was somehow involved.

In the entrance of the house, with Helena clutching her hand, Cindy fell to the floor, the sobs coming too hard and fast to control.

***

Jackson and Joe stood near each other at the edge of the driveway. At the sound of the cries, they both turned and looked at each other, and Jackson saw his own questions reflected in Joe's countenance. Neither said a word, but both broke into a run, heading toward the front door of the house. Jackson, younger and in better shape, beat Joe to the front porch. He looked inside and saw his sister cradling Cindy in her arms while Cindy's sobs filled the cold, starry night.

Without asking permission of either of the officers, Jackson went inside and dropped to the ground. His eyes implored his sister for answers, but she merely shrugged and shook her head.

"Cindy," Jackson said quietly. "Come on. I can take you to Mama's or to Andi's, wherever you want to go." He tried to take her arm and pull her up, but she knelt on the floor, crying in Helena's arms, like an unmovable fountain raining droplets of water. "Please, Cindy," he pleaded. "Let me take you somewhere. Whatever is wrong, we can work it out."

At that, she looked up at him, her red-rimmed eyes filled with tears. "They're gone. They're all gone. And this is all my fault."

"What's gone, sugar?" Helena asked.

"My father's letters. They're all I have of him, and I hadn't even finished reading them. Now, they're gone, and I think he's the one responsible for this." Her words were punctuated by choking sounds, and Jackson felt her anguish as painfully as if it were his own. She looked at Helena. "This is all my fault. I'm so, so sorry."

Dale stooped down beside them. "Cindy, what was in the letters? Why would someone take them? What does this have to do with your father?"

"I don't know. I only read the first few. There were others. I was reading them slowly, one at a time. I didn't even know about them until after Gloria died. I f-f-found them hidden under her bed."

Dale looked questioningly at Helena.

"Gloria was her mother. She passed away about a year ago. The situation was…not good."

"Cindy, this might be important. Do you remember anything in the letters that somebody would want to know? Any reason at all why they would take them?"

Jackson looked at Dale. "Do you think that's what they were after? A bunch of letters?"

"Why?" Helena asked. "Why would someone do all of this for a box of letters?"

For the first time, Jackson took a long look into the house. He was horrified by the destruction he saw. How could someone do this? His heart broke for his sister, and he wanted to be angry at Cindy for any part she played in this, but when he looked into her eyes and saw both grief and remorse, he couldn't be angry with her.

Eric spoke up. "Maybe they thought they were taking a jewelry box. You said it was locked," he looked at Cindy. "Maybe they thought something valuable was in it."

Cindy shook her head. "It had a lock, but it wasn't locked. The key doesn't fit. And there was nothing in it but the letters."

Dale and Eric exchanged a look, and Jackson wondered what they were thinking. It made no sense.

Why completely destroy an entire house for a box of letters?

"Let's go down to the station," Dale suggested. "I have some questions for Cindy, and Eric and the rest of the team need to finish up here."

With Helena holding her hand, Cindy managed to stand. Jackson could see the new wave of determination on her face.

"I don't know how I can help, but I'll tell you anything you need to know." She looked at Helena. "And I'll pay for this, all of it. I'll help you clean and redecorate and whatever else you need."

"Let's talk about that later," Helena said. She turned to Dale. "Do you want me to go, too? I'm not sure what you want to know, but obviously, I'll answer any questions I can."

"I will have questions, but I'll start with Cindy. Until we get a good inventory of anything valuable in the house, the missing box of letters is all we have to go on."

"Did they take my laptop? My iPad? The TV? Anything like that?"

"Not that we know of," Eric answered. "The TV is still hanging on the wall, and I saw a laptop and iPad on the desk in your room. There's another laptop on the kitchen counter. I wondered why he, or she, didn't take them. From what I can tell, this was a targeted hit. They were looking for something specific." His eyes darted toward Cindy, but she kept her gaze downcast.

"Dale, can I drive her? You don't need to take her in the police car, do you?"

"Sure. At this point, Cindy is a victim, not a suspect."

He saw her head snap up and her eyes go wide.

"A suspect? I might be considered a suspect? But I didn't do anything. I wasn't even here." Jackson heard the desperation in her voice.

Dale shook his head. "I'm not saying that. Let's go talk, and we'll see how this all pans out."

All the confidence Jackson had seen earlier was gone, and Cindy looked once again like the lonely, frightened girl who came to Andi seeking friendship and advice. Jackson had never felt such an overwhelming urge to care for and protect anyone or anything in his life.

***

Cindy's hand shook as she accepted the paper cup of water and took a sip. Neither she nor Jackson had said a word on the short drive to the police station. She tried to remember every detail of every letter, but nothing she had read was anything more than a father's expression of regret to his daughter. There was nothing in the letters that could be of importance to anyone but her. Of course, there were letters she hadn't read. Why had she done that? Why had she put off reading them? Why hadn't she just sat down, all at once, and read her father's only communication with her in ten years?

"Cindy, what can you tell me about the letters or about your father?"

"I don't really know much about my father. He left us when I was twelve. Well…" She stopped. Could that be it? The key to everything? "He didn't exactly leave." She looked at Dale and slowly said the words she had come to accept over the past several weeks. "He was arrested. For bank robbery with a deadly weapon and attempted homicide."

Dale nodded, and Cindy realized he knew that already. How long had he known?

Dale looked down at the legal pad in front of him, his pen perched in his hand as though he didn't know what to say. He looked back up at Cindy.

"The money was never recovered," he stated.

Suddenly, the fog in her mind lifted, and she took so deep a breath, she thought she might choke on the air. She gulped in several gasping breaths.

"Cindy, relax. Take a deep breath."

She did so and then spoke. "The other day, I got a call from Sheriff Ramírez. I didn't know anything before that, and everything about this has been so shocking. I didn't…" She looked up at Dale, still unable to catch her breath, feeling a full-blown panic attack coming on. "I didn't make a connection. I never knew anything about the money or the robberies or any of this. I never knew anything. And nobody has ever asked before or tried to contact me or broken into my house or car or…" She tried to get air, but her lungs didn't feel like they were working. She felt dizzy and grabbed onto the edge of the desk for support. Dale motioned to someone on the other side of the glass window.

"Cindy, calm down. I know you didn't know. I've talked to Sheriff Ramírez. He believes you, and so do I."

"You do? But why? I mean, you don't even know me."

Dale looked uncomfortable for a moment. "I've, uh, I've had someone following you."

"Me? You mean, someone really has been following me? Since when?"

"Since the sheriff called about a week or so ago to let me know your father was in Arkansas."

"My father got out of prison several weeks ago. He must think I found the money."

The reality finally kicked in. Her father was not the kind and loving man his letters portrayed. He was exactly the ruthless, violent man she remembered him to be. He thought she knew where his stolen money was, and until he found it, he was determined to continue ruining her life just as he'd been doing for the past twenty-two years.

***

Exhausted, worried, and confused, Jackson laid his head back against the wall and closed his eyes, his neck cradled by the back of the chair. He must have nodded off because it felt like only seconds later when he was jolted alert by the sound of an opening door. When Dale led Cindy out of the conference room, Jackson stood.

She looked even worse than when they first arrived. Her eyes were swollen, and deep, purple pools of skin puddled beneath her lower lashes, blending with the mascara that smeared above her cheeks. She was pale, and her hair was as limp as her body seemed to be. There was no life in her, no hope, no confidence.

She looks like a cancer patient. He winced at the thought, remembering that Dale and Cindy both knew all too well what that looked like.

"Can she leave?"

"Yes, but don't take her to your house. Take her to Joe's. I think she might be in shock."

Jackson blinked, waiting for Dale to say more.

"I can't tell you anything, Jackson. If she wants to, that's her call. Just make sure Joe keeps an eye on her. And Jackson, I've had someone watching her for a while. She can explain why. At first, I thought… Well, never mind that. There's a good chance she's in more danger than we thought."

Jackson looked at Cindy, but she didn't seem to register anything that was being said.

"Is she… is she going to be okay?"

"Emotionally? I think it will take some time. Physically? If I can help it, she's going to be okay. We'll do everything we can to see that she's safe."

Jackson put an arm around her, and she sagged against him as though she hadn't the strength to keep standing.

"It's okay, Cindy. You're okay. I won't let anything happen to you."

There wasn't even a movement of her head to acknowledge that she heard him. She simply leaned heavily on him and let him lead her out to his truck.

Jackson wasn't sure he was going to be able to get her up into the cab, but as though she were moving in a trance, when he opened the door, she climbed inside. Jackson closed the door and hurried around to the other side. He didn't get inside right away. Instead he called Joe and told him what was going on. Joe sounded as though he was still wide awake, and Jackson thought of Helena. Was she there or at their Mama's? Would she be okay with Cindy staying at Joe's? Would she and Cindy be okay after this?

Whether they were or not, Joe said he'd be waiting when they arrived. He had more than one empty bedroom and would take care of Cindy for the night. Jackson didn't know if that meant she couldn't stay any longer or if Joe was just assuring Jackson that it was okay for him to take her there. He didn't really have the time or the inclination to read too deeply into Joe's words.

Before he backed out of the parking space, Jackson looked over at Cindy. She hadn't buckled her seatbelt, so he gently reached around her and snapped the buckle into place. She stared out the windshield, motionless, her eyes hollow and unyielding. What did Dale know that Cindy had been hiding? What was it that put her in so much danger?

When they arrived at Joe's, the good doctor rushed outside and met Jackson at the passenger side door.

"She's not talking and barely moving. She just stares straight ahead. I don't know what's wrong or what she told Dale or what he told her. Oh, and Joe, I didn't tell you…" he began as a police cruiser pulled up across the street. "Dale has someone watching her."

"Was she behind this?"

"No," Jackson was quick to point out. "I mean, I didn't get that impression. More like, she knows something or has whatever this guy is after. Dale said she might be in danger."

Joe sighed. "I would be angry about having her in my home or around Helena except…"

"Yeah, I figured you'd understand. After all that stuff with your ex."

Jackson tried not to look down at Joe's hand which had undergone several surgeries after his ex-fiancé tried to maim him.

Joe nodded. "I'll take care of her. Help me get her inside, and then you go home and get some rest."

Jackson opened the door and climbed up to unbuckle her seatbelt. He'd been so afraid she might just fall over, he hadn't released it when they first arrived.

"Cindy, sweetie, we're at Joe's. Can you get out of the truck?"

She didn't nod or answer, but she turned and began to climb out. Joe took her hand, and Jackson slipped his arm around her waist. They helped her to the ground and then bent, looped her arms around their shoulders, and led her to the house. They led her inside and up the stairs, Joe leading the way to the second floor while Jackson supported Cindy. Joe turned down the bed covers, and Jackson helped her sit on the side of the bed before gently removing her boots.

He stood and looked at Joe, his cheeks growing warm. "Uh, should we?"

"I'll take care of it. It's not like I've never seen a half-dressed patient."

Jackson nodded. "Is Helena here?"

Joe shook his head. "I wanted her to come home with me, but she insisted on being taken to Andi's. I'm not sure if she wanted the comfort of her sister or the protection of a Navy SEAL." He gave Jackson a crooked grin.

"I can't blame her."

"Neither can I, but I can't help but wonder…"

"If she's thinking about Lindsay and all the stuff she put you through?"

"Yeah."

Jackson laid his hand on Joe's arm. "Don't worry. Helena loves you. It's all going to be okay."

Joe nodded and returned his focus to Cindy who still sat on the edge of the bed like petrified stone. "I've got this from here. I'll text you in the morning."

Jackson glanced down at his watch. "It's already morning."

Joe nodded. "I'll text you later this morning. Get some rest."

"I have to be at work in four hours."

"Can't you call in?"

"I could, but I doubt I'll sleep much anyway."

Joe nodded knowingly, and Jackson took one last look at Cindy before turning to leave. He stopped in the door and looked back.

"Take care of her, Joe. I don't know what's going on, but…" he choked on his words. "She's… I…"

Joe held up his hand. "Jackson, I know. I see it in your eyes. Don't worry. She's going to be fine."

Jackson nodded and headed out, feeling like he was leaving his world behind.

***

It wasn't quite light out when Cindy opened her eyes. She shot up in bed and took in her surroundings.

Where am I?

The faintest light was beginning to peek through the window blinds, and Cindy didn't recognize anything she saw. When she pulled back the covers, she was even more startled to see that she was in her white t-shirt, socks, and underwear. Alarmed, she looked for her clothes and saw her jeans, flannel, and coat neatly draped over a nearby chair. Her boots stood on the floor next to the chair.

There were no photographs in the room, and there were no decorative touches that made her think of Helena or Helena's mother, Grace. The walls were white, or looked white in the early morning light, and the comforter on the bed was a generic blue plaid. She definitely wasn't at Mel's or Trudy's, and Sarah didn't have a spare room. Not that she suddenly would have ended up at any of their houses.

The aroma of sausage and fresh coffee penetrated the room through the crack under the closed door, and her stomach growled. Her mouth was dry, but she didn't feel hungover. She never had more than one drink if she drank at all, and she certainly hadn't been drinking while she was working.

Working. She'd been working on the window display at the toy store. No, she'd finished working. Jackson was there. They talked about New York, and then…

Her breath caught in her throat. Dale. He'd gotten a call. She went with him, and they'd gone back to Helena's. The rest was a blur.

Where the heck am I?

She pushed herself out of bed but felt unsteady on her feet and stumbled toward the chair. She hastily pulled on her jeans and shirt, fastening the buttons as she walked toward the dresser on the other side of the room. She looked terrible. Her hair was stringy, her makeup was smeared, and under her eyes was so purple and puffy, she thought at first she might have been in a fight. She ran her fingers through her hair and tiptoed to the door.

When she entered the hallway, she looked around, still unable to place her whereabouts. She ducked into the bathroom across the hall, splashed water on her face, and removed what makeup she could using moistened toilet paper that shredded in her fingers. There was a tube of toothpaste on the counter, a brand-new toothbrush in the wrapper, and a small stack of paper cups. She brushed her teeth and swished her mouth with water.

After pulling the covers back up over the bed and tugging on her boots, she made her way quietly down the stairs. The first floor was immaculate and stylishly decorated, and even Cindy knew the pieces of furniture were not reproductions.

"Good morning."

Cindy jumped and felt her heart in her throat. She turned around to see into Joe's gourmet kitchen. It was like standing in a magazine.

Joe stood at the stove, a red and black apron over his dress shirt and slacks, and a spatula in his hands.

"I've got sausage cooking and was going to make pancakes. The coffee is ready, unless you'd like tea. In that case, I can put on a kettle."

Her eyes followed the tantalizing smell that her nose had detected, and she saw a real coffee percolator, not a Keurig or a jar of instant grounds.

"I hope you slept okay," Joe said, and Cindy turned back toward him.

"I did. Um, thanks. Can you, I mean, I'm a bit fuzzy on…"

"Jackson brought you by last night after you left the station."

"The station…" She tried to figure out what he was talking about.

Joe put down the spatula. "Cindy, do you remember what happened?"

"I remember working at the toy store and Dale saying something happened. I remember doing some work at the house and doing the display at the toy store."

She frowned. "Jackson was there, and then Dale showed up…"

Joe nodded. "Is that all you remember?"

She held her breath, lips tight, eyes squeezed together. Suddenly, she saw Dale in the police station, heard him talking about the letters, her father, the missing money. She opened her eyes and looked at Joe.

"My father. He did this. He's been following me, I think. Or was that Dale? Anyway, my father broke into the house and my car. Maybe. He…" visions of Helena's house swarmed her mind, and she reached for a chair. She pulled it out and sat down, placing her elbows on the table and her head in her hand. "He destroyed Helena's house."

She felt Joe come up beside her, smelled the coffee he put in front of her, felt the steam rise to her face. She looked up and tried to smile. "Thank you."

She didn't usually drink hot coffee and never black, but the bitter taste brought her some inexplicable comfort. She took two more sips, blowing before each one, and then sat the mug down on the table.

"Did they catch him yet? My father?"

"I don't know anything, Cindy. All I know is that when Jackson brought you here last night, you were in shock. I kept an eye on you off and on all night, and a police car has been parked outside since you arrived."

"A police car? In case he comes after me? My father, I mean."

"I don't really know."

She nodded and took another drink.

"Do you think you can eat something? You really should. Being in shock takes a toll on your body."

"Um, sure. I'll have whatever you made."

He made the pancakes, and they ate together in silence. Joe was too polite to pry, and Cindy had too many things on her mind to make conversation. When she finished, she looked up at Joe and asked, "Now what? Where do I go?"

"Andi texted this morning and said you can stay with them. Helena's there, too. They have plenty of room."

Cindy nodded. "Yeah, I've stayed there before. The house is huge." She looked at Joe. "Do you think Helena will mind? Is she mad at me?"

"For what? For having a crazy father?" He laughed "If that were the case, she never would've agreed to marry me. Has anyone ever told you about Lindsay?"

***

"You look like you spent the night standing up with the lights on. What happened?"

Jackson adjusted his hat and gloves before answering Mac.

"I had a rough night."

"I would say so. Anything you wanna talk about?"

Jackson looked at the man. How had this stranger become his confidant and sounding board? About ten years younger than Jackson's father, Mac was not somebody Jackson would've ever thought of as a friend. He was rough around the edges, hard to put a finger on, and often lapsed into long periods of silence. Despite all that, Jackson had grown to like the man.

He opened up about his developing feelings for Cindy, about them dancing together, and about how much fun the two of them had on the dance floor before she ran out. Between customers, Jackson told Mac about his doubts about his future career, and his desire to stay in Buffalo Springs. He even admitted to Mac that he thought he might be falling in love with Cindy.

Through it all, Mac remained silent, allowing Jackson to talk as much or as little as he pleased on each subject. He made grunts and noises, smiled and frowned, and let Jackson know he was listening without saying a word. Then Jackson relayed the call Dale received, what they found when they arrived at the house, and how Cindy had gone into shock. At this news, Mac's face went white.

"Is she okay?"

"Joe texted me earlier to say that she'd eaten breakfast and eventually remembered what happened. He thinks she's going to be okay, all things considered."

"What exactly made her go into shock?"

Jackson thought it was strange that Mac had remained quiet through all Jackson had told him but seemed more than eager to hear about Cindy, worried even, but he'd talked so much about her that he figured Mac felt like he knew her as well as Jackson did.

"Some letters she had, they were from her father. They were the only things, as far as we know right now, that were taken." Jackson looked at Mac and gave a slight shake of his head. "Strange, don't you think? That all the thief would take was a box of letters? Unless it was her dad and there was information there that he needed or that he wanted to keep secret. Anyway, there seems to be more to the story, but I don't know the details. They think she's in danger, from her father of all people. I knew he abandoned them when she was young, but to think that a father—"

"Jackson, I'm sorry." Mac jumped up and frantically looked around as if he needed to find something. He felt in his pocket and pulled out his keys. "I've got to go. I can't explain right now. Tell Cindy…tell her everything's going to be okay. I'm going to make it okay."

Jackson watched as Mac bolted through the back door into the store.

What the heck just happened?

And then…it all became clear.

***

Cindy sat at Andi's kitchen table after being dropped off by Joe. Boomer slept at her feet, and she wondered if he sensed how comforting that felt to her. She'd changed into a pair of Andi's leggings and a sweatshirt and was trying to keep busy. Since she had taken her laptop and work bag with her when she went to the toy store, they had been in her car when the house was ransacked. She thought perhaps she could take her mind off things by working on some ideas for a potential client who had made an appointment for after Christmas, but her heart wasn't in it. Besides, it was impossible not to think about Helena's house or her father or the police officer outside. When the doorbell rang, it was a welcome distraction. Boomer barked and ran toward the door ahead of her.

She heard voices in the hall. One was Wade's and one was a man's she didn't recognize. She couldn't hear what they were saying, but then she heard their footfalls coming down the hall.

"Cindy," Wade said. "This is Officer Rob Hansen. He needs to talk to you."

"Ma'am, we've had some developments in the case, and Dale asked if I would bring you down to the station."

Cindy stood on shaky legs.

"Developments?"

"I don't know all the details. Dale said he got a call from Jackson Nelson telling them that he thought your father was on his way to the station."

"Jackson? How would he—"

"I don't know, ma'am. Dale said not to let you out of my sight. I kept watching the house, and then Dale called back and said a man claiming to be your father had just showed up and turned himself in. Dale said you should come."

Cindy looked from the officer to Wade. She didn't know what to say.

"I need to get my coat. It's upstairs."

"Yes, ma'am. I'll wait."

As Cindy walked up the garland-draped staircase, she looked the portraits adorning the wall. In every picture, there was a smiling family with a happy mom and a doting father. True, maybe that wasn't the way it was in real life, but everyone sure looked happy in the pictures. All Cindy ever wanted was to be part of *that* family. The ones she scoffed at on TV, the ones that caused her to change the channel because they were too good to be true. She never thought they actually existed, but she still wanted it so badly. And then she met Evan, and she thought, maybe… But that wasn't meant to be, and she was alone again. Then she came here.

She saw the Nelson family, heard about Wade's family, met Mel's parents, and marveled at Dale's family. Even though Dale was a widower, he still had his loving parents and his brother, and he seemed to be doing okay. Those families really did exist—the ones who went to church and actually lived according to their faith, the ones who looked out for each other, opened their homes to each other, and even opened their homes to strangers!

On her way back down the stairs, Cindy stopped and looked at the last photograph in the line, the one at the bottom of the steps that everyone could see when they came into the house. There was a much younger Wade, the little sister who had died, and smiling parents. Someday, he and Andi would be able to add to the wall another smiling family with so much love to go around. Would it ever be her turn? Would it ever be Cindy posing for a portrait next to her husband with her children gathered around them? An image of Jackson appeared in her mind, but she shook it away. Now that they all knew the truth, why would his family want someone like her—someone tainted, someone with the blood of a felon in her veins—to intrude on their perfect family?

"Ready, ma'am?"

Cindy turned from the photograph and nodded. She hadn't seen her father in over ten years. She guessed this was her Brady Bunch moment. Welcome back from the slammer, Dad.

***

Jackson paced back and forth in the lobby of the police station. When he saw the car pull up in front, he stopped and went to the door. Rob Hansen followed closely behind Cindy as she walked toward the building. Jackson opened the door, and Rob ushered her in. When she was inside, she came face to face with Jackson. Her countenance was unreadable.

"Cindy, are you okay?"

She nodded. "I'm fine. How did you know?"

"I didn't. Not for sure. I just put two and two together today when I was telling him about last night, and he kind of freaked out. It occurred to me that all the other times we talked, he was always really interested in you, in us, in whether or not I heard from you, took you out—"

"Jackson, stop. What do you mean he freaked out and was interested in me? You were talking to him? You were talking to my father, and you never told me?"

He wasn't sure if the look on her face was surprise or disgust. He had to make her understand.

"I didn't know he was your father. It never even occurred to me. For all I knew, your father was dead."

"You talked to him about me? How could you? What did you tell him?"

"Cindy," Dale called from the other side of the station. "Can you come back here, please?"

"Cindy," Jackson grabbed her arm, and she looked at him like he was a stranger or worse, like he was someone who would hurt her. He let her go. "We need to talk."

"Not now, Jackson," she said coldly. "It's *my* turn to talk to my father."

He watched her walk away, her head held high, her expression as hard as steel. Anyone else would look at her and think she was confident and bold and willingly going in to face the man who had wronged her all those years ago. Jackson had gotten to know and understand her, though, and what he saw was a frightened girl who knew that her past and present were about to collide. Where would Jackson stand once the fallout had been assessed?

Fourteen

"Please, take a seat." Dale closed the door behind her, and Cindy took a seat at the conference table. Dale sat across from her. A sudden sense of deja vu crept over her. They were the only ones in the room, but she still felt unsettled.

"Where is he?"

"In a holding cell. We're checking now to see if he's done anything against his parole. He doesn't have an alibi for either of the nights the house was broken into, but I have a question for you. In my notes, I have that you mentioned someone following you and someone breaking into your car. Can you explain those statements?"

"As far as someone following me, it was just a feeling I had. Sometimes, I felt like someone was watching me. Jackson felt it, too, once when we were leaving the movie theater in Harrison. I thought maybe it was my imagination, but then someone broke into my car."

"When did this happen?"

She thought back. "Do you mind if I check my calendar app?"

"No, go ahead. We're going to need the exact date and time to check your father's alibi and to rule out our guy."

She pulled out her phone and scrolled back to the night she was at Melanie's. She told Dale about going out to her car only to find the trunk open and the contents rifled through.

"Why didn't you report it?"

"I was afraid to. I was worried that Helena would tell me to leave and that my new friends would be afraid to be around me." She looked away, both embarrassed and sad.

"Cindy," Dale said quietly. "Haven't you figured out that's not the way we do things around here? This town, those of us who've lived here our whole lives, we've seen a lot, been through a lot. Look at Wade and Andi. Look at Helena and Joe. One thing that never changes is that we all do our best to look out for each other. We're all family."

"But don't you see? I'm not. I'm not family. I don't have a family. I don't belong here or anywhere."

Dale stood up and opened the blinds on the windows. He pointed to a very worried Jackson pacing in the lobby. "I'm willing to bet a month's salary that the guy you see out there looking like he's lost the most important thing in his life would disagree with you. In fact, all the Nelsons would disagree with you. You *are* family to them, don't you see that?"

She looked at Jackson. Even from where she sat, she could see the circles under his eyes, the dejected expression, the way his shoulders slumped, and his brow creased. He looked up, as if sensing her looking at him. When their eyes met, she knew. She wished she could get up, run out the door, and tell him how she felt, but that would have to wait. She smiled faintly and nodded slightly, and with just that small acknowledgment, she saw him breathe a sigh of relief. He nodded back, and she smiled a little more.

"Do you see?" Dale said. "He'd do anything for you."

Would he? I know I would do anything for him.

At that moment, she had no doubt she would, but she wasn't sure where he stood.

Dale closed the blinds and sat back down. "Now that we've cleared that up, is there anything else you'd like to share?"

Cindy reached her hand up to her throat but hesitated. Sitting at Joe's table, trying to remember everything that had occurred, trying to process all that happened since she had found the letters, she had a thought. She reached into the collar of Andi's sweatshirt and extracted the chain on which she wore the heart pendant from Evan and, alongside it, the mysterious key.

"I don't know what may have been in the last few letters, but I think this is what he was looking for. I was in too much of a daze last night to think clearly." She unclasped the necklace, removed the key, and handed it to Dale. "I have no idea what it goes to. There are no markings on it, and I tried every lock I could find in Mama's house when I first came across it. I thought maybe it went to the box that the letters were in, but it doesn't."

"It wouldn't." Dale looked up at her. "It's a safety deposit box key."

Cindy tilted her head and looked at him. "A what?"

"A safety deposit box key. You know, at a bank." He stood and opened the door, calling someone to come in.

"I don't know what you mean."

"You've never heard of a safety deposit box?"

She shook her head. "I mean, maybe I've heard the phrase, but I have no idea what one is."

Dale handed the key to the other officer. "Take this to MacCallum's cell and show it to him. Ask him if he knows where the box is and how to access it." Dale closed the door and returned to his seat.

"It's a box in a bank used to keep valuables. The owner of the box has a key, and the bank has a key. You can only access it if your signature is on the card corresponding to the box. You take it into a locked, completely sealed room and open it in private. Nobody, not even the bank, knows what's in it. They used to be used for things like social security cards, birth certificates, wills, that kind of stuff, sometimes expensive jewelry, coin collections, whatever people thought was valuable enough to lock away in a safe."

"Wait, you mean like what Jason Bourne accessed in Switzerland? That's where he found his passports, money, and all that. Those are real? And they have those here?"

She could tell he was suppressing a smile, but she was too surprised to be embarrassed.

"They do. All banks have them."

Cindy's eyes widened. "Do you think that's where the money is? Maybe my father assumed I had it and was looking for it. He might have thought the key was in the box with the letters. Or maybe one of the letters tells me where to find the deposit box and how to access it."

There was a quick knock on the door, and the officer opened it and stuck his head inside. "He wants an attorney."

"Did he say anything?"

"Nope. Just took one look at the key and asked for an attorney."

Dale sat back. "Great. That's going to take all day. There's only one attorney in town, and I hardly think he's going to take the case."

"Tell him to take it. Tell him I said to."

"Cindy, I can't do that. You don't want me to do that. What if you decide to press charges? You're going to want Wade on your side."

She shook her head. "But he's my father." The words were out before she realized it. His letters had gotten to her. Despite all she knew about him, she was desperate for a connection, even after all he did to her.

"It's not a good idea, Cindy. Let me call the county DA and see if we can get someone to come down."

She watched him start to leave but called out, "Dale, wait. Can I… can I see him?"

Dale sighed. "Are you sure?"

She nodded.

"Okay. Steve, take her to see her daddy while I make a call to the DA."

Cindy stood, unsure if this was the right thing, but after all these years, she had a few things to say to the man who called himself her father.

***

Jackson watched as Cindy was led toward the stairs at the back of the station. He was exhausted, but he wasn't going to leave her. He felt his phone vibrate and looked down at the text.

Got your message. Give me a call.

Jackson tapped on the phone and waited for his boss to pick up on the other end.

"Hey, Jackson. How's your friend?"

"She's okay," not that he knew the answer, but he wasn't calling to talk about Cindy. "Did you know Mac served time in prison?"

The question was met with silence.

"Dan? You there?"

"Jackson, my brother spent time in prison. It was years ago, and I was pretty young. When he got out, he had a hard time getting a job. Nobody wanted to hire him. They didn't care that he was a kid himself when he went to jail and that he'd learned his lesson. The answer was always no. He bounced around from odd job to odd job, never able to make a living. He never got married, never owned a home, and at the age of thirty-seven, he took his own life. I made a promise to never let another man go through what he did. If I can offer someone a second chance, it's my obligation to my brother to do so. A few years ago, I encountered a group that helps former prisoners find work. I told them that I'd take anyone they believed deserved a second chance. Mac is one of those men."

"How did he end up working with me?"

"I couldn't start him on a register. I'm forgiving but not stupid. I figured if he did well outside, he could move inside eventually, work his way up. He had to earn it. That was my part of the bargain."

"So, you had no idea his daughter had come to town and was living with my sister."

"Holy sh—are you serious?"

"Dead serious."

"I didn't even know he had a daughter. I take it that's why you and Mac both had pressing emergencies at the same time."

"Yeah. I'm sorry about that. I didn't mean to leave Pete high and dry like that."

"Hmph. Just watch it when you come back. It's blowin' up a storm, and he's been swamped with pickups of pellets, horse feed, hay, salt, you name it. People go crazy when they think they're going to be housebound for a day which is usually all it amounts to around here. But with Christmas Eve being tomorrow, everything is crazier than normal."

"Sounds like the storm could be bad," Jackson said.

"I guess we'll have to wait and see."

"Yeah. Anyway, thanks for the info. I appreciate it"

"Take care, Jackson. And I hope I wasn't wrong about Mac. He seemed like a decent guy."

Jackson felt the same way, but his concern was for Cindy. Mac could fend for himself.

Jackson looked around for Dale and spied him talking to his administrative assistant. Jackson waited for them to finish before waving to him and gesturing for them to talk. He tried to read Dale's body language as he approached, but the man was all business.

"What's up, Jackson?"

"Where did they take Cindy? Is she going to see him?"

"Yes. She asked to see him."

"Is that a good idea?"

Dale raised his shoulders and blew a long breath. "I don't know. I wasn't sure he'd agree. He's lawyered up."

"So, he confessed to everything?"

"Not exactly."

Jackson waited, but that was all Dale said. "What does that mean?"

"That it's an open investigation, Jackson. I can't tell you any more than that. Go home. Go to work. Whatever. When she's done, I'll have someone take her back to Andi's."

"I'd rather wait."

"Suit yourself, but I'm not sure how long she'll be here." Dale started to walk away, but Jackson grabbed his arm.

"Dale, you're not holding her, are you? I mean, she's not a suspect, is she?"

Dale took a moment to answer, and Jackson didn't know what to think.

"Look, I don't think she did anything wrong, but again, this is an active investigation. Let me do my job, and you go do yours." With that, Dale turned and headed back to his office.

Jackson debated his options, but in the end, he knew what the right thing to do was. The woman he'd gotten to know was not a criminal. She was kind and caring and had been dealt a raw deal in life in so many ways. She'd been abandoned too many times, purposefully or by fate, and Jackson wasn't going to be the next person to just disappear when she needed him the most.

***

He sat on a wooden bench attached to the wall with chains. He held his head in his hands and didn't look up when they approached. Cindy studied the man from her spot outside the cell. There was something about him.

"MacCallum, you've got company," Officer Hansen said before looking at Cindy. "I'll be right at the end of the hall." He gestured toward a chair not far away, and she nodded.

When Mac looked up, Cindy blinked in surprise. "It was you. I saw you. At the theater. You were following us."

"Hello, Cindy."

"That's all you have to say? You've been following me for weeks, broke into my friend's house, searched my car, and all you can say is 'hello'?"

"It's not like that." He sat back against the wall. "You have to believe me."

"Then tell me. You owe me that much."

Mac winced. "It wasn't me. I didn't do those things."

"Sure. You get out of jail—jail! Don't even get me started on that—and find your way to the same town I'm living in, and suddenly someone starts stalking me. Tell me - it's not like what?"

He stood and rushed forward, grabbing the cell bars in front of her so quickly, Cindy took a large step back. Her heart rate accelerated.

"I did follow you here, but I'm not stalking you. I just wanted to see you, get to know you. I was waiting for the right time, but now, all I'm trying to do is protect you."

"What do you mean, 'protect me'?"

"I can't say more right now, but you've got to believe me."

"You used Jackson to get close to me."

"That's not true. I had no idea you knew each other. I had no idea you were living with his sister. Me working with him, it was pure coincidence."

"Oh, really?"

"Yes. But once I knew, then I guess I did use him. But I just wanted to know that you were happy, that you were safe, that you—"

"I know about the missing money. Sheriff Ramírez told me."

Mac scoffed. "He never did believe me when I told him I didn't have it."

"But you did have it, didn't you? Or you knew where it was. I found the key that you left for me with Gloria. It's a bank key. You asked her to keep it safe for you."

He shook his head. "You've got it all wrong."

"Then tell me the truth! What's in the box? Where is the money? Is that why somebody is after me? Do they think I have the key or the money?" She laughed. "If they saw how I live, how I've always had to live, how Mom and I could barely make ends meet, how I had to get a job at the age of thirteen. Thirteen! My childhood ended when you walked out the door, and I had to beg and borrow for everything we had because Gloria spent every dime she made on alcohol. You wrote that you wished you could've seen me on the night of my prom. You know what I did the night of the prom?" Her voice grew loud and shrill. "I served burgers to my classmates when they all stopped by McDonald's after the dance. That's what I did the night of my prom! While Gloria tied on another one, and you sat in prison."

"Cindy, I'm sorry. I—"

"Save it, *Dad.*" The tears were coming on, and she refused to let him see her cry. "You chose that life and those people over us. Well, I guess like father like daughter because now I'm choosing me."

She turned and walked quickly toward Officer Hansen who was standing and ready to react.

"Cindy, wait. Please listen to me."

She stopped, a myriad of retorts coming to mind, but rather than respond, she simply turned toward the staircase and walked away, just as her father did when she was twelve years old.

*****

"Wade, it's Jackson."

"How are things going?"

"I'm not sure. There's a chance Cindy might need a lawyer."

There was no hesitation like with his boss, no moment of silence. "Sure. Let me know if I need to head over."

"Thank you."

"You're welcome. Hang in there."

Jackson breathed a sigh of relief as he disconnected the call. He looked up when he saw movement in the back of the station.

Cindy returned from the holding cell with her head held high, but even with the distance between them, Jackson could see that she held back tears. As though she knew he would still be there, she turned toward him and offered a feeble smile. Jackson prayed that she had forgiven him for not telling her about Mac, that she believed that he hadn't known the man was her father.

Dale met Cindy outside the conference room door and motioned toward Jackson. He saw Cindy nod her head before Dale opened the door and ushered her into the room. He turned toward Jackson and waved his hand for Jackson to join them. Jackson didn't hesitate. He rushed through the desks, past the two uniformed officers, and into the room.

"I'll leave you two alone for a bit," Dale said before he closed the door.

Cindy stood by a chair, and Jackson resisted the urge to go to her and hold her. He wasn't sure where they stood, but he knew how he felt. He'd had plenty of time to think things over in the past twenty-four hours. What a fool he'd been to think that he could leave her.

"Dale said you wanted to talk."

"Are you okay?"

"Hmph. What's okay? I don't know what to think or believe. I don't know if he's lying or telling the truth. I don't know how this is all going to turn out."

"Cindy, for what it's worth, the man I've gotten to know over the past few weeks—"

"What? Is a good guy? Is a caring father? Save it, Jackson. The man is a con, a crook, a criminal. He almost killed a little boy. Did you know that?"

Jackson's mind reeled at the statement. The man he'd worked with had been gentle, kind, wise, courteous, and helpful. He couldn't reconcile that with the vision of a killer.

"Nope, it looks like dear old dad didn't tell you that, did he?"

"He didn't tell me a whole lot about himself. He said he lived in Arizona before coming here."

She laughed. "In a federal penitentiary."

"He said that he had a wife and daughter and that he screwed up and lost them. He told me not to make the same mistakes."

"The wise old sage, huh? Like he's one to give advice."

"Cindy." He drew near her. "I think he meant it. I think he knows he messed up."

"So, what? You're defending him now? You're on his side? He robbed, he shot at someone, he spent years in prison, and the first thing he does when he gets out is follow his own daughter and terrorize her! Do you really think that sounds like a man who is repentant?"

"I don't know. I just don't know. And I don't care. All I care about is you. That you're okay, that you're safe." He reached for her hand, but she moved away. "Cindy, please. Let me help you."

"Nobody can help me, Jackson. I've lived my whole life taking care of myself. I've tried to leave my past behind. I even got engaged and look how that turned out. My mother didn't love me, my father left me, my friends abandoned me, my fiancé died on me. Don't you get it? I'm meant to be alone. I thought you and I...I thought maybe. But it's not going to work. You've got a future in New York, and I've got a father who tries to kill people. I can never be who you want me to be."

"I want you to be you, nobody else. It's you that I want to be with. It's you that I'm…"

He took a step toward her, expecting her to step back, but she remained still. She leveled her gaze on him, her eyes dark and cold, with not even a hint of the smile he'd seen earlier. She was challenging him, and he wondered if she even knew it. Her anger at her father was spilling out onto him, but he would not back down. She was wrong about her ability to overcome her past. She'd already done it.

"When you came here, you were lost and scared and vulnerable. In only a month's time, you've become confident, strong, and brave. I've watched you transform, and I've seen who you are. You say you can't be what I want you to be." He took another step and thought he saw a slight crack in her armor. He watched her swallow. "But you are exactly who I want you to be. You aren't your mother, and you aren't your father." He lowered his voice, and his words became gentle. "You are the woman I'm falling in love with, and that's all I want or need you to be."

Her lips parted, and she gasped a short intake of breath. She blinked, and her eyes glazed over with moisture.

"What about New York?" she whispered.

"I don't know," he said honestly as he took her hand. "I don't know what I want any more, but I do know that I want to be with you. The rest can be worked out."

She gave a small nod. "And my father?"

Jackson shook his head. "Is not our problem." He leaned toward her, his eyes darting from her eyes to her lips and back again.

The door opened behind them, and Cindy jumped.

"Cindy, I've got a list of banks in and near La Mesa. If he doesn't talk, we've got somewhere to start. I can start proceedings to get a warrant. In the meantime, a defense attorney is on the way."

Jackson turned toward Dale. "Can she leave?"

Dale hesitated before nodding. "Don't leave Buffalo Springs. Answer if I call. And be careful. We don't know if he was working alone."

***

Cindy put on her coat, Jackson took her hand, and she let him lead her through the station. A cold, blustery wind whooshed by as they opened the door, making an eerie whistling noise. She shivered, pulling her coat tighter to ward off the chill.

"There's a change in the weather," she said.

"It's blowin' up a storm. I got an alert while I was waiting for you. Supposed to be a blizzard. Are you hungry? We can get food and take it back to Andi's, or we can go to my house."

Cindy realized that she was hungry, practically famished. "I could really go for a pizza right now. I'm starving."

"Pizza it is. I hope you're good with frozen though. La Forna doesn't have pizza."

"That's fine, but let's get to your truck before *we're* frozen."

They hurried down the sidewalk, and Jackson led her to the truck. Once inside, he turned it on and cranked up the heat. They waited, blowing on their hands until they felt the warm air surround them.

The Shop-A-Lot was mobbed, but they managed to find a frozen pepperoni pizza and a few other items Grace asked them to pick up after Jackson called her to see if she needed anything. Luckily, the store had a small section with socks and underwear, and Cindy grabbed a pack of each. They weren't glamourous by any means, but beggars shouldn't be choosers, she supposed. She found a toothbrush and hairbrush and then grabbed some deodorant.

As they checked out, Cindy felt a shiver roll across her shoulders and down her back, and the hair stood on her neck. She straightened and looked around.

"What's wrong?" Jackson asked her.

"I, I don't know. Probably nothing." She tried to shake off the feeling that something was wrong, but as they loaded the groceries into the backseat of the truck, she couldn't help looking over her shoulder and thinking about what Dale said as they left the station. What if her father hadn't been working alone?

"Hey," Jackson said gently, cupping her chin in his hand. "What's wrong?"

"I just have this weird feeling. What if Dale was right? What if there's someone else?"

"Then I'll protect you. I promise." He leaned in and gave her a quick kiss. "I promise," he repeated, and she nodded, wanting to believe him but not sure how he would handle a hardened criminal.

He closed the back door and guided her into her seat, closing the door behind her. She watched him push the cart into the corral and run back to the truck as the first flakes began to fall. For the first time in her life, she found herself praying to a God who, only a couple months ago, she hadn't known existed.

***

Grace Nelson welcomed them with open arms, as Cindy knew she would. Whether she knew about Mac or not, Grace wasn't the kind of person to turn her back on anyone. For that, Cindy was profoundly grateful.

"Come in, come in," she said, taking the groceries from Cindy's hands. "You must be freezing. Go, sit by the fire. Jackson and I will take care of these."

Cindy took off her coat and hung it in the closet as she had seen Grace do before and joined Joshua in the living room.

"Hey, Mr. Nelson. What are you watching?"

"The history channel. No more bowl games to watch, and I like the history shows."

"I do, too," she said though she hadn't seen many, if any at all. "I like history. I like learning."

"I can see that. You're a reader like Helena. She's always learning something new. Loves reading and research. I think that's why she became a librarian."

"Did you encourage them to learn and study history when they were growing up?"

"I did. Never went to college myself, but I wanted my kids to be well educated. I guess my love of history, especially anything military related, rubbed off on Andi the most."

"Did you serve?"

"I did. Navy. It was hard on Grace once Andi was born though, with me being at sea all the time. When she was pregnant with Helena, I put in for my discharge."

"How long were you in?"

"Almost ten years. Joined right out of high school. Grace was a lot younger, so she was still in school then. She was my sister's best friend, you know."

Cindy smiled. "I didn't know that. So, you met through your sister?" How ironic, she thought.

"Sure did. I was already in the Navy when they became friends. My sister kept writing to me about this friend of hers, but I hardly remembered her. I never paid much attention to her friends. They were just kids to me. Then I came home one weekend, and Grace was at the house. They were seniors in high school by then. The three of us spent the whole weekend together, and by the end of the weekend, I had Grace's address. We wrote letters for months, and then on one of my weekends home, we got married."

"Did you elope?" She was fascinated by his story, but more so by the look on his face as he told it. She saw so much of Jackson in him, and Joshua's expression was the exact same one Jackson had worn when he told her he would protect her.

"Nah, but when I left her that first weekend I was home on leave, I knew. I never wanted to be away from her again. It was agony, those months before I returned home on my next extended weekend. I asked her then to marry me, then she and her Mama spent the next several months planning the wedding. They wanted a church wedding, but I wasn't much on religion. I just wanted to marry her."

"Wow. You didn't waste any time."

"No need to. When you know, you know."

She felt Jackson's eyes on her and turned toward the hall. He was leaning against the doorjamb, his arms crossed in front of him, gazing at her with the most beautiful expression, and she felt warmth course through her entire body and settle in the pit of her stomach.

"The pizza's cooking, and it looks like you might be stuck here." He nodded toward the front windows.

Cindy turned and gasped. The few flakes that fluttered through the air on their drive to the house had turned into sheets of falling snow. She could barely make out the front yard. Like a child, enchanted by the sight, she turned on the couch and knelt, her face pressed to the glass.

"It's so pretty. I've never seen anything like it." A sudden thought occurred to her. "What about Christmas? It will be ruined."

She felt the cushion sink as Jackson joined her. "You can't ruin Christmas. It's not a day or an event. It's more than that."

"But I thought…"

"Christmas Day was chosen as a day to celebrate the birth of Christ, but it's the birth itself and everything that surrounds it that matters. We'll celebrate Christmas whether we're snowed in or not. We don't need all the commercial stuff that goes with it—the food, the presents, the wrappings and bows, or a big gathering."

"But we'll have all those," Joshua chimed in. "Your mother has been working overtime since she heard the forecast."

Jackson laughed. "Why am I not surprised?"

He put his arm around Cindy and pulled her close to him, and she instinctively laid her head on his shoulder. They watched the snow, breathing in time with one another, and she allowed herself to forget about everything that was happening outside of the cozy house with the warm fire and the aroma of pizza filling the air.

They might have stayed there for minutes or hours. She didn't know and didn't care. Nothing felt more right than to be watching the falling snow with Jackson's arm around her, their breath fogging the windowpane.

"You kids ready to eat?" Grace called from the kitchen, and Cindy thought the mood would be broken, but when Jackson took her hand and led her down the hall, she held on tight—to his hand and to the feeling that she belonged with him, with this family, to this life that she held onto so tentatively.

***

It was well past dark, but the orange glow lit the room, keeping it toasty while the blanket of white piled up outside the door.

Grace and Joshua had gone to bed, and Cindy and Jackson sat on the rug in front of the fire. Cindy leaned back on him, and Jackson kept his arms wrapped securely around her, his cheek pressed to her strawberry-scented hair.

They had a lot to work out, a lot to discuss, but for tonight, Jackson only wanted to concentrate on this, on them, on the way it felt to finally hold her like he'd wanted to for so long. They might not be dancing, but his heart beat to a steady cadence, his arms held her tight, and the rhythm of their breathing filled the night with sweet song.

"I wish we could stay like this forever," he whispered into her hair. He felt her cheeks expand into a smile, and he couldn't wait a moment longer.

He gently shifted and turned her so that their faces were close. "I meant what I said earlier. I'm falling in love with you."

She didn't answer, but her eyes danced, and the firelight lit her face, turning her expression into something ethereal. She looked at his mouth, and he was gone.

When their lips met, he thought his chest would explode. Not mere butterflies, but a whole flock of birds took wing in his gut. He wanted to spend the entire night kissing her. He felt her fingers brush the side of his face, and his kiss grew deeper.

He had no idea how long they kissed, but eventually he pulled back and looked longingly into her eyes. "I think we'd better call it a night."

She pressed her lips together in a tight smile and nodded. "I think you're right." But neither of them moved.

Finally, Jackson pressed one more soft kiss onto her mouth and took her hands, pulling her up as he stood.

"Mama raised me to be a gentleman, so I'm going to say goodnight here and let you go get yourself ready for bed. Do you need anything?"

She shook her head. "I think we got everything I might need at the store." She looked down at the sweatshirt. "Maybe something to sleep in though."

Even in the dim light, he could see her blush.

"Knowing Mama, that's already been taken care of. In the morning, I'll give you a clean shirt to wear. I'm sure Mama left a towel in your room, so you can go ahead and shower when you get up if you want. Or now if you prefer."

"Tomorrow is fine. Thank you, Jackson. For everything. And about today, I'm sorry for—"

He laid a finger on her mouth and shook his head. "No need. Christmas is a time for new beginnings and forgiveness." He gently ran his finger across her bottom lip and gave her another quick kiss. "Good night."

"Good night, Jackson."

She let go of his hands, and he watched her go to the staircase, turn back and smile, and then ascend the steps like an angel, leaving his heart leaping for joy.

Fifteen

"Oh, no you don't!" Cindy grabbed a handful of snow and balled it up, pressing the snow together until it was nice and hard. Then she flung the snowball as hard as she could toward Jackson who easily deflected it with his hand before throwing another ball her way.

Cindy had never seen anything like the wonderland she now stood in. It had snowed for sixteen hours straight, and everything was blanketed in white as far as the eye could see. Even the trees were covered with fluffy white mounds that, every time the wind blew, made it seem like it was snowing again. Her gloved fingers were wet and numb, her cheeks felt like ice, and she wasn't sure she still had toes on her feet, but for the first time in her entire life, she actually felt like a carefree little kid. Her only lament was that this feeling had come about twenty years too late.

She ducked behind a wall of snow as another snowball was hurled in her direction. She patted together another weapon and stood, ready to lob it at Jackson, but he was nowhere in sight. She craned her neck, but she couldn't see him. Just as she was about to go looking for him, two strong arms grabbed her from behind and pulled her down into the snow.

"Ambush!" Jackson yelled, and they tumbled into the thick white mattress of white.

"No fair," she protested, looking up into his soft, brown eyes.

The war game forgotten, Cindy let the victor claim the spoils and wrapped her arms around him as his lips met hers. When Jackson pulled back and looked at her, she no longer felt like a child. She reached and stroked his face, and he quickly withdrew, but laughed.

"That's freezing!" He stood and pulled her up. "Your gloves are soaked. Let's go inside and warm up." He took her hand and led her into the house.

When they walked into the back door to the kitchen, the aroma of chocolate filled her senses.

"It's about time," Grace scolded, but she smiled at her son. "I guess you never outgrow some things." She looked at Cindy. "I never could get Jackson to come in out of the snow when he was a little boy."

Jackson walked to the stove and inhaled deeply over the saucepan simmering on the burner. "But your homemade hot chocolate was always the best enticement."

Grace looked out the window. "I can't believe we're going to have a real white Christmas. I think we should watch that movie later. How 'bout it, Jackson?"

"That's a great idea, Mama."

"I don't think I've ever seen it," Cindy said. "Just bits and pieces."

Grace laid her hand on her heart. "Oh, saints preserve us. We can't let that go on for one more day. After lunch, we turn it on."

Jackson made each of them a mug and reached into the fridge for the Reddi-Whip they'd gotten at the store.

"I wondered what she wanted that for," Cindy said as she watched him top off the drinks with a mountain of whipped cream.

"You can't have hot chocolate without whipped cream."

As Cindy took her first sip, Grace asked, "Is this your phone on the counter, Cindy? You have a call coming in."

Cindy reached out her hand and took the phone. The number was local, and she slid her finger across the screen and answered as Grace slipped out of the room.

"Cindy, this is Dale." While he spoke, she put the phone on speaker and took a seat at the table. Jackson joined her. "I just wanted to let you know that your father is out. His attorney showed up and said we had no grounds to hold him."

"But what about the break-ins?"

"He's adamant that it wasn't him, and we've got no evidence to the contrary."

Jackson spoke up. "Hey, Dale, you're on speaker. If it wasn't him, why'd he turn himself in?"

"I can't really tell you. When he came, he said he wanted to turn himself in so that you were no longer in danger, but then he clammed up as soon as I showed him the key. That's all I know."

"Where is he now?" Cindy asked.

"Back at the campground, I guess. I told him he wasn't allowed to leave the area. Just in case. Eric did dust for prints on your car and again at the house, but it might take a while to get a hit. It's not like on TV. We had to send them to the experts at the state level, and it will take them a while to actually match them, and it's Christmas. It'll take several hours, best case scenario, before we have any information, but we probably won't know until after the holiday. There's one thing we do know. Your father's prints are not a match to any we found in the house the first time."

"None?" She wasn't sure if she was relieved or even more concerned.

"None. But that doesn't mean he wasn't involved," Dale was quick to point out. "He could've hired someone or been working with somebody. We just don't know at this point."

"Okay, thanks for the info, Dale."

Jackson spoke again. "Listen, you said that Mac told you he was turning himself in to protect Cindy. Did he say from whom?"

"Nope. If there's someone else we should be looking for, he's not saying. I urged his attorney to convince him to work with us, but so far, I haven't heard anything. I'll let Cindy know if I do."

"Okay, thanks," Jackson said.

"Thanks, Dale. I appreciate you calling."

"No problem, Cindy. Be careful. And merry Christmas."

"Thanks, Dale. Now get home to those kids. Have a merry Christmas yourselves."

They said goodbye, and Cindy took a drink of the now lukewarm chocolate. She drummed her fingers on the table.

"What are you thinking?"

"About something my dad said," Cindy told him. She looked up and frowned. "He was so insistent that he followed me here to get to know me and now wants to protect me. When I brought up the money, he told me I had it all wrong."

"And you believe him." It wasn't a question.

"I," she sighed. "I think so." She shook her head. "I don't want to. Or maybe I do want to, and I shouldn't. I don't know. It's just that… the man who wrote me those letters, the one who said how sorry he was, the man who begged me to believe him last night, that's not the man I remember, and it doesn't sound like the man the newspapers described."

"Mac told me once that when he found God, it changed him."

Cindy sat back in her chair. "You know, the sheriff said that he got time off for good behavior and that he'd 'found God'." She used air quotes. "Sheriff Ramírez said that his attorney argued that he was a changed man."

"Maybe he is."

"But what about the money?"

Jackson puffed his cheeks and blew as he sat back. "Maybe he's not lying. Maybe he doesn't know where it is. Maybe, like you, somebody else thinks he does or thinks he told you in one of those letters."

"But if he doesn't know, why won't he just tell Dale that?"

"Maybe he just thinks nobody will believe him."

She looked at Jackson, her heart filled with pain and her mind with uncertainty. "What do I do?"

"I wish I knew."

"Well, that makes two of us."

***

Jackson was surprised to hear the front door open. He reached for the remote and pushed pause on the Bing Crosby classic just as Boomer rushed into the room followed by Wade and Andi. Boomer ran straight to Cindy as though he'd known she'd be there.

"It's freezing out there," Andi said, unwrapping her scarf. She looked at Jackson and Cindy sitting snugly together on the couch and arched one brow. Cindy leaned up and scratched Boomer behind the ear. "You two look cozy."

Jackson picked up a pillow and threw it at his sister who ducked and laughed.

"Hey, watch it," Wade said. "She's carrying precious cargo." He took off his coat and helped Andi with hers.

Andi elbowed Wade and made a shushing sound as she stooped down, picked up the pillow, and threw it back at her brother.

"I meant the presents," he said, pointing to the bags she held in her hand.

"Andi, Wade, you made it." Grace walked into the room, wiping her hands on her apron. The aroma of baking cookies seemed to follow her into the room. "I was just taking a break from the movie to bake one last batch of Christmas cookies."

"We made it," Andi said, giving her mother a hug. "I'll help you in the kitchen. Wade wants to talk to Jackson about something."

"No trouble making it down your driveway?"

"Mama, we live on a farm. Wade has a tractor. It wasn't that hard."

"Says the woman who watched from the window."

Andi playfully punched Wade in the arm.

"Is this about Cindy?" Jackson asked.

"Nope, it's about me and you," Wade said. "Do you mind if we talk?"

Jackson had no idea what this could be about. He untangled his arm from Cindy's back and stood. "Where do you want to talk?"

"Ma, is the dining room okay?" Wade asked his mother-in-law.

"Of course. Cindy and I already set it for dinner, though, so don't mess anything up."

Jackson followed Wade down the hall and took a seat at the table. Probably sensing that food might be involved, Boomer followed.

"What's up?"

"Jackson," Grace called. "Be sure to offer Wade a drink."

"Drink?" Jackson asked with a grin.

Wade returned the smile and shook his head. "Thanks, Ma. Not yet," Wade called as he sat down opposite Jackson. "I've made a decision about some things."

"Okay…" Jackson dragged out the word, unsure as to what Wade's decisions had to do with him.

"I hate my job."

Jackson laughed. "Don't we all."

"No, I mean it. I've hated it since the day I took office. When Andi came to town, and we started working on the revitalization, things got better, but the more we worked on bringing business to the town, the more I missed what I used to do."

"Mergers and acquisitions."

"Yes, that and all the law that went with it. I miss what I did in New York, but I don't miss working seventy to eighty hours a week, the shady deals, or the cut-throat backroom stuff. I miss using my degree, making deals, and helping create empires. Not that I'd go back to all the wheeling and dealing between giant corporate conglomerates and stabbing people in the back."

Jackson still had a hard time seeing Wade as the ruthless M&A attorney he supposedly was, but he guessed that anytime you were making multi-billion-dollar deals, it was hard to stay grounded. Was Wade really looking to go back to that world?

"So, what are you saying? Are you and Andi moving to New York?"

Wade let out a harsh laugh. "Heck no. Just the opposite. With all the growth here and in neighboring counties, there's a lot I could do with my knowledge. I've been looking into hanging out my shingle. I'd practice small-town law, which Buffalo Springs desperately needs, but I'd also deal in business law. Eventually, I'd like to bring in an attorney who could do the routine stuff, and I'd concentrate on brokering deals between businesses. I look at all the potential around here and think, why should New York have the monopoly on mergers and acquisitions?"

"Okay, that all makes sense. What does it have to do with me?"

"I'd like to add another component to the business. I'd like to not only broker the deals but be part of them. I'd like to open an investment firm, find businesses around here that are for sale, and either be part of the sale or buy the business myself, build it up, make it viable, and then resell it. It's not really all that different from what I did with the mergers and acquisitions I handled. Only this time, I'd be buying some of the businesses for myself."

Jackson was beginning to see where this was headed. "Wade, if you're offering me what I think, how can I do what you need me to do without any experience? I've got the education but none of the hands-on. I never even did an internship. I've only overseen the piling of one bag of manure on top of another in the back of a pickup truck."

"I know what you mean, and that's an issue, but I think I've got a solution. I've got a lead on an internship at a New York investment bank with an office in Little Rock. If you're willing to make the hour drive every day and do the internship for a year, which by the way will pay substantially less than that offer you're waiting for in New York, I'll hire you at a competitive salary to work for me right here in Buffalo Springs. It won't be the same as getting the New York experience, but there will be times when you'd be able to tag along with another banker when he or she goes up there."

Jackson could hardly believe what he was hearing. "You mean, I could do real estate investing from right here?"

"At the end of a year."

"Understood."

"And I have to make sure the internship is still open, and you'll have to apply."

"Sure. No problem. I'm ready to apply as soon as you give the go ahead."

Wade reached his hand across the table. "Then we have a deal. Welcome to the world of real estate investing and corporate law."

As Jackson walked down the hall, he felt as though the weight of the world had been lifted from his shoulders. He could feel his cheeks growing wider and wider as his smile expanded.

"Well, you look happy," Cindy said when he sat beside her on the couch. Andi was in a nearby chair, and Grace was on the other end of the sofa with her crochet needle moving faster than a hummingbird.

"Jackson and I are going to open our own business," Wade said. He stood by Andi's chair, and she beamed up at him, taking hold of his hand.

"What?" Grace exclaimed. "What kind of business?"

"A mixture of sorts. Law, finance, and investing. A little of what I did in New York along with the stuff Jackson studied in school."

"Where?" Joshua asked. "Are y'all moving to the city?"

Wade shook his head. "Nope, we're staying right here in Buffalo Springs. My wife won't have it any other way."

"I guess I can call North American Bank on Monday and cancel my second interview," Jackson said, still reeling in a cloud of disbelief.

"Jackson, do we still have that other bottle of champagne left over from your graduation?"

"I believe we do, Mama."

The timer sounded again.

"I'll get that," Grace said, laying aside her yarn. "I'll be right back with the champagne and a plate of cookies."

"Because every glass of champagne should be served with fresh baked cookies," Jackson said.

"Mama—"

"I've got it, Andi. You stay put."

Jackson looked at Cindy. "This Christmas just got even better."

***

"Cindy, it's Dale."

Cindy excused herself and slipped upstairs to the guest room. "Hi, Dale. What's up?" She started to close the door only to find Boomer trailing behind her. She let him in and shut the door as Dale filled her in.

"He's ready to talk, but he says he'll only talk if you're there."

"Why? What difference does it make?"

"I don't know, but his attorney says that's the only way it's going to happen, and to be honest with you, they hold all the cards. We don't have anything on him, so either he talks, or we keep moving blindly ahead."

She sat on the bed and took a deep breath, twirling a strand of her hair. "I guess I don't have a choice, do I?"

"Sure, you do. You don't have to do anything you don't want to do."

"But there may still be someone out there trying to get to me."

"Yes. Do you want me to send a car?"

"No, Jackson can drive me in the truck. Can I bring Wade?"

"You don't need to. You're not the one who needs an attorney, but it's up to you."

They agreed on the time, and she disconnected. She sat on the bed for a few minutes more, stroking the soft golden fur of the dog who had curled up beside her. She went back downstairs, and all eyes turned her way when she stood in the doorway.

"He wants to talk, but only if I'm there. That's his term."

"No way," Jackson said. "You told him no way, right?"

"Jackson, I don't know what he has to say or why he insists I be there, but if I want this to end, I don't think I have a choice. I told him you'd drive me." She looked at Wade. "Can you go with us? Dale said it was okay."

"Sure." Wade put down his glass. "We'll have to continue the celebration another time."

"Good thing we only had that one toast," Jackson said, placing his glass on the table. "Let's go see what he has to say."

"You'll be back in time for dinner, won't you?" Andi asked.

Wade kissed Andi goodbye, "Yes. I promise. Don't worry."

Cindy noticed an odd look pass between them and wondered what was going on. Was something wrong?

"Dinner will be ready when you get back," Grace assured them.

"Where's Helena?" Cindy asked as they put on their coats.

"We dropped her off at Joe's," Andi said. "He's hosting Christmas dinner tomorrow, so they're working on some of that today."

"I'll call and let them know what's going on," Grace said. "I'll tell them not to rush over. I'm sure they're enjoying the time with Joe's family. Y'all get going and let me know when you're on your way back."

"What about church, Mama?" Jackson asked. "Are we going to try to get there?"

"If you all can get to the police station, we can get to Christmas Mass."

***

They rode in silence with Cindy sandwiched between Jackson and Wade. Main Street had been plowed, and the side streets were being worked on. Jackson drove past the parking lot where enough spots had been cleared for a few cars. Walls of snow stood all around the lot. He dropped Cindy and Wade at the front door of the station and went back to the lot to park.

Cindy could see her father through the glass windows of the conference room. A man she assumed was his attorney sat beside him.

"Can we wait for Jackson?" she asked Wade, suddenly unsure of her decision to meet with her father and feeling the need to have Jackson by her side.

"Sure. You wait here. I'll let Dale know you're coming."

He walked through the station, saying hello to the other officers as he went. It sounded odd to hear them greet him as 'Mayor Montgomery' when she'd only heard the Nelsons and Trudy refer to him as Wade.

The door opened, and the wind and cold accompanied Jackson inside. He took her hand, and they made their way to the conference room. After they entered, Dale closed the door and the blinds, and they faced Reginald David MacCallum.

"Hello, Cindy. Jackson." Mac nodded his head but didn't get up.

Jackson nodded. "Mac."

His gaze fell to their interlocked hands, and a small smile formed on his face. He looked at Cindy and nodded as if he approved. The gesture confused her. Did she want him to approve of her choices?

"Take a seat, y'all, and we'll get started." Dale pulled out a chair for Cindy, and she sat down. She kept a tight grip on Jackson's hand until he released her and laid his arm protectively on the back of her chair.

"Mr. MacCallum, I understand you'd like to make a statement. With your permission, I'd like to record this conversation."

Her father's attorney nodded, and Dale pressed the record button on his phone.

"Statement of Reginald MacCallum, December 24, 3 p.m." Dale said. "Go ahead."

"First," He turned to Cindy. "Cindy, baby, I'm sorry. I'm so sorry that you got dragged into this. You gotta believe me. I never wanted you to be in danger."

Cindy just sat there and looked at him. What was she supposed to say?

Mac shifted his gaze back to Dale. "Okay, the key. It's not what you think." He looked back at Cindy. "Baby, do you remember when you were little, maybe eight or nine, I took you to the bank with me?"

Cindy shook her head. She didn't remember ever going anywhere with her father. She reached up and rubbed her temple. A headache was coming on, and she wanted this to be over. She listened as her father continued to speak.

"We got a box, you and me. We put your grandmother's jewelry in it—her wedding and engagement rings, her sapphire necklace, and the pearls her daddy gave her when she got married. You used to love to look at her pearls."

A vague memory came back. Cindy was eight, maybe nine, and she was sitting at the old metal and glass dressing table her mother had. Cindy was looking in the mirror, her lips plastered with lipstick, and she was wearing something… pearls maybe? Gloria came into the room, found Cindy playing with her makeup and jewelry, and went berserk. Cindy remembered her yelling and screaming and telling Cindy to never touch her things again.

"I, I think I remember the pearls. They were Gloria's…"

Mac shook his head. "No, they weren't. I took those and some other special pieces from my mother's house the day of her funeral. I put them away for you, but Gloria found them. She was furious that I'd kept them from her. The next time she went out, I took them, all my mother's jewelry, and I took you, and we went to the bank to get a safety deposit box for them. I asked my lawyer to send the key to you on your twenty-first birthday. I didn't want to say what it was for in case Gloria got a hold of it. I guess it was stupid of me to think that you'd remember that. You were so little."

"You, you saved them for me? You didn't try to sell them or—"

"They belonged to my mother. I wanted you to have them." His face and his tone were full of pain, and Cindy believed him.

"Mac," Dale broke in. "Do you remember which bank they're in? Could you give us permission to have the box opened and checked to see if that is what's in there?"

Mac nodded. "Yes, of course. I want you to have them." His eyes implored her to listen, to understand, to believe.

"What about the money, Mac? Where is it?" Dale asked.

Mac looked down at his hands, interlaced in front of him on the table. He shook his head and looked up at Dale. "I don't know. Honestly, I don't know. Gloria is the only one who knew."

Cindy gasped. "Mom? She knew about the money? All those years that we lived in squalor and I had to work every hour I wasn't in school to buy food and pay the bills, and she had all that money?" Cindy was suddenly struck by what she had said. She looked at Dale. "Not that I'd have wanted stolen money, but it makes no sense."

"She knew. After the kid, well, after what happened on that last job with the little boy, I wanted out, but I knew it was too late. I knew we were done. I knew we'd never get away with it. Taking money was one thing. Taking lives was another." He looked away and let out a long sigh. "I gave my take to Gloria and told her everything. I told her I was leaving and that she needed to turn it in." He looked at Dale. "I woulda turned it in myself, woulda turned myself in, but I was a coward. I was a yellow-bellied coward who ran instead of doing the right thing for once in my life. It wasn't until after I was arrested that I realized she hadn't turned it in, but what could I do? I couldn't tell them. They'd arrest Gloria, and even though I didn't care anymore what happened to her…" He looked at Cindy. "She was all you had."

"So you lied. Told the police you didn't know where it was," Dale said.

"I wasn't exactly lying. By that time, I didn't know. The cops searched the house. They didn't find it. I didn't know what Gloria did with it, still don't."

"Mac, who else might know that Gloria had the money? Who might think Cindy knows where it is?"

"Beats me. As far as I know, I'm the only one who got out."

"I have to ask you something," Cindy said, trying to control her voice and her emotions. "That little boy…did you shoot him?"

Mac hung his head, and she saw a tear fall from the bridge of his nose. "No," he said quietly. "I've never shot anyone." He raised his eyes to hers. "I was a bad guy. I did some bad things. I robbed, and I lied, and I cheated, and I know I hurt you and your mom, but I never, ever shot anyone."

"Then why didn't you tell the police or the judge who did?"

"There were three of us. We all had guns, but we didn't keep them with us. After each job, we put them in a bag and buried them in Roger's back yard until the next job. We never bothered checking to see which gun we had, so there was no way to know which one of us held the gun that fired the shot, and all our prints were on all of 'em. One of them knows, whichever one did it, but I don't know, and whoever did it ain't saying."

Dale sat back and puffed out his cheeks, blowing air across the table. Cindy got a small whiff of stale coffee.

"Is there anything else you need to know?" her father's attorney asked.

"I don't think so. Unless…" He leaned across the table and looked Mac square in the eye. "Mac, someone is after your daughter. They've broken into the house where she's living twice and into her car. By the looks of the last break-in, they're getting desperate. Cindy may be in grave danger. Is there anything, anything at all you've left out? Is there anyone you can think of who might be doing this? Please, Mac, you've got to tell us."

Cindy's father turned to her and held her gaze. "If I knew anything, if there was anyone I thought might be trying to hurt you, I'd say so. I love you, Cindy. No matter what I've done, that has never changed."

***

Jackson felt useless during the entire exchange. He could see and hear the pain Cindy was suffering, but he could do nothing to make it better. He knew she wanted to believe Mac, but their history was sordid, and he'd never really been there for her. A stack of letters doesn't make a father.

He thought about the time his father taught him to play catch, the jokes his father used to make at the dinner table when they were kids, his patience when he taught each of them to ride a bike or bait a line or cast a fly just so across the river. As far as Jackson knew, Mac had never done any of those things. From what he'd gleaned from Cindy, Mac had been borderline abusive physically, and outright abusive verbally and emotionally. He had no idea what it meant to be a father.

On the other hand, Jackson had gotten to know a different side of Mac. Though the man sitting across from them looked different without his trademark lambskin-lined denim coat, his calm, quiet demeanor and expression were the same. He looked at Cindy with the same regret Jackson had seen in his eyes and spoke with the same longing in his voice. Mac wanted to make amends, Jackson thought, he just didn't know how.

Once Mac signed a release for the safety deposit box, Dale told him he could leave. Dale thanked Cindy for meeting them and told her he'd let her know what they found in the box. They thanked Dale, put on their coats, and walked through the station in silence.

Jackson, Cindy, and Wade climbed into the truck. Once Jackson was settled in the driver's seat, and the heat began to blow, Cindy turned to him.

"You believe him, don't you?"

"I do. The question is, do you?"

She bit her lips together and inhaled through her nose, releasing the air in a long, slow stream. "I don't know. I want to, which in itself is, I think, a big step. It's just that…" She looked down at her hands and shook her head. "He hurt us. Over and over again, he hurt us. Not so much with bruises, though there was some of that, but with words and actions. And then he did this horrible thing and left us to deal with the consequences. I mean, even before he was arrested, he left. He admitted that today. He just left. Gloria was no saint, believe me. But how much of the way she treated me was because of him?"

"Cindy," Wade said quietly. "Whether you forgive him or not is up to you but take it from someone who knows. We all do things we regret and must atone for. Everyone deserves a chance to make things right."

"Thank you, Wade. I'll think about that."

Jackson hoped she remembered what he said the night before. *Christmas is a time for forgiveness.*

***

Cindy was so full, she thought she might burst. Grace's Christmas Eve dinner consisted of both ham and turkey, cornbread, browned-butter green beans, deviled eggs, collard greens, candied yams, oyster dressing, black-eyed peas, and was topped off with bread pudding, rum balls, and pecan pie. It was the largest feast Cindy had ever seen by far.

"Great meal, Mama," Andi said.

"I'll second that," Joe's father, Henry Blake said, raising his glass. "To the chef."

Everyone echoed his sentiments, and Grace flushed with embarrassment. "Oh, come now, it's just a meal."

"Wait until you all see what Joe has prepared for tomorrow," Helena said. "We won't need to eat again until Easter."

"Speak for yourself," Andi said. "I'm going to be doing a lot of eating for the next eight months or so." She looked around the table expectantly.

A silence fell over the room before everyone exploded with excitement. Cindy looked at Grace who sat quietly with a look of sheer joy on her face.

"You knew," Cindy whispered.

Grace shook her head. "I suspected. Andi wouldn't admit anything though."

Cindy looked around the table. Parents, grandparents, and siblings, all growing up together. What a wonderful life they all must have had.

"I'm not sure any of our presents can top that one," Helena said.

"You might be right, pumpkin," her father said with a wide grin. "But speaking of which… Grace? The night's not getting any younger, and we'll need to get to the church by 11:15 if we want to get seats for Midnight Mass."

"Well, I guess it's present time then," Grace said with a smile.

"Presents tonight?" Cindy asked.

"It's a tradition we started when the kids were little," Grace told her as she began clearing dishes. "Family presents on Christmas Eve and Santa presents on Christmas morning."

Cindy kept her jaw from dropping at the thought of presents from family *and* from Santa. She rarely had one or the other.

Thirty minutes later, Cindy sat back on the couch in the crowded living room, content to watch everyone else open their gifts and was surprised when a perfectly wrapped present landed in her lap. By the time all the gifts were handed out, Cindy had nearly as many as everyone else. She fought back tears as the thought hit her that she'd never gotten this many gifts in a lifetime of Christmases.

"Who's first?" Andi asked.

"Same rule as always," Grace said. "Youngest first."

All eyes turned to Cindy, and she felt the heat in her cheeks and the tears in her eyes. "No," she said quietly. "It's your family celebration. One of you should go first."

"You're the youngest," Jackson said. "I'm almost two years older, I believe. That means you go first, or you'll be breaking the family tradition."

She looked at the gifts that surrounded her. "Well…" She sucked in a breath and let it out. "Which one should I open first?"

"Open mine," Helena said. "It's the one with the blue ribbon."

Cindy dug through the gifts until she found the right one. With all eyes on her, she tugged at the ribbon and then carefully pried open the paper.

"Oh, come on!" Jackson said with exaggerated annoyance. "We'll be here all night. Just rip it open."

She looked at him with wide eyes. "It's too pretty to rip." But she smiled as she worked the paper open with a quick motion to reveal a leather-bound copy of *Anne of Green Gables*. "Oh, Helena." She fought even harder to hold back the tears. "It's my favorite."

"And now you have a copy of your very own."

Cindy had told Helena that she loved the series so much, she'd contemplated stealing it from her elementary school library. Instead, she just checked out each book over and over, reading and rereading the series until she moved on to middle school. Her mother believed that books were a waste of time and money and never bought any. This was the very first brand-new book she had ever owned—not the library's, not Evan's, and not a hand-me-down from someone else or from the Good Will.

"You have no idea what this means to me." It didn't matter what else was inside the other boxes. This was a gift Cindy would cherish for the rest of her life.

***

With the strong possibility that parking would be limited, if the lot was even clear, they decided to walk to Mass. After checking with the rectory, they were assured that even a blizzard couldn't prevent Midnight Mass, so they all bundled up and began the long, cold walk to the church. Joshua insisted on joining them, so Wade left early so that Joshua, Grace, and Joe's parents could be dropped off at the door. If need be, Wade would take the truck back to the house and meet everyone at the church.

While Cindy and Andi chatted about Andi's pregnancy, Jackson took the opportunity to whisper to Helena, "Hey, that book, it's a children's book, right? You had it when you were a kid."

Helena looked at him for a moment, her eyebrows knitting together in confusion before her mouth formed a round O. "The one I gave Cindy? Well, technically it was written for children, but by today's standard, it hardly ranks as a child's book. Children today wouldn't make it through the first chapter on their own without putting it down for something more exciting with fewer words and more pictures."

"But why that book? For Cindy, I mean?"

Helena relayed to Jackson the conversation she and Cindy had one evening while searching for something on TV. They were both delighted to come across the Megan Follows classic rendition of the beloved orphan.

Jackson listened intently, recalling Cindy's stories about her childhood. "I'd like to give her what she's been missing all these years. That is, if I can."

Helena looked at her brother with love and admiration. "I think you might be just the right person to do that, little brother."

Jackson glanced at Cindy, noticing the big smile on her face, and made a Christmas wish that she would never be sad again.

The steeple loomed in front of them, and light poured forth from the little brick church. Grace and Joshua waited just inside, and Jackson followed his family up the aisle. He couldn't take his eyes off Cindy as she looked around the church, clearly captivated by the nativity scene, the glowing candles, and the festive flowers and greenery that decorated the sanctuary around the altar. They held hands during Mass, and Jackson prayed that this nightmare she was trapped in would be over soon. He added a prayer that she and Mac would find a way to start over. After all, it was the season for miracles.

***

Cindy had heard many things about Christians, particularly Catholics, and she'd never known what was true and what was fabricated. As she sat and listened to the readings, the speech the priest gave—she was told later it is called a homily—and the songs, she felt a contentment that she had never known. The prayers were comforting, and the soft glow of the candles reflected in the beautiful windows brought peace to her whole being.

On the walk back to the house where Andi, Wade, and Joe and his family would depart until the following day, she asked Jackson, "All that stuff about Christ being born to a virgin and being God's own son sent to die for our sins, that's really for real? I mean, it's not just some made up mythology?"

"It would be more than strange, more than two-thousand years later, to find people still believing and spreading something that's only a myth, don't you think? I mean, after Jesus died, the Romans wanted to kill all the disciples and put down what they saw as a dangerous rebellion. They decided not to because they knew that the legend of Jesus would die on its own. Yet here we are, all these years later."

"In my house, Christmas was all about buying expensive liquor at holiday prices." She gestured toward a house wrapped in lights. "We never did that. We never sang Christmas carols. We never had a dinner like your family had tonight. The holiday came and went, and if I was lucky, I might open a box with a doll or something bought from a thrift shop. That stopped when I was, oh, maybe about ten."

Jackson turned to her, surprise showing in his wide eyes and open mouth. "You haven't gotten a Christmas present since you were ten?"

She smiled faintly, trying her hardest to hold back tears, and reached for the heart-shaped pendant she wore around her neck before remembering that it was no longer there. She had removed it that evening when she dressed for Mass, right after Jackson fastened a bracelet on her wrist under the Christmas tree. She had no idea when he found the time to buy the silver band adorned with two entwined, gem-outlined hearts, but she loved this simple reminder of their growing feelings for each other. When she removed the necklace, she waited for the sadness to hit her, the melancholy that always came with thoughts of Evan and their lost love, but it didn't come. She realized then that she hadn't thought about Evan much at all lately.

"That necklace I have," she said quietly, "the one with the heart pendant, Evan gave it to me our first Christmas together. We weren't supposed to be buying presents at all." She shrugged. "I was used to that, so I didn't really think anything of it when he made the suggestion. I didn't buy him a thing, but on Christmas morning, he handed me a little box wrapped in gold paper with a red ribbon around it. I remember I was shaking so hard, I could hardly open it. He wiped my tears as I opened the box, and he said, 'No matter where

I am in this world or the next, you will always have my heart.' I never took it off until tonight."

She saw the look of surprise on his face as he glanced at the spot where the pendant normally lay.

"I'm sorry about Evan. I don't know if I've ever told you that. Andi said he was a great guy."

She smiled. "He was."

"Jackson," she whispered. "Thanks for making my heart whole again."

Jackson brought her gloved hand to his lips and kissed the back of it. She felt the bracelet slide up her wrist.

"Thanks for letting me," he whispered back.

Cindy held back a sigh of contentment but grinned the entire walk back to the house.

Sixteen

It was the Wednesday after Christmas, and Cindy was just wrapping up a consultation with a client in Eureka Springs. She clipped her phone onto the mount on her dashboard and pulled out onto the main road. She turned up the radio and tapped her fingers on the steering wheel. The local stations mostly played country music and were back to their regular non-Christmas playlist, and Cindy found that she liked the genre more than she thought she could, especially the older songs, which surprised her to no end. She listened to George Straight singing about his exes in Texas and laughed at the lyrics, so different from the songs she used to listen to.

She sang along with the songs she knew, but her thoughts were mostly on the package she was waiting on. Her grandmother's wedding and engagement rings, a necklace with a blue sapphire pendant, and the string of pearls had been retrieved from the safety deposit box, and at Mac's instructions, were being FedExed to her. Like he told them, there was nothing else in the box, which she learned was a small and inexpensive box right in the Bank of America in La Mesa. As much as she wanted her grandmother's jewelry, nothing could compare to the bracelet dangling from her wrist. She smiled and thought about all that had taken place in the past few days.

Jackson called New York and cancelled his interview. Wade was beginning the process of starting their business while planning a press conference to announce that he was not seeking re-election. Grace and Andi were already scouring Pinterest for nursery ideas, bouncing their decorating ideas off Cindy. She and Helena had been allowed back into the house, and the cleanup had begun.

Cindy planned to head straight back to Helena's to be there when the new living room furniture and mattresses arrived. Though it would take some time before the insurance would be sorted out and a check would be issued, Cindy used what little she'd made so far to order replacements for the couch, chairs, and bedding. It was the least she could do. Helena then insisted that the furniture would belong to Cindy since, not only was she paying for it, Helena would move into Joe's house after the June wedding. Cindy still felt obligated to pay Helena back, and they were working that out as best they could.

About halfway to Buffalo Springs, she felt the hairs on her neck rise in that familiar—and not very reassuring feeling—that something bad was about to happen. She lifted her gaze to the rearview mirror, expecting to see Eric or Steve behind her. Though she convinced Dale to call off the twenty-four-hour surveillance—she knew he didn't really have the resources for that—she still saw one of the officers now and then checking up on her. She agreed to let Jackson, Andi, Dale, and Eric all access her location on her new, up-to-date phone—a Christmas gift from Wade and Andi—and she knew they used it liberally to track where she was and make sure she was getting to where she was supposed to be safely.

The car behind her was neither Eric's nor Steve's. And it wasn't Dale's either, but she thought she'd seen it before. It was a black, late model Ford, not unlike many others on the road and very much like the unmarked cruisers police often used, but this one had a long scratch across the front bumper that was clearly visible in the mirror. Where had she seen that before?

Cindy reached for her phone and held in the button that activated the automated system.

"Call Dale, on speaker."

Within seconds, Dale picked up. "Hey, Cindy. What's up?"

"Dale, do you have someone following me today?"

"Not at the moment. Why?" She heard the click of his office door as it closed, and the background noises ceased.

"There's a car. I've seen it before, but I don't know where. Anyway, I'm pretty sure it's been behind me since I left Eureka Springs. It's probably nothing, but..."

"Can you see the plates?"

Cindy tried her best to get a look at the license plate in the rearview mirror, but the car sped up.

"No, it's too close."

"Okay, listen to me. How far are you from town?"

"I don't know. I can't see the GPS while I've got you on the phone." She saw a sign go by. "Wait, I just saw a sign. I'm about twenty miles out."

Suddenly, she felt a bump that jerked her, throwing her head forward. She screamed.

"Cindy, what's wrong?"

"He just hit me! He just hit the back of my car!"

She felt another jolt and pressed hard on the gas.

"Dale, he's hitting me! What do I do?"

"Cindy, do you see a gas station, a store, anything?"

"No, I'm in the middle of nowhere. He hit me again! I'm trying to speed up, but he's..." She jerked the wheel as she came to a sharp turn on the mountain road. "He's going to kill me! I'm going to smash into the side of a mountain!"

"Cindy, calm down. I've got someone on the way. Just try to stay ahead of him. If you see someplace to pull off, someplace where there are people, then do that, and let me know where you are."

The car hit her again, and another sharp turn loomed ahead. Her tires squealed as she took the turn and swerved into the other lane. A passing car laid on its horn, and Cindy jerked the wheel back. She could hear Dale calling her name, but she needed to concentrate. She wasn't used to these winding roads, and though the snow had melted, it was still slick in places.

Finally, she spotted a bait shop ahead and sped up. She could smell rubber when she turned off the road and slammed on her brakes in front of the store. The car kept driving as Cindy sat, her hands braced on the wheel, her breathing coming hard and fast.

Dale was screaming into the phone, but it took her several seconds to catch her breath and find her voice.

"He's gone," she managed between breaths. She told Dale where she was and what had happened in those terrifying minutes before she saw the store. She jumped when someone tapped on her window.

"You okay, Miss?" an older man asked, leaning down to peer at her through the glass. He had leathery skin, a long, grey beard, and a red hat with a political slogan on it. She nodded and picked up her phone.

"Dale, hold on."

She rolled down the window just an inch and tried to smile. "I'm fine. Thank you. I was, uh, a little lost and pulled off to check my directions."

He looked at the phone on the dashboard, and his worried expression turned into a scowl.

"You came flying in here like a bat out of hell. You lousy out-of-staters, coming in here talking and texting and not watching the road. It's a wonder you didn't kill someone." He walked away, muttering to himself, and she rolled up the window.

"I'm sorry about that. I think I'm okay now."

"Just hold tight, okay? Eric is almost there. He can follow you back. Are you good to drive?"

"I will be by the time he gets here."

"Good. It won't be long. I'm going to hang on until he arrives."

She sat there for another ten minutes before Eric's cruiser pulled into the lot. He stepped outside and looked around before approaching her car. Cindy thanked Dale and disconnected the phone.

"You okay?" Eric asked when she rolled down the window.

"I'm fine. Just a little shaken up."

"Can you drive?"

She nodded.

"Okay. I'll follow behind."

She thanked him, and he went back to his car. Cindy took a deep breath and laid her head briefly on the headrest before shifting gears and heading back to town, her police escort following closely behind.

***

Jackson looked up when Mac entered the warehouse. For a moment they just looked at each other, but then Jackson stood and extended a hand.

"Why don't we start over. My name's Jackson Nelson, and I'm in love with your daughter."

Mac grinned and took Jackson's hand. "Reginald MacCallum, but my friends call me Mac. How's she doing?"

"As well as can be expected. She's scared, confused, not sure about what's true or real in her life."

Mac nodded, a pensive look on his face. "I guess that makes sense."

"Did you come here to find her?"

"I guess you could say that. I figured I'd stick around long enough to make sure she was okay, happy, getting along all right in the world."

"Did you know she was in danger?"

"Not until you told me about the break-in."

"That's when you started following us, huh? She told me she saw you at the movies that night."

"I was worried she might have recognized me, but I guess it's been a long time…"

"Why didn't you just say something to her? To me? Why keep it a secret?"

"She's got her own life, and she'd made it clear she didn't want me to be a part of it."

"What do you mean?"

A truck backed up to the closed doors, setting off the bell, and Jackson and Mac filled the order. Two trucks arrived after the first, and a steady flow of people restocking after the storm kept them busy for a while. They were eating lunch when Jackson returned to their earlier conversation. "So, what did you mean that Cindy'd made it clear she didn't want you in her life?"

Mac chewed his mouthful of sandwich and washed it down with a long swig of Coke. "In my last letter, I told her I wished she would write back. I asked her to let me know what she wanted, if I should keep writing to her. I never heard from her. I guess she didn't want to acknowledge that her daddy was in lock-up."

"Mac, Cindy never saw your letters."

His hand stopped halfway between his lunch bag and his mouth. He put the sandwich down. "What do you mean, she never saw them? She had them. She said she read them."

Jackson shook his head. "Not until recently. Gloria hid them. It wasn't until just before Cindy came to town that she found them. She was cleaning out the house and found the box her mother kept them in. I don't know why she bothered keeping them. Guilt, maybe?"

Mac stared ahead, his expression blank and his breath fogging the cold, mountain air. "So, she didn't read them until now?"

"No, and she didn't read them all. She said it was too painful to read them all at once, and the box was stolen before she finished."

Mac winced, either at the thought of causing Cindy pain or at the thought of the break-in. Jackson didn't know which.

"You're telling me that Cindy never knew I wrote to her all those years?"

Jackson shook his head. "She had no clue. She didn't even know you were in prison. She thought you'd abandoned them."

"In a way, I did. And I was going to if I hadn't gotten caught." He scrunched his face in anguish. "I was so selfish."

"We're all selfish at times."

"Not you, though. I don't think you have a selfish bone in your body."

Jackson snickered. "I don't know about that."

Mac looked at him with hope. "Do you think me and her could start over? Do you think she could forgive me?"

"That's not my call, Mac. She's confused and hurting and still trying to process everything. Give her some time, and then reach out to her. I can't promise anything, but it's worth a try."

Mac nodded appreciatively as the bell sounded, and they stood to load another purchase.

***

As Cindy drove, she thought about all she had to do at the house. Dale said he'd be by later to take her statement, but she could go home as long as Eric was watching the house. Cindy was grateful. She had a lot to accomplish before Helena got home. She wanted to have the entire living room put together and the kitchen organized. They'd spent two days cleaning and hauling stuff to the dump, and they were both ready for the house to feel like home again.

When they arrived, Eric went in first and made sure everything was okay. Cindy thanked him and assured him that the doors would be locked, and she would only open them for the delivery man.

"Nice try. I know Dale told you I was staying. I'll be right outside."

Though she wanted to protest, she was relieved. She was more shaken than she wanted to admit.

When Dale showed up, he took her statement and assured her that whoever was after her had screwed up. They now knew what his car looked like, and it was only a matter of time before they caught him.

Shortly after Dale left the house, the new doorbell rang, and Cindy hurried to answer it. She looked at the fancy monitor and spotted Wade standing on the porch. She opened the door with a lump in her chest.

"Wade, come in. Is everything okay? Andi? The baby?"

"Yes, everything's fine, but Dale called me. He's worried because you told him you didn't want police protection, and after what happened today, I don't think that's a good idea."

"Well, Eric's out there now, but Wade, you of all people know that the town can't afford to put someone on me twenty-four-seven."

"Agreed, but I can."

She took a step back and placed her hand on a nearby chair. "You would do that?"

"Of course. You're Andi's friend, Helena's roommate, and Jackson's...?" He looked at her with a raised brow.

"We, uh, we haven't really put a label on it, but I guess you could say we're…together?" They'd only just admitted their feelings for each other, but she wondered if everyone would think it was too soon.

"Right. Well, I have the resources and the contacts to hire someone, and actually, I already have."

"You what? Wade, I really can't ask you to do that. I could never repay you."

"I don't care about that. I only care about protecting my family, and how it looks from here, that includes you."

She didn't know what to say, and she couldn't have spoken if she did. A huge lump filled her throat.

"I went to college with a guy from Little Rock. His name's Lance Calhoun. He's a deputy US Marshall. He's working to obtain permission from his supervisor to guard you until we catch this guy."

"Is that allowed?"

"That's a bit of a grey area. The US Marshalls do typically protect federal witnesses, and though you're not technically a witness to anything, there is the matter of the missing money, and bank robbery is a federal crime. He's pretty sure he can make a case for it."

"Wow. I guess I hadn't thought that much into it. I've been focused on my father and where all that's heading, but a federal crime…?"

"That's why Mac was in Phoenix. It's a minimum-security federal prison."

She nodded. "When would this protection start?"

"As soon as Lance gets the okay."

"Okay. Until then?"

"Until then, Eric and Steve will take turns. Don't argue," he said when she opened her mouth to protest. "It's their job. Let them handle this for now."

"I guess so."

"And another thing, one of the guys who helped us with the drug operation, Ryan Stewart, he works for Treasury and is a friend of Andi's. He's now involved, too. I wouldn't be surprised if the FBI joins in. Everyone wants a piece of this. That money has been missing for over ten years."

Cindy could hardly wrap her mind around the fact that she was involved in something so big. She thanked Wade and watched him leave. She could see Eric parked in front and wished, for the hundredth time, that this would all just go away.

***

"Why didn't you call me?" Jackson was furious. When he had arrived at the house and seen Eric out front, he'd nearly panicked. He immediately asked Eric what was going on, and though he tried to stay calm, he could hardly see past the image of Cindy nearly being run off the road. He said a silent prayer of thanksgiving that Wade had stepped in to provide protection.

"And say what? Oh, I don't want you to worry, but I almost got killed today."

"Yeah, something like that." He opened his sister's refrigerator and took out a Coke. "And why is there never any beer in here?"

"Because neither of us drinks beer, and it's not your house. Now, are you going to keep yelling at me, or are we going to talk like civilized human beings?"

Jackson gulped down a mouthful of soda before apologizing. "You're right. I'm just worried about you."

"I know, and I love that you want to protect me, but I'm okay. Nothing happened." She went to him, and he encircled his arms around her.

"It wasn't nothing. You could've been killed. Now that I have you, I don't ever want to lose you."

"You won't. I promise," she spoke into his chest.

He rested his cheek on the top of her head and inhaled the scent of her. He couldn't stand the thought of someone trying to hurt her. After a moment, he pulled back. "The house looks good by the way. You must've spent all afternoon working nonstop."

"Pretty much. Honestly, I was grateful to have such a huge project to focus on."

She had the living furniture moved into place and both mattresses settled onto the beds which she had made with new linens she and Helena ordered online on Christmas Day. She'd finished organizing the kitchen cabinets and was putting the finishing touches on the counter when Jackson arrived.

"I hope you worked up an appetite. I figured you might not feel like making anything, so I picked up dinner."

She looked past him to the bag on the table, finally noticing the scent. "Do I smell barbecue?"

"Ribs, cornbread, green beans, and sweet potato fries." He grinned.

"That sounds heavenly."

They sat down to eat, and Jackson waited for the right time to bring up what was on his mind. "So, your dad was at work today."

"Oh?" She raised her brow as she took a bite of a fry. "And?"

"He's hoping you want to have a relationship with him, but he understands if you don't."

"He said that, huh?" She broke off a piece of cornbread and ate it.

"He did. He didn't know you hadn't seen the letters until recently. He told me that in his last letter, he asked you to let him know if you wanted him to keep writing. When he never heard back from you, he gave up." Jackson was grateful they'd already discussed the possibility of the two men continuing to work together until Jackson's potential internship began, and Cindy was okay with Jackson talking to Mac about her.

"So, he thought I didn't want to hear from him anymore."

Jackson pulled a chunk of meat from a rib bone. "Would you? I mean, if you had read the letters back then, would you have wanted to stay in touch?"

She took a long drink of water. "I don't know. I was so young. I might've been embarrassed, or I might've been a girl who just wanted to know her father. It's hard to say. It's not like we had any kind of relationship before he left."

Jackson acknowledged that.

"Is he planning on sticking around town?"

"I think that's up to you. He won't stay if you don't want him to."

She turned and stared off into space, and Jackson was struck by how similar they were. "You have his eyes, and a lot of his expressions. I don't know why I didn't realize it before."

She turned back to him. "Do I?"

"You do. The way you stare off like that, and the way you hold your head and squint your eyes when you're confused, or when something is bothering you. I've seen him do all that."

"I never looked much like Gloria. I think I got my hair from his mother."

"The one with the jewelry."

"Oh! You were so upset when you came and I told you about the car, I completely forgot." She stood and went to the counter. She picked up a FedEx package and pulled out a small plastic bag. She unzipped the bag and let the contents fall into his hand.

"Wow. These rings are something else." The diamond wasn't big, but even after years of sitting in a box in a bank vault, the luster was stunning. It was surrounded by tiny blue stones that matched the ones in the pendant. "I wonder if her husband had these made to match."

"I wondered that, too," she said. She picked up the pearls and looped the strand across her hand. "I remember playing with these when I was little. Nana died when I about seven, I think. Gloria had these in her jewelry box, and I used to take them out and wear them when she wasn't home. One day, she caught me with them and beat the tar out of me." A sudden light went on in her eyes, and she gasped. "And Daddy came in and pulled her away. The next day, I think, we went to the bank. He told me that these were mine and that Gloria would never take them away from me again."

"You just remembered all that, didn't you?"

"Most of it, yeah."

Jackson picked up the diamond ring between his fingers and held it up and wondered if Cindy would want it to be her engagement ring.

He watched her place the ring on her finger and hold up her hand, inspecting how it looked. It was a perfect fit. "I guess I should put this somewhere for safe keeping."

"I think that's a good idea." Jackson slipped the wedding ring and necklace back into the bag and held it open for her to add the diamond and the pearls.

He sealed the bag. With thoughts of engagement rings on his mind, Jackson pulled Cindy down onto his lap. "I know it's too soon to talk about the future, but is it too soon to practice 'You may kiss the bride'?"

"It's never too soon for that."

***

Cindy tossed and turned as the full moon glowed outside, casting a bright light through her closed window blinds. The events of the morning replayed in her mind, images running wild like a pack of wolves—snarling, howling, snapping at heels, threatening her with their jaws and claws. Around two in the morning, she dragged herself from bed and peeked between the slats of the blinds.

Either Eric or Steve was still out front, and she made a mental note to take whichever one it was breakfast in the morning. That made her think about the kitchen and how pleased she was with how she'd been able to organize it. In fact, she'd been pleased with all her work, and Helena was delighted when she returned from seeing Joe after work. They'd worked in unison all day Monday and Tuesday cleaning up the mess, but Cindy assured Helena that she should go to work on Wednesday and let Cindy take care of the final stages of getting the house back in order. Though the house belonged to Helena, it gave Cindy a sense of pride and accomplishment to be able to set up everything.

Cindy tiptoed out into the main living area of the house and looked around. Helena did a beautiful job of decorating, but Cindy saw much more potential in the house. The dividing wall between the kitchen and living room should be cut out so there was a bar between them rather than a wall. It would open up the house so much more and would provide a great space for entertaining. The backyard was big enough that a sunroom could be added onto the back of the house, and the loft Helena used for storage would make a wonderful bedroom for a child or two. Perhaps it was what Jackson said about kissing the bride that had her thinking this way, and she smiled at the image of filling the house with a family. Though it was much too soon to entertain the notion, she began wondering if there might be some way to make Helena an offer when the June wedding got closer. Cindy felt like she was on the brink of having all she ever wanted in life. She just had to get past this whole situation with the money and the stalker or robber or whatever he was, and…her father.

The peace and quiet of the night was broken by the hooting of an owl, and a shiver ran across the back of Cindy's neck. She peeked outside into the backyard, fully illuminated by the moon. She wondered where the man was who tried to run her off the road. What did he want? Was it really the money he was after? And was her father as innocent in the recent occurrences as he claimed to be?

Shifting clouds caused shadows to dance across the yard, and ominous shapes began to appear here and there, looming larger until the clouds parted, and moonlight shone again. Cindy hugged herself tightly, feeling the chill of the winter and the eeriness of the night. She busied herself with rekindling the fire, and then returned to bed where, for the first time in her life, she prayed herself to sleep.

Seventeen

"See you later tonight," Trudy said over the phone. "We can talk about the party. I think I've got everything ready, but I want to run it by y'all."

"Trudy, it's a New Year's Eve party. There's not much to do." Cindy took the brownies from the oven. Helena said the gals could hang out at the house that evening, and Cindy was anxious to talk to them in person. She had so much to tell them.

"It's my first big party, and I want everything to be perfect. See you in an hour." Trudy hung up, and Cindy looked at the clock. It was already five. She was exhausted from a week of little sleep, and she was afraid to leave the house, certain she would be followed despite the presence of Lance Calhoun, US Marshall. At least she would be with Jackson and all their friends at Trudy's party. Tonight, Jackson was playing online video games with the guys, and Cindy was hanging with the girls.

Cindy was looking forward to Trudy's party the next night, but the nightmares that plagued her snatches of sleep made her more nervous than a long-tailed cat in a room full of rocking chairs.

She smiled at how easily the phrase had come to mind. It was one of Grace's favorites, and she'd heard Jackson use it a time or two. She closed her eyes and pictured the scene. Yep, that was exactly how she felt, like she was dodging danger at every turn and just trying to keep herself intact both physically and mentally.

The sound of the doorbell caused her to start, and she wondered who could be dropping by. When she checked the monitor, she was surprised to see Mrs. Imogene Baker standing on the porch peering right back at her. She pulled open the door and was met with a howling wind and the commanding presence of the former mayor. Mrs. Baker entered before being invited, and Cindy closed the door to the cold.

"I came by to see for myself that you're okay. Word around town is that you haven't left the house since Wednesday. Don't you have a business to run?" Mrs. Baker unfurled the scarf around her neck and hung it on the coat rack. She surveyed the little house, taking in every inch with her roving eyes. "This is quite nice. I like what she's done with the place. I haven't been inside since my childhood best friend, Marcy, lived here."

"Helena really has done a good job. She's very good at planning and organizing, and I know she worked hard to create just the right space for herself."

Mrs. Baker turned to Cindy and gave her the same scrutiny she gave the house. "Then you two must complement each other well here. Speaking of complementing each other, I hear that you and Jackson finally made it official."

Cindy was taken aback. Official? "Excuse me?"

"I saw it on that Facebook thing. He says you're a couple now."

"He did?" She felt a flush in her cheeks and couldn't help but smile.

"He did, and from the looks of you, that admission comes as no surprise."

Cindy suddenly remembered her manners. "Mrs. Baker, can I get you something to drink?" She went toward the kitchen.

"No, thank you. I just wanted to get a good look at you, make sure you're not letting this situation get you down. What's your next job?"

"Well, I'm going to help a woman in Eureka Springs who has become a bit of a hoarder. Not as bad as the ones on TV, but she's collected too much stuff just the same. We've got a big job ahead of us."

"Good. That should keep you busy and provide a nice payment. And after that?"

"I've had a couple people reach out for quotes on my website, but I can't really give them a good estimate until I see the job for myself."

"Then why are you home today? You should be out there, looking at the jobs, giving out quotes, and making money."

"I…" Cindy looked away. "To be honest, I'm afraid to leave the house." She closed her eyes, embarrassed that she admitted this to a woman who seemed to have no fear of anything.

"'For surely I know the plans I have for you, says the Lord, plans for your welfare and not for harm, to give you a future with hope.' That's Jeremiah, chapter twenty-nine, verse eleven. I assume you're familiar with him."

"Um, no, not really. I've gone to church twice now, but I don't really know anything about God or… Who did you say?"

"Jeremiah. He was one of the prophets, a controversial man who spent his life preaching obedience to the word of God. He wrote letters to the exiles in Babylon, pleading with them to be patient and wait for God to set them free. That quote is from one of his letters."

Cindy took a seat in the armchair and beckoned for Mrs. Baker to sit. "What does it mean for me?"

The woman sat down on the couch. "God has plans for you, my dear. He didn't bring you to this town in the middle of nowhere, so far from where you grew up, for you to cower and give in to fear. I can only imagine what fortitude it took for you to come all this way by yourself. Look at all you've done in the short time you've been here. You established not just a career but your own business. You've become part of one of the most honored families in town. You've fallen in love. All of those take courage. Am I right?"

Cindy smiled. "I can say a resounding yes to the last one. The others… I'm still working on those."

Mrs. Baker waved her hand in the air as if Cindy's thoughts on those matters had no bearing. "Cindy, God has given you a great thing—a vision. He has given you the ability to make a new start, to show people how to see things in a new way, and to see that we all are worthy of love and acceptance. He has not brought you this far to snatch it all away. He has shown you your future, and in that, you must find hope."

"Mrs. Baker, how did you get to be so wise?"

"At my age, you're one of two things—wise or dead."

"Can I show you something?" Cindy was inspired to ask.

"By all means."

Cindy jumped from her seat and went to the bedroom. She opened her dresser drawer and took out the plastic bag, then hurried back to the living room, taking a seat next to Mrs. Baker on the couch.

"These belonged to my grandmother. My, uh, father had them sent to me." She poured the contents of the bag into her hand and showed them to Imogene.

Picking up the diamond ring, Mrs. Baker held the piece of jewelry up to the light and carefully inspected it. "This is real, a mighty fine specimen."

Cindy laughed. "Why am I not surprised that you know about jewelry, too?"

"My parents owned a fine jewelry store for many years. I took it over when they retired. I sold it years ago when I realized I would never have children to carry on the business. When the town began to decline, the doors closed for good. Darn shame, too. It was a grand old store."

"Remember my grandmother I told you about? The Painter? These were hers. My father said she wanted me to have them."

"They're all remarkable pieces."

"I imagine that my grandmother was like you, though I was too young when she died to know for sure. I feel… Well, it's silly, but…you've become…" She bit her lip, unsure of what she was trying to say.

Mrs. Baker laid her hand gently on Cindy's leg. "I know, dear. I feel it, too. I never understood why God didn't see fit to give me children, but when I was elected mayor, it became clear. This town, all its citizens, they're my children. That's why I've always kept a close watch on everything that happens, even now." She patted Cindy's leg. "And I think God has seen fit to give you a grandmother, if you'll allow it."

Not even trying to hold back the tears, Cindy leaned over and threw her arms around the elderly woman. "I think it's the best gift God has ever given me," she said, and she felt Mrs. Baker's rigid frame yield to her embrace.

After Mrs. Baker left, Cindy took the jewelry back to her room. She started to put the bag away but then stopped. She looked at her reflection in the mirror and the blank space where the heart hung around her neck for so long.

She looked at the jewelry for several minutes before removing the sapphire necklace from the bag. She unclasped it and slid it around her neck. She smiled at the sight of it, a sign of a new beginning. For her, for Jackson, and even for her father.

***

"Jackson, what's your problem?" Tanner's voice rang in Jackson's headphones. "This is the worst you've ever played, and I'm usually fighting to be on your team."

"He's lovesick," Austin teased from Nashville. "And I can't blame him. You know, Jackson, if I'd stuck around, you wouldn't have had a chance."

"Yeah, yeah, yeah. Quit talking and concentrate on the game."

"Look who's talking," Tanner admonished. "Seriously, what's going on? Did something else happen since Wednesday? Is Cindy okay?"

"She's fine as far as I know," Jackson said as he wielded a sword at an approaching beast. "I hate that I'm not with her and don't know if she's safe."

"She's got someone watching her back, right?" Austin asked.

"Yeah, but… I don't know. I worry all day and all night when she's not with me."

"And what could you do to stop something from happening that a police officer or marshal couldn't do? Watch it! There's a flame thrower!"

"I know. You're right. I just—shoot! I lost a life!"

"Hang in there," Tanner told him. "I'm right behind you."

"I told her I loved her," Jackson suddenly blurted out. "I meant it. I've never felt this way before."

Tanner laughed. "I could've told you that weeks ago. And?"

"And I think I want to marry her."

"Slow down, buddy," Austin said. "I'll give it to you that she's a catch—nice-looking, smart, funny, great personality, but marriage? That's not something any of us has ever even talked about before, not even when I dated Rosemary for three years. She talked about it, but not me."

"Come on, you know that's not true. If she hadn't gone off to graduate school and met that guy—what's his name?" Jackson asked.

"Mike."

"Yeah, him. Anyway, if she hadn't left, you'd be married now. We all want what our folks have, and you know it."

"I do," Tanner said. "I just haven't found the right one. Not sure I will around here. I can't believe that your perfect woman just dropped into your lap right here in Buffalo Springs. Raptor!"

"I got lucky, all right. I just pray we find this guy soon. I hate that she's in danger."

"You're the one who's in danger right now. Look out!"

Jackson fought the sentinel and won. He wished all bad guys and monsters could be so easily defeated.

***

"Can I take a few slices to Lance?" Cindy asked, already piling slices of pizza onto a paper plate.

"Sure. Ask him if he wants a beer," Trudy offered.

"Um, I don't think he can drink while he's guarding someone," Melanie told her.

"True. How about a Coke?"

Cindy grabbed a can from the refrigerator and walked the drink and the pizza out to the car. "I thought you might be hungry," she said when he rolled down the window.

"Thank you, ma'am." He took the plate and can that were offered. "Mighty obliged."

"You're welcome, but it's Cindy. I was never called 'ma'am' in my life until I came here."

"It's what we do, ma—I mean Cindy."

"Let me know if you need anything."

"Um, ma'am? I hate to ask, but do you think I could use the facilities?"

"Of course! Come on in."

He put the plate on the dashboard and the drink in the cup holder and followed her into the house. She noticed the firearm at his side, reminding her that this wasn't just some guy she was becoming friends with. He was there to protect her. It was an odd feeling.

"Ladies, this is Lance. He needs to use the, uh, the bathroom."

"Well, I'll be," Trudy exclaimed, batting her eyes. "You go right ahead, Lance. Our bathroom is your bathroom."

"Ignore her. It's right through there." Cindy gestured the way.

"Cindy," Trudy hissed. "You didn't tell us that your marshal was a dead ringer for Jesse Metcalfe. You've been holding out on us."

Cindy laughed. "Trudy, you are the most boy crazy female I know. Leave Lance alone. He's trying to do his job."

They all looked toward the door at the sound of the toilet flushing and water running. When Lance reappeared in the doorway, he smiled and said thanks to Trudy before his eyes fell on Sarah.

"Sarah? Sarah Wyles? Is that you?"

"Hi Lance." All eyes turned to Sarah who was as red as Santa's Christmas suit.

"Sarah, it's been ages. How's your mama and all?"

"Just fine. And your family?"

"Doing well. Your brother, Sean?"

"Married with three kids. He works for FedEx."

"Yeah, I knew that. I'm happy for him."

"You two know each other?" Trudy asked, her eyes wide in amazement.

"Lance was friends with my brother, Sean, back in high school."

"You were what? Ten when we graduated?"

"Younger than that." She looked at the other ladies. "There were five of us. Sean's the oldest, and I'm the youngest." It was rare that Sarah talked about her childhood or any part of her life before moving to Buffalo Springs, and they all looked at her with wonder.

"I've seen your picture on his Facebook page. Otherwise, I would've never recognized you."

"Yeah, I guess I've changed a lot since then."

"I'll say," he said, his face reddening. "Well, I'd better get back to my post. It was nice seeing you. Tell Sean I said hello."

They watched Lance walk out the door before pouncing on Sarah, and Cindy was glad she was no longer the focus of attention.

***

By Saturday night, all the snow from the previous weekend was completely gone, but more snow was predicted for New Year's Day. Jackson and Mac decided to keep the bay doors open while they worked and enjoy the sunshine and the above freezing temperature.

"So, you're going to keep working here once you start your internship?"

"That's the plan. At first, I thought I'd quit, but if I get the internship, I won't be making much more than a stipend, so I've got to make a living somehow. Mama doesn't work, and Daddy won't be able to work again. Medicare doesn't do much for them, and they're not old enough for social security. Luckily, their house is paid for."

"So, you support yourself and them?"

Jackson shrugged. "We all pitch in, but I do as much as I can."

"Tell me about this Lance guy. Is he good?"

"Don't know. I reckon so if Wade hired him. Wade and Andi have some pretty high connections, so I trust their judgment."

"And no more on the car?"

"No, but the Feds are involved now, so hopefully soon."

"Do you think…" Mac looked down at his boot and kicked at a bag of feed. He looked up at Jackson. "Do you think she'd meet with me? For dinner or something? To get to know each other, I mean. You could come along."

Jackson sucked in a deep breath and let it out. "I don't know, Mac. She's trying to forgive you, trying to accept that you've changed. It might take a little longer."

"I figured that. Just thought I'd ask."

"Why don't you reach out to her? See if she's willing. I can't tell you she'd say yes, but I think it would be better coming from you than from me."

"How can I reach her?"

Jackson thought it over. "We're going to a New Year's Eve party tonight, but we're having dinner at

Rick's tomorrow. Just the two of us. You might could stop by our table."

Mac nodded. "I might just do that. And Jackson?" Jackson looked up at Cindy's father. "Thank you. It means a lot to me that you're willing to give me a chance."

"I was raised to give people the benefit of the doubt. But I'm not Cindy."

He hoped his point hit home.

***

New Year's Eve at Trudy's had been a blast, and Cindy was happy they'd all talked her into going. She wasn't so sure about tonight though. Rick's Place was crowded, very crowded. Almost every table was taken, the dartboard and pool table were swarmed with players, and the waitresses looked exhausted even though the dinner rush had barely started. Cindy figured everyone was out partying two nights in a row since January second was a Monday and an extra holiday this year for some.

"What can I get you?" Arlene asked, blowing her bangs from her face.

"A Captain Renault for me," Jackson said.

"I should've known. You and your daddy always order the same burger. And you, sugar?"

"Um…" Cindy looked at the menu, all pub foods, all greasy and high in calories, but boy were they always good. "I think I'll have the Bogart burger."

"Good choice. That's our most popular. Anything to drink?"

"Yuengling for me. Cindy?"

"Can I just have a glass of water, please? Lemon, no ice."

"Sure thing. I'll be right back."

Jackson reached across the table and took her hand. "You okay? You seem nervous."

"First time out in public since…"

"Cindy, it's okay. There's a huge crowd of people. Nothing's gonna happen."

She let the warmth of his touch and the love in his eyes wash over her. He was right. Nothing was going to happen with this many people around.

They talked about nothing and everything, touching on the subject of her father for just a few minutes before Cindy changed the subject. She wasn't ready to think about him yet. They talked about the weather, Jackson's internship application, the consultations she had scheduled this week, and her interest in buying Helena's house.

Cindy detailed all the changes she would make, beginning with the sunroom and moving on to the loft. She told him she'd want to replace the gas fireplace with a woodstove and the electric stove with a gas range. After several minutes of telling him her desires for the house, she noticed that he was nervously tearing apart his napkin. She nudged his arm.

"Earth to Jackson. What's wrong?"

With the back of his hand, he pushed the pieces of the napkin into a pile, then took a pull of his beer. "You know, Mama and Daddy are still pretty young. Daddy won't even be able to collect social security for a couple more years."

"Okay." She took a long drink of water and waited for him to continue.

"It's been me and them for a while now. Ever since Helena went off to college. She went right to library school and came home and bought her house. She'd been saving her money since she was fifteen, and she's a shrewd saver."

"I can see that. So, what's bothering you? Is your father okay?"

"He's fine. Getting stronger every day, but I don't know if he'll ever be able to work again. I think he wants to, but he won't be able to make enough money to support them both."

Arlene arrived with their food, and Jackson quietly said grace for them both before they picked up their burgers.

"I still don't know that prayer. I don't know any prayers actually. You'll have to teach me."

Jackson smiled at her. "Sure. I can try to teach you whatever you want to know. But you know who really knows her stuff?"

They spoke at the same time, "Mrs. Baker," and Cindy laughed.

"How did you know that?"

"She was my Sunday school teacher for years. How did you know?"

"She kind of gave me a little lesson on…" She rolled her eyes back and twisted her mouth. "Jerome? A prophet who told the people to be patient and wait for God to lead them out of exile."

"Jeremiah?" he asked, wiping mustard off his chin with his napkin.

"I think so. That sounds right. Anyway, she told me a little about him and how he said that God has a plan for everyone to give us hope for the future."

"Smart man, that Jeremiah."

"Anyway, back to your parents," she prodded.

"I meant what I said to you the other day about wanting to make a future with you, but I don't know if I can leave them behind. I mean, they depend on me. I do so much for them, and I know that's not fair to you, for me to always be at their beck and call."

Cindy reached for his hand just as he had reached for hers earlier. "Jackson, you forget. It wouldn't be you at their beck and call. It would be us. If we have a future together, I'll be making a future with your whole family. Besides, it's not like Gloria is still around, and my father, well, I think he's proven that he can take care of himself. Though I hope he's improved his means of doing so."

And speak of the devil, look who just showed up.

Cindy put down her burger and looked up into the face of her father.

"Good evening, Jackson. Cindy." He nodded at them both. "I hope you're having a good dinner."

Cindy nodded. "We are."

"Jackson mentioned you might be here tonight, and I thought I'd just stop by and say hello. I won't stay. I ordered carry-out. Just wanted to, like I said, say hello."

Cindy cut her eyes toward Jackson who was suddenly very interested in his coleslaw.

"Thanks. I hope you have a good meal." She looked down at her own plate, hoping to convey a message.

"Cindy, I, uh, I was wondering if we could get together sometime. To talk. You and me, or the three of us." He motioned to Jackson. "No strings or anything. Just a nice talk to get to know each other again."

"Again?" She looked up and gave him a look of disbelief. "When did we ever know each other to begin with?" As she said the words, she thought of the letters and how much her father seemed to have observed over the short twelve years he was around, but she brushed the thought aside, not ready to accept him back into her life just yet.

"Yeah, well, the invitation still stands. I'd like to get to know you now. If you're willing."

Cindy wanted to tell him no. She wanted to tell him to leave her alone. She wanted to tell him to leave town and never come back, but instead, she closed her eyes, took a deep breath, and said what she hadn't expected to say.

"I'll think about it. I'm not saying yes," she was quick to add. "But I'm not saying no."

Mac nodded, a slight smile growing on his face. "That's good enough. I'm here whenever you're ready to talk." He looked at Jackson. "You all have a real nice night."

"It's y'all," Cindy said.

"Excuse me?"

"If you're going to stick around town, you have to learn to say, y'all instead of you all."

Her father laughed. "I'll remember that." He walked away, and Cindy felt a tug at her heart.

"He grows on you, you know."

"I can see that," she said. "I guess I'll have to consider his offer."

"I think you should," Jackson said. "I think it would be the right thing to do."

"We'll see," she said. "Doing the right thing is not a phrase often associated with Mac MacCallum."

***

After they'd eaten, paid their bill, and taken part in a game of pool with Wade and Andi, who also showed up for a greasy dinner and a night out, Jackson told Cindy to wait by the door while he pulled the truck around. She watched for him to pull up from inside the front door of the saloon. A waning moon hung overhead, and streetlights lit the town. Christmas lights still glowed from every storefront and house. When Cindy saw Jackson turn the corner from the side street where they'd parked, she opened the door and took a step into the chilly night.

Jackson pulled up as close as he could get and came to a stop outside the theater next door. As Cindy approached the theater, a hand reached out from between the two buildings and pulled her into the dark alley, flattening her against a wall. She tried to scream, but he cupped her mouth. She tried to kick him, but his legs were like tree trunks, thick and solid, and the dark alley was covered with the day's fresh snow, making her feet slide in the effort.

"Don't move." He placed a gun against her temple. "Now, I'm going to move my hand, and you're going to tell me what I want to know. No funny business. Is that clear?"

She nodded and wondered where Jackson was. Had he seen the man grab her, or was she in the shadow of the building when it happened? Did he even know she'd left the saloon?

The man took his hand away and pressed the muzzle of the gun deeper into her forehead.

"Where's the money? Don't lie to me. I know your father left it for you. I read the letters. I know he told you that he'd left something for you in the secret box the two of you had. What box? Where is it?"

"It…it was a safety deposit box, but it wasn't the money."

"Don't lie to me, girl."

She fought to breathe. His gorilla-like arm was lodged deep in her throat, and the longer he held her, the tighter his hold became.

"Cindy!" Jackson yelled from the truck, and she felt her phone buzz.

The man pressed the gun and his arm even tighter. "Don't call out. I'm warning you."

"I won't," she squeaked.

He asked again where the money was, using words she hadn't heard since she and Evan hung out with the other SEALs.

"I'm telling you the truth. I don't know where it is."

She heard someone coming, and the man yanked hard. She felt the necklace chain snap and fall into the snow. The man pulled her deeper into the shadows. She watched in horror as Jackson walked right by, heading toward the saloon. Cindy tried to yell, but the man's arm was constricting her throat.

"Come on," the man said, yanking her so hard, she lost her footing, and he was forced to drag her through the alley.

By the time they exited the alley onto the next street, she could hear Jackson frantically calling her name. She wanted to call back to him, but the man's arm was still on her throat. She grabbed at his arm, and he slammed her against the side of something—a car. His car. They were at his car, the one with the scratch on the bumper. It was parked next to a building where Cindy had seen a For Sale or Lease sign in the window. On the opposite corner was a hair salon, dark and empty on a holiday night.

The man opened the car door, and Cindy knew he was going to force her inside. Everything she'd ever learned in school about stranger danger came roaring back to her. She could not get in that car. She would never make it back alive.

He lowered the gun and released his hold in order to turn her around, and she made her move, kneeing him as hard as she could just as she'd done to Jackson the night of the first break-in.

He cussed at her, releasing a string of insults and blasphemies, and she ran. She was almost to the next block when the shot rang out.

***

Jackson looked down the dark alley. He thought he saw movement ahead, but it was too dark to see who it was. He switched on his phone's flashlight, and the ground in front of him lit up. Something glittered in the white snow, and Jackson bent to pick up the sapphire necklace.

"Cindy," he breathed, putting the necklace in his pocket as a shot rang out, followed by a blood-curdling scream. He looked down the dark alley and saw shadows at the other end. There was movement near the outline of a dark car. The expletive came without thought, and he raced down the darkened road.

Jackson saw the man raise the gun and heard Cindy crying as the man aimed to take another shot. Jackson charged ahead, using his head as a weapon. He felt like he'd hit a brick wall, but he heard the clatter of the gun on the sidewalk. He looked up into the eyes of a madman and looked back down, scrambling for the gun.

Before he was able to reach the weapon, he heard a shot. The man pitched forward then fell, narrowly missing Jackson. When he looked up, Jackson saw Lance Calhoun, who was supposed to have the night off, standing several yards away. His legs were spread wide, his arms were outstretched in front of him, and his gun was perched between his hands.

"Back away," he said to Jackson who slowly stood and backed off, his hands raised. That was when he noticed another body lying on the ground between him and Lance. Cindy was on her knees beside the body, and her sobs rang out in the night.

Jackson heard the wail of the siren from the volunteer fire station across the street, and several men ran from the building, hurrying toward them.

Jackson looked at the figure on the ground next to Cindy. He recognized the lambskin-lined denim jacket, and his heart lurched. He heard Cindy's frenzied prayers.

Lance moved closer to the man he'd shot, the gun still pointed. He reached out and rolled the man over, and Jackson saw the hole in his chest. Lance lowered his gun.

"Go take care of her. I'll call the police chief."

Jackson looked over at Cindy, her chest heaving as she breathed and looked up at him. Her glistening tears glowed with the reflection of the streetlights.

Before Jackson had a chance to move, the sound of police sirens could be heard. The ambulance pulled out from the bay of the fire station into the street.

Jackson ran to Cindy. She was frozen in place, her hands covered with blood. She moved as the EMTs began working on her father. "Is he? Is he?" Her words were choked by her heavy breathing.

Jackson looked on as the men rolled Mac over. Blood pooled from his chest just below his right shoulder. An EMT ripped open his shirt and cut his jacket out of the way.

"He's got a pulse," a man called, his fingers pressed to Mac's throat. Another man opened the stretcher beside them. They packed the wound tightly with large gauze pads and inserted an IV into a tattooed arm. They placed a board under Mac and a collar around his neck and lifted him onto the stretcher. Two men loaded him into the back of the ambulance while another called the hospital.

"We're taking him to Washington Medical," he called back, and Jackson hollered his thanks.

"He saved my life," Cindy said. "He jumped in front of me when that guy shot." She looked up at Jackson, and he saw the grief and worry in her face. "I don't know who that man was, but my father took the bullet for me."

Eighteen

Cindy was sound asleep in the waiting room chair. Around three in the morning, she was awakened by a nurse. "Dr. Ortega will be in shortly."

It was almost thirty minutes later when the surgeon appeared in the doorway. "Ms. MacCallum?"

She stood. "Yes, that's me," she said, acknowledging the name for the first time since she was a child.

"You're his daughter, I'm told."

"Yes, is he going to be okay?"

"Better than okay. The bullet tore through his right sternum and into his pleura, but it lodged there and stopped him from bleeding out or collapsing his lung. He's one lucky man. He's going to be asleep for a while, but he'll be awake in the morning. He's going to be in a lot of pain, and recovery won't be easy. He won't be able to do a whole lot for quite some time, but he should make a full recovery."

She felt her knees buckle as relief washed through her. "Thank you, thank you."

"I'll give you a few minutes with him, but then you're going to have to leave. You can come back during visiting hours."

"Okay, thank you again."

"A nurse will be right out."

Once in Mac's room, Cindy went to her father's side and took his hand.

"Daddy, I don't know if you can hear me, but you're going to be okay. We're going to be okay." She wiped away her tears with the back of her other hand, but they kept flowing down her cheek like a waterfall. "We're going to be okay, Daddy. You and me. We're going to be okay. And if Jackson and I do get married someday, you can walk me down the aisle, and our kids will call you grandpa, and we're all going to be okay."

"Miss, I'm sorry, but you're going to have to go. He needs his rest," the nurse said from the doorway.

"Yes, yes, I'm coming." She brushed away more tears and squeezed his hand before leaning down and kissing him on the cheek. "I'll be back tomorrow, Daddy. And we'll make a new start. I promise."

She gently laid his hand on the blanket and went to the door. She looked back once more before leaving and whispered goodnight to her father.

***

Jackson arrived in the ER lobby just as Cindy walked off the elevator. She rushed to him beaming with happiness.

"He's going to be okay. The doctor said he was lucky and that he'll make a full recovery."

Jackson wrapped his arms around her and felt her melt into him.

"I was so unfair to him, Jackson. I didn't know if I could trust him, if he had really changed, if he really loved me, but he, he was willing to give his life for me."

"'There's no greater love than to lay down one's life for one's friends,'" Jackson quoted.

"No greater love," she repeated, her face still buried in his chest. "Is that from the Bible?" She lifted her gaze to his.

"It is. It's from the Gospel of John. Jesus is telling his Apostles that his love is as great as his father's love, and that anyone who loves that greatly should be willing to give his own life for those he loves."

"And he was willing to do that for me."

"Your father and Jesus. Both of them made the decision to give their lives for you." He took her chin in his hand. "You know, I would do the same."

She nodded. "I know, and so would I. I guess we're all lucky to have so many people willing to give our lives for each other."

"Lucky isn't the right word. We're blessed, Cindy. Blessed in so many ways. Oh!" He reached into his pocket and pulled out the sapphire necklace. "I found this in the alley. I fixed it while I was waiting to be questioned." He looped it around her neck and clasped it. "It looks like it was made to hang right there."

Cindy reached up and held the stones between her fingers. She blinked back tears, and Jackson pulled her into his embrace.

With his arm wrapped around the woman he loved, Jackson made his way into the dark night. He had gone from terror to grief to relief and now joy in the knowledge that they were all blessed.

***

Dale stood beside Mac's bed. Cindy was in the chair. Mac was awake and alert, and Cindy could barely believe she was in her father's hospital room, thanking God that he was alive.

"Sutton's son, huh? Doing his daddy's dirty work or acting on his own?" Mac asked.

"Who's Sutton?" Cindy asked.

"One of the other men I…uh…was involved with. Back then." Mac looked away, unable to say the words, and Cindy felt more than ever that her father truly regretted his life of crime.

"We'll never know if he and father planned this together or not. Based on what Junior told his ex, he was acting on his own. He'd hit rock bottom. Lost his job during the pandemic. Wife left him and took the kids. He lost his house. Some online news show picked up on the news that you were out of jail and did a whole update on the bank robberies and everything that went down. Apparently, the show framed the story as a kind of treasure hunt, challenging watchers to find the money. He decided that he deserved it for himself seeing as how his father had been one of the ones to take it."

"And the ex-wife didn't see fit to let anyone know?"

Dale shook his head. "She didn't think he'd actually do anything. Said she thought he was all talk."

"And Sutton? Still in prison?"

"Died of pancreatic cancer six months ago." Dale held out his hands in front of him and shrugged. "So, he may have known what his son was planning, or he may not."

Mac was pensive for a moment. "I guess it is kind of a treasure hunt. There's no telling what Gloria did with it." He looked over at Dale. "I really don't know where it is. Would have told someone long ago if I did. I've been trying hard to live according to the Gospels. I've made my peace with God, and now I need to make my peace with everyone else." He looked over at Cindy.

She smiled at her father and nodded. "There will be plenty of time, Daddy. We've got years ahead of us to make up for lost time."

"I wish you luck," Dale said to Mac. "It's not every day that somebody gets a second chance at life, and from where I stand, it looks like you just got a third chance. Don't screw it up."

"I don't intend to," Mac assured him.

Dale told them goodbye and left them alone.

"I've got to go, Daddy. Jackson and I are going to daily Mass this morning to show our thanks, and he's waiting for me downstairs. I'll be back later."

"Daddy. It's been a long time since you called me that."

"Get used to it."

"I'd like nothing more."

Cindy stood to go and gave her father a kiss on the cheek.

"Cindy," Mac called as she reached the doorway. "Say a prayer for me."

"I will, Daddy. I will."

***

Jackson and Cindy sat on the front porch swing, their laps covered with only a light blanket. The temperature had reached fifty-one, and it was predicted to be sixty the next day.

"The weather here is crazy," Cindy said.

"It's pretty fickle," Jackson admitted, "but it keeps you on your toes."

"How was the first week on the job?"

"I liked it. I'm going to be pretty busy. I'll have to accompany one of the investors to New York in a couple weeks, and believe it or not, I'm looking forward to it. How about you? Did you get registered in time?"

"I did. Classes start on Tuesday. Can you believe it? I'm a college student."

"Of course, I believe it. You can do anything you set your heart on."

"I still can't believe the college awarded me that scholarship. I didn't even apply for one. They just said I was chosen because of my stellar academic record in high school."

"You deserve it. You worked hard and didn't reap any of the benefits. It's about time you get to collect on all you did to get where you are."

A car pulled up out front, and Mrs. Baker stepped onto the sidewalk. Cindy stood, letting one of the blankets fall to the floor.

"Mrs. Baker? It's awfully late for you to be out. Is everything okay?"

"Everything is perfect. I just came from Fayetteville. I had a board meeting this afternoon at my alma mater. They said that one Cindy Nelson received a full scholarship to attend online classes beginning next week. I just wanted to make sure you accepted and got registered."

Cindy's mouth fell open. "I did. Tell me, Mrs. Baker, did you know I applied to go to school there?"

"I told you before Cindy, I make it my business to know everything that goes on here in Buffalo Springs. Now, do you have everything you need for class?"

"I think so."

"Good. If there's ever anything you need, you let me know. Got it?"

"I do."

"Very well. Jackson," she said as if just noticing he was there. "See to it that she doesn't stay out too late once classes start. She's going to need to keep her grades up."

Jackson stood. "Yes ma'am."

"You two have a good night." Mrs. Baker got back into her car and drove away.

Cindy turned to Jackson. "You don't think…?"

"I most certainly do. And you know what? She's got as much money as Wade does. Let her spend it however she wants. Come on. Time to head inside."

Cindy helped him pick up the blankets and then accepted his hand. Her father would be coming home tomorrow. They'd secured an apartment above the hardware store for him, courtesy of Tanner's family. Jackson and Wade were making arrangements for Wade to open his law firm while laying plans for Jackson to join as an investment officer once he finished his internship, and Cindy would be going back to school.

There wasn't anything else in the world she could ask for. Between her father, Jackson and his family, and even Mrs. Baker, she finally had the family she always wanted. Her heart was full, and she was forming a strong faith, not just in her family and in God but in herself. She knew the plans God had for her, plans to prosper and not harm, and for the first time in her life, she had hope in the future.

About the Author

Amy began writing as a child and never stopped. She wrote articles for magazines and newspapers before writing children's books and adult fiction. A graduate of the University of Maryland with a Master of Library and Information Science, Amy worked as a librarian for fifteen years and, in 2010, began writing full time.

Amy Schisler writes inspirational women's fiction for people of all ages. She has published two children's books and numerous novels, including the award-winning Picture Me, Whispering Vines, and the Chincoteague Island Trilogy. Amy enjoys a busy life on the Eastern Shore of Maryland.

The recipient of numerous national literary awards, including the Illumination Award, LYRA award, Independent Publisher Book Award, International Digital Award, and the Golden Quill Award as well as honors from the Catholic Press Association and the Eric Hoffer Book Award, Amy's writing has been hailed "a verbal masterpiece of art" (author Alexa Jacobs) and "Everything you want in a book" (Amazon reviewer). Amy's books are available internationally, wherever books are sold, in print and eBook formats.

Follow Amy at:
http://amyschislerauthor.com
http://facebook.com/amyschislerauthor
https://twitter.com/AmySchislerAuth
https://www.goodreads.com/amyschisler

Book Club Discussion Questions

1. Buffalo Springs has changed a lot since Andi and Jackson first envisioned a new future for the town. What do you think the town still needs?

2. Jackson did what many young people today are forced to do—he deferred college for a time to save money. Luckily for him, he managed to return to school and graduate, but it must have been difficult for him to go back to school just when his friends and peers were graduating. How do you think he felt, and what do you think motivated him to continue?

3. Cindy left behind everything she knew to find the one person she thought could help guide her to a new life. What do you think Cindy was thinking on that long drive to Buffalo Springs to see Andi. Did you think she was making the right choice? How do you think Andi felt about Cindy's need for Andi to help make everything all right?

4. Cindy discovers that a hobby and coping mechanism could also become a lucrative career. Were you surprised she was so good at decorating and organizing when she came from a sparse home where money was more than tight? Why do you think she was so good at what she did?

5. Jackson has always dreamed of moving to New York City and pursuing his dream of being a multi-million-dollar real estate investor. Once he arrived in the big city, though, he began questioning his dream. Have you ever wanted something until it became a reality? What did you do?

6. While in New York, Jackson was surprised to see that modern technology has replaced creativity and ingenuity in the store windows. He regrets that he couldn't see the sights the same way his grandmother did when she was younger. What modern-day changes leave you wishing you could have experienced something the way it used to be?

7. The father Cindy knew, and the father she discovered, were two very different men. What do you think changed Mac while he was in prison? Is it possible to become a changed person? Do you think Cindy was right to question his motives, or should she have given him the benefit of the doubt?

8. What do you think Gloria did with the missing money? Where do you think it is now?

9. How did Jackson grow as a person from the beginning to the end of the novel? What or who do you influenced him the most? His mother? Cindy? Wade?

10. In what ways did Cindy grow and change as a person by the end of the novel? Who or what most influenced her growth?

Praise for Award-Winning, *Island of Miracles*

"I can already see the Hallmark Channel movie!"
  Anne, Goodreads

Praise for Award-Winning, *Island of Promise*

"[Amy] draws you in to the lives of her characters…she paints the picture so eloquently it's almost like you are there.
  Cindy, Amazon

"I love Amy Schisler's books. I cried tears of both sadness and joy while reading this. I read this book in a day!"
  Mitzi Mead, Goodreads

Praise for *Seeking Tranquility*

"The romance in this book was pure, refreshing, and beautiful, completely believable and just the right level of sweet. At the same time, it was heady and exhilarating–in short: it felt like falling in love–and I was delighted by it."
  Jessica Castillo, Catholic 365

Praise for Award-Winning, *Whispering Vines*

"The heartbreaking, endearing, charming, and romantic scenes will surely inveigle you to keep reading."
  Serious Reading Book Review

"Schisler's writing is a verbal masterpiece of art."
  Alexa Jacobs, Author & President of Maryland Romance Writers

Praise for Award-Winning, *The Good Wine*

"'The Good Wine' written by Amy Schisler is a beautiful love story about overcoming loss, reconnecting, and finding forgiveness."
  Reader Views Reviews

Also Available by Amy Schisler
Novels
A Place to Call Home
Picture Me
Whispering Vines and *The Good Wine*
Summer's Squall
The Devil's Fortune

Buffalo Springs
Desert Fire, Mountain Rain
Mountains, Moonlight, and Magic

Chincoteague Island Trilogy
Island of Miracles
Island of Promise
Island of Hope

Chincoteague Sunsets trilogy
Seeking Tranquility

Children's Books
Crabbing With Granddad
The Greatest Gift

Spiritual Books
Stations of the Cross Meditations for Moms (with Anne Kennedy, Susan Anthony, Chandi Owen, and Wendy Clark)
A Devotional Alphabet
Meet The Saints From A-Z, An Introduction to the Saints for Children